Also by K. Aten:

THE ARROW OF ARTEMIS SERIES
The Fletcher
The Archer
The Sagittarius

THE BLOOD RESONANCE SERIES
Running From Forever

OTHER TITLES
Rules of the Road
Waking the Dreamer

The Sovereign of Psiere
Book One in The
Mystery of the Makers series

K. Aten

Mystic Books
by Regal Crest

ISBN 978-1-61929-412-7

First Edition 2019

9 8 7 6 5 4 3 2 1

Cover design by AcornGraphics

Published by:

Regal Crest Enterprises

Find us on the World Wide Web at
http://www.regalcrest.biz

Published in the United States of America

Acknowledgments

This book wouldn't exist without the prodding and support of my beta reader, Ted. He was with me from the beginning, brainstorming different ideas until I settled on this world, with these women. Thank you, Brother. I'd also like to thank Regal Crest Enterprises for letting me tell my stories to a wide audience. And finally I'd like to give a shout out to Micheala for reading through one crazy story after another, and for putting up with my persistent further/farther confusion.

Dedication

I took a handful of themes/tropes that I love and crammed them all into one book. I suppose that I'm an overachiever like that. But I did it for a reason, at least on a subconscious level. This book is my tribute to every sci-fi and fantasy book I read as a kid. Science fiction is the genre I love most and it feels good to put my own star in the sky.

Chapter One

DAEMON SHENDO HAD hated his job for the past twenty-two lunes and it was no coincidence that he'd also been the captain of Her Royal Sovereign Connate Olivienne Dracore's Shield Corp unit for the same amount of time. It wasn't that the heir apparent was a bad person, she was simply impossible. "Connate Dracore, I highly recommend that you allow the engineers to test the cycle before you attempt a solo ride. No one knows what it will do at speed with that much power."

"If you're afraid to accompany me on this test, Captain Shendo, you're more than welcome to wait here with your Shield team." Olivienne glanced at the half a dozen guardians that were milling around off to the side, all dressed in the infamous black uniforms of the Psi Shield Corp. She raised a single dark eyebrow at the grizzled man who was in charge of her safety. Nothing he could say would steer her away from testing the new cycle, but she was curious if he would attempt to follow her into what was sure to be an extremely dangerous ride. She was used to risk. But having enhanced awareness as one of her channels went a long way to mitigate the dangers of her many adventurous undertakings. Capt. Shendo knew that. As the head of her royal guardians it was his job to know all of her channels and their strengths, as well as those of the men and women that made up her Psi Shield Corp unit.

Every person born on Psiere displayed one or more different power channels of the mind when they reached puberty. The amount of channels varied, some had more and some had less. The strength of those abilities also varied on the six-point scale. Every Psierian went through rigorous testing as soon as their channels opened and were given a strength rating for each. The more channels a person had, the more power they were capable of. It was as if each person were a receptacle for stored power that replenished slowly throughout the oors of the dae.

Soft channels were those powers that didn't exert physical change on the world around, therefore they didn't really pull much power. Soft channels included things like telepathy, empathy, clairvoyance, enhanced awareness, and intuition. The hard channels were the ones that physically taxed the Psi, like telekinesis, apportation, levitation, pyrokinesis, and others. More than once Olivienne had exhausted herself on an adventurous mission from the use of her channels alone.

If a Psierian pulled too much too fast, they could burn through their reserve before it could be replenished, winding up with channel strain, which in turn would result in overall weakness and a headache. If they tried to pull more than they were capable of, the person would be rendered unconscious and that was not a good thing to happen in a dire situation. But Olivienne wasn't doing anything that would pull that much power.

As the commanding officer of her Shield team, Shendo would also know that the rating of her enhanced awareness was six. While her two rating teleportation was next to useless, her five rated telepathy and four rated apportation channels were very good skills to have. And her six rating pyrokinesis was excellent but none contributed toward her safety quite like that awareness.

Capt. Shendo was a five rating telepath so he was well aware that the Connate was testing him. She'd never made a secret of the fact that she hated having a Shield team assigned to her, but it was protocol for all the royal family members. Olivienne disliked it so much she often went out of her way to prove that they couldn't keep up with her. It was often a sore point in the unit that the highest trained individuals in the land couldn't at least keep pace with one of their sovereigns. It pricked the pride of the entire unit but not nearly as much as it infuriated their Shield Corp captain.

It had become a game to her and Shendo had grown tired of playing games somewhere along the way in his twenty-five roto career as an officer. He knew that she was blessed with five, medium to high level, channels. For generations, royals had always been powerful Psi. But that didn't excuse her from so publicly defying his authority. His anger at her willfulness grew and pressed on those around him like a dark cloud. "Your parens entrusted me with your safety and I will not allow you to take that cycle!" To further drive his statement home, he snatched the keys for both experimental cycles from the hand of the hapless lead engineer.

Being the first heir to the Divine Cathedra of Psiere, there were only two people the Connate took orders from and they were her parens, Olivara and Keshien Dracore, the Queen and King of Psiere. Olivienne had a presence about her, with the black hair and dark purple eyes of her mother. While the Connate's attractive face and mannerisms were obviously from the Queen, her height and spirit were all from the King. She wasn't known to abuse her authority as the Connate, but she also didn't let anyone but her parens dictate what she could and could not do. As a result she ignored a lot of advice, specifically from Capt. Shendo.

Rather than acknowledge the captain's declaration, she merely smirked at the older man and mounted the gleaming cycle. The saddle was padded and comfortable, the copere and stele piping along the sides of the illeostone tank was smooth and fluid. There were gauges where the steerage bar mounted over the tank. One read 'MPH' for mahls per oor, and the other sported the letters 'CHG' to show the percentage of illeostone charge pressure. The cycle screamed speed and Olivienne was not going to let one worn-out officer dictate her actions. She had put a lot of time and effort into retrieving the schematics for the new cycle on her most recent adventurist mission and was not to be deterred. Olivienne put on the helmet that was hanging from the steerage bar then turned to look up at him. "This is your last chance to come with me and maybe save a little honor in front of your unit."

The captain's face reddened at her implication that he was afraid, standing out against the stiff black color of his uniform. Then he laughed and held up the key to her cycle. "And how exactly are you going anywhere?"

The Connate rolled her eyes at him. Shendo should have known better at that point. She held out her palm face up and merely focused her mind on the key. In an instant it disappeared from Shendo's hand and appeared in her own. Olivienne used it to start the cycle and shot the gaping man a triumphant look. It was apportation at its best. "Be back in a bit." She gave him a quick salute then roared away down the test road. When the engineer realized what she'd done, he scrambled to set up the speed tracking equipment. There was no way he was going to waste an opportunity to make history with the newest application of the Maker's texts.

The shock quickly wore off and Capt. Shendo cursed her impertinence. "Sheddech!" He hopped on the second proto-cycle, quickly donned the helmet, and sped after the Connate. As much as he was convinced her rebellious nature would mean his own death, he knew he couldn't let her be unaccompanied during the ten mahl long loop she would take to test the cycle and gain speed for the measurement team. On a normal cycle with a normal Psi, ten mahls would take about ten meens. But nothing about his current situation was normal. He increased speed recklessly in an attempt to catch up with the Connate but she continued to accelerate away. Their path along the special test road took them out through heavily forested land until it made a great loop and returned back to the engineering facility.

The captain didn't have a tinted visor on his helmet, it was a standard issue. However, Olivienne's did. When they made it through the series of winding turns that eventually looped them back toward the original starting location, the morning light of both suns glared into their eyes. Archeos was the worst with its larger golden-white glow, but the smaller bluish-white Illeos certainly didn't help.

Two mahls out from where the measurement would occur Olivienne increased the throttle and shot forward. Her hair had been twisted into a tight knot at the base of her neck but the wind quickly unraveled it. Inky blackness trailed the rider like the darkest of smoke. The Connate lived for the speed and thrill of the cycle and the captain was just praying to the Makers that he would simply live. Half a mahl out Olivienne kicked up the speed again until the markers on each side of the test track became a blur. She watched as the gauges and dials between her hands increased into the red indicator zone and smiled.

It was often said that there were three kinds of people in the world–people that avoided danger, people that thrived on danger, and people that created it. Capt. Daemon Shendo was definitely of the first variety. For the most part he enjoyed life and wanted to make sure he had as long of one as he could get. While he was a tested soldier, he didn't make it to his age and rank by giving in to the recklessness of youth, or succumbing to the foolish pursuit of pride.

Just as he decided it was safe to let off the throttle and slow, his attention was diverted to a railer running in the distance along tracks that were parallel to the test road. The brightly gleaming aerodynamic cylinder had windows along the sides of the passenger segments and the light reflected off those windows into his eyes. Capt. Shendo's control of the cycle wobbled in that instant and his speed was simply too much to avoid the   impending crash. The cycle began to swim tail even as he brought his nearly blind eyes back to the front. Both speed and momentum were unmanageable with his concentration momentarily lost and eventually the front wheel cranked hard to the right, pitching the captain from the saddle.

As Olivienne flew across the finish line, breaking a multitude of land speed records on her cycle, Shendo flew through the air as well. It would be no broken record for him, but rather two broken ribs, a dislocated shoulder, a broken arm, and a broken upper leg bone. It would have been much worse but Spc. Devin, one of the guardians in the Connate's Shield unit, was a three rated telekinetic and managed to slow Shendo's roll half way through the crash. Too little too late perhaps. As he lay there gritting his teeth in agony, he thought that maybe it was finally time to retire. Then the pain became too much and everything went dark.

Capt. Shendo woke oors later in a med bed. He wasn't in agony like he expected to be. Though that was probably a bad sign because that meant his injuries were severe enough that a doctore with the telesana channel had been called in. Healing with the mind was a rare channel to have and the people who held the ability always became doctores. But there were limits to even a Psi healer's abilities so he still wore an immobilizer on his leg and arm, and his ribs ached. A medican came into the room shortly after and looked at him in surprise. "Oh, you're awake!"

He shut his eyes and sighed, feeling every one of his combat rotos. "Unfortunately."

"I'll be right back, I was told to inform General Renou when you woke, and she's just out in the waiting area."

In anticipation of his visitor, Capt. Shendo opened his eyes again. When the door swung open to admit the general, Daemon Shendo wore a look of resignation. He never even gave his commanding officer a chance to speak. He simply met the trim woman's eyes and admitted defeat. "I'm done and I want out."

General Camen Renou nodded, both accepting and expecting his answer. "I'll inform the Queen and we'll start searching for your replacement. Thank you for your rotos of service, Captain." And just like that, she walked back out of the room.

LT. COMMANDER CASTELLAN Tosh had always been known as a soldier's soldier. She was strong, loyal, capable, and controlled. After spending four long rotos at the Psi Officer Academy, four in a stint in the western grasslands of Endara, and a little more than four fighting against the Atlanteens in southern Dromea, she had certainly earned her title. With one hundred soldiers under her command, plus another one hundred automatons, she was kept plenty busy. Grabbing a rag from her back pocket, Castellan wiped the sweat from her brow. The center of Dromea was located directly over the equatorial line of Psiere so it was always hot. But during the rainy season it was both hot and humid. The daetime temps averaged more than ninety pyrs or greater, only falling with the binary suns at night. There were plenty of daes she wished for the plush life of an Academy instructor or a royal guardian, and it was no secret to the men and women serving her that those daes occurred most often when the suns burned hottest.

Castellan hated being hot and she hated being sweaty even more. But the lt. commander had dealt with the conditions of her post without complaint over the past handful of rotos because of one reason, and one reason only. There was a promotion promised if she could help stabilize the region around Ostium, the largest city in Dromea. Ostium was situated on the southeast coast of the smaller southern continent. The city itself was bisected by the Mir Ostium River, which came down out of the distant mountains and emptied into the sea. The Atlanteens frequently caused havoc along the entire coast and would send their leviathans to harry the fishing ships put out from the ports in the area.

The Psierians weren't the only sentient species that occupied Psiere. They were just the only land-dwelling one. Atlanteens were a bloodthirsty race that lived deep below the surface and had the appearance of half Psi and half swimmer. While their upper body was Psierian in appearance, there were a few noticeable differences. Castellan had always thought they were beautiful in an alien sort of way. The Atlanteens' skin was a mottled combination of gray, blue, and green, and they had little gills at the edges of their jaws. They had strong arms that ended in strange web-fingered hands. Their species was not discernable in their gender because they didn't have any external sexual characteristics, though their size varied widely. They had a fin ridge that bisected the top of their skull, and another larger fin on their back. Both fins were finer than the large scaled swimmer tail that was located where a Psi's legs would normally be.

While the aggressive sea race had never developed any aether tech that the lt. commander had heard of, they had very strong mental telepathy that they used to control all the creatures that dwelled below the surface. Giant leviathans were only one of the many species that were sent to attack the land dwellers. All manner of other land capable sea creatures would come out of the depths and attack citizens, night or dae.

Her thoughts were interrupted as she stared out over the glittering blue expanse. "Commander Tosh!" Noticing movement to her right, she turned her gaze to the approaching private. His trademark khaki uniform was crisp, as was the rest of his appearance. When he reached her, he gave a single closed fist salute. His elbow was bent and left arm across chest, held rigidly in place perpendicular to his body and parallel to the ground. Castellan saluted him back and he gave his report. "Ser, we have two leviathans sightings reported to the northeast, toward the island of Puer. So far they are staying away from the bridge to the south."

She nodded at him. "Move two rail guns to cover that section of the wall and send word to the 'ton sergeant to be wary. Have him line up the automatons along the bridge now, don't wait until the last supports are attached. We don't want those suckers pulling down all our hard work now do we?"

"No, ser! I mean...yes, ser!" Clearly flustered, he stood there for a few secs longer. She smiled at him, thinking he'd be on his way, but he just smiled awkwardly back.

Finally the lt. commander rolled her eyes. "You're dismissed, Benya."

"Yes, ser!" The man quickly saluted and ran off to hand out her orders.

Castellan shook her head then turned back to the sea. "They get younger and younger..." Every citizen of Psiere had to go through advanced academy training after their primary education. Though the four rotos of service were mandatory, people were allowed to choose if they wanted to go to Officer Psi Academy, or just Base Academy. Base was for people that didn't want a career in the military or any other corps that required combat training. Academy did two things for Psierians. It provided essential support for the military, and it also allowed people to select the course of their final education where they received training in their future career. Every Psi was tested upon entry to the institution located in the city of Scola and were given a list of options as to where their talents best lie. Want to be a chef? As long as it was within your test rating then you'd simply choose the culinary track where you both cook for hundreds of soldiers and get advanced culinary training. It had worked well for generations, probably because for the most part, people got to choose their own career.

It was a little more than twelve rotos ago that Castellan walked into Base Academy with an interest in metalworking. But channels and the fact that she tested abnormally high on her academy exam, the Psi Defense Corp practically begged Castellan to switch schools so she could go into the officer program. Even after four miserable rotos in Dromea, she never once regretted her choice.

Despite the heat and humidity, Castellan Tosh presented perfectly no matter the time of dae. Her hair was smartly parted and combed to the right, the back and sides cut to military regulation length of shortness. The wind blowing in from the water never even mussed the sun-bleached hairs out of place. Castellan had a strong jaw but unexpectedly fine eyebrows that had also bleached nearly white in the hot suns over the southern continent. Her eyes were deep and brooding like she held the weight of the world, or at least knew all its secrets. It was those eyes though, combined with full lips and her tall soldier's body that meant she never lacked for company in her off oors. One of Castellan's lovers once said that while her eyes competed with Illeos's blue beauty, her smile was as radiant as Archeos.

Castellan didn't know about that, but she was well aware that nobody appreciated a big head. Having come from a family of illeostone miners, she knew that life wasn't made on looks alone. It was built on the back of hard work and perseverance. Her maman would tell stories of manually hauling carts of illeostones to the special temple room that was designated for recharging, even when she was pregnant with Castellan. By the time her younger sibs came along, the Resource Corp engineers had perfected the automated carts that would take illeostones in and out of the chamber. But the work ethic Castellan had learned from her maman and papan was exactly what made her such a good officer.

Her Psi Defense Corp success was certainly aided by the fact that she had an absurdly high channel track. Rivalling past royals, she had a rare five channels, all of which were of good rating or better. She was the highest strength of any telekinetic and intuitive that the academy had even seen. But she also had five ratings in both, levitation and telepathy, and a three rating in ferrokinesis. So she could intuit any situation, she could read minds, she could move objects with her mind, she could move herself with her mind, and she could manipulate metal. All good skills to have.

Movement out of the corner of her eye drew her attention back to the bridge. She brought her spyglass up and watched as one lone tentacle rose from the blue depths. She grabbed her voteo from her belt and called out to all the troops. "'Ware the bridge, leviathan on the southern end!" Rail guns moved swiftly along their track to the opposite end of the wall and within five secs from her warning they began laying down fire. The large brass shells made almost no sound, being propelled by compressed aether alone. But they could accurately target and fly at least a mahl. Average cycle speed on the speedway was only sixty mahls per oor. It was an impressive distance when talking about weaponry that would blow the tentacle off a creature easily as large as three fishing vessels. Castellan watched as that questing tentacle was indeed blown completely off. It landed harmlessly back into the water below the bridge, rippling the surface as it sank again. No other tentacles came up. She grinned and called out to the woman working the rail gun that had hit the beast. "Nice job, Bombardier Gant!"

The woman spun in her rail seat and gave the lt. commander a thumbs-up. "Thank you, ser!"

She grabbed the voteo again and called off the alarm. The small device was perhaps the best thing that had ever come from the Psi Divinity Corp. She would never have guessed that the engineers, interpretists, and adventurists devoted to the Divine Mystery could come up with such an amazing invention. Before the discovery of voteos, they had to resort to primitive electrical pulse signals, or light and mirror signals over long distance. The new voteo was nothing more than a box the size of two fists. She knew the basics of the design, having studied a number of tech items while still training. As long as the thumbnail sized illeostone inside was charged, it would release aether that powered a miniature speed turbine. That produced electricity that created voteo signals. Those signals would be sent and picked up by other voteos. There were larger ones of course that could send signals much farther. But they took even more illeostones to power and were quite heavy. A com soldier would only be able to carry the voteo pack and their rifle.

Castellan nodded as the bombardier turned around again, ever wary during the final phase of bridge completion. The bridge itself had been a regional dream for many rotos. The island of Arafa was massive and lush at nearly seven hundred and fifty mahls at its longest, but it lacked any good ports for ships. Lord Pon Havington started out as the magistrate of the southeastern most state of Dromea and had worked his way up to Praefectus of the entire southern continent. He had been pushing the bridge project for rotos. The Queen finally signed off on it a roto and a half before and automatons were brought in to aid in construction. Of course Queen Olivara Dracore would have never signed the allowance had Castellan not secured both sides of the straight between the island and mainland ahead of time. Large walls ran along the coast of both, and each wall had a rail gun line along the entire length. Once the bridge was complete, weaponized automatons would be stationed on the expanse every ten yords or so along to further discourage the Atlanteens from attacking.

A shadow rose up from the ground by her feet and she turned to see the imposing bulk of Lord Havington himself approach. He had only been Praefectus for two rotos and Castellan had never taken a liking to the powerful continental governor in the entire time that she had been stationed in Dromea. But she knew that both their successes hinged on the other so she remained cordial and diligent with her duties. "Ah, it's nice to see plans come together at last! Well done with the oversight on this one, Tosh. I'll be sure to personally let the Queen know how indispensable you've been for the people here in Dromea."

He was busy looking out toward the crowning glory of his career so he missed the eye roll Castellan tossed over her opposite shoulder. "Thank you, ser." She didn't acknowledge his title because he didn't acknowledge hers and it was within her right to give such a response. It was true that while they were always polite to each other in public, both were high enough telepath rating to know that they despised each other. Because of that knowledge, Castellan assumed he was merely spouting a line of lies for the benefit of information specialists and the rest of the soldiers. But a person could not lie mind to mind and some of his mental thoughts about her had been less than respectful.

However, Lord Havington had excellent Psi shields and because his shields were so good she also knew that she had only overheard the slanderous thoughts because he wished her to hear them. It would have surprised the lt. commander completely had she known he was being completely serious with her about the recommendation.

What Castellan Tosh did not know was that Praefectus Havington *would* put in a good word with Queen Olivara because he desperately wanted the intelligent and highly capable Lt. Commander gone from his continent. He had plans and they required a more...lenient approach at military awareness. Yes, it was nearly time for him to begin.

Chapter Two

OLIVIENNE WOKE AND stretched then glanced at the clock on her bedside stand. It was a beautiful piece with complicated gears and levers all moving in synchronized harmony. It featured an ornate winding mechanism, though she never had to wind it herself. The cleaning staff took care of such things. It was early still and thinking about the beauty of motion made her turn her head in the other direction toward her bedmate. Benicia was a rising star in the world of professional pipeball and had made no secret of her admiration of both Olivienne's body and her position. With short brown hair, big eyes, and lush lips, she was sought after by many. But Olivienne wasn't lured by a pretty face alone and had rules for such dalliances. Before the Connate took anyone to her bed, she made it quite clear that it was for sport only, not for anything more serious or promising. Despite being the heir to the Divine Cathedra, Olivienne Dracore simply had too many other interests and pursuits to be tied down in some sort of royal consorage.

Being driven in her profession, she spent wekes and sometimes even lunes traveling around the continents searching for artifacts and information relating to the Makers and the Divine Mystery. The information she uncovered was often given to the interpretists and inventors to create more devices for use in everydae society. It would surprise many to know that Olivienne herself was the one who discovered and helped translate the schematics for the devices dubbed 'voteos' by the various Psi Corps. They had revolutionized the communication industry across the continents. The biggest discovery before that was for the wind and water turbine schematics that brought power to the cities via underground copere lines.

Olivienne was frequently impulsive when it came to her adventures. She also hated apologizing to people, and loathed goodbyes. All three of those character traits made for a bad potential par so she avoided such things. No, consorage was certainly not for her...at least not for many rotos. There was still too much to do before she inherited the Divine Cathedra and was required to settle down.

The Divine Mystery alone was enough to keep her busy many lifetimes over. No one knew where their race had come from or why they had the powers they did. Each continent had a colossal pyramid with a network of tunnels and rooms inside. The Temple of Archeos was located at the mouth of Mir Tessere, just outside the largest city of Endara. Tesseron overlooked the beautiful Bindle Bay and was the capital of the largest continent, just as Ostium was the capital of Dromea. But Tesseron was also the location of the royal palace and over-arching government of Psiere. The other known major pyramid, the Temple of Illeos, was just to the northeast of Ostium. There were rumors of a third great temple but it was yet to be discovered or even proven.

The pyramids were full of oil-sealed schematics in encrypted code. It took tens of rotos for the scienteres and interpretists to discover the cipher located in each pyramid and twice as long to figure out the key for each pyramid's documents. However, nothing found had yet explained who built the temples or where the mysterious builders had gone. The temples had only been unlocked for five generations, long enough for the interpretists and historians to begin decoding the secrets of the illeostones and archeostones, but not nearly long enough to solve the mystery.

The only certainty was a race that may or may not have been like their own had built temples and other civilian structures on the two known continents of Psiere. Besides the temples, citizens and adventurists had been finding encrypted documents and other artifacts scattered throughout the land. Some were easily translated with one or the other of the two known encryption keys, but more than a few remained indecipherable.

Growing up in the capital city, Olivienne had spent a lot of time exploring the great pyramid and unlocking a few secrets of her own. Even at a young age, she vexed her guardians to no end with the things she'd get into. It was that fascination as a child that led to her occupation as an adult, besides that of the Royal Sovereign Connate. Olivienne Dracore was a historical adventurist, investigating clues and translations about the Divine Mystery. Her favorite part about the job wasn't just going out and finding lost information and artifacts. The thrill of adventure was easily rivaled by seeing the creations that came from her discoveries, like the voteo or the proto-cycle. Adventure was in her blood, and the drive to solve the Divine Mystery was in her heart, neither of which left room for being a sovereign. That was why she was labeled as difficult by her past Psi Shield Corp captains, because she resented all the pomp and protections that came with being Connate to the Cathedra. She resented the duties that took her from her career and the adventures that she loved so much.

It was because her adventures and duties took her far afield that she greatly appreciated those nights she could sleep in her own bed. She liked it even more when she didn't have to spend the evening alone. No matter her personal preferences on attachment, Olivienne couldn't help appreciating Benicia's smooth lines and her cleanly muscled body. And the woman didn't just look the proper form for an athlete, she had the stamina to match. The Connate smiled remembering how they writhed together for oors until they both fell asleep in a sweaty tangle. As if sensing the Olivienne's hot gaze, long lashes raised and the Sovereign's gaze was met with a pair of dark yellow eyes. She grinned at the woman in her bed. "Good morning."

"Morning." Benicia stretched, drawing Olivienne's eyes to the small breasts that had come out from under the coverlet. She wanted to taste them again, but before she could act on her impulse, the chime to her royal residence rang. If she still lived in the main palace, she would have illeostone powered air flutes to announce her guests, but she opted for the semi-autonomy of the guesthouse located near the outskirts of the royal property. She raised a single dark brow at the fact she had a visitor. If her parens wanted to speak with her, they usually called on the teleo, rather than send a messenger.

She sighed and gave her bedmate a regretful look. "I must apologize for not following through with my promise of breakfast in bed but it seems I have company."

Benicia smiled at her seductively. "I could wait here if you like..." Both the statement and intent were left open and Olivienne took a few secs to consider the option. Finally she shook her head and crawled out of bed.

"No, I wouldn't have a visitor unless it was important. Perhaps we can schedule our breakfast on a later date."

The famous pipeball player pouted but understood the rigors of duty so began dressing as well. "My season is just beginning so it will be a trial to find the time for meals, or dalliance, but I think we can manage." The Connate smiled at her.

When they were both finished dressing, Olivienne saw her down the stairs to the front entrance of the guesthouse. Benicia opened the heavy wood door as she looked over her shoulder at the Connate. "As always, dinner was excellent but dessert was better. I look forward to breakfast next time." She ran a finger across her lower lip before licking the tip with her tongue. It was lewd and naughty and Olivienne knew exactly what was promised.

"It is nice to know our daughter keeps her guests well fed."

Benicia immediately blanched when she realized who was at the door. She spun her head around and bowed deeply to the Queen of Psiere. "Cathedress! My apologies for being so crude in the presence of your greatness..." She rambled quickly, appalled that the ruler of the known world had witnessed her bawdy display.

Olivara waved a negligent hand through the air. "It is of no consequence, Psera Demeer." The Queen of Psiere laughed at the look on the younger woman's face. "Surprised I know your name?" Benicia nodded mutely. Olivara answered her but her gaze was for her daughter. "Olivienne is the Royal Sovereign Connate, heir to the Divine Cathedra, nothing she does is unknown to those that wish to keep her safe." She turned her eyes back to her daughter's guest once she could see she'd made her point with Olivienne. "Now if you will excuse us, we have much to catch up on. Good dae, Benicia Demeer, and good luck on your upcoming season." While the Queen was as polite as could be expected, she made it quite clear that Benicia was being dismissed.

Benicia took the hint and quickly exited the guesthouse. Olivara shut the door behind her and muttered under her breath. "Service Corp are certainly a thick bunch, aren't they?"

"Really, maman? You have all the subtlety of a railer trying to make schedule. Now what was so important that you had to interrupt my first morning home in three wekes?"

The Queen's riding boots clacked on the polished stone floor as she made her way into the cozy receiving room. Wearing a cream colored blouse covered by a hardened leather corset and dark brown riding pants tucked into her boots, she looked more like her adventurous daughter than ruler of the people.

She had a small satchel resting at her hip, its strap slung across her chest. There was also a pistol holder and pistol on the left side of her waist, ready for an instant cross-draw. She may have been the Queen but she hadn't been helpless since she was old enough to fire a pistol in the right direction. Despite the casual dress, Olivienne had no problems seeing the station rather than the mother she had come from, with Olivara's carefully pinned up hair and regal mien. Her mother interrupted her thoughts when she spoke. "That's precisely why I'm here. I haven't seen you for nearly a lune, and when I do I only get a quick nod during events of state."

Olivienne scowled. "So is this an official visit or a familial one?"

The Queen patted the lounge next to her and smiled. "It's just me wanting to visit with my daughter. Do you have some time to spare?"

If it was an official visit, she knew her mother would grill her about replacing the captain of her Psi Shield unit. It had only been a few daes since his accident but they were bullish about security for the royal family, especially the sovereigns. Her mother would also try to encourage Olivienne to pick up more royal duties and adventure less. Such conversations always led to a fight that in turn led to more adventure and even less royal duty. Perhaps her mother was starting to understand the truth of who Olivienne Dracore truly was on the inside. But since it was not an official visit, the tense set of Olivienne's shoulders relaxed and she smiled back at her mother. "Of course I have time for you, maman."

Olivara gazed at her daughter for long secs and moved her hand up to brush an errant strand from her brow, tucking it behind the younger woman's ear. "So, how have you been? Your father says that the managing engineer of the Divinity Corp test facility informed the Imperium of a new cycle design. Was that yours?"

The Connate stretched out and put her feet up on the stone and wood table that sat in front of the lounge. "Well not mine, as you know. But yes, it was based on a design I found in a small cave located at the southern end of the Dara Mountains. The schematics showed an enforced illeostone tank and differently configured piping from the standard design. It allowed for the power of four stones in the tank instead of the usual max of two."

"Cave? What cave?"

Olivienne smiled at her mother. Even though they didn't share the same view on a great many things, they both loved a mystery. "I found old documents in a book from Pentole that referenced a cave of untold treasures. The maps were rudimentary, so much so that I wasn't sure exactly which range of mountains they referred to. But once we had the translations complete, we narrowed it down to an area about two mahls square."

The Queen looked at her in astonishment. "How in the world were you able to do that from such crude maps?"

The younger woman laughed. "The translation referenced a distinctive arrow-shaped rock formation that was known to the locals. It stated that the formation would cast a shadow to the west at middae during the first lune of summer. The end of the shadow was said to rest at the opening of the sacred cave."

A dark brow wend up. "But its only spring!"

"That's why it took us three wekes to run the numbers on the angle of the sun to extrapolate an approximate search area and then scour that area. But we did it and eventually found a cave carved into the hillside. We had to use aether-powered winches to move the large stone blocking the entrance and sadly animals had gotten into some of the oiled schematics. But others were fresh as the dae they were made. It was a magnificent find!"

"Traps?"

The Connate shrugged. "Minor ones only." It had long ago been translated that the reason the Makers left their caches of artifacts and documents puzzle protected and oft times booby-trapped was because they believed knowledge should be earned. One translated text referred to the challenges as both test and rite of passage.

While the Queen would never admit it, she lived vicariously through her passionate and driven daughter. Olivara wasn't old by any measure of the word. Most Psiere citizens lived to be around one hundred and fifty rotos. But she was a third of the way through her life and her daughter seemed so young and full of vigor at the age of twenty-eight. "How exciting! Any devices or stones?" Olivienne shook her head and her mother continued on. "I assume you went straight-a-way to the interpretists in the temple?"

Olivienne shook her head again. "No actually, I was anticipating a big find so I cajoled Interpretist Solgin into coming along. He's one of the better ones and I only had to pay his way on the railer and bribe him with a gallon of golden mead. It was just dumb luck that the first schematic we figured out was recognized by one of my guardians. Specialist Soleng has a secondary degree in cycle and moto engineering and said it looked like the plans for his cycle at home. Rather than board the railer back to Tesseron, I made the decision to take a moto out to the test facility southeast of Pentole. Captain Shendo was not happy but the gamble paid off. The modifications dictated by the new schematics weren't extensive, that was how they managed to complete two bikes in just a matter of daes. But, while they seemed rather minor, the increased performance was significant. I can only imagine how it will change all our engines moving forward!"

Olivara nodded. "Engineers are an intelligent group of men and women, it's only a matter of time before the adaptions to current modes of travel begin." Then the Queen sighed and shifted in her seat. "Speaking of Captain Shendo...we're having some trouble filling his post as the head of your Shield unit. Apparently your reputation precedes you and no one who is qualified wants the job."

The Connate shrugged. "So don't fill it. I've got plenty of guardians, they do well enough."

"'Vienne, not one of them would know a real threat if they saw it! You're not just my daughter, you're the heir to the Divine Cathedra and there are separatist factions on both continents who resent the royal rule. As much as it chafes you, your security is of the utmost importance! Did you at least go see the man that you nearly got killed?"

The younger woman felt her temper rise. "Of course I went to see him! It's only been four daes since his unfortunate accident."

Her mother snorted. "And?"

"And what? He threw a waste pan at me! It's not like it was my fault he was injured. He was too old and simply couldn't keep up with me while I was testing the cycle. He should have stayed at the facility like I suggested."

Olivara closed her eyes and pinched the bridge of her nose. "'Vienne...that is your excuse for all of them." When she opened her eyes again, she caught the smallest flash of triumph on her daughter's face and suddenly she understood the situation completely. "You're doing it on purpose!" Olivienne didn't say anything and the Queen's voice rose in volume ever so slightly. "You are purposely trying to make them quit! Captain Shendo was the seventh leader of your Shield Corp unit in six rotos! They've all either quit or become too injured to continue with a career in active duty. This is a dangerous game you're playing, Daughter! These are people's lives, including your own!"

The Connate put her feet back on the ground and stood from the couch, her ire having risen too fast to stay seated. "What you don't seem to realize is that this is not a game, this is my career! I find it sorry indeed if professional soldiers cannot keep up with one historical adventurist! I will not coddle hardened military men and women. If they cannot keep up with me then they are not fit to protect me! Maman, they are too old and used to the creature comforts of their station, it's not my fault. I didn't create the system, I'm merely trying to live within it." Olivienne was prepared to argue further but was stopped by a long sigh from her mother.

"You're right." When Olivara looked up at her daughter and heir, apprehension was written clearly on her face. "A soldier's ability to protect is worth nothing if they can't at least outperform you. But it's more than that, 'Vienne. I worry about you."

The Connate resumed her seat and gazed curiously at her mother. "About my safety, or something else?"

Olivara smiled. "I will always worry about your safety. But I also worry about you." She reached out and touched Olivienne's chest above her heart. "I worry for you here. You have chosen a hard path in a life that is already made difficult by your inherited station. I worry that you will never find a match for your passions and spirit. I just want you to be happy."

"I am happy. I mean, I love my job and I have evening company when I wish. Everyone gets lonely sometimes but you don't need to have to par up to be happy."

The Queen looked at her daughter curiously and the weight of decades of experience seemed to settle over her shoulders. "I'm never lonely."

Olivienne laughed. "That's because you have the perfect par! Papan is the best anyone could ask for. How could I hope to find someone as good as that? He is the perfect King to your Queen."

The Queen smiled sweetly at the love that Olivienne carried for her father. Before he became King, and before they had even gone through the Ceremony of Consorage, Keshien too had been an adventurer. But despite his free spirit and love for thrill, he had grown into his role as King and her chief advisor. She had confidence that her daughter would grow into the role of Queen as well, though hopefully not for many decades yet. Despite her appreciation for Olivienne's words she shook her head. "No one is perfect, as you should well know by now. The key is to find someone that not only compliments us, but that will grow and change with us as life makes and remakes our spirits anew. Neither I, nor your father, are the same people as we were when we first met. We have both grown as individuals. But we have grown together over the rotos rather than apart." She placed a hand on the younger woman's arm. "You don't need perfection. You simply need love, passion, understanding, respect, and a drive to explore the world together no matter the challenge in your path."

Olivienne looked at her mother in a new light. "And you have all that with papan?"

The Queen nodded. "All that and more."

The younger woman sat silently for half a meen while she took in her mother's words. "Well you don't have to worry about me, maman. I'm sure I'll recognize my par when I meet her. It just hasn't happened yet."

"History is full of the foolish and the blind. Perhaps you won't recognize it when it happens...but it is your decision to make I suppose. I just want the best for you, I always have."

The Connate smiled at her sometimes meddlesome mother and Queen. "I know you do."

Olivara stood and her daughter followed. "If we can find a better fit for you as Shield Corp captain, will you at least try to give them a chance?"

Olivienne thought for a few secs and finally conceded that her mother was right. Despite how much she loathed to have guardians and handlers, she knew that her position demanded nothing less. Finally she nodded at Her Supreme Sovereign. "If you can find someone that is able to keep up with me, I will give them all consideration and respect."

The older woman pointed a finger at her. "I'm going to hold you to that!" She got an eye roll in return. "How long will you be in the city? Perhaps you can have dinner with me and your father tonight?"

Olivienne walked her mother to the front door and gave her a hug. "I leave for the southern continent tomorrow morning but I can certainly spare this evening for my family. Safe riding, maman." Her mother smiled and waved after she mounted the horse that had been tethered to the gate outside, then she rode off with Capt. Torrin by her side. The rest of the mounted guardians that had been waiting for her trailed along. Olivienne scowled at her own guardians that were posted around the property.

Dinner that evening was familiar and full of the gentle laughter and teasing that Olivienne had grown up with. Her younger sib, Kesharan, was also home for the meal. At seventeen, he would be entering the Academy in less than a roto. While he spoke of his interests and exam fears, Olivienne looked hard at him trying to recognize the boy she once knew. He had grown up so much. While they both had to deal with a daily life that involved guardians and royal duties, he was only the Sub-Connate. He would not inherit unless Olivienne were to die before she could produce a Connate of her own.

The Divine Cathedra always passed to the female heirs unless one did not exist. Then the male heir would hold the position of supreme leadership until a female heir could be produced. For the length of their history, it had always been so. The words of the rule were carved into the Divine Cathedra itself, the massively ornate throne that sat in the largest room of the palace. The Cathedra was both mysterious and powerful. Carved into it were the same texts and letters found in the main chambers of the temple pyramids. The throne also featured permanently affixed archeostones, a rarity in the world of Psiere.

There were only ten known archeostones in existence. Four in each temple, and two in the Divine Cathedra. It was the archeostones that recharged the illeostones. There were chambers in the temples dedicated only to the task of recharging the millions of dissipated illeostones from all over the contents. Depots existed in all the cities where you could turn in your exhausted illeostones and get recharged replacements.

Once charged and in the presence of water, the illeostones gave off aether. It was an amazing thing to see the reaction occur. It was even more surprising to realize that the stone only needed a drop of water to trigger release. The smallest of devices used just that, while larger ones like motos, railers, and cycles, had entire tanks of water with multiple stones inside. The aether reaction was incredibly strong and could power even the largest turbines. When the stones were dissipated then they were replaced by charged ones. Simple yet mysterious.

Devices and machines running on illeostones could be limiting for certain modes of travel. Railers and haulers had it easiest because they could readily carry supplemental stones. Dirigibles were the most versatile forms of transportation but also one of the slowest. Because of the weight of the illeostones, the dirigibles could only carry so many if they hoped to also transport passengers and equipment. That meant that while they could fly anywhere, they had a max range of about fourteen hundred mahls at about forty mahls per oor. So it was railers with their max speed of one hundred and fifty mahls per oor and no limits on goods or passengers that became the most common and economically feasible method of transport.

"Your mother says you're taking the railer down to Dromea tomorrow." Olivienne nodded. "Has there been another discovery?" Her father addressed her while they were eating traditional end-of-meal fruit tarts.

She held her hand out horizontal and wobbled it a bit while she chewed her dessert. "Somewhat. One of the documents I brought back from the mountain cave was like so many others we've found. It didn't yield to either encryption key. This more than ever convinces me that there must be a third temple. Everybody knows by now that each temple's documents have a specific key that is based on the temple name and for neither Archeos nor Illeos to work, it must mean there is another!"

Her papan chuckled. "Well not everyone knows that, Daughter. But I agree with you actually. I've always believed in the third temple theory."

Olivienne smiled at him and continued. "So at the bottom of this particular document there are a matched pair of temple symbols whereas all other documents only have a single symbol. I surmised that there must be a sib document to it. I used the railer voteo to call ahead to the Temple of Archeos and had them check the archives for any documents with the same pair of symbols but they found nothing. I thought then that perhaps the document from the cave was originally located in the temple here in the city and someone had removed it long ago and hid it in the countryside. To what end I know not. I made an educated guess and called Roz Gosten, the head of the interpretists at the Temple of Illeos and she has her team searching through their archives for a double symbol document while we speak. I'm hoping to hear something on my way down."

Kesharan spoke up, clearly interested in his sib's work. "What happens if they don't find the linked document in Ostium? And what makes you think that if you do find it you'll be able to translate? The other undecipherable sheets don't have a double temple symbol, right?"

She cocked her head to the side and contemplated his questions. They were very good ones. "All documents have had a single temple symbol, with the exception of the one I've just found. I don't know anything solid at this point. I'm not sure why there is a double symbol. Maybe it is another mystery temple document, maybe it is something altogether different. The real truths will come out once we can get the pair together. If the hypothesized linked sheet isn't in Ostium then I think perhaps I will find the largest town nearest the western end of the Mea Mountains. Um..." She paused, trying to picture the map in her head.

It was her father who supplied the answer. "The actual tail of the range lies nearly equal between Gomen and Cordeesh. However, Cordeesh is another coastal river mouth city like Pentole so may be what you're looking for."

Olivienne nodded. "Yes, I think you're right. So that will be my backup plan. However I really hope to find the document safe in the temple archive in Ostium. That way I would avoid tromping through the hot and buggy jungle of Dromea." The other three laughed at her characterization of the notoriously wild and tropical southern continent.

The Queen lifted her glass of honey mead and the others followed suit. "Well then, I wish Olivienne the best in her search!"

The royal family continued the salute around the table. Keshien went next. "I wish Kesharan successful testing and placement within the Academy!"

The youngest Dracore raised his glass. "I wish papan success with the crusty men and women who hold elected places in the Imperium!"

Olivienne was the last to raise her glass and she made eye contact with her mother as she did so. "I wish maman the greatest of luck finding a suitable replacement for Captain Shendo, and the softest of seats on the Divine Cathedra for all her royal audiences." The entire family laughed, knowing that both the task and the seat would be much harder than the Queen would like.

Chapter Three

"SER! ARMICRUSTES ARE coming ashore at Temple Beach! Report says well over two hundred." Sergeant Beng stood at attention in front of her desk.

Always bad news with the good. Lt. Commander Tosh was in the middle of re-reading a telegram from Lt. General Tenet, head of the southern forces. It was a recall notice back north, to the Defense Corp headquarters in Tesseron. While she was excited to leave Endara behind, Tesseron surprised her. Typically new assignments would be given via telegram or they would just recall her to the Academy located on the island of Discentem, for supplemental training. Both academy schools, officer and base, were located on the island and because of that, the office of military reassignments was located there as well. Some assignments required supplemental training but usually the training was done in preparation for a promotion. It wasn't a good sign if they were recalling her to Tesseron rather than pull her back to Scolla on Discentem Island.

She was promised a promotion for putting up with the hellish southern continent for four long rotos. Perhaps what worried her the most was that she would only have one dae with her replacement before heading north. To have so little time to brief an incoming commanding officer was not protocol. Castellan looked up from the neatly printed page and addressed her sergeant. "Instruct First Lieutenant Cando to ready her troops plus thirty automatons and load them on haulers. We'll make better time getting through the city that way." The man hesitated. "What are you waiting for?"

He chewed his droopy mustache. "How many haulers, ser?"

Lt. Commander Tosh sighed. "Ten platoons of five men each should be simple enough maths, Beng!" She waited a sec taking in his confused face. "Twenty bodies per truck. You will need four trucks. Now move!" She had no idea how the man made it to sergeant but it happened before she came along or it wouldn't have happened at all.

Still the man hesitated. "But what about you, ser?"

All patience lost, Castellan stood and waved him off as she holstered the pistol she had set on her desk. "I'll be there before you, now go!" Besides the pistol, she grabbed a few shell magazines and a couple extra illeostones, then walked over to the far wall. Her company sword gleamed, its razor edge drawing her eye along its length. She snatched the blade from the wall and shoved it into the nearby sheath, then took off out the door. The chance that she'd need the blade were pretty low but one never knew what could happen in a battle against Atlanteen-sent creatures of the deep.

As predicted, her cycle pulled into the cleared lot at the top of the beach well ahead of the haulers. There were no people left down below even though it was a beautiful dae for swimming. Despite the danger of the water, many couldn't seem to stay away from the ocean's refreshing effects in the hot climate. As a result, many cities and municipalities had built seawalls to keep the deepwater denizens out of their swimming areas and away from the beaches.

Defense Corp soldiers were the primary protectors of land and infrastructure, while the men and women of the Security Corp focused on Psierians and society. However, something like a public beach fell into a bit of a gray area where it came to protection. Safeguarding of the beach itself didn't fall under the regard of either Corp. Instead the city relied upon the seawall and the few Salvo Corp members assigned monitor the people and water. Preservists were highly trained in search and rescue, and also had basic medican knowledge. They were stationed in tall lookouts to facilitate visibility, but the standout red uniforms were missing when Tosh arrived at the scene.

The sheer size and number of the armicrustes took her aback. Rarely did anyone see more than a few in a lifetime. To see so many of the moto-sized armored crustaceans at one time was daunting. They had yet to begin making their way up the stairs and off the beach, instead wreaking havoc on all that had been left below. Wooden lookout towers were pulled down, blankets, baskets, and umbrellas were all destroyed by the rampaging monsters.

Tosh heard the haulers pull up behind her and knew her soldiers and automatons had arrived. She was about to turn around and start giving them orders when she heard a scream down on the beach. The lt. commander brought her hand up to block the glaring light of the two suns and scanned the distance.

Movement near the headland at the far end of sand caught her eye. She quickly pulled out her spyglass and focused on the spot. There was a woman and a small child halfway up the rocks. Three armicrustes were less than two yords away. "Sheddech!" She collapsed the spyglass and took off running along the lot, toward the point where the woman was attempting to climb the rocks. It was the only way to get to her. Going by the beach would be suicide. Castellan hoped that at least a few enterprising soldiers would follow when they realized where she was headed.

When she reached the woman's location, Castellan looked down the rocks toward her to assess the situation once again. One giant pincer was reaching for the little girl and the officer had no choice but to utilize her channel. The pistol would do no good against their armor plating unless she were close enough to aim for something sensitive. Using telepathy, she spoke to both the woman and the child at once. *"Be calm, I am coming down to save you. Do not scream because that will draw more of the beasts."*

They both looked up at her fearfully but each nodded. It was the woman's voice who answered. *"We understand. Please hurry!"* Unfortunately for them, their previous screaming only served to draw more of the creatures to their location.

Lt. Commander Tosh was not just good at commanding other soldiers, she was one of the best soldiers herself. And she was powerful. She paused and stared down at the creature closest to the trapped civilians. It was a stretch but she was able to lift the massive crustacean with her telekinesis and fling it backward down the rocks, taking out two along the way. While her power was great, she only had a couple moves like that in her. It was more tiring than she expected and she knew she'd have to change tactics sooner rather than later. Using the hard channels was easier when one was close so she needed to eliminate some of the distance between them.

Concentrating again, she utilized her levitation channel and moved above the ground toward the woman and child. She alit atop the largest boulder below the pair and faced off against the next approaching armicrustes. Castellan pulled her pistol and looked for a weakness she could utilize. The creatures weren't fast moving on the crawl, but they were tireless and could climb just about anywhere. In the front center were eyestalks and mandibles and that was where she aimed. The sound of the pistol going off wasn't loud but the shrieking of the armicruste was shocking to her ears. In pain and blinded, the creature took two steps back until it went over the ledge behind it. It managed to take one more on the way down.

Out of the corner of her eye she saw the soldiers and automatons line up above the beach and begin firing down on the armicrustes with heavy caliber rifles and sling grenades. She had a brief absurd thought that the beach was going to be a mess and wondered if the crustaceans were edible before the next sea-bug was coming up the rocks toward her.

"Ser!" Castellan looked over her shoulder to the top of the rock wall she had come down. First lieutenant Koryne Cando was standing there with a dozen other soldiers and three automatons. She had a high-cal rifle at the ready but wasn't taking aim yet. "We can't fire until you and the civs are out of the way, the angle is bad. You want me to send the 'tons down for them?"

Tosh shook her head regretfully. "No, they can't navigate the rocks, it's too treacherous. Are any of you high channel telekinetic or apport?" The woman shook her head. It was the slight stiffening of her facial features and Castellan's own high-rated intuition that had her duck at the same time a large pincer swung over her head. She spun around and took aim again but the creature's reaction was surprisingly fast. The pincer came back around and knocked the pistol from her grip. Her hand stung but it wasn't incapacitated so she drew her sword and hacked at the nearest joint. She nearly lost her balance when the joint separated easily to the speed and sharpness of her blade.

The armicruste gave a shriek and she ducked another swing of the massive claws. When the claw switched and came forward to catch her in its pincer, she swung the sword again and took out the other front facing leg. The loss of support on the rocks was too much and the sea-bug fell backward down the break wall. Her relief was short-lived because another came crawling over the rock ledge. Castellan was forced to use her telekinesis to lift that one away and she immediately felt the drain of it. Lifting more than three-thousand punds of monster, even for so short a time, was exhausting. More were coming to take its place so she started picking up stones that were twice her body weight to fling down on to them. The massive rocks made loud cracking sounds as they slammed against the armicrustes exoskeletons.

Even though a Psi's energy was constantly replenishing itself, there was no way it could keep up with the demand Castellan was putting on her channel. She had only been skirmishing with the giant creatures for ten meens but sweat dripped from her brow and exhaustion tugged at her. Her head started to throb so she had to think of another plan. Lt. Commander Tosh was heartened by the fact that she wasn't the only one inflicting damage by the sound of shrieking along the beach and the muffled whumps of the grenades.

Castellan knew she had to get the civs out of the line of fire so she took a chance with her remaining reserve of power. Taking advantage of the space she'd cleared she used her levitation channel to lift herself from the rock and moved up to the woman and child. First she turned her back to the child. "Climb onto my back and hold me tight around the neck. Tight as you can!" Once the girl was situated she instructed the mother.

"Try to do the same thing from the front. Lock your legs around me if you can." The next armicruste was less than a yord away when Castellan was sure the two civs were secure. Levitating the three of them at once didn't use nearly the amount of power as lifting and flipping a tun and a half of armored crustacean, but it required a lot more concentration. Just as she got ready to lift them the woman in her arms yelled.

"Look out!"

Castellan didn't even have to think about it. She pulled from her dwindling channel reserves again and flung another large rock behind her, then boosted all three of them straight up in the air. Taking them so high above the rocks was more difficult because of the pull of grav and the distance from the ground. As soon as they were out of the way, the soldiers and automatons started firing down on the armicrustes. When she set them all safely on the ground behind the determined line of fighters, her knees buckled slightly but she held steady until both her passengers were standing on their own.

She could tell she had given herself channel strain with that last boost, based on the throbbing in her head and near-fainting spell, but everyone was safe. Castellan wiped the sweat off her brow and drew in a deep breath before addressing the two civs she had saved. "Are either of you injured?"

The mother shook her head. "No, just scared. My name is Endie and I can't thank you enough for what you did."

Lt. Commander Tosh felt a tug on her shirttail where it had come untucked. She looked down to meet the dark orange eyes of the little girl. "Thank you, ser! You're brave like my papan."

Castellan looked at the little girl and couldn't help smiling at the gap in her teeth. The girl reminded Castellan of her sib's daughter. "It was my pleasure, little one. And who is your papan?"

Endie answered. "Private Second Class Markis Kavin. He's down at the big island this weke." She was referring to Arafa, of course. The island was actually about three oors south of Ostium and soldiers were required to rotate down for an entire weke to save travel time. Since the completion of the bridge, both Psi and automaton patrols manned the walls along the narrow straight as extra protection for the new span. She knew Kavin, he was a good soldier and he spoke frequently of both his par and his little girl.

"I know Private Kavin, he speaks of you both often. He's a good man and a brave soldier, you should be proud. Now if you'll excuse me, I need to see to my troops." The little girl saluted Castellan and it warmed her heart. Most of the fighting was complete by the time she walked up to her lieutenant. Castellan Tosh stared down at the beach taking in the carnage and destruction, then she sighed and shook her head. "Such a waste."

First Lieutenant Cando looked at her curiously. "Ser?"

Castellan pointed at the beach where automatons had gone down to verify that none of the armicrustes remained alive. "What do you see down there, Cando?"

The answer came back with a certainty that was found only in those that were afraid or prejudiced. "Monsters."

"Do you know what I see?" Cando shook her head. "I see wasted life. The Atlanteens knew that it would be highly unlikely that the armicrustes would advance beyond the beach, our security is much too good for that. They needlessly wasted the lives of those creatures for what? To instill a little fear in the people of Ostium? It makes me question the motive of our nemeses of the sea. I would think that each one of these sea-bugs were probably three times our age or more. Yet the Atlanteens sent them ashore to die. It makes me sad."

Cando's look went from one of fear and loathing to that of introspection. "If I may speak freely, ser?" Castellan nodded. "I don't think I've ever seen a soldier look upon a monster of the deep and feel regret for their death. You seem ver—almost...tenderhearted. You hold more respect for your enemies than anyone I've ever met." She paused for a few secs, organizing her thoughts. "I've never had a senior officer like you. I think I will miss you when you're gone."

The lt. commander looked at her subordinate sharply, wondering if someone had been reading her mail. Cando was a fairly new transfer and had only been with her a few lunes but she was very good and highly recommended. "When I'm gone?"

"Oh, yes, ser! You're a legend back at the Academy. People talk about your power and your deeds in the lower classes. And everyone knows that you've practically turned this region around and won it back from the clutches of the Atlanteens. Surely they will be promoting you soon or the generals are nothing more than a bunch of arselicks!" Shock stole over Cando's face and she scrambled to defend her words. "Speaking candidly as you requested, ser!"

Castellan chuckled at the woman's words, relieved and more than a little embarrassed. "Well, Cando, from your mouth to the glowing incandescence of both suns, I certainly hope you're right!" She called out to a few of the longest-term soldiers of the region. "Anyone know if these suckers are edible? No sense letting them go to waste."

One of the more grizzled veterans who was near to retirement called out from the beach just below. "They're great in stew, ser!"

"Thanks, Lieutenant Tep!" She turned back to Cando. "I think this lot is good now. Will you let both the council and the base cooks know that they should send some folks down here to collect meat? Tell the hospitals too!" She paused. "And have someone grab my pistol from the rocks before you pull everyone back to base. Just leave it on the desk in my office, if you will."

First Lieutenant Cando saluted smartly and didn't question why the lt. commander would choose to go without her weapon when she could simple grab it with her channel. Castellan Tosh's channels were legendary. "Ser, yes, ser!"

Castellan began to walk away then thought of something else. "Tep!"

The older man straightened from where he was securing rifles and ammunition in the back of one of the haulers. "Ser?"

"Do the locals know of a use for the exoskeletons?"

He grinned and nodded his head. "They make for good fertilizer if you grind it up. Got a coz'n in the Stock Corp and he raves about the stuff."

"Do me a solid and call your coz'n, will you? Tell them if they haul it away they can have it, just make sure they wait until the meat is harvested first. Clear?"

"Yes, ser!"

Seeing things well in hand Castellan mounted her cycle

again. Rather than head straight back to base on the southeast side of the city, she decided to continue farther up the road toward the Temple of Illeos. Even though she'd been in the area four rotos, the site of the massive structure never failed to leave her in awe. Lt. Commander Castellan Tosh was more than just a soldier, she was a thinker of high level. She loved to solve problems and puzzles in her spare time and often pondered the Divine Mystery. She'd seen many of the texts and translations, and she even bought books to read when time allowed. Even though Castellan wasn't an interpretist in the Divinity Corp, she still took the classes when she was at the Academy and impressed her teachers with her ability to puzzle out meanings.

There was a moto lot a small distance from the temple where interpretists, visitors, and other Divinity Corp workers could park. That was where she left her cycle. She didn't want to enter the temple proper, just walk the terraformed and plotted grounds around it. The temple itself was an enormous and imposing structure. It looked like a series of steps layered on top of each other. At least from a distance. It was only up close that it became evident that each layer was a hundred yords tall. There were actual Psierian-size steps up the center all the way to the top but they were kept blocked off for security and safety reasons.

All around the temple were canals and fountains, Psi-made waterfalls and bridges. A small channel of the Mir Ostium had been diverted to create the beautiful landscape and design around the temple. It also fed the gardens and flower beds that surrounded the structure. While the origin of the great temples were still a mystery, it had been the people of Psiere that had built and landscaped the area around their bases. Some thought the canals and bridges added serenity to the space but Castellan thought that it only emphasized the mystery of it all. It was as if the temple itself were a puzzle and instead of solving the puzzle, the modern people of the land added pieces here and there. It was both baffling and beautiful.

She walked the stone paths and bridges, enjoying the breeze and low-set double suns. It was late afternoon going on evening and the sky was starting to turn colors as they made their descent from the vastness to the land below. If Castellan were needed back at the base, they would call on the voteo, but failing that she was her own woman for the rest of the night. As she passed near the smaller entrance, she was surprised to see the imposingly black-uniformed Psi Shield guardians standing at attention outside. While they were too far away to make out which royal they were protecting, she could surmise who it was. The Royal Sovereign Connate Olivienne Dracore was a well-known adventurist and historian. Her sib, the Sub-Connate, was not even at Academy yet, and she would have known if the King or Queen were on the continent. But the Connate frequently traveled around and was known to be difficult about following protocol. At least that was the news Castellan heard amongst the military gossips. "Curious." She mumbled to herself then began the trek back to her cycle.

Perhaps it would be a good night for a cup of golden mead and a book on the Divine Mystery. There were worse ways to spend her time and she knew Lt. Commander Seevert Bello would arrive in the morning thus beginning the hand-off of command so she could make the return trip north.

THE FOLLOWING DAE went by faster than anticipated for Castellan. Like a highly-oiled automaton, her replacement arrived at exactly seven hundred, as the previous dae's recall notice had stated. Lt. Commander Bello had a look about him that she didn't appreciate. Her intuition channel had given her fits from the moment she met him stepping off the railer. But it wasn't her call to put Bello in charge of the forces around Ostium and she would have no say in the matter once she boarded the railer back to Tesseron. All she could do was impart as much information as possible in such a short time and wish the lt. commander luck. She did take a meen to debrief First Lieutenant Cando though.

"Ser, you wished to speak with me?" Cando had come to Castellan Tosh's office near the end of her final dae. Rather than speak in the office itself, she gestured to the first lieutenant to precede her back outside. There was nothing left of hers in the office so she closed and locked door behind her. Once outside, Castellan led them around the back of the building and over to a nearby copse of pelma trees. One never knew if there were spies about and in the small grove they only had to watch for falling coacas.

The light breeze carried the ever-present salt tang that she'd grown used to in Ostium. Tosh gestured for the other officer to have a seat on the bench and she took one as well. "You've worked with Lieutenant Commander Bello throughout the dae now and have had a chance to see his command style. What is your first impression of him?"

Cando thought for a sec then she leveled a serious look at Castellan. "Permission to speak freely, ser?"

"Of course."

A dark look came over Lt. Cando's face. "I don't trust him. I mean, I've always had...vaguely negative feelings toward Praefectus Havington, but Bello twangs my intuition channel even more."

Castellan looked at her curiously. "What's your strength again?"

"It's a five."

The ranking officer sighed and ran a hand through her hair. Cando was startled at the gesture because she'd never seen her commanding officer anything less than neat and professional. She found it endearing and even more attractive if possible. "That's high enough to know then. I have my concerns but for obvious reasons there is nothing I can do or say about them. It is abnormal to only have one dae to train an officer replacement but I also found the half-hearted attack on the beach yesterdae to be highly suspicious. There was simply no reason for it on the Atlanteen's part."

Tosh made a face. "Something here smells worse than the stink of the harbor and I will no longer be around to unravel the mystery. However, if you ever see anything that you know to be wrong or improper, contact me. I will give you my personal voteo code. Following the way of the just is a hard road, Cando. But know that you have an ally. I worked hard to put this region together, I have no want to see it fall apart again. Even if I am on the northern continent, I will not abandon you to the wills of wicked men. Understand?"

"Thank you, Commander, that means a lot to me. You know there is an impromptu going away party for you at the south hall...do you plan to attend?"

Castellan stood and grimaced at her junior officer. "Unfortunately. However I have no plans to stay late because I have to be on the railer first thing in the morning. It leaves at eight hundred oors and I have no wish to travel the dae away with a sick head."

"But, Commander Tosh, a sick head is the only way to properly say goodbye!"

The senior snorted. "I don't think so."

Cando smirked back at her. "We shall see, won't we?"

AT EIGHT HUNDRED the following morning, Castellan Tosh was safely aboard the railer. Her items were packed away in a single large duffel and stored in her sleep cabin, leaving only a small satchel for personal items and entertainment. Even though she was technically between assignments she was perfectly put together in her casual uniform of tan pocket pants and a short sleeved tan shirt. Her tall black boots were polished to a high shine. She wore her pistol holstered at her side but her sword was stowed with the luggage. As always, her hair was perfectly combed without a strand out of place. Lt. Commander Tosh was leaving Ostium the same way she came in, every ince of her the soldier's soldier. And she never once gave any indication that misery washed through her in waves with every sec that passed.

Rather than let common sense dictate the actions of her night, she got carried away with her friends from the town and the other officers that had previously been under her command. Even First Lieutenant Koryne Cando was feeling clearer that morning, which was surprising indeed considering how drunk they had gotten together the night before. It was a fun evening made more fun by pleasant company. And none of it was against reg since Castellan was no longer Koryne's senior.

Castellan figured that she'd try to lie down once the railer got underway but by eight mins after the oor it was still sitting at the station. Finally at quarter after, her patience and temper broke, most likely exacerbated by the pain lancing through her skull with each heartbeat. She went to the nearest door and swung down off the railer. The First Pilot was standing off to the side joking with two porters and she called out to him. "What seems to be the hold up? This railer was supposed to depart at eight hundred sharp!"

He was a military pilot so he acknowledged the lt. commander's rank with a smart salute. "Ser, we are still waiting on the arrival of the Royal Sovereign Connate. She got detained at the temple but should be here shortly. I apologize for the delay, ser!"

Castellan snarled and waved him off. "Of course we are! No, don't apologize, it's not your fault some people think that the randomness of birth allows them special privilege above all the rest." She turned away and marched back to the railer, unaware that the Connate had heard her entire diatribe and was fuming.

"And just who the deep sea darkness was that?" While she was too far away to see who had said the words she certainly heard them. Olivienne Dracore was livid that someone had all but called her spoiled. She worked hard for her position and she had been quite successful in the rotos since she'd finished academy and her military service. Not to mention that her delay was caused by the Queen herself. Her mother had contacted her to request a few sensitive cases of documents from the temple, which is what threw off the railer schedule. But you don't say no to the Queen.

The pilot cleared his throat nervously. "Connate Dracore..." Angry purple eyes turned to the shorter man and he continued with much trepidation. "By your leave, that is Commander Castellan Tosh. She is one of the best soldiers I've ever seen and this region wouldn't be half of what it is without her stabilizing presence over the past four rotos. I'm sure she didn't mean to imply anything untoward about your pedigree or work ethic."

Olivienne was not to be swayed from her ire. "I don't care if she is the general of the entire Psi Defense Corp, she's rude and needs a lesson in respect!" She looked toward Lt. Savon, the man who was temporarily in charge of her Shield unit with no proper captain at the helm. "Are all the cases loaded?"

He nodded. "Yes, Connate Dracore."

"Good." She turned to the nearest porter. "Can you show me to my sleep car? I was up all night searching through the archives and desperately need some rest."

The younger woman stood in awe of the sovereign before giving a quick bow and swallowing down her nervousness. "Yes, Connate Dracore! If you'll follow me?"

They entered through a different door than the one Castellan Tosh had taken, which was how the Connate never realized that the first class sleeping segment only held two cabins. One was occupied by the Royal Sovereign, the other by a certain Lt. Commander. The First Pilot knew though and he mopped his sweaty brow with the rag he kept in his pocket. It was going to be a long couple daes back to Tesseron. He predicted that he'd be hiding in his own cabin much of the time the other pilots were on duty.

Chapter Four

THE FIRST DAE of travel was fairly quiet. The Connate stayed in her cabin sleeping the entire morning, then ordered noon meal in so she wouldn't have to deal with marching around the railer segments with a trail of black clad guardians scaring the other passengers. She also wanted to put some time in on the document they had found at Ostium. It had a pair of symbols at the bottom that she was certain meant a match to the one they found at the cave wekes before. Unfortunately it wasn't yielding to the usual encryption key and she suspected that it was another undecipherable message from the Makers.

Olivienne thought about the impossible task of trying to find the new translation key. Six daes a weke, four wekes a lune, and ten lunes a roto. Solving the mystery of the rumored third temple would give her letters of a new encryption key thus possibly releasing a vast amount of knowledge currently locked within the untranslated texts in each temple. It could make her career.

Her newest artifacts and documents alluded to that old rumor of a third temple and she desperately wanted to find such a thing if it existed. She was one of the believers and she wished more than anything to deliver proof. With that thought in mind, she shoved the remains of her noon meal away and redoubled her efforts at translation.

Castellan managed a few oors of sleep herself before she finally ventured out to prowl the different segments of the railer. As soon as she exited her cabin, she knew immediately who the other first class guest was. Unlike the standard passenger segments, the sleeper segment had a hallway that ran toward the back of the railer on the right side. Castellan was in the first private cabin, then there was a small lounge area, and the second private cabin was at the end of the segment.

Even if her powers of deduction were drastically off, she would have guessed her fellow first class passenger by the black clad guardians seated in the small lounge. There were also two more cluttering up the hall in front of the other suite and at each end of the sleeper segment. Their segment had been hitched last on the railer, probably to cut down on foot traffic near the

Connate, as well as make the space easier to secure. They obviously trusted Castellan, most likely because she was a ranking military officer.

It was half past fourteen hundred oors and just after the stop at Cordeesh when she finally ventured out for food with a book in hand. As Castellan passed through each seg on her way toward the front of the railer, she got quite a few curious looks. And the dashing soldier drew more than her fair share of appreciative glances. She was attractive but beyond that she carried herself with a certain dignity that people responded to. Many on the railer were from Ostium and knew who she was. Lt. Commander Tosh had become almost famous for her ability to bolster the frequently Atlanteen-harassed region. Because of her accomplishments, Castellan made them feel safe. Even though it hadn't been long since she got the recall notice, news had spread fast throughout the region. They simply didn't know what to make of the fact that their long-time protector was being called back north. No matter what continent one was on, Psi didn't like change.

Castellan was recognized and hailed as soon as she stepped into the dining segment. "Lieutenant Commander Tosh, what a pleasant surprise!"

The woman who spoke was seated at a table near where Castellan entered the seg. She had a smooth brown mug held casually in one hand and the remains of her meal lay cold on the plate in front of her. Castellan smiled when she saw her. "Doctore Shen! The pleasure is all mine."

Dre. Shen waved to the seat opposite her. "I've finished with my meal but you're more than welcome to join me. We haven't caught up in ages. Besides..." She paused and glanced around her. "Tables are at a premium here, apparently."

Sure enough, Castellan looked up at the rest of the railer segment and saw that all the tables were indeed taken. "I wouldn't mind sharing a table but I'm afraid I'm not the best company right now. Strained my channels two daes ago and I'm only now feeling well enough to eat some food."

The doctore raised an eyebrow. "Strained channels wouldn't keep you from eating, Castellan."

The lt. commander blushed and scratched her ear. "Well, stone brew and my reassignment party might."

Gemeda Shen laughed gently at her long-time friend. "I see...so a sick head on top of the rest?" The tall soldier nodded.

"That hardly seems like you, my dear. Well get yourself some food and you can tell me all about it after I patch you up."

Castellan held up her hands in dismay. "Oh no, I couldn't ask you to do that!"

"No? So it wasn't you who made sure the hospital and orphanage in Ostium got a significant donation of armicruste meat after your now infamous battle? Information travels fast my friend. The news reached Cordeesh by evening meal. Come now, it's the least I can do for the Hero of Temple Beach."

Castellan made a sound of discomfort low in her throat at receiving such a horrible moniker. But rather than engage in a battle of wits or words she was not fit for at the moment, she turned and walked farther down the aisle to the food station. Quiet laughter followed her.

Once she returned and settled onto the bench opposite Gemeda, the fair-haired woman held out both hands palm up. "Before you start eating let me see if I can alleviate some of your discomfort."

"You mean you can promise never to call me that awful name again?"

Gemeda shook her head and grinned. "Oh no, I'll be using that for many rotos to come, if only to annoy you. Now hold out your hands." Castellan complied and placed her hands palms down and let Gemeda clasp them in a casual grip. Not only was she a doctore, but she was one of the few with the telesana ability. Dre. Shen was a Psi-healer but also carried three other channels, all of which helped to make her one of the most renowned medicans on either continent. She carried both telepathy and empathy, as well as eidetic memory. It was as if the fates wanted to build the perfect medican and that Psi was Gemeda.

Proving her ability and reputation, Castellan started to feel significantly better within secs of their initial touch. Lt. Commander Tosh sighed when the doctore pulled her hands back a meen later. "Ah, that is much better. Thank you, old friend."

Gemeda waggled a finger at her. "Friend yes, old never! I was able to take care of your sick stomach and head, and alleviate the pain of your strained channel, but you should avoid using it for a dae or two."

The lt. commander laughed. "Well, as it's highly unlikely I'll face down a tun and a half of armored sea-bug while on the railer, I'd say complying with the doctore's orders shouldn't be a problem." The savory bowl of tender grain, fungi, and shredded fowl were beckoning her empty stomach so Castellan began eating. She spoke between bites of the surprisingly tasty railer food. "So what brought you down to the southern continent? Or are you posted here now?"

"I'm stationed on Dromea for the time being."

Castellan made a face. "And you never contacted me?"

The doctore shrugged. "You've clearly been busy. Besides, I'm posted up at Gomen and I've just finished a tour of the facilities in all the major cities down here. It was requested by the Queen herself that I instruct the other doctores with telesana in best practice techniques that will allow them to heal longer and cleaner." Her indigo colored eyes twinkled as she took in the palest blue of Castellan's. "All work and no play I'm afraid. I just finished my final weke in Cordeesh and now I'm finally headed home." She played with her utensils while Castellan continued to eat. "What about you? You're venturing a little far from the southeast province, won't your soldiers miss you?"

The lt. commander shrugged and swallowed. "Not my soldiers anymore."

A pale eyebrow went up at her words. "Oh? Where are you headed now and aren't you about due a promotion?"

"Tesseron. And I'm surprised you haven't already heard about my recall the way rumors fly." Castellan grimaced and pushed her empty dish aside. "And yes, I was promised a promotion if I stabilized the region around Ostium."

"And?"

She shrugged again. "I don't know. The missive just said I was being recalled to Tesseron with no mention of my next post. I guess I'll find out when I get there."

Gemeda touched her hand. "I'm sure it will work out, Castellan. You are a magnificent officer and news of your accomplishments have even reached the Queen."

Castellan looked at her curiously. "And how do you know that?"

"A few lunes back I happened to be at dinner with the Queen Olivara and King Keshien, as well as a variety of other esteemed guests, when talk of Ostium came up and your name followed soon after. It was all effusive praise, I assure you."

"Effusive or not, I refuse to waste my time pondering and worrying. I'll find out what my next post is when I report for duty in a few daes." She leaned forward and let some of her non-officer character shine through as she whispered to her friend. "Between you and me though, I really don't care what happens as long as I'm off this sun-scorched continent!"

"I don't mind it so much. Spend a rotation in the mountains and you'll be glad for the heat."

The soldier shook her head. "Not me. I've been down here four long rotos and I never got used to the high heat. So when does the railer reach Gomen? I haven't had time to look at my schedule yet."

Gemeda pulled out a small tele-typed slip from the satchel that hung at her waist then made a face as she read the time. "Nearly twenty-two hundred. Just in time to get home and get about six oors sleep before I have to be back at the hospital."

Castellan looked at her curiously. "Why so early?"

The doctore sighed. "I have a full dae of surgery scheduled, most of which I'll have to do the hard way as it is partly a teaching session. No rest for the wicked I say!"

"Well that is completely unacceptable! You should get some sleep on the way there."

Gemeda shook her head. "I only have a standard ticket, love. It's a short hop after all...you know how Medi Corp doesn't like to waste cred."

The lt. commander stood and gathered her trash. "You'll sleep in my cabin, I insist. I have plenty of space since the powers that be saw fit to put me in the first class segment. No one will bother you there, not even me. I can while away my time anywhere."

The good doctore stood as well and quirked a smile. "What if I ask you to bother me?"

Castellan shook her head in consternation. "Not even then. You know I love you dearly but the time for that is long past, Gem. And you need your sleep much more than you need a quick tupping."

Gemeda pouted but was secretly pleased that her good friend cared more about her welfare than about sexual gratification. She stood and tossed her own trash in the receptacle. "All right then, lead the way, ser!"

They didn't have any problems until they reached her sleeper segment. One of the two guardians stopped them as soon as they came out of the pass through and into the door of their segment. The taller of the two serious, though young, looking guardians blocked the hallway. "I'm sorry, ser, but no guests are allowed in the Connate's seg."

Castellan stood fast in the face of his young surety. "Do you know who this is?" He shook his head. "This is the renowned medican, Doctore Gemeda Shen. And since this is also my segment, I say this woman is allowed." He gave a shake of his head and she narrowed her eyes as she took in his rank insignia. "We seem to be at an impasse. What is your name, Lieutenant?"

He stood straight in the face of her authority then and gave a proper salute. "Lieutenant Gentry Savon, ser!"

She looked around at the other guardians that had come from the small lounge area to see what the disturbance was about. Gemeda put her hand on Castellan's arm. "I can just go nap in one of the passenger segments. There is really no need for a fuss."

"No, you will do no such thing." She glanced around, looking for the person in charge. "Where is your captain? I wish to speak to them."

Savon swallowed nervously. "I am the acting unit leader, ser. Our captain has not been replaced since the unfortunate, er...cycle incident."

Lt. Commander Tosh settled her authority around her like a cloak. "Well then, Lieutenant Savon, I suggest you will need to ask permission for me to bring a guest aboard this segment."

"But who do I ask, ser?"

She smiled. "I would imagine that you should ask the ranking officer."

He swallowed. "Erm, that would be you, ser."

"So it would."

The fellow to the left cleared his throat and held up a single finger. "Um..."

Castellan turned her icy gaze to him and Dre. Shen held back a snicker at the look of fear that washed over the young man's face. "Yes, Specialist?"

"Actually, ser, the ranking person on this segment would be the Royal Sovereign, Connate Dracore."

"Of course it is." Tosh sighed and rubbed her forehead. She turned her gaze back to the hapless lieutenant. "I suggest you go ask permission then because I'm not growing any younger." They continued to hesitate and she had a feeling the Connate left instructions not to be disturbed. But it wasn't her problem. "Now, Lieutenant! Because you either elicit permission from Connate Dracore or I will write my own permission slip and you will not like the ink I use."

Lt. Savon knew exactly who Castellan Tosh was and he had

no want to be on her bad side. "Yes, ser!" He saluted then spun on his heel and marched down the hall toward the Connate's cabin.

Dre. Shen and Lt. Commander Tosh watched as the soldier in charge of the Shield unit timidly knocked on the Connate's cabin door. Gemeda leaned closer to Castellan and whispered in her ear. "Is this wise...possibly incurring the wrath of the Royal Sovereign?"

The lt. commander just laughed. "She'll get over it." She quieted when the Connate answered her door and they both listened to the conversation. They couldn't see Connate Dracore because she remained in her cabin but they heard her voice well enough.

"I thought I left instructions not to be disturbed, Savon!"

"Yes, Connate Dracore, but I was sent to ask your permission to allow a guest onto the first class segment." He shifted nervously from foot to foot.

The Connate's voice came back sounding both annoyed and curious. "A guest? For me?"

He shook his head regretfully. "No, Sovereign. It is Lieutenant Commander Tosh's guest. She wishes to bring a woman into her cabin but we had explicit instructions not to let anyone else on the segment. With the exception of you and the Lieutenant Commander —"

"By the ocean depths...this is what you've interrupted me for? I don't care who this Tosh is tupping. She's on this segment so she must have proper clearance. Let her have honey and leave the bees alone, Savon! Now off with you!"

Sensing an imminent explosion from the honorable soldier, Gemeda immediately grabbed Castellan's wrist to catch her attention and delay the angry outburst. "Tosh..." When she had the other woman's attention, she continued. "Let me. I've spoken with the Connate on a few different occasions. She is bright but gets utterly involved in her work. Let me speak with her." Castellan nodded but her teeth remained clenched. Gemeda pitched her voice loud enough to be heard at the end of the railer segment. "Connate Dracore, you may want to watch who you call honey in the future!" As soon as the words left her mouth there was an exclamation down the hall.

"What the..." Olivienne's head popped out of the door and stared down at the other two women. "Doctore Shen? I had no idea that was you Savon was going on about!" The Connate left her cabin and walked toward Castellan and Gemeda.

The medican gave her sardonic grin. "Clearly. Do you always leap to assumptions so?"

The Connate grinned back. "Do you always pick up handsome soldiers on the railer?"

A noise something like a pained growl came from Castellan's throat. "I would appreciate it if you wouldn't speak about me as if I weren't here."

"And I would appreciate it if you would keep your assumptions to yourself in the future!"

Dre. Shen looked back and forth between the two women and sensed some deeper strife beyond the meeting of the past few meens. She turned to her long-time friend. "What have you done now, Tosh?"

"It wasn't me! The almighty Royal Sovereign Connate Dracore kept the entire railer waiting because she couldn't be bothered to be here on time!"

Blood rushed to Olivienne's face as anger began to rise. "How dare you speak about matters you know nothing of! There was a very valid excuse as to why we were late to the platform!"

The good medican sensed something building that was going to lead to no good, and the Connate's guardians clearly had no clue what to do with the arguing pair. Both women were above the men's pay grade. She tried to interject. "Ladies..."

Castellan snorted. "Oh yes, I'm sure there was. Not used to getting up before nine hundred are we?"

Gemeda tried again with no effect. "Ladies..."

"For your information, *Lieutenant Commander* Tosh, we were late because the Queen requested a number of secured cases be removed from the Temple of Illeos to be brought back to the Temple of Archeos. We were nearly to the railer platform when we got the missive and had to turn back. I will be sure to let my mother know that we inconvenienced your travel plans when I return!" Olivienne's last few words ended in a shout, which caused all the guardians and the medican to step back. The only one that held her ground in the face of the Connate's anger and threat was Castellan.

It was in that moment, as she took in the flushed face and heaving chest of the angry sovereign, that Castellan Tosh was struck by the strangest wave of attraction. Castellan wanted to shake Olivienne Dracore, to push the woman against the wall of the railer until she could make her see reason. It was an odd urge and it made her pause. She normally liked her acquaintances a bit less bold, and quieter for sure. Connate Dracore was neither of those things, squared. But despite all that, and despite the fact that the stubborn sovereign had infuriated her to no end, Castellan had the suicidal urge to move closer to the irate woman. But she didn't. Typically being one of level head and sound mind, the lt. commander could see that she herself was in the wrong.

While Olivienne Dracore may have made an assumption about the nature of her guest, Castellan made the first assumption before the sovereign had even boarded the railer. She was at fault first. In a move that startled all parties present, Lt. Commander Tosh took a step back from Olivienne and saluted her then moved into a low bow. It was a symbol of deepest respect, or apology. "Please forgive me, Connate Dracore. You are correct in that I made assumptions about you this morning, and I said things that were both inappropriate and unjust. You have my sincerest apology. As for Doctore Gemeda Shen, she is a longtime friend who has a busy schedule tomorrow so I was going to let her use my cabin to rest on our way to Gomen."

Olivienne looked at the medican and Gemeda nodded her head. "It is true, I did come here to rest." She got a twinkle in her eye and added a little more because she knew it would embarrass the good lt. commander. "Though only after she shot down my attempts at seduction."

Castellan sighed and looked up toward the celling of the railer, silently reciting every line of the Code of Archeos. Olivienne merely laughed at her embarrassed countenance. "My apologies as well, Lieutenant Commander Tosh. It seems we were both guilty of false assumptions." She turned to face Gemeda and bowed slightly. "And to you as well, Doctore Shen. I didn't not mean to cast aspersions on your character."

"No harm done, Connate Dracore. I accept your apology." She looked back and forth between the two previously arguing women. "Well I don't know about you, but I'm certainly not going to sleep just yet. Your little row has energized me quite a bit. Would either of you happen to have some portea or golden mead?"

Olivienne smiled at her suggestion. "I happen to have a full bottle of portea given to me by the largest vinier in Ostium. I see no reason not to share it with friends." Castellan made a pained face at her words but conceded that becoming acquaintances with the stubborn woman was significantly better than screaming at each other. "Besides, I'm ready for a break." She held out her elbow toward Gemeda and, charmed, the medican accepted the escort down the short hall to the segment lounge. Castellan sighed again and paced stoically behind them.

The lounge had one comfortable couch bolted to the floor of the railer segment, as well as three more low-slung and well-padded chairs. Once Olivienne deposited Gemeda on the couch, she excused herself to fetch the bottle of portea. There were glasses already secured in a cabinet next to Castellan's chair, so she set the book she had been carrying on the low central table and made herself useful by retrieving three of them. Her mind whirled in strange eddies, thoughts about the Connate, and their interaction. They were interrupted by her friend. "So what was that all about? I don't think I've ever seen you lose your calm."

Castellan looked up at Gemeda. "It's not completely unheard of you know. I am just an average Psi after all."

The doctore laughed loudly and startled the nearest guardians. "You were never average, my dear."

"Have I missed all the humore, or did you save some for me?"

Gemeda waved her hand dismissively. "Oh, it wasn't really a funny thing, merely a funny response. Castellan here was being humble like always, despite the fact that she makes even the most upright soldier look unsavory."

"Oh?" Olivienne turned her violet gaze to the officer in question realizing that she had indeed committed a grave injury to the attractive woman's character. "And here I accused you of bringing back a woman to tup! I am double sorry for my accusation and offhand remarks then."

Castellan snorted with laughter and had to move the now full glass of portea away from her mouth. "Oh, I am hardly that upright, Connate Dracore. But I will admit you besmirched my honor a bit with your words. No worries though, I'm right as rain now."

Olivienne smirked back at her over the top of the burgundy liquid in her glass. "Oh, you certainly are." Tosh was startled by the bold flirt of the sovereign's words and Gemeda hid a smile behind her own glass. Right that moment she would have given anything to continue traveling all the way to Tesseron, if only to see where the two women in her presence ended up. Sparks like that didn't happen without some sort of chemistrae.

The silence turned awkward after a meen. Castellan's book caught Gemeda's attention when she set her glass of portea down on the low table. "What are you reading, Tosh? Still whiling away your time puzzling out the Divine Mystery?"

Castellan shrugged and leaned forward to move the book out of sight. "When I have time, which isn't often."

Before she could reach the novel it was snatched up by the Connate. "What is this, you follow the Divine Mystery? Seriously, or just as a curiosity?" She flipped the book over and her dark brows rose up when she read the title. "By the depths...serious it is then! This is a great book. I think you'll like it a lot since it pieces together much of the literature concerning the Maker's motivations."

Tosh looked back at her both surprised and interested. "Oh yeah? I can't wait to get further in then. Sadly I'm only at the beginning." Part of what made the Divine Mystery so intriguing wasn't just the fact that no one knew who the people were that built the great pyramids, or where they came from. They also didn't know where the Maker's had vanished to. And it wasn't easy to translate the documents as one would assume either. It was tedious and painstaking work. Each new vellum of information only deepened the mystery. It was like putting together puzzle pieces in the dark, when the picture kept changing. All people like Olivienne could do was to keep gathering those puzzle pieces for the interpretists to translate. Somedae they would solve the mystery, but that dae was nowhere near.

The trio of women drank their portea and spoke on a variety of subjects. Both Olivienne and Gemeda informed Castellan of all she'd missed in the four rotos that she'd been living in Dromea. In return she told them of all her observations about the Atlanteens and her thoughts of their motivations. After nearly two oors of conversation, Gemeda excused herself to go rest in Castellan's cabin. Olivienne also apologized to the lt. commander and said she had to get back to her stack of untranslated vellum and the document she had found in the Temple of Illeos. Left to her own devices, Castellan reclined on the couch and dove into her book. Every so often she'd look up in the direction the Connate had retired, wondering about the unusually fast flame of her ire earlier. She eventually shrugged it off. After all, everyone had buttons to be pushed and some were better pushers than others. She sighed and tried her best to put Olivienne Dracore from her mind.

Chapter Five

CASTELLAN HAD ONLY been reading a short time when she was interrupted by the Connate's senior guardian. "Commander Tosh..."

She looked up at him and immediately knew something was gravely wrong. "What is it, Lieutenant Savon?" She marked and closed the book, placing it carefully on the low table, then stood and straightened her uniform.

He swallowed nervously. "Ser, I've had a precog. We need to stop at the next town but we don't have much time."

Immediately concerned, she grilled him for details. "What are your channels?"

"Intuition, but lower. Prescience and telesthesia, both average."

She thought for precious secs. "Do you know what the problem is, or is it not distinct enough yet?"

He shook his head. "I'm sorry ser, I don't know yet."

Castellan held out her hand. "If you'll allow me to touch you, I believe I can see the precog with my telepathy. Do you consent?"

Sure of her capabilities and strength, he held out his hand. As soon as their skin met his telesthesia channel unexpectedly opened and they both saw a hazy image of an island in the middle of a rapidly rising river. Five Psi, children by the size, appeared to be trapped. Lt. Savon gasped and pulled his hand away. "It's you! You triggered my remote seeing so you must be the one they need!"

Rather than answer him, Castellan strode over to the teleo that was mounted on the wall of their lounge. She rang the pilot and he answered right away, aware that the call was coming from the Connate's segment. "Pilot Thot Binier, how may I assist?"

Castellan wasted no time with pleasantries. "Pilot Binier, this is Lieutenant Commander Castellan Tosh. We need to make an emergency stop at the next town. Do you know what it is called and if it's near a river?

"Yes, ser. The town is called Vesper. It's not a regular stop so they only have a small platform. The platform is right before we cross the Mir Altaq. It's a good thing you called when you did, we're less than ten meens out. I'll voteo ahead and let them know we are stopping. Binier out!"

Feeling a vague sense of urgency, Castellan jogged down the hall to the Connate's cabin door. She knocked and kept her emotions under tight control. "Connate Dracore, we have a situation."

There was the sound of shuffling on the other side of the door then it slid open. "Situation?"

Lt. Commander Tosh nodded, ignoring the flutter of attraction that was as unwelcome as it was inappropriate. "Yes, Connate. Savon had a precog and it seems I am needed at the next town. There are children in danger."

Olivienne leaned over and grabbed her pistols from the work space. She slung a satchel across her shoulders, then stepped out of the cabin. No matter the situation, her mother trained her to never go anywhere unarmed. "I assume you informed the pilot?"

"Yes. But it's not necessary for you to leave the railer, Connate Dracore. You would be better protected by staying here with your Shield unit—"

"Bollux! I'm a powerful Psi, and well trained in emergency situations. I will be there in case someone needs me." She looked over at Savon. "Is this like the rock slide?" He nodded. "Just as strong?"

Savon made a face. "Stronger, Connate. I hope we are in time for Lieutenant Commander Tosh to help."

Olivienne spun her gaze back to Castellan. "You?"

"Yes, it seems that my touch prompted an episode of telesthesia immediately after his precog, indicating that I am the one the vision relates to. He was able to see children on an island in the middle of a rapidly rising river. The precog says a flash flood will occur soon so we need to get them off that island."

The Connate raised an eyebrow to take in the well-built Lt. Commander. "Interesting." Olivienne continued to stare for secs longer then shook herself as if she were in a daze. "Well, whatever the challenge may be, we won't meet it standing here like a couple of milling gozens. Let's head toward the front of the railer where the pilot will most likely line up with the platform. If I remember correctly, the town is on the river right before we cross the bridge."

As soon as she finished speaking, the pilot's voice came over the speaker system located in every segment of the railer.

"Attention citizens, we will be making an emergency stop in five meens. Please remain seated and do not exit the railer. Do not fear, the emergency is not related to the railer or any of her passengers. We are simply stopping to assist the town. Again, please do not leave the railer and remain in your seats."

Castellan, Olivienne, and all but two guardians made their way toward the front of the segment as they felt the railer begin to slow. Before they could pass by Castellan's cabin, the door slid open and a sleep tousled Dre. Shen popped her head out. "Tosh? What is going on?"

"Emergency in the next town, Gemeda. Lieutenant Savon is a precognitive and says they need my help."

Gemeda looked alarmed. "But Castellan..."

Castellan knew her friend was about to bring up the strained channel and for whatever reason, Tosh didn't want the others to know. She interrupted the good doctore before she could traipse any further down her line of questioning. "Come along if you wish, Gem, but we need to leave now."

It only took a few meens to make it to the front of the long railer. Their jog through the aisles of each seg was assisted by the fact that citizens were remaining seated, just as the pilot had requested. A porter directed them to the door that would line up to the platform and it was only a few meens longer for the railer to eventually slow to a stop. It was raining outside and two people stood in the middle of the downpour, soaked to the skin and waiting to meet the departing group. The clouds were so thick that the dae was cast into a gloomy haze, despite the afternoon light of the two suns. Of the people waiting, one was a woman of middling rotos and wore an insignia on her cloak so Castellan addressed her. "Our precog says you have a situation with trapped children."

The middle-aged woman took in Castellan's rank insignia curiously. "Yes, Commander. Five of them took a boat out to the picnic island earlier todae and when the weather kicked up sudden like, they were unable to come back. Eventually the parens contacted me and when we investigated we found the water impassible." She paused as if remembering something vital then held out her hand. "My name is Stelle Gordy and I'm the elected town Representative. I'm sorry you stopped for nothing. The island has a small shelter, we figured we'd just let them stay the night out there and retrieve them in the morning once the storm passes and the water slows again."

Castellan's hair had wet enough that a lock fell down into her eyes. She took a sec to slick it back off her face, then she clasped Rep. Gordy's hand in her own. "Lieutenant Commander Tosh, and behind me are Royal Sovereign Connate Dracore, Doctore Gemeda Shen, and the Connate's Shield unit. It is Lieutenant Savon who is responsible for this stop. Your plans to wait will not work since he had a precog of a flash flood coming down from the mountains. I'm afraid your children are not safe where they are."

Rep. Gordy didn't know which shock to respond to first. The fact that the royal heir was soaking in the rain in front of her, or that danger was at their doorstep. She bowed toward the sovereign. "Connate Dracore, it is an honor to meet you!" She turned her attention to the man that had accompanied her. He was young and had a similar look about him so Castellan thought maybe he was Rep. Gordy's son. "Gevin, take the moto and go round up your papan and the rescue crew. And hurry! Have them meet us at the dock."

She turned back to their group. "If you'll follow me, the dock isn't far from here." She gestured down a path that ran perpendicular to the railer tracks. Nearly twenty yords farther down the railer line there was a bridge that crossed the Mir Ataq. The river wasn't very large but the bridge itself was quite high, a testament to the fact that spring floods were not that uncommon in the region.

The group took off at a fast jog down the slippery path. Castellan glanced at the Connate out of the corner of her eye, surprised that the royal was keeping up with no effort. Dre. Shen had no problems but Castellan knew that her friend kept up a strict exercise regimen that started back when they served on the east coast of Endara together. Gemeda acted as though she were a hundred rotos old with her proper seriousness. But in all actuality they were the same age and had come through the academy in the same class. They both went to officer school together then on to serve in the Psi Defense Corp. But when the Psi Medi Corp was low on members, they recruited Gemeda and she left with the chance of faster advancement rather than continue along the military track. She had more opportunities and better appointments through the Psi Medi Corp as well.

About five meens after they started out, the path brought the group to a park. Rain and wind lashed at them, soaking Tosh's shirt and causing it to stick to her skin. The dock itself was on floats, another indicator that the river rose up and down with some frequency. Castellan could immediately see why they decided to wait on rescue. The water was both fast and deep, running from right to left. On top of the hazardous current, there was also a lot of debris in the water, including entire trees. Any boat attempting to cross would be on a suicide mission. Olivienne was thinking the same thing and turned to the Representative of Vesper. "Does your town have a high telekinetic or teleporter?"

Rep. Gordy shook her head regretfully. "No, our last high channel went off to Academy this past spring."

"So you have no hard channels that could help?"

The older woman grimaced. "I'm sorry, Connate Dracore, but no we don't."

Castellan looked at the Connate curiously. "You're a royal, and you mentioned being high Psi. What are your channels?"

Olivienne frowned but listed them off anyway. "Awareness, telepathy, pyrokinesis, and apportation, and low channel teleportation. I'm afraid none of those could help this situation. I could wish a million times over for my teleportation channel to be higher, but unfortunately I can't pull more than a small animal if it's something alive. I'm stuck primarily with the inanimate."

Lt. Commander Tosh straightened, a determined glint in her eye. "Don't be too sure that your channel is so useless, Connate Dracore." She peered across to the island, driving rain impeding her view. "Do you think you could apport float vests over to the island?"

Olivienne gazed out over the tumultuous water. "Do you have a spyglass?" Castellan pulled one out of her pouch and handed it over. After a few secs of struggling to peer through the wet gloom, the Connate collapsed the device and handed it back to Castellan. She could just make out the shelter on the small island and the huddled children inside. "Yes, I could do that."

Tosh looked around and spied a boathouse. She removed her pistol holder and her ever-present leather pouch and handed them to Gemeda then addressed the Connate. "Come!" She broke into run, knowing that every single sec counted. Seeing her intention, the Connate handed off her own gear to Savon and made haste after her. She was followed closely by her Shield guardians. When they reached the boathouse ten yords away, Castellan found it locked. She abruptly pulled up and gave a great kick to the door, splintering it open. Inside they retrieved the only five float vests stored within. It would do. She handed them one by one to the Connate and just as fast Olivienne apported them out to the island. At the same time Castellan reached out with her mind to make contact with any of the children in the group.

She found one mind with the telepathy channel and pushed slightly to make her presence known. The child, a boy on the cusp of puberty, responded. *"Hello?"*

"Do not be frightened. My name is Castellan and we will get you to safety. But you must put the float vests on just in case the water rises further. Okay?"

Castellan didn't have the empathy channel but the colliding thoughts in the boys head indicated relief. Indistinct words like happy, sad, scared, and cold bombarded her through their connection. *"Thank you, and please hurry. Water is almost to the shelter!"*

"We will hurry. Tell me one thing, is your boat still there?"

"No, the river took it."

She pulled out of the connection and turned to the Connate as they jogged down to the floating dock. "Did you hear?"

Olivienne nodded. "What is your plan?"

"There is only one thing I can do. I'm going to have to go get them. I will levitate across the river to the island with a boat, load them up, and bring them back."

The Connate looked Castellan up and down with surprise. "You can do all that?"

Ever the unflappable professional, the lt. commander responded with confidence. "Of course. I'm a five channel high Psi. My telekinesis is rated a six, I think I can manage a few kids and a boat."

Olivienne's eyebrows rose with the commander's words as they joined the rest of the group at the edge of the dock. "You! You're the Hero of Temple Beach?"

"Yes she is, why do you ask?" Of course Dre. Shen only heard the Connate's question, not the preceding conversation.

"She's going to levitate a boat out to the island to get the kids and bring it back."

Gemeda looked like she was going to protest but Castellan held up a hand. "This needs to be done, Gem, damn the consequences." The sense of unease she had been feeling since being on the railer increased and she knew she had to act. Without another word to the group, she jogged over to the nearest boat that looked like it would hold five kids and cut the line with a knife on her belt. It was the only item she hadn't removed when she stripped her tools and devices. Then before the river could rip it away from the dock, she lifted the boat into the air.

As the boat rose above the river, so too did she. It was harder than she thought it would be. Though her strength had long returned to her depleted channels, using her telekinesis felt a lot like touching a hot brand with an already burnt hand. Castellan's channel throbbed sickly and pain flared through her temples. Her face a study in concentration as she went, all the group on shore could do was watch and wait.

Curiosity niggled at the back of Olivienne's mind and she addressed Dre. Shen. "What were you going to say to her when she stopped you?"

Gemeda clenched her fists, knowing exactly how much pain Castellan would be in. "Her actions at Temple Beach strained her telekinetic channel yesterdae, practically burned it out and depleted her reserves at the same time."

"What? Is she insane? If the pain overwhelms her she'll drop them all!"

Dre. Shen shook her head. "She'll drop herself first, unconscious into the water if need be. We should stand ready just in case."

The entire group moved to the top of the hill nearest the dock as rain continued to lash at them. Lt. Savon gave warning when another precog hit. "Connate Dracore, we only have meens until the flood. Perhaps we should move back to a safer distance—"

"No! We will stay here and wait." Mentally she sent warning to Tosh. *"Hurry, Savon says we only have meens 'til the flood!"*

"We are on our way."

Sure enough, within the next meen they saw the small boat appear through the gloom, floating just above the water. Castellan and the boat barely cleared the frothing waves below. The pain of her strained channel was preventing her from expending the amount of effort that a greater height would require. The salvo team and medicans, arrived while they had been waiting. The trained men and women were ready to swoop in and tend to the kids the meen the boat landed. Much to the dismay of them all, the boat full of children and Tosh stopped about ten yords out from the shoreline. Even from that distance in the rain, Castellan's face showed the agony she was in.

"She's not going to make it...can't make it..." Olivienne wasn't sure who said it, but she hated the words. It was Gemeda who countered them.

"She'll make it or die trying. There is no can't in Castellan's lexicon."

A great roar sounded upriver to the right. Castellan's face turned toward the sound and with the motivation of fear for the kids she gave a great mental shove that sent the boat halfway up the side of the hill. Unfortunately that push stole her consciousness, plunging her into the icy water below.

Olivienne didn't even think about the consequences of her actions. She apported two of the float vests from the kids that were safely ashore and sprinted toward the water. Savon called out to her just before she dove in. While the Connate was an excellent swimmer, nothing had prepared her for the raging and abusive current. When she broke the surface, she saw Castellan's head pop up as well, the plunge having brought her awake again. She screamed into the other woman's mind. *"Catch!"* Then she apported the other float vest into her hands.

Olivienne took valuable secs to secure her own vest, ever conscious of the wall of water that she knew was coming. She winced when a small tree limb glanced off the back of her head but she didn't take her eyes off the lt. commander. Tosh had only succeeded in draping the float vest around her neck, but it was not secured. The Connate swam as hard as she could, angling toward the barely conscious soldier. By a stroke of blind luck, she made it to the lt. commander and wrapped her arms securely around the woman just as the flood hit. She held on as tight she could, not only to Tosh, but to the strap of Tosh's vest as well. It wouldn't do to lose the one thing that was keeping her afloat.

Castellan roused slightly, struggling in the unfamiliar grip as they were tossed about. "What...?"

Olivienne soothed her mentally. *"It's okay, just don't let go."*

The soldier twisted her head to look upon the Connate with dismay. *"If something happens to you the Queen will kill me — look out!"*

A large tree trunk was coming right at them, but Olivienne had seen it too and before it could strike, she concentrated and apported the deadly projectile downstream from them. She continued apporting the largest stuff away for desperate meens while the river tossed them like leaves in the wind. Her awareness and apportation channels were working at their limits as Olivienne tried to keep them alive and intact.

The duo was approaching another high bridge when multiple things happened at once. The Connate was distracted by another large tree trunk in the water and while she took care of that the back of Castellan's head struck a boulder just below the surface. Olivienne saw it but there was nothing she could do to prevent the blow. She screamed when Castellan's eyes rolled back and shut. "Tosh!" But the roar of the raging water drowned out the sound of her voice. She tried again. *"Tosh!"* Her mental calls too went unanswered.

Another large piece of debris struck the Connate in the back while she was distracted causing her to loosen her grip. That was all it took for Castellan to be washed away from her. Olivienne felt a slight pressure in her head and the mental voice of Spc. Devin came through. *"Connate, we are here!"*

Before she could respond, Olivienne was caught up in a large net of some kind. She was relieved to see that Castellan was caught with her. The pressure of the river was immense but slowly the two women began to rise, the net pulling them back together. When Lt. Commander Tosh was within reach, Olivienne tried to ascertain her condition. The soldier was clearly unconscious but it was impossible to check her breathing or pulses until they reached the safety of the bridge. It felt like aeons before they were lifted over the rail and deposited on the stone surface.

The rain had let up to a light sprinkle but Olivienne wasn't concerned about any of that. As soon as they were released from the tangle of netting she scrambled to Castellan's side. The woman wasn't breathing and a check of her neck yielded no pulses. "Sheddech!" Olivienne looked around desperately. "Where is Doctore Shen?"

Lt. Savon was breathing hard and his face was flushed. "We had to leave behind the group to sprint ahead in time to catch you at the bridge, Connate. They should be along shortly. Is she not breathing?"

"No pulses either! You take chest compressions and I'll breathe, okay?" He nodded and they went to work on Castellan, trying to bring the life back to her abused body. They worked for precious meens until Tosh's body spasmed and a rush of water coughed up from her mouth. Relief washed through Olivienne and she helped roll the other woman to her side to facilitate the evacuation of river water from her lungs. Pounding steps sounded nearby and suddenly Dre. Shen was in her face.

"What happened?"

Castellan continued to choke out the water so the Connate answered. "Lieutenant Commander Tosh's head struck a boulder just before my guardians pulled us out. She was wrenched from my grasp and took in water. When we got to the bridge, she wasn't breathing and had no pulses. We were able to resuscitate her though."

Gemeda looked at her longtime friend with concern and immediately placed her hands on either side of Castellan's face. Olivienne stood while the doctore worked and salvo personnel from the town arrived with a couple of dry blankets for them both. Five meens later, Castellan was able to rise and stand on her own two feet, though still shaky. Gemeda turned to the Connate and grabbed her hand. A warm rush of energy swept through Olivienne's body and all the aches and hurts from the time in the river faded away. "There, that should be fine for you. I'm afraid Lieutenant Commander Tosh is a little worse off but she should make it back to the railer now."

Stelle Gordy offered hospitality, it was the least she could do for all the Connate and Lt. Commander had done for them. "We have lodging and warm baths that can be drawn—"

It was Castellan who interrupted her with a voice that was roughened and not as strong as normal. "Thank you Representative Gordy, but we must decline. The railer has been stopped long enough and we really shouldn't hold up the schedule any longer."

Dismayed, Olivienne protested. "The railer can wait! You've been injured and should—"

Castellan cut her off with a negligent wave of her hand. "I should get back to the railer. Our job here is done and the good people on board deserve to get to their destination without too long of a delay." She turned her attention to Rep. Gordy. "If you have a moto to take us back, that would be greatly appreciated."

Stelle Gordy nodded. "Of course, Lieutenant Commander Tosh. We have motos and a larger hauler in the lot this side of the bridge. We'll get you back post haste."

The group started back down from the bridge with Castellan walking next to the representative. Olivienne stood frozen for a meen longer. The guardians milled about clearly ready to get the Connate out of the rain and into the safety of her railer segment. Gemeda stayed behind to study the Connate. The sovereign's face showed a multitude of emotions. Exhaustion, confusion, and irritation seemed to be the main ones. She understood what Olivienne Dracore was feeling because she had been friends with Castellan a long time. "She is a creature of duty, Connate

Dracore. Castellan will always put the will and needs of others above her own."

Olivienne looked at the doctore. "She is infuriating!"

Gemeda nodded sagely. "She can be, for sure."

"Seriously, she nearly died! I can't believe she would carry on as if..."

"As if nothing happened? That's just her way, Connate Dracore. Even when she removes the uniform from her body, it never fully leaves her mind. She is a soldier's soldier, through and through."

The Connate shook her head ruefully. "Please, after all this I think you can call me Olivienne."

"It is an honor. And in return I insist you use my name as well, Gemeda."

They started back toward the lot with the guardians in tow and Olivienne couldn't keep her thoughts from the hardheaded Lt. Commander. "She's going to get herself killed with that mentality."

Gemeda smiled up at her. "Won't we all?"

Chapter Six

SOMEONE FROM REPRESENTATIVE Gordy's group had clearly voteoed ahead to the railer because the aether-powered engine was warmed up and chuffing by the time they arrived back at the platform. Not only that but when the intrepid group of heroes walked onto the first segment, all the passengers stood and applauded. Olivienne used her pyrokinesis to warm and somewhat dry the group while in transit to the platform, and Lt. Commander Tosh had taken the time to straighten her uniform before they got on the railer. Olivienne wasn't sure how the officer did it but by the time they greeted the other passengers, Castellan Tosh's hair was slicked back and she was the consummate professional once again. It was only Dre. Shen's frequent worried glances toward her that let the Connate know Tosh was still in pain.

Once they were back in the first class segment, it was Dre. Shen who attempted to take charge. She took hold of Castellan's arm and tried to direct her into the first cabin. "I need to finish your healing."

Castellan pulled her arm away and shook her head. "No, you need to get some rest. The entire reason I brought you down here was so you could be fresh for your surgeries first thing in the morning. You need to be resting, not tending to me. I'll be fine." When the medican leveled a stern look at her she continued. "I have daes on this railer to do nothing but read my book and heal. Why don't you lay down for a bit...unless you're hungry?"

"No, I'm not hungry since I ate later than normal but—"

"Go get some rest then, Gem. I'll take a powder if the pain gets worse."

Olivienne had been watching the exchange go back and forth between the two stubborn women. Eventually the medican's features took on an irritated but resigned set and she ground out one last word. "Fine." Then she slid open the door to the lt. commander's cabin and went inside.

The guardians had left them alone, with half going up to get their own food from the dining segment and the other half retreated to opposite ends of the first class seg. Castellan stood there while she took stock of her remaining injuries. Her head throbbed in time with her heartbeat, and her left ankle was slightly sprained. She could also feel bruises on various parts of her body. Gemeda told both her and the Connate in the hauler that she only healed the worst of their injuries and took care of the effects of being dowsed in the icy water. They wouldn't get sick but there was still a lot of pain. Then as if thinking about Connate Dracore reminded Castellan of her presence, she turned her head to the right and met those dark purple eyes. "Is there something you need from me, Connate Dracore?"

Olivienne smiled at the enigma that was Lt. Commander Castellan Tosh. She was a mix of stubborn and brave, fascinating and controlled. But it didn't take an empath to know Tosh was suffering. Olivienne could see it in the slight crinkle between her pale eyes and the tense set of her shoulders. "I have some powder in my cabin, for the pain." She watched the officer stiffen and had a feeling Tosh would deny being in discomfort. "I'm going to take it now myself. And please, after all we've done todae, I would be honored if you would just call me Olivienne."

Castellan hesitated, then finally nodded her head. "I would appreciate the powder and thank you for gifting me with your given name. I would be honored if you would do the same in return." She held out her hand to the Connate. "Lieutenant Commander Castellan Tosh, at your service, psera."

Olivienne took the offered hand and clasped it warmly in her own. "Brave, handsome, and polite...such a rare combination to have." Castellan startled at the compliment but didn't say anything in return.

Once they were inside the Connate's cabin, Olivienne finally relaxed. As a sovereign, she always felt as if she had to put on a mask in front of everyone, with the exception of her family. Strangely enough, she felt no need for such masks with Castellan Tosh. To keep from overanalyzing the feeling, she began searching through one of her leather satchels until she came up with a palm-sized waxed pouch. She grabbed two glasses from the sideboard and poured a finger of scotch in each, then added two pinches of powder. She turned around and Castellan raised a single pale eyebrow at her. "What, you don't like scotch?" Castellan smiled. Her teeth were white and straight, her lips the perfect amount of fullness. The seemingly carefree action transformed the officer's face from serious to swoon-worthy and Olivienne was not unaffected.

"No, I like scotch just fine. I'm surprised you do though."

"You'd be amazed at the things I like." Olivienne handed over the second glass.

Tosh laughed and downed her drink in one swallow. "I probably would." Either the powder or the scotch was of the highest quality because she started to feel better almost immediately.

Olivienne saluted Castellan and downed hers as well. "We should have done a toast to a job well done. Five children saved...not bad for a dae's work. Do you do such things often?" She got a curious look in return.

"Such things?" The Connate refilled both glasses and waved for them to be seated on the lounge.

Castellan stiffly complied, feeling a little out of place in the sovereign's private cabin, as if she were doing something taboo by hobnobbing with royalty.

Olivienne noticed the awkwardness but ignored it, hoping the other woman would relax. "I meant saving people every dae. Like you did at Temple Beach two daes ago. Running around throwing your all into every task to ensure that the job gets done and done well." The Connate was aware that her words and tone of voice came out with the potential for double meaning. They were both going to be on the railer for daes and she was testing the dashing officer to see if she had potential for dalliance. Soldiers had a reputation after all, did they not?

Castellan cocked her head and gave Olivienne an appraising look. She had a choice to either play the game or feign ignorance to the Connate's deeper meaning. On one hand it was the heir to the Divine Cathedra sitting next to her, which in itself was a little intimidating. On the other hand it would be daes more on the railer with not much to do and an uncertain future once she reached Tesseron. If Olivienne Dracore was willing then perhaps a little tupping would go a long way to distract her from her worries. The Connate was certainly beautiful enough, if a bit hot-tempered. Castellan ran an index finger around the rim of her glass and looked into those startlingly dark violet eyes when she answered. "Well I wouldn't say every dae. And I learned many rotos ago that if you want something to have a satisfactory outcome, your all is what should be given. With great effort often comes great reward. Wouldn't you agree, Olivienne?"

"If I didn't, we would certainly have daes ahead of us for you to convince me." The Connate took a slow sip of her scotch and watched Castellan with pleased eyes. Eventually they ordered evening meal into the Connate's cabin. Castellan was able to finally relax and it turned into one of the more pleasant dinners she'd had in the past few rotos. When the meal was complete and both women were sipping glasses of portea, it was the lt. commander who moved the conversation to something that interested her just as much as a dalliance with a beautiful woman. "So tell me more about your current project. Did you find something of interest down in Ostium?"

Olivienne let her move them past the blatant flirting into a subject she both loved and knew well. "I did actually. We found a document and numerous schematics in a cave at the western tail of the Dara Mountains. I have been searching for proof of the third great temple for the past few rotos. We occasionally find documents that reference a third temple but nothing that gives a name or location. We also find quite a few texts located outside either temple that cannot be translated at all. One of the documents we found in the cave is such."

The lt. commander nodded sagely while she savored the flavor of the strong vineo on her tongue. "I've read a few journals about the lost temple of the Makers. It has always been hinted at and rumored but no one has found proof. Do you really think you have a lead as to its whereabouts?"

"I don't have anything solid. The document we couldn't decipher is slightly different from any others we've found before. Here —" She set her drink on a nearby table then got up and rifled through another satchel until she found a hardened leather tube. She pulled out a rolled piece of oiled vellum and carefully straightened it, weighing down the corners with items on the desk. "If you look here in the bottom right corner, there are two temple symbols instead of just one." She grabbed another tube that was just sitting on the desk and unrolled a similar document. "The bottom of both have the same double temple symbol and that is why I think they are linked somehow. But neither page yields to either of our known decryption keys."

Castellan stood and walked over to look at the two pages that were side by side on the desktop. Both looked to be about the same age but were incredibly well preserved. Whoever the Makers were, they had technology and skills well beyond the modern Psi. "If I remember correctly, the cryptograph is always the same, right? It's only the key that changes. The key is 'ARCHEOS' for documents and texts that were found in the Temple of Archeos, and 'ILLEOS' for the ones found in the southern temple?"

"Yes but it is more complicated than that. The original text is translated to different letters based on the cryptograph. Then those letters are assigned numeric value. The key word is repeated over and over throughout the text, but it is converted to alternate letters just like the original text based on the same cryptograph. That too is converted to numeric value. The values are added together to form a sum and that sum is modified for the twenty-six letter alphabet. And to make it nearly impossible to decipher without the correct key, those final sum numbers are converted back into the cipher alphabet. It is quite ingenius really, but the maths frustrate me to no end."

"It's madness! No great wonder that it took generations for us to start decoding the ancient texts!"

Olivienne shrugged. "I suspect that is the point. There is a lot of power in the illeostones if utilized correctly and the Makers probably didn't want us to find the texts and understand them until we were ready."

Castellan nodded at her common sense observation. "You make a fair point. So how does one go about deciphering the ancient texts? Do you do it, or is it only something an interpretist can do?"

The Connate lifted one of the pages in question and beneath it was another page printed with evenly spaced graph lines, a multitude of perfect little squares. Along the top was their alphabet, and in the row below that was another set of letters that appeared to be a rearranged version of their alphabet. The subsequent rows in the first column were labeled as to what part of the decryption that row was relevant to. "This is the alpha sequence that has been discovered in both the great pyramids. It took rotos for the scienteres and historians to figure out that there was a key needed to break the code. With the name of each temple carved above every arched doorway, eventually someone was bright enough to try that."

"I think I read about that one. It was someone playing around with the crypto one dae and they stumbled on it, right?"

"Yes." Olivienne nodded then pointed at the first line of the document she retrieved from Ostium. "Normally I would let the interpretists do this work because it is tedious and my mind is not well suited for all the maths involved." She gave Castellan a sly look. "I am after all more a woman of action. Too many oors stuck inside gives me fits."

Castellan laughed having already assumed as much based on

the sovereign's personality. "I would never have guessed."

Olivienne smirked and continued. "Anyway, I can do it, but it doesn't come as naturally to me like it does for those who study such things. First you need to write the words you wish to translate on the 'encrypted text' line. On the 'numeric conversion' line you convert the letters to a number based on the original alpha sequences." She rifled through the papers on the desk until she found a different document. "I'll use one that I know is from the Temple of Archeos."

She wrote out some of the beginning text into the squares at the top of her worksheet. "Let's say the first letter of the encrypted text is an 'R'. So if a real letter 'N' equals an encrypted 'R,' and 'N' is the fourteenth letter of the alphabet, then the encrypted 'R' would be converted to a '14.' You follow?"

The soldier looked at the squares, the top one with an 'R' filled in and the one below it with a '14'. "Yes, I believe so. And after that you enter in the name of the temple?"

"Yes, the name of the temple repeats over and over throughout the text. That too gets converted to the encryption letter, then on the fifth line the encryption letter is converted to a number and that is where the maths come in that I hate. On the sixth line you subtract the temple number from the original encrypted text number if it is less. If the numbers are the same you write '26,' and if the temple number is more then you add twenty-six to the original encryption number before subtracting the temple number out. On the seventh line you convert it back to a letter, and that letter will be a cipher letter so on the eighth line you will need to convert that to the standard alpha letter again."

Castellan reared back her head from where she'd been leaning over the page watching Olivienne fill in the numbers and letters. The final letter written on the eighth line was an 'L.' "By the depths! That is as tedious as anything I've ever seen! People actually do this for a living?" Olivienne nodded. "And they enjoy it?" Just the thought of such a concept was appalling to the officer.

The Connate smiled. "Believe it or not they do. One of my regular interpretists, Dzin Solgin, loves his job. There is nothing he enjoys more than tackling a newly found sheet and turning it into decoded text."

Tosh shook her head. "Madness. So you did all that work for one letter, do you know what the text actually says on the document you've just started?"

Olivienne nodded and smiled. "Oh yes, it's a list of proverbs

I acquired many rotos ago. It was the first document I found after I got my Adventurist designation. It says, 'Last of the risers eats least.'"

Castellan laughed. "That one is certainly true." She slid the sheet aside so they could see the two double-temple symbol documents. Before she could ask any more questions, a great yawn nearly split her jaw in two.

"I had no idea my company was so dull."

A slight blush crawled up the lt. commander's neck and stained her cheeks. "My apologies, Connate—"

"It's Olivienne, please."

Castellan inclined her head toward the sovereign. "My apologies, Olivienne. But I fear the last two daes are catching up with me." She pulled out her pocket watch and was shocked to discover that they had been enjoying each other's company for oors.

Before they could say another word, the speaker crackled and the pilot's voice came on. "Attention passengers, we will be arriving in Gomen in ten meens. The stop will last half an oor while passengers and baggage are unloaded. For those continuing on to the city of Kemit, please remain seated and a porter will come around a check your ticket again once we are underway. Be advised that this railer is continuing on to the northern continent with a final destination of Tesseron. If you find your ticket in error and are headed for Soflin, speak with the nearest porter immediately so that you and your luggage can be offloaded with haste."

"I had no idea it was so late! I should bid you good evening and go see Doctore Shen off the railer, then perhaps retire to my own cabin for some much needed rest."

Olivienne smiled and gathered the documents into a neat pile. "Actually, I'd like to say goodbye to the good doctore myself. If you don't mind, that is."

It took a sec for the lt. commander to realize that Olivienne's pause was the Connate's way of checking to see if she were stepping on any toes, in one way or another. Castellan's history with the medican was old history and she welcomed her fellow traveler to the farewell. "Oh, not at all. Gemeda is one of the most honest and trustworthy friends I've ever known, a true gem in more than just name." She winked at Olivienne. "But one can never have too many friends capable of telesana either."

The Connate laughed. "I can certainly think of a few times such a skill would have been nice to have at my disposal." She gestured toward the door. "Shall we then?"

Castellan strode the few steps to the door and slid it open with a bow. "After you, Connate Dracore." Olivienne rolled her eyes at the surprisingly playful side to the lt. commander. She looked forward to exploring that side over the coming daes. Seeing the doctore from the railer caused a bit of sorrow for the two intrepid travelers. Castellan of course refused Gemeda's final offer of healing. "I'm good Gem, I promise. Hopefully we don't wait another two rotos to catch up again, yea?"

Gemeda embraced her and kissed both cheeks. "Certainly not!" She repeated the farewell with Olivienne. Then in the next instant she lifted her case and was gone from the railer.

When the two women returned to the first class segment with four guardians in tow, Olivienne stopped with Castellan outside the officer's cabin. "I suppose this is where we bid goodnight." She waited to see what Castellan would do.

While Lt. Commander Castellan Tosh had no problems showing an attractive and intriguing woman exactly how she felt with the touch and taste of her lips, she knew that Olivienne Dracore was no ordinary woman. She had to imagine that one was not simply so forward with the Royal Sovereign Connate of Psiere. She was sure there must be protocols in place, even for dalliance. Rather than take a chance at breaking protocol, Castellan stepped close to the Connate and took her into an embrace much the same as she used with Gemeda. Then she kissed each of Olivienne's cheeks before stepping back again. "I had a wonderful evening, Olivienne. Thank you for taking the time to show me your work on the documents you've found. It was fascinating, to be sure."

Olivienne was a little disappointed that the dashing woman in front of her did not take more initiative, but she knew they were both exhausted from the dae's ordeal. While they had danced around the subject in her cabin earlier, she was unsure of exactly what the lt. commander would be interested in. Because of that uncertainty, Olivienne didn't give in to the urge to push the other woman against the door and thoroughly show Tosh what she was missing by retiring for the evening. Instead she smiled gracefully and inclined her head. "I had a wonderful evening as well. It was nice to be able to have intelligent conversation with someone on a wide variety of subjects. Refreshing really. Perhaps we can pick up where we left off tomorrow?"

Castellan's entire face lit with her smile and Olivienne was caught in the pale blue of the officer's eyes. "I think that is a grand idea!" She bowed slightly. "Until then, Connate Dracore."

"Until then." Olivienne watched Castellan disappear into her cabin then made her way farther down the segment until she reached her own. As she fell headfirst into sleep, she couldn't help thinking that the next few daes were certainly looking up.

THE NEXT MORNING Castellan woke early per her usual. She had trained herself to rise early in the first few rotos of officer school. She took stock of her body and was pleased to note that that her general aches and pains were significantly better. Her head still throbbed but that was to be expected with a strained and then re-strained channel. Despite her exhaustion the previous evening, she took the time to rinse the river water from herself before bed so all she had to do was get dressed the next dae.

Because of her throbbing head, she decided not to go through her normal morning exercise routine, which meant she didn't need another rinse. With her hair combed, uniform crisp, and boots shining, she left her cabin in search of breakfast. There were the usual two guardians at each end of the first class segment and she assumed that Olivienne was still abed. Rather than wake the Connate and possibly offend, she would simply pay a visit to her after morning meal.

As if a repeat of the dae before, her name was called the sec she entered the dining segment. "Lieutenant Commander Tosh!" She was both surprised and pleased to see the Connate seated at a table mid-way down, breaking her fast. She walked down the aisle and stopped out of the way near the Connate's table.

"Good morn, Connate Dracore. You look refreshed. I take it all is well after our impromptu dunking?"

Olivienne smiled at the perfectly put together officer. She briefly wondered what it would take to send the woman into dis-array and hoped she would soon be able to find out. "I could say the same to you, Tosh. I didn't notice a limp on your way down the aisle, and the dark circles are gone from beneath your eyes. I take it your rest was recuperative?"

Castellan nodded. "Definitely so."

"Would you care to join me?" The Connate was seated at a table all to herself while the four guardians that had accompanied her to the dining seg had appropriated another table to eat their own breakfasts.

The officer bowed with a twinkle in her eye. "I would be

most honored." She left and returned a few meens later with a simple fare of fruit and cooked grain and a thick piece of toasted bread slathered in jam and cream. She had two mugs on her tray, one of juice and the other of water. When she sat, Olivienne looked at her tray in dismay.

"I know a soldier's pay isn't nearly that of some private industries but is that really all they'll allow for official trips?"

Castellan smiled in good humor. "I make plenty, thank you. And they would pay for whatever I would wish to eat. This is all I have want for. Without completing my normal exercise this morning, I find that my appetite is less than usual."

Olivienne boldly plucked a small round fruit from a dish on Castellan's tray and popped it into her mouth. When she was finished chewing the sweet fruit, she licked her lips appreciatively. "And if you should happen to work up an appetite later?"

Clearly the Connate was still interested in dalliance and the officer was finding the sovereign's company more and more to her liking. She responded appropriately to show her interest. "Well, should my appetite increase later then I will be sure to assuage my hunger in the most pleasurable way possible. Perhaps with company, if company is so inclined."

"Oh, company is definitely inclined." There was a moment of heat while their gazes locked on each other, then by some unseen mutual signal they both resumed their meal.

When their meal was complete, Olivienne was reluctant to leave the intriguing woman's presence. "What do you have planned now?"

Castellan wiped her lips with the provided cloth napkin and set it on the table. "As it so happens, I currently have no plans. I wanted to stop and check our arrival time in Tesseron when I got back to our segment."

"I can help you with your inquiry." Castellan looked at the Connate curiously. "I travel by railer so often I feel as though I have not only the schedule memorized, but all the distances and travel times between major stops." She shrugged. "A hazard of my occupation I guess."

Without thinking, Castellan commented. "So much travel must make it difficult to engage in relationships."

Olivienne gave her a slow thoughtful look. "Perhaps as difficult as an officer who could be moved to a different continent with only a few wekes notice. I guess there is a reason why people like us are often single."

"I suppose you have a point. So when is our arrival in Tesseron?"

A smile from the Connate met her words, or rather met her lack of words. The officer didn't discount Olivienne's statement that neither woman had time for relationships. It was another indicator that they were both on the same page where dalliance was concerned. Neither woman knew where the future would take them and couldn't offer more than a little friendship with some tupping thrown in for good measure. "I believe our ticket said six-thirty tomorrow."

A pale eyebrow went up. "Another full night? I don't remember it taking so long when I went south four rotos ago!"

"Well, we will actually have a four oor layover in Penterole while the crew changes and the segments are re-supplied. It is there that passengers will be allowed to leave the railer to take in the sites of the beautiful port city."

Castellan laughed at her words, garnering even more attention from the people in the passenger segment they were passing through. "You sound like a travel intinerist with your seller's words."

"By the depths, no! I've seen the good parts and the less than savory parts of Pentole and I would never try to sell that city to someone. Their operae house and the Blue Bridge are the only two wonders as far as I'm concerned." When they reached the first class segment once again, Olivienne paused with her companon outside Castellan's door. "So..." Her voice trailed off as a bout of unusual nerves overtook her.

Castellan didn't make it any easier with her prompt. "So?"

"If you have nothing to do, you are more than welcome to come to my cabin and study my texts again. What say you?"

The dashing and not-so-upright officer slyly smiled. "That depends."

Olivienne's dark eyebrow went up in question and her violet eyes seemed darker in the artificial light of the narrow aisle way. "On?"

"On whether or not your use of the word 'texts' was merely a euphemism."

The Connate thought for a sec and responded. "And if it is?"

Castellan Tosh grinned. "I'd say lead the way."

Out of curiosity, Olivienne had to ask. "And if it is not?"

Castellan shrugged. "I'd still say lead the way."

The Connate laughed. "You are a most intriguing woman,

Lieutenant Commander Castellan Tosh. I almost think it is a shame that our trip together is over in the morn."

"Almost?"

A twin to the lt. commander's sly grin crept across Olivienne's face. "Well, we do tend toward...high passions. I'm afraid if we spent a significant amount of time together we'd end up raging."

Castellan remembered back to the moment they were face to face doing just such a thing the previous morning. "While I'm not normally one to lose my calm, I have to admit that you were more adept than most at pushing my buttons, so perhaps you are right."

"Of course I'm right." The Connate spun in place then and went farther down the hall to her own cabin. Castellan stood staring at her when the Connate stopped at her own open door. "Come along, Tosh. I thought you wanted to look at my texts?"

Chapter Seven

"WOULD YOU CARE for a drink?"

Castellan pulled out her pocket watch upon entering the Connate's private cabin. It was just after eight hundred. "It's a little early for liquor isn't it?"

Olivienne rolled her eyes. "I meant water, of course."

"Oh, of course." The Connate busied herself pouring water and Castellan walked over to the desk. "May I?" Olivienne nodded so she pulled the two coded double-temple pages from the pile. "So what happens when you have the wrong translation? Is it all unintelligible or do you stop part way when it looks like it won't work? If so, could the message just be hidden further down the text?"

"You certainly have a lot of questions but they're all ones I will be glad to answer." Olivienne handed over the glass of water and set her own out of the way on the desk. She shuffled through the stack until she found another translation sheet with little squares full of letters and numbers. She handed it to Castellan. "This is what the ARCHEOS key yielded when we used it on the document from the cave, one that I'm sure came from the northern temple."

Castellan looked over the document and her eyebrows went up. "Well that is strange, it looks like the translation started to work." She pointed at the first line of deciphered text. "See here, there are two words before it stops making sense." Castellan began reading the text aloud, if only to help herself work through the puzzle. "On the si...then it just goes to a series of random letters. K-X-C-B-H-Y-D, and on...but those couple words have to mean something, right?"

Olivienne shrugged. "Sometimes an incorrect key will yield actual words, the way you can draw letters at random from a bag and end up with a few. So it's not completely uncommon, though it is strange for it to be right at the beginning."

"Wait! Look at the where the translation stops working." Castellan pointed at the first seven letters of the translation sheet but rather than speak those letters aloud she spelled out the key. "A-R-C-H-E-O-S corresponds perfectly with 'on the si.' Is it possible that the key changed? Has that ever happened before?"

The Connate's gaze sharpened abruptly and she leaned closer to the worksheet. "By the depths, I think you're right! But what?"

"What about..." The full-time officer and novice historian trailed off, unsure of the merit of her idea.

Olivienne gave her a curious look and prompted the other woman to finish her question. "What about what?"

Castellan pointed to the bottom corner of the original encrypted documents. "You said yourself that you've never seen the double temple symbol before. What if the key was a combination of the two temple names?"

"That's just..." She trailed off then her face lit up. "Only one way to find out." Olivienne grabbed another worksheet and rather than copy the letters ARCHEOS repeatedly into the temple key row, she copied ARCHEOSILLEOS twice in a row. Then she grabbed the encrypted page and filled in the first thirteen letters. Castellan unconsciously leaned closer while Olivienne began converting the encrypted letters to numbers, then doing the same to the temple key words. Their breathing picked up once she was finished with the mathematic and first alpha conversion. By the time she got to the actual translation point they were both practically vibrating with excitement. Olivienne read them aloud as she started writing out the translated text. "On...the...sixth...dae...of...septa...in...the...y..."

She tossed the scribe down on the desk and looked at Castellan in amazement. "By the Makers, you've done it! That's brilliant!" She threw her arms around the jubilant Lt. Commander and kissed her straightaway on the lips. They pulled back in surprise, simultaneously realizing that they had successfully pushed through the invisible barrier that had been keeping them apart. Castellan was only about an ince taller than Olivienne, and as they stared into one another's eyes, they were very much on the same plane of thought.

Slowly, but deliberately, Castellan leaned in again and that time made the kiss last much longer. Both women moaned when Olivienne opened her mouth to the officer's questing tongue. Unable to help herself, Castellan Tosh moved both hands up to cradle her sovereign's face and deepened the kiss. All the excitement of translation paled in comparison to the blood that began to pound through their veins at such an innocent touch of the lips. Just as languidly as they began, Castellan pulled away again eliciting a whimper from Olivienne. The Connate looked at her in confusion and forced a sheepish admission from the dashing woman with kiss-darkened lips. "I'm torn."

Olivienne smiled, understanding Castellan's words completely. "Let's translate the documents then we can celebrate by continuing where we left off."

"That is a grand idea!"

The Connate smirked as she turned toward the desk. "Perhaps we can work you up to an appetite yet."

Castellan leaned over to whisper in her ear. "Perhaps I'm already there."

Olivienne shuddered. "Enough of that, time for you to earn your keep, soldier." She pulled a second chair up to the desk and moved the already begun worksheet in front of Castellan. "Do you think you have the process down enough to finish this?"

"I think so." She picked up the discarded scribe and Olivienne dug into her satchel for another. Then she too began working on the second translation. Unfortunately she ran into trouble right away. "I just realized that we have already tried the Archeos key on the second document and it yielded no intelligible translation."

Castellan looked at the worksheet in the Connate's hand. "You said the interpretists tried both keys, where is the one for Illeos?" Olivienne shuffled through more papers until she produced the attempted decoding using the Illeos key. Right away Castellan pointed out where the words started to translate then stopped six letters in. "Look here, it says 'perhap.' Maybe it too has the double key, only it is reversed because the document is from the Temple of Illeos. Try reversing the key."

Olivienne looked at her new acquaintance appreciatively. "You know, you're quite good at this. Perhaps you should travel the continents with me in search of answers to the Divine Mystery."

She got a smile in response and a slight shake of the officer's head. "I enjoy my job too much. You'll just have to find another amateur with an insatiable thirst for problem solving."

Seriousness overtook Olivienne in that moment. "I have a feeling that the information in these documents is going to completely change everything we know to date. There is something truly important here or they wouldn't have gone through all this trouble. I'm convinced of it!"

Castellan laughed at the historical adventurist's certainty and passion. "Well then, let's get them translated so we can find out what it is!" They worked steadily for half an oor translating each and every letter of the encrypted documents. Surprisingly, Castellan finished first even though the document from Archeos was twice as long as the other.

Olivienne wasn't kidding when she said that she hated the maths involved. When they were finished, she glanced at the page in Castellan's hand. "You have the Archeos document, want to read it?"

"Sure." Castellan scanned the page then cleared her throat to speak. Her voice was rife with wonder and solemnity while reading the words that no one of their society had ever read before. "On the sixth dae of Septa in the roto one hundred and six of Psiere, a great astaeroid by the name of Torae struck Antaeus. The resulting cataclysm destroyed our venerable celestial body and forever darkened the night sky of Psiere. The destruction hurled the pieces we call archeostones across the surface of the planet below. Antaeus was an entity of much power and as a result the fragments of the moon have the ability contained within to imbue that power to the illeo mineral found naturally all over the planet. The archeostones react with planetary oxy and emit aether into the atmosphere, and the illeostones absorb the aether." Castellan paused to take a drink and met Olivienne's wide eyes over the glass.

While some of the information contained within the text was well known, other parts shocked her. "A moon? How can that be? I know our written texts only go back a few hundred rotos but it seems unlikely that we would have missed something so vital. The scienteres and historians have always assumed we were a young society. But no one really knows where we came from. It's like our past was simply washed away."

Castellan nodded in agreement. "Then there are the Makers. Who are they, where did they come from, where did they go? We are only so advanced as a society because of what they've left us. Are they responsible for our lack of past? It makes no sense!"

"I suppose that is why we refer to it as the Divine Mystery. Okay, now get reading, Tosh! I want to know more."

Castellan rolled her eyes but gladly continued. "The illeo mineral is not just found within the small stones and pebbles on the surface but is also contained within all living things. Most surprisingly it is also found within the third generational progeny or later of the sentient species of both ocean and land, thusly granting them special powers of the mind the more contact with aether they had while in utero. Because of the potential of abuse, we have gathered as many archeostones as possible and left them in the Temple of Antaeus."

"Son of a sint!" They both spent long secs in shock at what they had learned. Olivienne was the one that broke the silence. "All the sovereigns of Psiere...we have always had a lot of power. There are two archeostones in the divine cathedra which means our mothers would always be near a source of aether." She looked at Tosh. "But how does that explain other people with more than average channels or ability? Like you."

"My maman was exposed, much like yours." Olivienne cocked her head curiously. "Both my parens are in the Psi Resource corp. My father runs the Tosh family illeostone mines but my maman oversees the recharging operation at the Temple of Archeos. To emphasize the importance of hard work to me and my younger sibs, my maman would tell us stories of when she used to manually move the carts of illeostones in and out of the recharge room, while she was pregnant with me."

The Connate's eyes widened. "I've seen those carts, your maman must be tough!" She paused for a sec and realization came to her. "Oh! She would have exposed you a lot. What about your sibs, are they powerful Psi too?"

Castellan shook her head. "No, by the time she was pregnant with Tellesen, they had switched over to an automated system. I guess I've always been a bit of a freak with my channel strength. That was actually how I met Gemeda Shen. We were in advanced academy classes together." She shook herself from the old memories and turned to poke at the paper in front of Olivienne. "I read mine, now it's your turn!"

The text on Olivienne's page was only half as long as the first message. "Perhaps the greatest discovery was that a number of rocks have been found which appear to be an amalgam of the astaeroid Torae, and the moon Antaeus. Those antoraestones hold the power of amplification. For whatever power that is contained within the illeo mineral, it will be increased by ten times over in the presence of an antoraestone. Because we have been unable to destroy such powerful artifacts, we took great pains to hide them until the Psi society is able to responsibly manage their energy and usage." Olivienne turned a shocked face to her companion. "By the divine and sublime! To find such a stone would be amazing indeed!"

Castellan frowned. "It could also be a weapon most fierce." The Connate gave her a strange look so the officer elaborated.

"Think about what would happen if the Atlanteens had some-thing like that in their possession. Or one of the meaner factions of our society. Imagine if someone like me or you turned to evil. What kind of damage could I wreak upon the people of Psiere if I could lift ten times my current capacity? I lifted nearly two tuns, twice within ten meens time! But ten times that...why, I could destroy a town! That sort of power is dangerous, Olivienne."

"I see your point, but think of the good it could do as well. We could travel ten times the distance by dirigible and truly explore our world! Where did we come from and where did the Makers go, Tosh? We know about the Atlanteens, but what if there is another race of peoples on this planet? Isn't the small risk worth the benefit in the end?"

The lt. commander thought about her many battles with crea-tures sent by the Atlanteens and all the lives lost on both sides as a result. But the ocean dwellers weren't the only trouble Psierians faced. There was always one faction or another who worked toward the dissolution of the current government. Some didn't like the idea of a royal family, some thought that the two conti-nents should be separate countries with their own rulers.

There were many men and women who had turned their backs on polite civilization and been sent to the islands, either Aetate or Iuvenis. It was all dependent on which law was broken and the person's intent. The punishment for a Codice Prime infraction, any premeditated action that causes death to a sentient entity, was always death. After Codice Prime, there were six other codes in the Psiere Legibus with varying degrees of punish-ment. A Code One infraction was premeditated action that caused permanent mental, physical, or emotional harm to a sentient entity, and the punishment for that was a life sentence on the island of Iuvenis. If anyone were caught trying to escape the island, they were immediately executed.

The Code Two through Code Five infractions called for time served at the prison on the island of Aetate with repeat offenders eventually getting sent to Iuvenis. And lastly, Code Six infrac-tions were assigned rehabilitation. Code Five and Code Six had the least severe punishments but they were for the accidental crimes, not premeditated ones. It may have seemed harsh to an outsider but criminals were handled by Psi Codice Corp and all went through the Process of Innocence.

Five independent teams would evaluate the person who com-mitted the crime. It was mandatory for one of the team members to have a high telepathic channel, and for the other to have a high psychometric channel. The investigators could both read the suspect's mind, as well as touch them to obtain information about that person, though it was against the Code to read or manipulate a mind against the Psi's will, even in the pursuit of justice. They could also touch an object and gain information that way. The investigators were thorough and in the past hundred rotos, there had never been a lack of consensus among the five investigative teams. Once hearing the results of the investigation the adjudicator looked up the crime and assigned a punishment based on the Psiere Legibus. Punishments were issued by rote, and the system worked extremely well.

It was only a hundred rotos before that, if the Psierian broke the Codice Prime, or even committed a Code One or Two infraction, and was too powerful or too dangerous to be imprisoned, they were tied into a boat and sent out to sea. The criminal faced a swift death by leviathan, for the Atlanteens would tolerate no one in their waters. It was a barbaric practice and had been abandoned long ago for more humane methods with the creation of the Psiere Legibus, the supreme laws of the land. Between the government and the royal family, no one would ever go without the basic necessities in life. So if someone committed crime, it wasn't out of desperation. It was either accidental or willful disobedience.

She looked at Olivienne seriously. "Can you imagine if a Code One infractor had such power? Or worse yet, someone who would willfully disregard the Codice Prime? One of those right-wingers calling for the execution of the royal family?"

The Connate paled slightly at her words but fired back anyway. "It's been rotos since any right-wingers have cropped up. Twenty-five to be exact. That was during the Politarian Uprising. They were all caught and sent to Iuvenis Island. I'm telling you, the gain far outweighs the risk!"

Castellan shook her head. "You read the history books just like I did and you know they were not all caught. The investigators never found the ringleader of the movement." Castellan didn't necessarily agree with the punishment of death but there was no other way to deal with the truly evil high Psi of their world. The use of telepathy and psychometry to definitively verify a person's guilt before punishment was what got the laws passed in the roto four hundred and two. Because of the all-encompassing ramification of the new law structure, it had to be unanimously approved by the Sovereign of Psiere and the entirety of the Imperium.

But beyond the criminal element, there was also the danger to those who went out every dae to provide for the people. Women and men of the Stock Corp who harvested from the ocean took a risk every time they sailed beyond the Defense Corp protected coastline. They were often well armed and armored to prevent destruction by whatever beast the Atlanteens might send to do their bidding. Lt. Commander Castellan Tosh shook her head. "As far as gain and risk are concerned, we are going to have to agree to disagree. As much as the idea fascinates me, and there is a part of me that wants to find such artifacts, I hope we never do."

Olivienne sighed. "You have always stayed well away from the edge, haven't you, Tosh?"

"I assume you're referring to my reluctance to subject myself and others around me to unnecessary risk? If so, then yes I agree. Risk is meant to be analyzed then mitigated or avoided. It is certainly not something to dive into straightaway without care of consequence."

The Connate growled and poked Castellan in the chest. "You are much too brave a person to be so timid! Is the real Lieutenant Commander Tosh all talk and no action?"

With rising color, Castellan faced her sovereign straight on. "Timid?" Her voice rose in volume as disbelief filled the word, bloating it into something much more intimidating than its mere meaning. "Timid? Just who do you think you're talking to?" She took a step closer until she was well within Olivienne's personal space. "I am not one of your guardians you can push around or ignore as you see fit! I am a soldier, an officer in the Psi Defense Corp and I...am...not...timid!" She practically ground out the words. When she finished her tirade both were breathing hard, so close the same air filtered in and out of their lungs.

Maybe it was Olivienne who moved first, or perhaps it was Castellan, but either way tempers smoothly morphed into passion of another sort. Olivienne gripped Tosh's waist tightly, crushing the material of the officer's shirt within her grip. She gasped as Castellan stole the breath from her mouth and used all her fire and control to thoroughly own Olivienne's lips. When Castellan's mouth left hers she whimpered at the loss. "No..." Her plea was quickly forgotten as Tosh moved down to bite and suck at her neck. Feeling out of control, the Connate needed something for her hands to do so she began untucking Castellan's shirt from the perfectly neat confines of the officer's trousers.

Castellan pulled her mouth away. "I can do that."

Panting, Olivienne watched as the other woman slowly unbuttoned her dark gray shirt. Her mouth watered the more flesh was revealed to her sight. When the buttons were down to Castellan's navel, Olivienne couldn't resist running both hands over the muscles and flat planes of the fit officer's stomach, then across her upper chest and shoulders. All thoughts of stripping stopped at the tantalizing touch. Olivienne prompted her. "Keep going." She got a frustrating grin in return.

"I think I'll stop right here and let you catch up. You appear to be a little overdressed."

"Overdressed hmm?" It took mere secs for Olivienne to focus her channel on one of the most sensual tasks she's ever under-taken. In the blink of an eye, Castellan's shirt was off her body and in Olivienne's hand. The Connate tossed it across the room where it landed on a starched heap on the lounger.

The proper soldier gave the garment a concerned look. "I should..."

Olivienne never let her finish. "If you say you should fold that shirt I'm going to apport it right off the back of this railer!" With those words Castellan's mouth snapped shut. As a reward for her silence, Olivienne apported her own shirt off next. They were left standing there in bosairs and trousers.

Castellan took charge again. "Close your eyes, 'Vienne." Deep purple irises looked back at her in surprise. Using the tight-est focus of her telekinesis, Castellan gently caressed the other woman's bottom lip. "Trust me." With an enormous amount of curiosity and the tiniest sliver of trepidation, Olivienne shut her eyes. The phantom touch started light at first, a gentle pressure against Olivienne's cheek. She swayed at the sensation when the pressure turned to another caress that trailed along her neck and down her shoulder, then along her ribs and stomach, and back up the other arm. She gasped as the invisible fingers of Castellan's channel worked their way down the center of her chest and pulled each side of the bosair until the clasps released.

She continued to tease the other woman until Olivienne was panting with arousal. "What are you doing to me?"

Castellan's voice was suddenly in her mind. *"Have you never been with a telekinetic of the highest level?"* Her phantom touch got bolder and a gasp was torn from Olivienne's mouth as she shook her head.

Olivienne's voice eventually responded in the lt. commander's mind. *"I want to touch you too."* She reached for Castellan's belt and unbuckled the shining metal, then she unfastened the button of her trousers.

Before she could get to the zip, Castellan stepped away and quickly removed her pistol from the holster, setting it on the desk. She turned back to Olivienne with a grin. "I wouldn't want that to accidentally go off."

The thoroughly aroused sovereign grinned back. "We don't want anything going off just yet." She crooked her finger at the officer. "Come here." Back together, Olivienne finished what she had started. Tosh returned the favor until they stood nude in front of each other. The Royal Sovereign smirked at Castellan. "This is your last chance to say nay, though you will miss out on a royal tupping."

Castellan stepped closer until their breasts pressed together. She paused for a sec as the sensation caused them both to sigh. "A royal tupping? Is that better than simply scratching an itch amongst us normal folks?"

Olivienne didn't answer, but instead used her apportation to remove the pin holding the trundle bed upright against the sidewall of her cabin. Then she carefully maneuvered Castellan backward until the officer's knees hit the bed and she gave a shove. Olivienne followed her onto the bed and sat firmly on the sprawled woman's hips, leaning in close to Castellan's lips. "There is only one way to find out." A strong soldier's hands pulled her the rest of the way down until their mouths met in an impassioned and thorough exploration. Heat flared between them when Olivienne ground against the woman below her and that was all it took for Castellan to flip her over.

Tosh held Olivienne's hands above her head and nestled her hips between the Connate's legs. She put her mouth to good use nibbling every available ince of flesh she could reach. The woman below her squirmed and moaned when Castellan got to a particularly sensitive spot on her neck. Both bodies followed their natural inclination to thrust against each other. When she'd explored all she could while holding Olivienne down, Castellan brought her mouth back to the writhing woman's lips. Olivienne struggled and spoke frustrated words against Castellan's mouth. "Let me free."

Castellan pulled back with a grin. "Why ever would I do that?"

"Because I want to touch you too!" The officer smirked and raised an eyebrow, prompting Olivienne to struggle more. "I'm going to give you a sound thrashing when I get loose!"

The officer laughed. "Promise?" Then as if she were acquiescing to the Connate's wishes, she released the struggling woman's hands. There was a moment of triumph on Olivienne's face at least until Tosh switched and began using her telekinesis to hold her down. Then before Olivienne could threaten further, she quickly made her way down the Connate's body until she could take a hard nipple into her mouth.

The woman on the bottom groaned with pleasure and thrust her chest upward. She closed her eyes at the sensation. "Use your teeth just a little...I like to feel it!" A bolt of arousal shot straight to Castellan's groin but she complied with the demands of her Royal Sovereign like any good subject would.

After she worked both nipples to red and aching hardness, she moved down Olivienne's body until she reached an area of sparse dark hair. She looked up into purple eyes gone nearly black with desire. "May I?"

Olivienne growled in response. "I swear to Archeos I'll teleport your tongue right out of your mouth if you don't put it to use right this instant!" The officer put her talented tongue to work and within mere secs, she had Olivienne moaning and writhing beneath her. Her head was thrashing back and forth and Tosh sensed she needed more. Sure enough after another meen passed, Olivienne was left to beg again. She struggled her hands against Tosh's immovable Psi channel and fairly shook with desire. "I need...Tosh..."

"I've got you." Castellan pulled her mouth away from its task and brought her fingers up to run them through the folds of Olivienne's quim. The Connate was so wet it took no time at all to lubricate her fingers for entry. She teased Olivienne's opening until the Connate stared down at her with those mesmerizing violet eyes.

Her expression brooked no question as to her need but just in case Tosh was particularly thick she spoke it aloud anyway. "Tongue on, fingers in!"

Castellan grinned and moved closer as directed. "You're so demanding!" Rather than reply to the comment, Castellan's mouth and fingers had Olivienne groaning out her pleasure. Tosh thrust first with one finger only, then added two within a few strokes. As Olivienne's clit hardened further beneath Castellan's tongue, she picked up the pace. Olivienne's legs began to shake and she got even more vocal as she approached the precipice of personal pleasure.

Rather than slow the Connate's rapid approach to the edge, Tosh curled her fingers inside her and redoubled her efforts until Olivienne screamed out her release. Unfortunately it was a sound that carried to the ears of every single soldier in the first class segment. Castellan kept up her ministrations while Olivienne rode the waves of her orgasm until the end. The officer only stopped when the twitching woman on the bottom feebly called out to her.

"No more, I beg of you!" Castellan immediately released her telekinetic hold over Olivienne's arms and moved up to kiss her on the lips. The Connate met her kiss with more passion that was expected after such a draining orgasm. "Mmm...you taste like me."

Castellan rolled to the side and looked at her curiously. "You like that?"

Purple irises met her pale blue ones. "I love the taste, touch, and sound of women, why would I not enjoy kissing my own flavor from your lips? I am a woman, after all."

The officer's eyes darkened slightly. "You certainly are." She took in Olivienne's flushed face and still-heaving chest. "Do you need a meen?"

Olivienne gave her a decidedly naughty smile in return before pushing Tosh all the way onto her back. "No, I don't." She immediately covered the soldier's body with her own and began kissing her, even as she dug her hands into the strong shoulders below her. Castellan kept herself exceptionally fit and Olivienne appreciated every muscle and line of Tosh's form. But even though the woman lying prone on the bed had a body of someone who worked hard and worked well, she still sported the soft feminine curves that Olivienne adored.

Tosh's breasts were small, but her nipples were large enough to make Olivienne never want to move her mouth away from their hard wonder. The highly capable officer was reduced to a whimpering and needy bundle of nerves by the time Olivienne slid her hand between them and slicked her fingers through Castellan's wet quim. Castellan stiffened when the Connate began stroking her flesh further and further until fingers were eventually swallowed deep inside the officer's depths. With that move, Olivienne shifted her body to the side in order to reach. She used her thumb to stimulate Tosh's clitoris at the same time she wrapped her lips around the writhing woman's nearest nipple. She bit gently before swirling her tongue around the sensitive flesh and Castellan arched her back off the bed with a cry. "By the depths!"

After thrusting for a number of meens and working both nipples to stiff peaks, Olivienne gave in to her need to taste the woman who was nearing the edge of orgasm. She pulled her mouth away from Tosh's chest and moved down between the panting woman's legs. Without even missing a stroke, she moved her thumb out of the way and took over with her lips and tongue. Olivienne hummed her approval at Castellan's taste and responsiveness, mumbling into the other woman's wetness. "Mmmm, so good."

Castellan Tosh was beside herself and was receptive to the Connate's touch indeed. "Yes!" She could feel herself tightening toward completion as pressure filled her head. She did not have to worry that Olivienne would move or stop before she could reach the end, she merely had to enjoy it. When orgasm struck, it was like a lightning bolt shook her body and stole her sanity in a mental scream. Just as all the guardians in the private seg had heard Olivienne's vocal shout earlier, they also heard and felt the pressure of the lt. commander's mental one. And for those that were empaths, the pleasure that radiated from the Connate's cabin was unmistakable, as Castellan's orgasm had brought Olivienne to a smaller peak as well. It was a good dae's tupping when pleasure was found simultaneously between partners, especially new ones.

The passion potential between the two strong-willed women carried over into round after round of the most exuberant and hot tupping between them. The oors between deciphering the sacred temple texts and the next railer stop melted into a mewling, writhing, wonder of pleasure. At one point Olivienne bit down on Castellan's hand when the officer tried to stifle the Connate's orgasmic screams. Both were established lovers and they took turns showing each other every trick they'd learned to wring pleasure from a woman's body.

Olivienne Dracore and Castellan Tosh may have been at odds just as often as not, but their connection in bed was unmistakable. Ten meens after they collapsed to the coverlets in sweaty exhaustion, the captain's voice came over the cabin speaker to inform the travelers they were a half oor out from Penterole. Castellan blinked to realize they had been engaged for so long. "Well," she said more out of surprise than anything, "had I realized you were such a...vocal lover, I would have used my channel on your lips instead of your hands. I fear my reputation is in ruins amongst your Shield unit!"

Olivienne started laughing as she lay there with her arm across her own eyes. "Mostly likely your reputation is greater than Archeos and Illeos combined. They have heard enough of my escapades that they are probably immune, however none before has compared to my morning with you! And to think I've been tupping athletes all this time for their stamina. I clearly should have been looking for a soldier!"

Tosh smiled as her heartrate began to slow to normal parameters once again. She glanced at the Connate as Olivienne moved her arm and opened those intriguing purple eyes.

"Athletes, really?" People that were placed into the Psi Service Corp, which encompassed both arts, athletics, and entertainment, among other things, were often joked to be of lower intelligence, or possibily even ability, than some of the other corps.

"Well to be fair, the last one was no ordinary athlete."

The lt. commander laughed and used her telekinesis to caress Olivienne's cheek. "Well to be fair, I'm no ordinary soldier."

The sovereign caught Tosh in an appreciative gaze. "No, you most certainly are not."

Castellan stretched her body and was well aware that she was being stared at. "All this vigorous 'royal tupping' has left me with an appetite. Would you care to take advantage of our long stop in Penterole and find a decent eating establishment?"

"What, tired of railer food already?"

"More like I'm tired of the railer. So, what is your answer, Connate Dracore?"

Olivienne looked at her seriously. "You may not want to have dinner with me."

Castellan sat up and gave the still-reclining woman a curious look. "Why ever not?"

"I'm a very public figure. If we sup together, people will link our names romantically...or worse. It may besmirch your serious officer character."

The sovereign got a shrug from the lt. commander. "Have you met a soldier? I would think our caterwauling of the past few oors would be enough to have your guardians wagging their tongues from here to Tesseron and back."

Olivienne stiffened slightly. "My guardians are always discreet."

"Discreet or no, they still talk amongst themselves, which means my reputation is already in tatters where it comes to a certain fetching sovereign." She smiled down at Olivienne. "Besides, I don't care about gossip. However I do care about stretching my legs, filling my belly, and having intelligent conversation. So if you're interested in those things as well, I would be happy to have you along. Besmirched character or no."

Olivienne sat up and apported their scattered clothes onto the bed with them. "You may regret those words, Lieutenant Commander Castellan Tosh. But I would be delighted to share all of those things with you. And perhaps..." She trailed off and Tosh looked at her expectantly.

"Perhaps?"

Olivienne gave her a less than innocent smile. "Perhaps after you've satisfied your appetite we can spend some time working up another."

A pale brow went up as Castellan began dressing. "I'd say that is a most satisfactory plan."

Chapter Eight

THEY EXITED THE railer after all the regular passengers had departed. It was nearly fifteen hundred oors and the railer was due for a six oor maintenance and restocking layover before continuing on to Tesseron. That meant there would be plenty of time to stretch legs and fill bellies. Just as before when the Connate left the railer, four guardians were left behind to watch the sovereign's first class segment and the remaining four came with them. For the first time, Castellan actually paid attention to the detail and questioned the lowered security. "Tell me, Connate Dracore...where is the rest of your Shield Corp unit?"

Olivienne looked at her as if she were mad. "Why, on the railer, of course!"

"But surely you have more than eight total?"

The Connate scoffed. "Of course I do! One is on leave at the moment and another had vacation that coincided with my trip to Ostium so I left her behind. I neither need, nor want, any more guardians than that."

Sensing that it was a volatile topic, Castellan did something she loathed to do and bit her tongue. After all, it was none of her business how the Connate's Shield unit was run.

"So what would you like to eat?" Castellan turned her head toward the beautiful woman she was escorting through the railer station. Her grin was roguish, which caused Olivienne to sigh and amend her statement. "You are a cad, Commander Tosh! I mean, where would you like to eat?"

Castellan tempered her teasing and shrugged. "I've been away from the north for five rotos, so I'm not familiar with the local eating establishments in Penterole. Do you recommend anything in particular?"

Olivienne thought for a meen as they exited the station and began walking through the large open square. The space was in part a marketplace and especially full of people. The group paused as a double handful of students crossed the path in front of them and the Connate considered the question. In the background the large clock tower *bonged* three times, for the three oors after middae. Olivienne's food contemplation was inter-

rupted by Lt. Savon. "Connate Dracore, would you like us to pro-
cure you a moto?"

Castellan was relieved to note that all four guardians were on
high alert as they stood in the busy square. Eyes scanned in every
direction looking for anything out of the ordinary, or of potential
hazard to the Royal Sovereign. She herself adopted a similar
stance and mentality, scanning the crowd that was ahead and to
the sides while they walked. Even though she was not dressed in
her uniform, it was a known fact the continents over that a soldier
could be taken out of the fight but the fight could never be taken
out of the soldier. Even in civilian clothes a part of Castellan
remained on duty.

Rather than answer Lt. Savon straightaway, Olivienne turned
to her dashing escort for the afternoon. "I know a place that spe-
cializes in food from the eastern province if you're amenable.
Khogalette's is also within walking distance."

Castellan Tosh was momentarily caught by the way the light
of the two suns gleamed on Olivienne's black hair. It reflected
nearly indigo highlights back to her eyes and was most alluring.
Unlike royals of old, the Connate's skin was well burnished by
the sun from her time spent as a historical adventurist. Her body
was toned from the career as well. "I think that sounds spectacu-
lar on all counts. Lead on, Connate Dracore." As an afterthought
she turned to Savon who watched from the other side of Olivienne. "It may be a good idea to teleo ahead to this Khogalette's
and see if you can request a private dining area for the Connate's
safety and privacy."

"Yes, ser, I was just thinking that." He moved a little farther
away from their group and rather than find a teleo, he unclasped
the voteo from his belt and contacted the local Defense Corp
operator for the city. The operator would easily call ahead and
make the reservations for the Connate's party.

It was good thinking on his part and Castellan admired the
man for his logical mind. Their dynamic was strange from the
moment she met the lieutenant. On one hand she was of higher
rank, but on the other hand the officer in charge of a sovereign's
safety always has the final say in any situation dealing with their
assigned royal. Yet time and time again Lt. Savon continued to
heed her word and look to her for guidance.

The walk was pleasant with the spring dae being neither too
hot nor too chill. Castellan had her sleeves rolled up displaying
tanned forearms. The strength of her arms alone was obvious by

the way the visible cords of muscle tapered into thick wrists. Most of that was from her regular sword work. Her shirt was also tight enough that if she turned just right, an observant person could note the pull of it against her muscles that were not shown.

Olivienne was most certainly observant of such things. Her own outfit was slightly scandalous for someone so high in Psiere society. It wasn't the flowing linen pants tucked into her tall brown boots, but rather the low cut blouse, which showed off her cleavage above the brown leather corset. She didn't feel like putting the bosair back on after their morning of debauchery, so she opted for the bosom lifting corset instead. Her double-holster pistol belt was slung on her hips, and she had added a brown leather pouch to the belt for other things she may need for a dae on the town. She noted that Castellan had donned her pistol belt as well. But then the officer seemed like someone who was well prepared at all times. Olivienne liked that trait in a person.

The Connate and lieutenant commander were seated as soon as they arrived at the eatery. The owner of the place even found tables for the guardians nearby so they could eat as well while they safeguarded the Connate. Over the leisurely meal, Olivienne and Castellan spoke on a great number of subjects but eventually circled around to the Divine Mystery and their discovery earlier that morning. "So what will you do now?"

Olivienne pushed away her empty plate and sat back in her seat, giving Castellan's question serious consideration. "Well, first I have to report my findings to the Queen and the Imperium. After that it will be imperative that we inform both temples of the newly discovered encryption key word. There are still rooms full of un-translated documents within both temples. An entire world has opened up with this new information."

Castellan cocked her head to the side as she watched the other woman's face light up with undisguised excitement. "Will you try to find the third temple?"

"Eventually. I think the Makers will not allow the task to be easy, considering they locked all those stones away for a reason. I suspect we will have to translate a lot of pages in order to start seeing clues to the location of the Temple of Antaeus."

A laugh met her words as Castellan shook her head in wonderment. "You know, I do believe I'm jealous that you are embarking on such an amazing adventure. There is a part of me that wishes I could be like the entertainment stars and go off in search of fame and fortune, solving the mysteries of the world."

"What is stopping you?"

Castellan shrugged. "Duty I suppose." She gestured toward herself with one hand. "This is who I am, for better or worse. All my knowledge and experience make me a good officer, but I'll be the first to admit that I'd be lost without the regimentation of the Defense Corp."

"Well you do seem very..." Castellan narrowed her eyes at the Connate and Olivienne finished diplomatically. "Precise. Very in control of your world, even when it spins away like it did in the river. I admire your calm capability."

Castellan lifted the remainder of her drink in a toast and Olivienne matched the gesture. "To calm capability then, and finding the adventure we both seek."

"Here, here!"

They spent oors in the eatery but still had plenty of time so Olivienne suggested a bit of shopping on her way back to the railer. Tosh laughed to see that their first stop was the pistol shoppe. Her service pistol was fine, so she stood near Lt. Savon while the Connate looked around. Seeing that Olivienne was going to be a while, she took the opportunity to question the quiet man. "How does one find himself in the Psi Shield Corp, Lieutenant Savon? Did you start as Psi Defense?"

The lieutenant made sure the other three guardians could adequately cover the small shoppe before answering. "I did start as defense, serving over in the eastern province near Baene. I was brought in by our previous leader on recommendation from my old Commander."

"And how do you find it here?"

Savon shrugged. "Sometimes I miss my old team and Commander Sheikha. Captain Shendo was a capable leader but sadly not a good fit for Connate Dracore's Shield unit. Speaking unofficially, ser?" Castellan nodded. "I'm not sure any of us really are."

The lt. commander's curiosity was piqued. "What happened to him and why do you say that?"

He waved discreetly toward their sovereign. "The Connate was determined to test an experimental cycle and Captain Shendo did not want her to go, concerned about her safety as he was. He made the mistake of forbidding her to ride one of the two cycles they had upgraded."

Castellan looked at him seriously. "She doesn't seem the type to do something that would be so dangerous. And knowing her even slightly I can certainly see how she'd not take lightly to such an action from him. Was his concern really so valid?"

"Begging your pardon, ser, but she jumped into a flash flood to save you."

Lt. Commander Tosh flushed at the memory of their narrow escape from certain death. "Fair enough, and good point but we both know how capable she is. As you were saying?"

"Anyway, I'm sure you've figured out by now that she hates her Shield Corp unit and has no patience for anyone that cannot keep up with her. But the problem is, ser, not many people can keep up with her. She is a sovereign and, as you said, highly capable at that. Between Connate Dracore's channels and her own level of training, she honestly runs us around a bit. And she makes it obvious that her only care is for whatever current adventure she is on."

"So back to your captain...I take it she left on the cycle and he followed her on the other?" Lt. Savon nodded. "And what, your captain quit simply because he didn't like his orders disobeyed?"

"Um...no, ser. It wasn't until after he wrecked that Captain Shendo quit."

Tosh raised an eyebrow. "Amicably?" She had never heard of anyone quitting the Shield Corp, had never even read about it in the history books. Being chosen for Shield Corp was considered the highest honor as they only took the best of what the Psi Defense and other Corps had to offer. Though she supposed that if people did quit it wouldn't be information that was spread around.

Lt. Savon shook his head. "I heard from Specialist Devin that he threw a waste pan at her."

"Sorry for keeping you waiting." Olivienne interrupted the conversation before Castellan could find out more. She glanced down at the pistol in the Connate's grip. The barrel was much longer than standard and she met the sovereign's eyes with a questioning look. Olivienne held it out to her, grip first. "It's a long-shot specialty. The barrel gives it greater accuracy at distance."

Castellan looked at the pistol in her hand then shook her head and handed it back. "Why ever would you need such a thing? Why not simply carry a rifle?"

Olivienne held up the pistol once again. "This is infinitely more portable and you never know when you may need the distance..." She trailed off and leveled a significant look at the head of her Shield unit. Savon's return look was dark and uncomfortable before he turned away to see to the rest of the guardians. Olivienne didn't even have a holster for the pistol; she carried it open in her hand. Weapons were only allowed in public spaces if you were of the correct authority, and un-holstered weapons were never permitted. Though any city would make special allowances for a Royal Sovereign.

When the group left the pistol shoppe, Olivienne declared that she was finished for the dae. She was kind enough to ask the lt. commander if there was someplace she wished to see but Castellan shook her head. The officer had never been one for superfluous purchases. Tosh found it curious that the closer they got to the railer station, the more tense the guardians became. She saw nothing out of the ordinary but she kept her guard up just the same.

All that tension came to a head when the group started across the busy market square. In an instant, Castellan's intuition channel flared at the same time Olivienne spun with the long pistol raised and fired toward the bell tower. A sec later Castellan caught sight of a man falling from the fifty yord height, a rifle striking the ground just ahead of him. Lt. Commander Tosh knew exactly what had happened and she found it foolish in the extreme. Lt. Savon was prescient and must have told Olivienne about the assassin ahead of time. Then when the time came, the rogue Connate decided she wanted to take care of the man herself rather than delaying their trip by following protocol and calling on the Psi Security Corp for assistance.

Castellan opened her mouth to berate the entirely too cocky group when her intuition channel flared again. She grasped in an instant what was happening and also knew there was no time to warn, only act. She dove for Olivienne, taking the Connate to the ground as the distinctive sound of a rifle shell speeding through the air hit them. Pain spiked in Castellan's back just below her ribs and she grunted. Then without thinking about the continued danger to herself, she rolled onto her back, pulled her pistol, and fired. A second body fell from the bell tower window just as the pistol fell from her hand. Sensing the danger had passed, the lt. commander closed her eyes as the agony coursing through her torso threatened to overwhelm her.

With the appearance of a second shooter, the Connate's guardians sprang into action. Two took off toward the tower while Lt. Savon and Spc. Devin moved close and stood over Olivienne, protecting her with their own bodies. There was a reason protectors of the sovereigns were called Shields.

In shock, Olivienne stood and brushed herself off then turned and looked down at Castellan. The lt. commander's eyes were shut and her breathing was significantly faster than normal. "Lieutenant Commander Tosh, are you well?"

Tosh swallowed the pain in order to speak and managed to grind out an answer from between her clenched teeth. "No, Connate Dracore. I've been shot."

"Oh bollux!" Olivienne spun toward her lead guard. "Get a doctore here now!" Lt. Savon pulled the voteo from his belt and made arrangements for the swift arrival of a medican while Olivienne knelt to examine the officer on the ground. She grew alarmed to see a rapidly spreading puddle of blood from beneath Tosh. "Stay with me now, Tosh!" She didn't get a response so she tried mind to mind. *"Tosh?"*

"I'm here."

"Hold on, okay? A medican will be here – " She glanced up at Lt. Savon and he held up two fingers. *"Two meens. Please, just stay with us."*

"I will." Castellan wasn't speaking aloud because she was trying to conserve energy. She was also doing special breathing exercises to help control the pain. She had learned many rotos before that controlling pain went a long way toward preventing shock. Just as promised, a medican arrived and began treating Tosh's wound. They were lucky enough to get the Penterole's only doctore with the telesana channel. Or maybe it had more to do with the fact that the initial voteo call said the Connate's group had been fired on and one person was hit. Taking no chances with a sovereign's life, they sent the best they had.

As soon as he saw that the shell was still in the wound, he called out to the group. "Any of you apport? I need this shell removed so I can do a healing!"

Olivienne quickly answered. "I am. What do you need, Doctore?"

He had already rolled Castellan over onto her stomach and cut a section of the officer's shirt away, displaying the grievous wound that was a handspan above her belt. "The shell struck her left kidney. I'm going to pry this wound open so you can see the shell, then I need you to apport it out. I can't start the healing until it is removed!"

"I can do that." She looked at where Castellan's head was turned with her right cheek pressed tight against the rough stones of the marketplace. "Do you need something to bite down on?"

Castellan groaned and managed one word. "No."

The apport only took a sec. As soon as the offending shell was removed, the doctore slapped his hand over the hole in Castellan's back and called forth the power of his healing channel. Sweat beaded across his forehead as he used his telesana to its limit in order to repair the damage inside. Meens passed and Olivienne was only vaguely aware that her small group surrounding them had expanded to more than quadruple in size as local Psi Security Corp units arrived at the scene. The Connate watched her companion fight through the agony of being shot and for the first time in her life, she regretted her casual disregard for standard Shield Corp security procedures.

The doctore finally pulled his hand away to reveal new pink skin beneath. Castellan appeared to be unconscious and he turned to Olivienne. "Connate Dracore, the shell expanded while inside and did a lot of internal damage before stopping. It was a good thing I was so near on business or she would not have survived. I recommend bed rest for the next few daes to replenish her lost blood, otherwise she is completely healed." He stood and swayed, clearly having drained himself to perform his duty. He was steadied by Lt. Savon.

The Connate stood as well and glanced back down at Castellan. "When will she wake? Does she need a med facility?"

"No, as I said she is completely healed. Just needs to remake a few flasks of blood is all. She should wake within a quarter oor. I activated her pineal gland and put her to sleep while I was working on the wound. I find it easier to have the patient unaware as they're less likely to distract my empathy with their pain."

Olivienne nodded and stood up from where she'd been kneeling on the ground next to Castellan. "Do you need us to call a moto, Doctore...I apologize but I do not know your name."

He held his hand out to her. "I am Doctore Bessing, and I am honored to meet you, Connate Dracore. I only wish it were under better circumstances."

"As do I, Doctore Bessing, as do I."

Five meens later, Castellan still had not woken but plenty had happened around her. For starters her body had been placed on a litter for transport back to the railer. Also the bodies of the two assassins had been collected by the Security Corp officers. Lt. Savon spoke with the head of the Security unit and arranged for

them to share any information found about the attackers. Assassination attempts on the royal family were of utmost priority and
there would be an extensive inquiry conducted. Shortly after their
conversation wrapped up, two of the Shield Corp team grabbed
the ends of Castellan's litter and the small group, with a much
larger force of Security officers surrounding them, proceeded to
the railer. When they reached the first class segment, the guardians holding the litter stopped outside Castellan's private cabin
but Olivienne waved them on.

"No, take her to my room please." The trundle bed had been
left down and Olivienne sorrowed to know that she was partly
responsible for the tragic turn the dae had taken.

Unfortunately for Spc. Devin, he was the closest one to her
person when Castellan swam toward consciousness. Her first
thought was of pain and danger. Before he could react, the lt.
commander had pulled her pistol and was pointing it at his head.
Thinking fast, Olivienne apported the weapon from Tosh's hand
and into her own. "Don't hurt him, you're safe. Everyone is safe."

Castellan opened her eyes then and as her memory returned
of the events in the market square, so too did the anger. Feeling
only marginally weak, she sat up in what she quickly realized
was the Connate's bed. "What were you all playing at back there?
I have never seen a more irresponsible and poorly organized
group in my life!" She stood from the bed and her anger seemed
to grow, causing the three Shield guardians to take a step back.

Lt. Savon knew well that he had not performed his duty as he
should have, but the Connate had commanded him and he was
bound by duty to take those orders from her. With much sorrow,
he bowed his head. "My deepest apologies, Lieutenant Commander Tosh. Our plan was carried out without enough thought
and preparation, therefore was foolhardy in the extreme. I shall
resign my commission as soon as we reach Tesseron..."

He was interrupted when Olivienne stepped forward. In her
own anger, Castellan failed to notice how drawn the Connate's
features had become. She only saw a selfish sovereign whose
reckless actions risked multiple lives besides her own. What if the
shooter had hit another person, or a child? What if there had been
no telesana-wielding doctore nearby, which was the only explanation for her quick healing? Both her mental tirade and Lt.
Savon's resignation offering were interrupted by the Connate's
solemn voice. "No, Savon. I'm afraid this entire debacle lies solely
on my shoulders." She focused her gaze on Castellan. "I was the

one who instructed him not to inform the local Psi Security Corp, as is standard procedure for a premonition of assassination. I was cocky and thought we could handle the shooter with the information provided by our channels—"

Castellan sliced her hand through the air in front of her to cut off the Connate's words. "None of you have any true idea of either the power of Psi channels, or the limitations. As you've just learned, nothing is infallible. Events like assassinations can be masked merely by putting two shooters in the same place. Unless your prescience is of the highest rank, you will not see two separate events but rather just one. Protocol is put into place to guarantee potential enemies can't use those limitations as a screen. Whomever sent those attackers clearly knew about the Connate's penchant for disregard of her Shield unit and counted on that fact when they set up this little trap." She turned her gaze to look straight into Lt. Savon's eyes. "Let this be a lesson to you going forward."

She took a step toward the door and Olivienne moved to block her. "Where are you going? The doctore said you need to rest!"

With minimal concentration, Castellan telekinetically pulled her pistol from Olivienne's hand to her own and re-holstered it. "I am going to rest in my own cabin where clearly I am safest. Good dae to you, Connate Dracore!" With those final words she turned and strode from Olivienne's room.

Chapter Nine

ONE OF THE main reasons that Castellan was so calm and cool in any situation was because she was a fairly mellow soul who was extremely slow to anger. To be fair, if events went so far wrong that they could burn through the wick of her temper, then surely they were wrong indeed. She was furious upon returning to her own cabin, though the heat of the anger had mostly left her as exhaustion set in. Her battered body had been through too much in the past few daes and there was not much she could do at that point but rest. It was nearing sup time but she had no appetite as they ate their middae meal quite late. Of course being shot played a large part as well.

She stripped the bloodied shirt from her body and fingered the rent that was originally made by the shell and enlarged by the medican. With a sigh of disgust, she balled the gray fabric and tossed it into the trash receptacle. She felt tired and dirty with dried blood so she opted for a quick sluicing in the shower before downing two large glasses of water and falling into her bunk. Before drifting off to sleep, she wound and set the fancy geared alarm clock next to the bed. She wanted to be up and ready to depart the railer as soon as it arrived in Tesseron. If she never saw the Connate again it would be too soon.

Back in Olivienne's cabin, her feelings ran the entire opposite gamut as the ones belonging to Castellan Tosh. She was well aware that her actions had not only endangered lives but had brought dishonor on her Shield unit. Honor was a concept that she had only recently been made aware of since becoming acquainted with Lt. Commander Tosh. It was almost surreal that they had known each other for so short a time yet Olivienne had been instilled with such a foreign awareness. Even though Castellan had survived the assassination attempt, Olivienne feared that their budding friendship had not. She needed to make amends and she wasn't sure how to go about it.

After an initial awkward silence when Tosh left her cabin, the three members of her Shield unit that had been in the room for the confrontation took their leave as well. Perhaps she could start there. Deciding on a course of action, she left her cabin in search of Lt. Savon. Olivienne found him playing a card game with specialists Devin, Soleng, and Qent. As soon as they caught sight of her, the entire quad stood and saluted. She waved them to take a seat again and Lt. Savon spoke up. "Is there something you need, Connate Dracore?"

She nodded and was more solemn than they'd ever seen. Gentry Savon was startled to see that the sovereign before them was not the same he had been dealing with for the past few rotos. She seemed...subdued somehow. "Actually, there is something I need. I need to apologize to all four of you. Lieutenant Commander Tosh was completely correct with her assessment of the situation todae. Not just that, but of her accusations involving me in general. I realize, perhaps belatedly, that I have made your job extremely difficult over the rotos."

Savon, being the good lieutenant and loyal subject, tried to prop her up. "It's not so bad, Sovereign. I could only imagine what it would be like to suddenly find people following me around everywhere, dictating where I could go and what I could do for safety's sake. I understand how you would think of us all as an inconvenience."

"You are right in that I've always found my Shield unit to be an inconvenience. I'm driven and my career means a lot to me. I loathe having to slow down for trivial things like protocol and security. And until todae, I'd never truly understood the necessity of it all." Olivienne took a seat on an unoccupied chair and got to the point of what she had to say. "My stubborn selfishness not only endangered your lives, but the lives of innocent bystanders as well. I want to apologize for that and for besmirching your honor in the eyes of Lieutenant Commander Tosh. You did everything you could to keep me safe, despite the situation I put you in, and I will be sure to put a recommendation for each of you in my report to the Queen and Imperium."

Olivienne stood once again and swept her gaze across all of them, landing on Lt. Savon. "Going forward, I will do my utmost best to follow protocol. There will be certain things I will need to do to perform my own job, but I will try to follow your recommendations."

Savon stood as well. "Begging your pardon, Connate Dracore, but when we get back to Tesseron, you will most likely have a brand new Shield Captain to break in."

"Then I suppose I'll have to repeat my words at that time because I mean every single one. Good night, pseros." With that, she left them to their game and returned to her cabin but not without one last regretful glance to Tosh's door.

THE NEXT MORNING Castellan was up earlier, feeling better than the dae before. She was scheduled to meet with General Leniste at seven hundred oors local time so her outfit choice was none other than her white dress uniform. She was always embarrassed to wear it, with the colorful patches on each shoulder and the medals clinking where they sat on her chest. The trousers had a royal blue stripe that ran down the outsides and disappeared into her tall dress boots. Her belt, holster, and pouch were all gleaming black to match. They were still twenty meens out from the station when she shouldered her accessory satchel and lifted the large duffel from the floor. It was heavy, as anything containing five rotos of a person's entire life could be, but she managed. She was just getting ready to go through the exit door of the first class segment when she was stopped by a familiar voice.

"Lieutenant Commander Tosh, a moment please?"

While her anger had faded overnight, it had been replaced by irritation and disappointment. She watched Olivienne striding down the hall and wanted nothing more than to ignore the infuriating woman. But she was an officer and an honorable one at that, and she was being hailed by her Sovereign so she waited. "Yes, Connate Dracore? Is there something you need?"

"I need to apologize."

Castellan sighed. "I assure you that an apology is not necessary. Let's just mark it up as a lesson learned, shall we?"

Olivienne stepped closer and looked upon Castellan with wounded eyes and unnaturally pale face. The distance between Olivienne and the lt. commander was maintained by the large duffel but they were still close enough for Castellan to notice that the Connate looked drawn. "I just wanted to tell you how sorry I am and that it was indeed a lesson learned. I have apologized to my Shield unit and promised to follow proper protocol in the future. I need to be a better person not just for them, but for myself and all the people who count on me."

"I'm sure they were relieved to hear that. Now if you'll excuse me..."

"Please, Commander...Castellan..." The officer turned her pale eyes back to the sovereign with barely disguised annoyance and Olivienne tried again. "Please, I don't want us to part as enemies. Can we not find our way back to friendship?"

Castellan straightened to her full height. "You are a sovereign of Psiere, we could never be enemies. As for a friendship, I don't know. You have callously disregarded beliefs that I hold dear. Beyond that, I have no idea where I will be stationed next. It may be that we'll never see each other again for as long as we live." Olivienne started to speak but Castellan held her free hand up to stay the Connate's words. "I hold no ill will, nor even anger toward you, but friendship is beyond me at this moment." She cocked her head to the side, considering Olivienne's pledge to think more about others in the future. "But if you truly mean the words you've said, then who knows what the future will bring. Perhaps we will indeed meet again on friendly terms. Good luck with your search for answers, Connate Dracore."

Olivienne gave the officer a sad smile. "And good luck in your search for adventure, Commander Tosh."

THE RAILER STATION in Tesseron was in complete chaos and it didn't take Castellan long to see why. Despite the early oor, both the Queen and the King had come with full units of Shield guardians to protect them. Certain that their arrival was out of concern over the assassination attempt on their daughter, Tosh thought it even wiser to slip through unnoticed. She didn't want any more attention drawn to herself where the Connate was concerned. She merely wanted to receive her new post and get on with life.

Outside the busy station it was easy enough to flag a delivery moto that could take her to the other side of Bindle Bay, where the Psi Defense Corp headquarters was located. Tesseron was a bustling metropolis, with buildings as much as ten levels high. Dirigible shipyards were on the south side of the bay, near the railer station so they ran no risk of catching on the beautifully carved spires and building peaks featured throughout the capital.

When they arrived, the driver stopped where the road ran in a circle around a grand fountain, just outside the steps leading up to the main entrance of the Defense Corp building. Castellan was irritated with herself that she didn't have the woman pull around to the side entrance but there was nothing to be done about it at that point. She handed over creds for the service then shouldered her duffel and made her way up the stairs. Castellan hadn't been in Tesseron for more than five rotos and seeing the grand building was a little overwhelming. She had forgotten how beautiful the edifice truly was. If there ever was a testament to the merging of function and art, it was the Psi Corp buildings. The only thing more beautiful was the royal manse that housed offices and the living space of the Sovereign family.

After a moment of disorientation in the grand entryway, Castellan made her way to the security desk. There were half a dozen soldiers spread throughout the lobby. A sturdy and serious looking young private was manning the desk and he stood and saluted as she approached. "May I help you, Commander?"

She set the duffel down and dug out the missive she had folded and placed in her waist pouch. "Yes, I have an assignment meeting with General Leniste."

The private ran his finger down the slate on his desk and stopped when he found her name. "Yes, ser. You are scheduled to meet with him and General Renou in General Leniste's office at seven hundred. His office is on the fifth floor, corridor G. There is a desk upstairs too, so if you get lost you can ask for directions there. Currently you are about thirty-five meens early, just enough time to break your fast in the eatery we have on site."

Castellan's pale brow rose. "General Renou? Are you sure?"

"Yes, ser." She was surprised enough to find out in the missive that she would be meeting with General Leniste himself upon her return to Tesseron. He was the head of the Psi Defense Corp and was not known to involve himself in the dae to dae placements of ordinary officers. But to find that she was also to meet with the general in charge of the Psi Shield Corp, that was most disconcerting. She wondered if the addition of General Renou had anything to do with her actions in Penterole. It made sense that Lt. Savon would have put her name into the report that would have gone to the Queen and the Imperium. The private interrupted her swirling thoughts. "Is there anything else I can do for you, ser?"

"Yes. Is there someplace I can store my duffel until after the meeting?"

He stood from his chair, then grabbed a ring of keys from the desk and came around the short counter that separated him from any visitors. "If you'll follow me, I can lock it in a storage closet until you return."

His statement seemed nearly like a question and the lt. commander nodded. "That would be acceptable, thank you."

Castellan kept her meal light in the eatery yet still the questions and concerns about the addition of General Renou to her reassignment meeting compressed the fruit and warm bread into a hard brick in her belly. At quarter to the oor, she made her way upstairs to the location of the general's office. There was another desk outside, manned by yet another private and she waited while he used the teleo to inform the general of her arrival. He listened for just a sec longer before disconnecting the line and waving her toward the plain wood door. "He is ready for you, Commander." As Tosh opened the door, she wondered if she was ready for the general.

As soon as she was fully in the room, both generals stood and she saluted them proper. She had only met General Leniste once, and never General Renou. Leniste was a big man, still imposing and fit despite being well into middle age and his nearly ten rotos as the head of the Psi Defense Corp. In comparison, General Renou was a woman smaller than even Gemeda Shen's sixty-four inces. What General Renou lacked in height though she certainly made up for with sheer crisp authority. With striking gray eyes and short white hair, she drew attention wherever she went. Leniste waved her toward an empty seat that was equidistant between himself and General Renou. She waited for both to sit before taking her own seat. "Sers."

Never one to skirt a subject, General Leniste started straightaway. "We heard you've had an eventful couple daes, Tosh." By using her last name only, the general was giving permission to speak informally with them.

"Yes, ser. I suppose you could call it that."

"Are you whole and hale now, Tosh?" General Renou seemed especially keen to hear the answer to her question as she leaned forward in her seat.

"Yes, ser. I strained my channel in Ostium the dae before I left to come north. Doctore Gemeda Shen is a personal friend of mine and healed much of the strain on the railer but events in a small town along the way strained me again. Whatever ails I may have been suffering from that second event were certainly healed by the doctore in Penterole when I was shot in the assassination attempt." She shrugged. "I am well now, if suffering slightly from blood loss. Nothing a few daes of rest and extra fluids will not cure."

General Renou looked pleased and Castellan grew wary. "Good, good!"

"I suppose you're wondering why you're meeting with me

about your next placement instead the head of the re-assignment division. You're probably even more curious as to why General Renou would sit in on our meeting."

Castellan's wariness tripled. "Yes, ser, I am."

He smiled in an attempt of reassurance. "I'm not sure if you remember, but we met once nearly six rotos ago. You were near the end of your term here in the north, right before being sent down to Dromea."

"Yes, ser, I remember."

"Yes well, even then I remember thinking to myself, 'that officer is going somewhere!' After consulting with your superiors, and reading through your transcripts, I see that your actions down south have earned you a promotion."

Relief coursed through Castellan as one of her dreams was about to come true. "That is what I was told, ser."

"Ah, well as luck would have it, you've come to the attention of more than just your superiors in the Defense Corp. It seems you, my dear Tosh, are a valuable commodity."

"Ser?"

Her gaze was drawn to General Renou when the trim officer began to speak in a voice that was like soft cotton. She was surprisingly quiet but Castellan had no doubt the woman could get her point across when she had to. "Yes indeed, Lieutenant Commander Tosh. We have been looking for an officer who is both highly capable and has a high channel rating. We are looking for someone whose dedication is unmatched and loyalty unquestioned. After much consideration, we would like to offer you leadership of a Sovereign unit in the Psi Shield Corp. With your new positon, you would also be promoted to full Commander." Her smile was wide and friendly, anticipating the excitement that her words would bring to Tosh.

Tosh had a feeling, but she had to be certain before she could make her decision. There was only one sovereign that was missing a lead for their unit and her stomach turned with the thought of having to see the Connate again so soon. "Which sovereign's unit would I be commanding?"

Renou looked surprised by her question. "Surely you knew that Connate Dracore's team is lacking leadership. I was informed that you two spent most of your time together on the railer during your trip north. Not only that, but I was also told you made a great team during the rescue and you even took a shell protecting the Connate herself. If that does not single you out for the role above all others, surely I do not know what would. Well done, Tosh!"

Despite the immense honor it was to be chosen for the Psi Shield Corp, Castellan Tosh was not excited at all. She swallowed the bile down as she realized she would have to derail her future purely for the sake of honor. "I'm sorry, sers, but I regretfully decline your offer."

"So beginning todae all your vellumwork will be transferred to—what did you just say?" Leniste looked at her as if she had just grown a second head.

Castellan cleared her throat and tried again. "Regretfully, I must decline this posting."

Renou looked dismayed. "Why ever would you do that?"

"It is personal. But suffice it to say I am unsuited to this duty."

General Leniste's face purpled. "Bollux! There is nothing personal in the Corp! Why would you feel unsuited?"

The officer sighed, hating the fact that her private life was going to be brought into the discussion. "Sers...the Connate and I had...relations on the railer north. Relations that were known by her guardians. It would not be honorable or appropriate for me to head up her Shield Corp unit."

Leniste sat back in his chair and glanced over at Renou. "Well I certainly didn't expect that."

Renou answered swiftly though. "We don't care."

Tosh looked at the head of the Psi Shield Corp more closely. The older woman was resolute, unaccountably. "But, ser, I thought only the rank of Captain could take control of a Shield unit?"

General Renou brushed a bit of dust off her sleeve before meeting Tosh's eyes. "It was decided unanimously that your capability and qualifications perfectly matched our need in this role and the requirement for captain's rank would be waived for you and you alone. Beyond that, in two roto's time, we would re-evaluated your performance and decide then if you would be suitable for a further promotion to captain."

Castellan leaned back in shock. To be made a captain before the age of thirty-four rotos was unheard of, as was only spending two rotos as a commander before another promotion came along. It was the pinnacle of career achievements and her heart sank. She looked down at her hands and sighed again. "Again, my apologies but I will still have to decline. Connate Dracore and I—

we did not part on the best of terms and I'd rather not be placed in charge of her protection unit."

"Lieutenant Commander Tosh..." With the use of her full and proper title, General Leniste had firmly taken the meeting back to professional business. Gone was the man who espoused pride in her achievements and skills. "Is this worth throwing away your career?"

Dread crept into her belly. "Ser? I'm not trying to throw away my career, but with all due respect, I'd rather advance through the ranks in my own Corp and not because the Shields are desperate."

Sensing a display of Leniste's famous temper, Renou tried to step in. "Germaine—"

Her words were cut off when Leniste's deep voice thundered through the office. "If you do not accept this post then you will not advance rank through *any* Corp!"

General Renou tried to salvage a situation gone badly. "Lieutenant Commander Tosh, I did not lie when I said you were exactly the person we've been looking for. Yes we are desperate but it is out of necessity. You witnessed that yesterdae in Penterole. But the fact stands that we feel you, above everyone else, are the perfect person to do this job. Please reconsider your decision."

While she respected General Renou and her honesty, Castellan had lost her respect for her own commanding officer. Anger replaced the sick pain caused by General Leniste's words and she moved her steady gaze from Renou back to Leniste. It was anger and lost respect that fueled the words that could have sent her straight to the prison island of Aetate. "I will not be bullied into a position that I find inappropriate and dishonorable. For my commanding officer to do so tells me that his own honor is lacking. You can drop me from a dirigible straight into the Caerula Ocean and I will still say nay."

"Why you insolent little—"

The head of the Psi Shield Corp cut off her counterpart before he could finish his threat. "Before we resort to anymore threats and *bullying*—" She spared General Leniste a dark look. "I would like you to take one full dae to think about your decision. I understand your position, Tosh, and I admire your honor greatly. But our need is also great and I truly do not think this post would compromise either your duty or your honor. You are too good an officer for that. So please, allow yourself a full dae of review before giving me your answer." She looked at General Leniste. "Is that acceptable?"

General Leniste deflated instantly, realizing how badly he had misjudged Tosh, and how poorly he had reacted to her words. He ran a hand through his short-cropped gray hair and met Castellan's eyes once again. "My apologies, Tosh. I fear that I let my temper get ahead of me and I took it out on you. We are under pressure from the Queen herself to fill this position and you were the name that came up again and again. Please try to see this situation from our side."

Tosh looked back and forth between the two Corp leaders. The fact that they were being pressured by the Queen put their reaction to her refusal into better perspective. "I can give you a full dae before I make my decision official. But I honestly don't see my answer changing between now and then." She looked back at her own general. "Without an assignment, I currently have no place to stay while in Tesseron. Is there a temporary bunk I can use?"

Leniste opened his mouth to speak but was interrupted by Renou. "I have a guesthouse you can use until this situation is resolved. Will that be acceptable?"

The Shield Corp general was trying to soften her up, to bribe a positive answer. It would not work of course but Castellan agreed to the guesthouse anyway. "That would be fine. Thank you, ser."

Camen Renou smiled at her before reaching into her waist pouch and pulling out a small card. She stood and walked to Leniste's desk and borrowed his stylus to jot something onto the back. When she was finished, she walked to where Castellan had stood from her seat. "This is the address for the guest house, and the combination for the gate lock is written on the back." She turned to Leniste again. "Is eight hundred oors good for meeting again tomorrow?"

General Leniste looked over at the slate that he had pushed off to the right side of his desk. He scanned the planner and then looked back at the two women in the room. "I have an oor of time then, so eight hundred is acceptable." He stood and nodded to Castellan. "You are dismissed, Lieutenant Commander Tosh."

"Sers!" She saluted both generals and walked out of the office in a daze.

Chapter Ten

IN NO TIME Castellan found herself in front of the imposing Psi Defense building holding her retrieved duffel in one hand and the card that General Renou had given her in the other. Her mind whirled with everything she had just learned and been offered. Castellan shook herself free from those confusing thoughts and peered closer at the card. She noted the address and called up the city grid in her head. If she wasn't mistaken, the general's guesthouse was less than ten squares away so opted to walk rather than call on another moto. She was still quite drained from her journey north and a few oors of rest might be good for her.

Despite Castellan's pride telling her otherwise, the large duffel she carried was heavy and within five meens the strain was making her sweat in her dress uniform. After another five meens she told her pride to take a flying leap and opted to carry the duffel with her telekinesis instead. The officer wasn't sure what to expect from General Renou's home but she had a clue as soon as she entered the upper class community. While it was true that no one in Psiere was allowed to go hungry, remain sick, or live in a poor quality house, some Psierians definitely fared better than others.

The gate to General Renou's property was a massive iron blockade that was bracketed on both sides by a tall stone wall. The top of the wall was lined with sharp metal spikes for as far as Castellan could see. It wouldn't keep out a diligent thief or ne'er-do-well but it would certainly deter the rest. Just as promised, there was a dial lock on the gate and Tosh used the code that Renou gave her to gain entry. Once inside, the paved stone walkway didn't go up to the house as expected. It was all lawn and gardens of immense topiatic delight. Rather than stare at the animal images that had been cut into the hedges along the front, Tosh followed the walkway around the right side of the medium-size manse.

As soon as she was behind the large home, she spotted another building that housed the General's motos. The fact that the general had more than one was telling as to the intimidating woman's wealth. But Castellan didn't stop there. She continued following the path farther back on the property until she came to a small two-story house. The stone and design perfectly matched that of the main house, just significantly smaller. The walkway ended at the front entrance to the guesthouse and she wasn't sure what to do except stare.

Before she could formulate a plan, the door *whooshed* open and a man of both middling age and middle height stood in the doorway. His hair was shockingly thick and white and he was dressed in normal civ clothes. The dark orange tattoo of consorage around his neck strikingly matched to his eyes. She'd seen the design duplicate of it around General Renou's neck, only hers was a less striking gray color. "Lieutenant Commander Castellan Tosh?"

She dropped her duffel bag and held out her hand. "Yes, ser, and you are?"

He clasped the offered hand and grinned. The smile utterly transformed the stoic and somewhat ordinary face into one of animation and joviality. "My name is Pendar Renou, I believe you've met my par, Camen Renou. She teleoed ahead and informed me of your arrival." He stepped back into the house once again. "Come in, I was just checking to make sure it was well stocked for your stay. If you'll follow me I can show you the amenities and let you pick out a room to leave your duffel in."

His name seemed familiar somehow but Castellan couldn't place it. He showed her around and afterward she picked out a bedroom to leave her gear. "You have a beautiful property, Psero Renou. If you'll forgive me, but your name seems familiar to me. What is your Corp?"

He grinned again and his entire demeanor brightened. "I'm Psi Service Corp. Does Pendaren sound more familiar?"

"Yes! That's it, you're the famous writer!" Tosh gave a slight bow, awed at being in the company of someone so well-known. "It is an honor to meet you, ser."

Pendar waggled a finger at her. "On the contrary, the honor is all mine. After all, it's not every dae I get to meet the Hero of Temple Beach, or the woman who took a shell for a sovereign of Psiere!" Tosh flushed at his unexpected praise and remained silent. His ever-expressive face changed yet again. "Oh! It seems I've embarrassed you, I really didn't mean to. I suppose you are tired after all your travails of late so how about I show you to the liquor case and leave you alone. Savvy?"

She nodded and he did as promised. When he was gone, Tosh

loosened the collar of her dress shirt, poured herself a glass of well-aged scotch, and took a seat on one of the reclining couches outside. It was there that the smell of spring and delicate sounds of birds lulled her into a fast and deep sleep.

"MAMAN, PAPAN!" OLIVIENNE looked up in surprise as soon as she exited the railer. Her pride was still stung that she had not won the handsome officer back to her good graces before they parted company. And the presence of her parens at her homecoming threw her off as well. "Whatever are you doing here?" Standing side by side, the iridescent tattoos around her parens' necks drew her attention. The royal tattoos of consorage were the only ones made with special ink that seemed to glow during the daelight oors.

Queen Olivara Dracore drew her only daughter into a firm hug. When she let go, Olivienne's papan did the same. Her mother gave her a disbelieving look. "Do you really believe we'd stay away after hearing about the assassination attempt yester-dae?" The Queen's eyes welled up before she pushed away the emotion. Olivienne saw it and recognized the technique for what it was because she used the same skill herself when dealing with overwhelming emotions. Growing up in the public eye had taught them all that the people wanted to see a calm and capable ruler, not someone whose emotions got away from them in a public place.

To break the heavy scene, Keshien Dracore grabbed his par's left hand and wrapped his free arm around Olivienne's shoulders. "Come. Let's not stand here making our Shields worry and sweat. We have a moto waiting to take you home."

They had just started walking and the Connate pulled up short. "You mean my home, right? Not back to the palace."

It was her mother who spoke. "Please, 'Vienne...can you not spend some time with your family? We feared we had lost you when the first reports came in about the assassination attempt. When we heard that one person in your party had been shot and it wasn't a member of the Shield unit...we feared the worst."

Olivienne sighed and chewed her bottom lip. She knew her parens worried and also knew she had much to tell them that she wanted kept private until the official announcement was made about her discovery. "Why don't you come to my place instead? I would like to unpack my bags and get a little more rest. Also, I have news—"

"*News?*"

"*What news?*"

The feel of Olivara and Keshien's voices in her head was as familiar as the sound of her own. She nodded and glanced around before briefly touching the center of her forehead with her thumbnail. It was a code known only to the royal family that said she had urgent secure information for them. Rather than reference the family telepathy session or the code aloud, the Queen responded with a nod. "What news could you have that is more important that our daughter's homecoming?"

Olivienne grinned and reached into her large shoulder satchel. When she withdrew her hand, she was holding the long-barrel pistol. She flipped it around and held it out to her mother, handle first. "I found this beauty in a little pistol shoppe in Penterole."

A single dark eyebrow went up as the Queen took the gleaming weapon. Besides the long barrel and polished teakwood grip, there were the usual openings for ammunition and illeostone. One small gauge on the side registered the illeostone's charge and a small marker on the other side let the shooter know exactly how much ammunition was still loaded. She stroked the finely crafted weapon reverently. Both she and her daughter were known sharpshooters and they shared their mutual love of pistols. The more unique the better. "Distance?"

The Connate shrugged. "I hit a clock tower thirty yords away when I needed to, and I was promised triple that." Olivara sighed and made to hand it back but Olivienne waved her off. "No, I bought it with you in mind. I apologize that I had to trial it out first though. First shot should always go to the gifted and not the gifter."

"I think we can make an exception this time. Come, we are holding up the railer and the rest of the fine passengers with all our overprotective guards. Let us head back to your dwelling where we can catch up."

Back at Olivienne's residence, she was going to let Lt. Savon send a detail inside for a security inspection but her mother stayed the order. "I already had Captain Torrin take a team though to inspect the entire place and two guardians were left inside to keep it secure."

"Thank you."

Once inside, Olivienne stood in the foyer and apported her

bags up to her room, with the exception of the shoulder satchel. That held the two special double temple documents and their translations that she wanted the Queen and King to see. They took seats around her entertainment room and she spread the original documents out on the low table. She immediately began recounting the tale of the past few daes to her parens. "You remember the undecipherable document I found in the cave, and how I went south in search of a match to it?"

Her father looked down at the table and grinned, excitement of his daughter's discovery taking ten rotos off his face. "You found it!"

"Yes. Unfortunately neither yielded to our two encryption keys and I was frustrated. The solution was actually discovered by an officer staying in the first class segment with me. She too has a fascination with the Divine Mystery and was interested in the documents so I let her take a look at them. They were doing me no good at that point."

Her mother glanced at her with a curious smile on her face. "Officer? Would this be the same one who accompanied you on your outing in Penterole, the one that was shot?"

Olivienne's face darkened with the memory. "Yes, that's the one. Lieutenant Commander Castellan Tosh, of the Psi Defense Corp. She was returning to Tesseron for reassignment and we struck up an acquaintance."

"Oh?" One thing the Queen, and perhaps all mothers across the continents, excelled at was speaking an entire paragraph of thoughts with just one word. Olivara knew her daughter quite well. She watched the way the younger Dracore spoke, and took in her facial inflections and understood exactly what she meant by *acquaintance*. Of all the things the Queen could have said in reply to Olivienne's words, the one that wasn't going to be mentioned aloud was that she recognized Castellan Tosh's name as one that had been brought to her a lune previous. There was a very small list of people that were both qualified and suitable to head up her daughter's Shield unit. On one hand, their "acquaintance" complicated things. On the other, knowing of Lt. Commander Tosh's similar interests as well as her sacrifice to save her daughter only convinced Olivara that the officer was the right one for the job. Time would tell.

Olivienne ignored her mother's weighted 'oh,' having heard it often enough. Either she would say what was on her mind eventually or not, but the Connate had learned that her mother would not be drawn into conversation about her thoughts prematurely. Instead of dwelling on whatever it was the Queen was considering, she went on with the story. "So Tosh pointed out that with a double symbol, perhaps they needed the key to be of both temple names. It worked on one, and after a false start where we had to reverse the temple names for the southern document, it worked on the other as well."

Keshien leaned forward abruptly. "So we have what, one or two more keys to translate documents?"

Olivienne shook her head. "No, not exactly like that. I think the double key will only work with documents with the double symbol. However, when we translated these two sib documents we made a discovery that will change everything! Here, I'll let you read for yourself." She shuffled the pages until the two translation sheets were on top of the pile in the correct order then slid them back across the table for her parens to read.

Meens of silence went by while they perused both sheets. Then nearly as one they sat back and stared at their daughter. It was Keshien who spoke first. "A third temple? But where?"

Her mother's mind immediately went to the harsher implications and for a sec Olivienne was reminded of Tosh. "I'm not going to lie, the power of antoraestones has the potential for immense destruction and it worries me that something like that will be discovered and fall into the wrong hands."

The King's opinion better aligned with Olivienne's own view. "But love, think of all we could do with that power! Why...we don't even know if there are other continents someplace beyond our current dirigible range on the ocean. We could better hold off attacks from the Atlanteens! With these special amplifiers, we would need less illeostones for the essential maintenance of our cities and people could have more access to power in their private lives!"

Olivara looked from her daughter back to her par, understanding that they were both optimists in life while she herself was much more a realist. "Have we already forgotten Ser Teloch?"

Keshien's lips turned white with the way he was pressing them together with anger.

Olivienne cocked her head. "Obviously before my time, but we learned about him at Academy. Wasn't he the rogue telepath that was forcing people to do his bidding on his estate during grandam's reign? He killed the most people with his channel of any other Psierian before or since. Something like thirty deaths, right?"

"No." While Keshien was a powerful man, strong, brave, and forthright when he needed to be, few knew that he was also very sensitive. The tone in her father's voice made Olivienne look at him with concern. After a few secs he continued. "They only knew about the people on his estate that he killed before the Psi Security and Defense Corps caught up with him. Your grandam was recovering from an assassination attempt and a lot of things were still in disarray within the government. After Ser Teloch's capture, word came to Tesseron of a small town that had simply disappeared. The buildings were still intact but no people. There was only one survivor, a small boy who had been sent to stay with his grandparens and was not there at the time."

Olivara took over the tale when it became too much for her par to continue. "Ser Teloch was from that small town. Before he was captured, he forced his mind on the citizens and made them all walk off a cliff to the ocean and rocks below. All one hundred and fifty-two died. When the grandparens brought the boy home to his parens they found an abandoned village. They reported the incident and brought the boy back to live with them. A weke later, what remained of the bodies were found at the bottom of the cliff and daes later Ser Teloch was captured and executed."

Olivienne raised her eyebrows. "I should hope he was executed, he violated the Codice Prime! We were well instructed in the laws of Psiere at academy. Any premeditated death to a sentient entity is punishable by life on Iuvenis Island. Unless that death was caused by channel, then the Psierian was deemed too dangerous to live. But what does this have to do with the antoraestones and why does the story of Ser Teloch upset you so much, papan?"

"Your papan was that small boy."

The Connate was too shocked to speak at first. Then she delicately reached out to her father, mind to mind. The request for speech was gentle and followed by the equivalent of a mental hug. *"I am so sorry for your loss. Why have you never told us?"*

He shrugged and answered silently as well. *"Because it is a sad tale and I never want to bring sorrow into my children's lives if I need not. Besides, I barely remember my parens or sib. It was long ago."*

"Sib? I have an amita or patruus?"

Keshien shook his head sadly. "Had an amita, 'Vienne. She was killed with my parens."

"My love..." Olivienne's attention was pulled to her mother once again. "Now do you see the danger presented by antorae-stones? If a man like Ser Teloch could kill nearly two hundred people with the power of his mind, what could someone do with something that amplified them to ten times the strength? What power would a telekinetic or pyrokinetic hold with such a stone if they were intent on evil deeds? None of us would be safe."

Olivienne shook her head not because she didn't believe in the danger, but because of how her mother came across. "Maman, you sound like Tosh. Truthfully, it is a bit disconcerting because I don't want to think about the Lieutenant Commander right now." She made a face of consternation.

Keshien's focus left the distant past and moved to the present and his daughter. "But 'Vienne, did you not say you and the officer became acquaintances on the railer? And Lieutenant Commander Tosh was also the one who helped you crack the code on the temple docs. Why would we not speak of her?"

"She was the one who was shot in the assassination attempt, wasn't she?" While the royal couple had not known about the translations of the temple docs or the news contained within them, they were well informed about the events that went down in Penterole. Not only did Lt. Savon voteo ahead his report on the incident, but so too did the local Security Corp. But even with all their advance information, they were still putting the puzzle pieces together.

Olivienne swallowed thickly and nodded, still picturing the bloom of blood as it ran from beneath Castellan's pain filled body. "She was. We—" She stopped, suddenly realizing the extent of her foolish actions in the marketplace.

"I acted with foolishness and dishonor and I'm afraid I forever disgraced myself where Lieutenant Commander Tosh is concerned. Lieutenant Savon knew about the assassination attempt ahead of time and I thought that I could handle the problem myself rather than delay our trip by following proper protocol and calling in the Security Corp. I was wrong and only Tosh saw the danger of the second assassin. She saved my life and possibly others by taking the shell that was meant for me. On top of that she managed to kill the shooter while she lay in agony on the ground."

She sighed and scrubbed her face while Olivara and Keshien Dracore remained silent. "When she woke from her healing, she gave us all, but especially me, a thorough dressing down for our senseless plan."

Keshien reached over and clasped her hand within his. "I can imagine the entire event frightened you, being that it was the first overt attempt on your life. I only wish we could have had a chance to interrogate one of them to see who the supplied the cred for such a thing."

Olivara addressed the subject as well. "We obviously heard nothing of this event ahead of time but I can assure you that we have our best Shield investigators on it. General Renou said she was sending two top agents with the psychometry channel to go through the assassins' effects. Hopefully we'll find out something soon."

The King shook his head in frustration at the lack of information and returned to the subject at hand. "What happened after she reprimanded you?"

The Connate shrugged. "She went back to her own cabin and refused to speak with me. I was able to catch up with her when we arrived at Tesseron to apologize and beg forgiveness but she said friendship was beyond her at this point." Olivienne shook her head regretfully. "I'm afraid that my mistake will surely stay with me on this one."

The Queen had to work hard to keep from giving anything away as her face was notoriously expressive, at least to her family. But she managed because to do otherwise would jeopardize everything she and the generals had set in motion. "It does seem a shame. After all, it's not every dae that one meets someone who both shares an interest in their life's work and would take a shell for them. This Tosh must be quite the soldier."

Olivienne remembered back to those few oors of passion and sighed wistfully. "Oh, she certainly is."

Olivara mentally groaned at the fact that her daughter certainly hadn't made it any easier for their plan to succeed. But rather than dwell on potential issues, she turned to the next steps of Olivienne's discovery. She sat up straighter, prompting close attention from both her par and her daughter. "This is what I want to happen, first I don't want the information on the second document known. 'Vienne, you can keep it with you but if you think that your security could be compromised again give it to me for safekeeping. Second, we will announce the information from the first document to the Imperium and the general population of Psiere. People are always thirsty for new information about the Makers and the Divine Mystery."

Keshien could see the direction that his par's mind was going and picked up the narrative when she stopped speaking. "Knowing the name of the third temple will kick off an immediate round of translation of all the as of yet un-deciphered documents in the Temple of Archeos and the Temple of Illeos. We don't know what those documents will say so if we really want to keep the antoraestones a secret, we should limit the interpretists working on the project to just the ones with top security clearance. We need a task force."

"I was just going to say that!" Olivara looked fondly upon the man she had fallen in love with so many rotos before. While his appearance was attractive enough, she was first enamored with his intelligence and wit. "I want an analysis done on the potential political, societal, and economic ramifications should these antoraestones be discovered. Keshien, I will entrust you the task of putting together such a team but if I had to make a recommendation I'd at least include General Renou of the Shields and General Leniste of Defense."

Olivienne dug in her satchel for a blank booklet of vellum and a stylus. "Why don't we run down the list of different Corps and decide which should be involved with the third temple task force and list the names of who should be on the team." She quickly wrote in both Shield and Defense, and added General Renou and Leniste after each. She moved down a line and looked up at the Queen. "Who else? If you need research done, I would think you'd want to include Academic Corp. Do you want Instrae Keeley Greene added?"

Olivara glanced at the King. "You know Instrae Greene better than I, what do you say?"

Keshien shrugged. "She has done similar such projects for me in the past. She is trustworthy. My only concern is whether or not she has time to serve on this task force."

"Instrae Greene may be neck deep in responsibility but she is as passionate about the Divine Mystery as I am. I bet she makes time." Keeley Greene was one of Olivienne's favorite instructors when she went to Academy, back before the highly intelligent Psi advanced and became the youngest head of the Psi Academy Corp. It was a massive division that oversaw not just all lower education of Psiere, but all the higher education and job training that university provided as well. When both parens nodded, she added Academy Corp with Ins. Greene's name.

The Queen spoke up, ticking off each different Psi Corp on

her fingers. "I think we can safely eliminate Service, Resource, and Stock. This is not something that we will need feedback from the arts, farms, or mining. I also think for obvious reasons we will eliminate the Politia Corp since we will not be telling the Imperium, nor the local governors and representatives about the second document. What about Security, Salvo, and Codice?"

The topic flipped back to Keshien. "Local law enforcement and local fire and rescue need not be in this. I think we can safely exclude the adjudication and penal system head as well. Psi Medi Corp?"

Olivienne shook her head. "The document didn't mention any physical side effects from its use and I think that if they were a danger to us it would have mentioned it. We probably don't need anyone from the medican's group. That only leaves my own Psi Divinity Corp, and the Engineers." The Connate cocked her head to the side. "Templar Zane Aislyn knows a lot about the Divine Mystery, and she may have unique insight on the question of both the third temple and the mystery stones. I've spoken with her a number of times over dinner and I would trust her with the secret."

The Queen stared off into nothing and tapped her bottom lip in consideration. Finally she returned her gaze to Keshien and Olivienne. "I say yes to Templar Aislyn and no to the Psi Engineering Corp. We'll wait on that one for now until we have more data."

When Olivienne was finished writing in the vellum book, she handed it to her father. He read the names aloud just to confirm one last time. "So we have Shield, Defense, Academy, and Divinity Corps. I've actually spoken with Instrae Greene recently and she's pretty busy right now. I don't know if she will want to be on the task force or if she will assign someone who can better help us with time and information. I trust her judgement with a replacement if it comes to that."

The Queen nodded. "I'm all right with that."

"And what am I to do?" Olivara looked to Keshien and Olivienne sensed communication between the two. That knowledge worried her. She was afraid that they may attempt to limit her career after the assassination attempt. She didn't want to be left out of the loop on this new development. It was her discovery and she felt a drive to solve the mystery that went beyond that of most people. Before she could worry herself any further her mother spoke aloud.

"I want you to see this though. I feel like you are the best adventurist for this particular job and you have always been particularly successful with all things related to the Divine Mystery. I also know that you've been one of the few people who was certain of the existence of a third temple." Surprise and elation crowded for room on Olivienne's face until her mother added the dreaded "but." "But, before you can go on any more trips, you will need a fully staffed Shield unit. You've been running too low for rotos. Unfortunately, we cannot staff the unit for you; that is the job of your Shield unit leader."

Olivienne looked confused. "Lieutenant Savon?"

Her father's deep voice cut in. "No 'Vienne, Captain Shendo's replacement."

Hope turned to dismay. "But how long will that take? You've been trying to find a replacement for wekes now! Maman...papan...this discovery is big, I cannot afford to be tied down right now while we wait to fluff out my guardians!"

Olivara held up her hand to stall her daughter's rapidly rising tirade. "I understand how you feel, 'Vienne, but this is non-negotiable. Security will have to be tight for all of us now, and on the new information. And think for a meen, there isn't much you can do until we put together the task force and we get a secure team of interpretists started translating those stored texts that were never decrypted. It's going to be at least a weke, maybe two before we start seeing results from them. Consider yourself on holidae." Olivienne started to sputter angrily but was stopped by her mother's voice in her head. *"Please, love...I couldn't bear it if something happened to you."*

Olivienne knew when she was beat. She sighed and nodded. "Fine, holidae it is I guess."

"Thank you..." The Queen was interrupted by a knock at the door. She used her telepathy to see who was on the other side and called out to him. "Enter!"

Her Shield unit captain walked through the door and saluted all three royals. "My apologies to you all but I have urgent news for Queen Olivara." She cocked her head curiously at him and the captain cut a glance sideways toward Olivienne then looked back to the Queen. "It is a message from General Renou."

"Oh!" She stood and turned to both her daughter and par. "Keshien, can you get started right away on what we were discussing?" He nodded and she turned her gaze to her only daughter. "And you stay out of trouble, savvy? I'm sorry I can't stay to talk any longer but I have business I must attend to." She leaned down to kiss Keshien on the lips, then did the same for Olivienne and followed Capt. Torrin out of the house. Keshien was well aware that the Queen had been meeting with General Renou to find a solution to their daughter's Shield unit dilemma. But Olivienne had no clue and was left feeling more than a little curious about her mother's sudden departure.

Chapter Eleven

CASTELLAN TOSH SWAM up to consciousness fairly quickly despite being sound asleep in the noon sun. She wouldn't have fallen asleep to begin with if she had not felt secure in her surroundings. But as she mentally cast her awareness around her, she was surprised to find someone near. With slow precision she opened her eyes to greet her guest. It took a lot to shock the intrepid officer and dashing lt. commander, and when she was startled she never let it show on her face. But even so, when she realized the Queen of Psiere was sitting in a lounger less than ten paces from her, Castellan visibly twitched.

Luckily her scotch glass was empty at that point or she would have spilled the amber-colored liquid all over her dress whites. She set the glass aside before quickly jumping to her feet and giving the proper salute. "Queen Olivara, it is an honor!"

"Relax, Lieutenant Commander Tosh, I'm here in a less than formal capacity."

Once her heartrate had returned to normal, Castellan did what any guest turned host would do. "Would you like a drink, my Queen?" Olivara smiled at her offer and for a moment Castellan was caught up in how similar she looked to her daughter. Both had the same dark hair pinned up on their head, and the same deep violet eyes. But where the Queen's eyes seemed to smile more, Olivienne's expressiveness was all in the sweep of her dark brows as well as the fullness of her mouth and set of her chin. The Connate was very much a child of both parens but the similarities between mother and daughter caused a spark of discomfort in Tosh's mind.

The Queen motioned toward Castellan's discarded glass. "What were you drinking before your nap?"

"Scotch, my Queen. The stuff that Psero Pendar Renou showed me in the house is very good. I can fetch you some if you'd like?"

Olivara nodded and smiled at the younger woman. "As long as you don't mind, I would be delighted to try Renou's scotch. They have certainly sampled enough of mine over the rotos."

Unsure how to react, Castellan could only nod and snatch her own empty glass from the small patio table. "I'll return shortly, my Queen." Just as promised she was back meens later and handed the two fingers of amber liquid to the Cathedress of Psiere. Olivara lifted it in salute and as custom, Castellan touched the Queen's glass with her own before taking a healthy swallow. "So what brings you to see me, my Queen?" She was smart enough to guess that the Queen had heard about her refusal of the Shield Commander position but she wanted to hear it from the woman herself.

"Please, call me Olivara, I insist."

Tosh dipped her chin in acknowledgement but her military training wouldn't allow her to be so informal with the highest leader of the land. Instead she resorted to official military address. "Yes, ser."

The sovereign smirked at the officer's response then thought hard on how she would broach the subject of her daughter's security while enjoying the comfort of the Renou estate. There was intelligence written in Castellan Tosh's pale blue eyes but she sensed a healthy dose of stiff military stubbornness lingering beneath the surface. "Let's not pretend we don't know why I'm here. I'm aware of how difficult my daughter can be at times, and of exactly how rogue her mentality is when it comes to personal security. But I also know she deeply regrets her actions in Penterole yesterdae."

Castellan sighed. "Be that as it may, she is reckless and insufferable with her hard opinions regarding proper procedure. May I speak openly without incurring the wrath of both Queen and mother?"

"I would prefer that actually."

"It is well known that the Connate is...difficult to work with, I'm not surprised half her previous captains have quit. And after witnessing the events yesterdae I'm also not surprised that the rest were injured out of active duty. Not everyone can be lucky enough to have a doctore with telesana nearby. I will not have my career or life cut short by a reckless woman with no regard or respect for the people around her!"

The Queen took a sip of her scotch, savoring the burn of it while she contemplated her next words. "What you don't understand is that until yesterdae you would have been correct with your assessment of her personality. But after speaking with her this morning I can see that has changed, things have changed in her that I don't see going back in the future."

"Well, it's understandable that she would gain new insight after the assassination attempt but that doesn't really alter my assessment regarding her attitude and lack of respect."

Olivara gave the officer a knowing smile. "On the contrary, I don't believe that it was the assassination attempt that elicited this change in my daughter. It was you."

Castellan looked back at the Queen in shock, drink forgotten in her hand. "Come again?"

"I have never seen it before but there is certainly something about you, Lieutenant Commander Tosh, which has gained from Olivienne what none of her captains have before...respect." Tosh snorted but let the Queen continue. "She has railed against her security detail from the time she entered the Academy. It has only gotten worse over the rotos as she became established in her career. No matter the experience, every single captain that has been placed at the head of her Shield unit has been met with disdain and disregard." She leaned forward with scotch glass in hand. "I'm well aware that they can't keep up with her. Between Olivienne's high channel rating and her career, I've come to realize that my daughter is different, Tosh, and she needs a different kind of team."

Despite her irritation with the woman who had nearly gotten her killed, Castellan was intrigued by what the Queen was saying. "How do you mean?"

"As you may or may not already know, I had a successful career as a judex before ascending to the Divine Cathedra. The job of judging other's crimes and assigning punishment as dictated by the Psiere Legibus made it fairly easy to guardian my personal safety at all times. The great Hall of Decretum itself is quite secure. I cannot say the same for Olivienne's profession, nay...her passion. She needs a Shield unit that can not only keep up with her, but can also contribute to her team in some way."

Castellan thought on the Queen's words and slowly they began to make sense. "I begin to see your point. To be truly successful, her team would need to be adventurists as much as Olivienne. In order to protect her, they would all need to be trained and capable in the middle of the fray. Why, it would nearly require rebuilding her team from the ground up in order to put together such a mix of talents to accomplish the task you're suggesting."

Olivara nodded. "Not only that, but the team would require a leader who understands the requirements needed to guardian both a sovereign and an adventurist. Even better if that leader carried the same fire of discovery within them..." She trailed off, letting her words sink in and spent the next few meens enjoying her scotch.

"And as a commander I would have control of the entire process? You could assure me that she would not go haring off to another mission before her team was properly assembled?"

Sensing she was on the cusp of success, Olivara nodded. "She has agreed to remain on holidae until a leader of her unit was found and her team expanded to proper size."

Castellan was deeply interested in the position but she had doubts about the intentions of the Connate. Before she could dwell any further on the ramifications were she to accept the position, she needed to provide full disclosure to the Queen. It was made more awkward by the knowledge that the Queen was also Olivienne's mother. "Before we go any further down this path of inquiry, I informed the generals, Leniste and Renou, that honor precluded me from accepting the post of Shield Commander."

Olivara cocked her head at the officer. "Honor?"

"Yes, ser. Olivienne and I have had...relations. We were intimate on the trip north to Tesseron and I believed that it would be inappropriate to accept a position as her senior protector. General Renou told me it was of no consequence but I would like your opinion on the matter. To perhaps make things worse, I fear that with the way our personalities clash we may never achieve something close to friendship."

"Hmm...clash? How do you mean?"

Castellan thought of the first moment they met. "From the beginning, our acquaintance was fraught with disagreement and verbal sparring. Before and after our intimate relations. I don't know if we would be as successful a team as you seem to think and I wanted to be completely honest with you about the why of it."

Olivara sighed and tapped her bottom lip thoughtfully. "I'm not going to lie and say that it doesn't complicate things but I stand by my decision that you are the best person for this job. I have complete faith in your professionalism as an officer in all matters. And if we are being completely honest with each other, I have another task for the unit leader alone, one that has nothing to do with Olivienne's safety."

"Oh?"

"I know that you and my daughter translated the new documents while on the railer. She mentioned that you and I shared similar concerns about the potential for destruction and abuse of the antoraestones. I have no doubts that 'Vienne will be the one to find the third temple, but for my own peace of mind I would like someone on the ground with her who takes a more practical approach when dealing with world destroying artifacts."

Tosh drained the rest of her scotch and sat forward on the chair. "What exactly are you saying?"

Olivara's violet gaze met Castellan's with all seriousness. "I'm saying that I don't ever want the antoraestones found. And if such a discovery were to be made, I'd be just as happy if they could be destroyed or locked away until we were capable of dealing with their power."

"And you don't trust Olivienne to carry out this task?"

The Queen looked at her knowingly. "I know my daughter, she usually sees the good in something and forgets that there are often two sides to everything. She is much like her father in that way."

Seeing that their glasses were empty, Castellan offered to play host once again. "Would you care for a refill?"

Olivara held out her empty glass. "Actually, I would appreciate some water."

Lt. Commander Tosh's mind whirled with the Queen's words even more than after her meeting with the generals. As she rinsed the empty scotch glasses and filled the Queen's with water, she thought about what the sovereign was truly asking of her. Could she push aside her and the Connate's contentious past and become the professional Shield officer that was needed? Castellan drew in a deep and calming breath before heading back outside. She handed the Queen her glass and rather than sitting down, Castellan straightened her uniform and drew herself up to full height. "If accept this post, I need reassurance on two points."

"Go on."

The officer held up a single finger. "The first time the Connate violates protocol resulting in the injury of her or another, I will be reassigned from this position."

Olivara scowled. "Give her three chances to prove herself."

A pale eyebrow went up in response. "You have assured me that your daughter is a changed woman. Are you really willing to risk three citizens to Olivienne's willful disobedience?"

The Queen sighed and rubbed her temple. "You're right, of

course. My apologies. What was the other thing?"

Castellan held up a second finger. "If I need to be reassigned to a different post, I keep my promotion to Commander and it will not affect my potential for advancement down the road. That promotion was promised to me for stabilizing the region around Ostium."

"That seems more than fair, Lieutenant Commander Tosh. Why would you think that you'd be penalized for reassignment?"

Tosh's face darkened. "I have already had my future career threatened by General Leniste if I do not take this position."

It was the Queen's turn to be surprised. "And still you turned it down?"

"I have my honor, ser!" Castellan's reply was nearly indignant and Olivara smiled to hear it.

The Queen set the glass aside and stood to face the officer dressed in blinding white. "I can assure you on both points. Now, do we have a deal?" She held her hand out and with only a sec hesitation, Castellan clasped it within her own. When the Queen released her, she smiled at the younger woman. "I will personally let General Renou and General Leniste know of your decision. I will also tell them of your conditions and that they were approved by me. As for now," Olivara looked around the tranquil estate then turned back to Tosh, "I will tell you to relax until you next meet with your new Corp leader. I would like this transition to be as smooth and fast as possible because you will have your work cut out for you when it comes to putting together the right team. But I trust you to handle it all with skill and panache."

Tosh bowed to her, ever so slightly. "Thank you, my Queen."

"I think I will take my leave now after all...I can never escape the office for long. My advisors are convinced that my face alone governs Psiere, rather than my intellect."

Castellan gave her a rakish smile. "Well then, they are seeing only half your substantial charms."

Olivara laughed and pointed at the daring woman. "Oh, how smooth you are, Commander." The Queen paused to take in the soldier before her. "You know, my daughter spoke well of your brilliance...she never mentioned how dashing you were. Had I never met my wondrous Keshien, someone like you would have surely turned my head to oathing. Good dae, Commander!" And with those last words, the Queen teleported away. Castellan could only stand there in disbelief with a blush rapidly staining her cheeks.

AFTER THE QUEEN'S visit to the Renou estate, everything moved quite fast. Before Castellan knew it she was given a completely new wardrobe and assigned an office in the Shield Corp headquarters, as well as given Capt. Shendo's old room in the bottom floor of Olivienne's home. It was originally meant as service quarters but Olivienne had no need for such things so she just turned it over to whatever Shield captain she had at the time.

As for the Connate, at first she was overjoyed to find out that Castellan Tosh would be assigned to her Shield unit. However that joy soon turned to blinding intractability when she discovered to what extent Tosh would be changing the unit. They clashed of course but Commander Tosh remained firm with her course of action.

Perhaps what annoyed Olivienne more than all the changes was that Castellan had become like a stranger with her no-nonsense professionalism switched on one hundred percent of the time. Gone was the woman who had started to become a friend and more on the railer. No matter how many times Olivienne made her interest in more personal pursuits known over the course of Tosh's first weke as Commander, the officer never once acknowledged the offer.

For her own part, Castellan thought she would go insane between Olivienne's hot attraction and her cold protests against team changes. It was enough to give her a headache most daes. On top of her issues with the Connate, she was saddened by the fact that four of the ten original members of Olivienne's Shield unit asked to be reassigned. She assessed the remaining six to verify their fit in the newly revamped team.

The six that remained were Lt. Gentry Savon, Spc. Ben Devin, Spc. Gar Soleng, Spc. Zed Qent, Spc. Gren Holling, and Spc. Eliseo Calderon. All but Calderon had been on the railer for the trip south. Spc. Calderon was the unit pilot that had been on leave at the time and Holling was their medican. It was too bad that he was one of the four that remained on the railer when Tosh was shot. She really had gotten lucky with the proximity of the telesana channel doctore.

Shield Corp members were considered the best of the best. They had to be in order to qualify to protect Psiere's royal family and all the interests of the sovereigns. There were only two routes that led to a person wearing the infamous black uniform. You could test in straightaway after completion of an advanced Academy track. Or you could be invited to join like Lt. Savon and Tosh were.

But it wasn't as simple as a mere invite. The Psi Shield Corp required a minimum telekinetic channel rating of four, and an all-channel average rating of four. That put them well beyond the average citizen of Psiere. Shield specialists and officers also needed to pass stringent physical and psychological evaluations, as well as have a commission specialty or advanced specialist training. There was no better soldier than the ones in the Shield corp. The black uniforms were truly a symbol of pride and excellence.

Tosh sat at a desk in her office at Shield headquarters with two files in front of her. The first one contained a collection of Shield Corp records for each specialist currently unassigned to unit duty. The second was full of Defense Corp officers that were eligible to be invited into the Shield Corp. Castellan felt pretty accomplished with the way she had already filled five of the eight empty positions within the unit.

One thing she noticed with the previous units for Olivienne was that they were almost predominately male. Since the team was responsible for guarding a woman, it made sense to have guardians who could follow her wherever she went. That meant Tosh had to not just plan around security and career, but she had to balance the team as well.

Lt. Savon was excellent at planning as well as being a tinkerist and Tosh brought Lt. Auda Madlin on board to act as his balance. She too had tinkerist training as well as being a senior officer. Spc. Devin had advance training in salvo and rescue so she brought Spc. Tian Meza on board with the same training. Spc. Soleng was an engineer with focus on mechanics and the addition to balance him was Spc. Branda Leggett with her generalized engineering commission.

The medican, Spc. Holling, was joined by Spc. Almeta Yazzie. Yazzie had been serving in the Defense Corp prior and had recently transferred to Medi Corp, much the way Gemeda had. Both women stated that the reason they were leaving Defense was because they felt a lack of challenge in their careers. While someone like Dre. Shen was much too valuable to pull into the Shield Corp, Castellan was delighted that Specialist Yazzie had both accepted her invitation and passed all the proper tests.

Tosh was surprised to note that Spc. Qent not only had a commission as an adventurist, but he also had advance specialist water training. When she looked through the un-assigned file two daes previous, she found another specialist who would be a good balance. A woman by the name of Veva Dozier also had an adventurist commission and advance training in caves and mountain work. Specialists Qent and Dozier were sure to come in handy as the translations of Antaeus documents sent them on more and more missions. Adventurists were known to travel all over the two continents and she wanted her team to be ready.

Five daes into her new promotion and Cmdr. Tosh was quite pleased to be left with three positions to fill. But those three specialists were taking a considerable amount of thought process. Occasionally she would rifle through a stack to look at a current team member before making notes and going back to her selection stacks. When she was done, she looked down at the vellum she had been making notes on. She was interrupted from her rumination by a knock on the door.

"Enter!" As soon as General Renou had cleared the doorway, Castellan stood and saluted her superior officer. She was a little surprised by the unexpected visit, but not completely so. The clock was ticking down on the amount of time she had to build her team. She knew Olivienne would want to go out sooner rather than later and she wanted to be ready, if only to prove that neither she nor her Shield unit would slow the adventurist down. "Ser! What brings you to see me?"

General Renou took a seat in a guest chair near Castellan's desk. The small woman looked around at the spare office, not at all surprised that Cmdr. Tosh had not wasted any time on personalizing it. She suspected the only reason the commander was even using the office was because she needed the files that were available within headquarters. "I stopped to check on your progress. How goes the hunt?"

Tosh straightened a stack that was less than square on her desktop, then looked up to meet the general's silver-gray eyes. "Well enough, I believe I'm nearly finished. You heard that four opted for transfer?" General Renou nodded. "My original objective of staffing up to the full fourteen members was of course made more difficult when I suddenly found myself down to six."

"And how do you find those six? Are they all acceptable within the plan of this proto-type team the Queen has requested?"

The commander nodded. "Luckily, they are all well-qualified and good fits for what I envision. Noting a lack of gender diversity, I'm adding a significant amount of female specialists. I surmised that with our assigned sovereign being female, we should have specialists prepared to go wherever she goes without awkwardness or discomfort."

Camen Renou smiled to see Castellan Tosh living up to her full capability. "The fact that you are seeing these things right from the beginning tells me that you will be a different sort of Shield Corp leader from all the captains we've had in the past. Where are you now in the process?"

"I have been attempting to not just balance the gender of the team but also match existing resources as well as add people with resources that can directly help with the Connate's occupation as a historical adventurist. I never realized how many people came out of Academy with an adventurist commission. While most likely not practical for standard Defense service, or even standard Shield service, I think it is a great addition to this team. My current status is that I've filled eleven out of the fourteen slots."

General Renou motioned toward Castellan's vellum. "May I see your list?"

"Sure." Tosh slid the page across the desk to her senior officer.

"I see you've added another lieutenant to supplement Lieutenant Savon. Good call on that." She pointed to another section of the page. "What is this section here?"

Tosh leaned forward to see the page. "That is a list of all the resources I currently have. I was hoping that if I wrote everything down, anything missing would be obvious. I'd be happy to hear any suggestions you may have."

Renou squinted. "Where is your communication specialist?"

"What?" Tosh peered at the page in shock. "How could I have missed something so vital?"

The older woman chuckled. "Don't worry, it happens to the best of us. I see you have one pilot already, what about another? I always find it handy to have people that can fly or drive anything. You never know what will happen out in the field."

Tosh nodded. "Both great suggestions. Just one meen..." She rifled through the stacks until she pulled out a file from each. She opened the first one and scanned down the page. "Specialist Dante Lazaro has commissions in both communications and chemistrae." She set that file aside and opened the next. "Specialist Necole Lear just spent four rotos on the eastern side of Endara and has only recently returned to Tesseron. She's currently serving in the Psi Defense Corp but her file is flagged for a Shield invite and she's also due for reassignment. That leaves me one short."

Interested, the general leaned forward slightly. "What do you have in mind?"

Castellan sighed and rubbed at her forehead tiredly. It had been a long morning of staring at files...a long weke. "I was hoping to bring an interpretist into the unit because I've witnessed how vital that role is in the Connate's dae to dae investigations. Unfortunately, I found no one in my files that had that commission."

Renou rubbed her lower lip thoughtfully. "I may have someone that would fit the bill. She is commissioned as both an interpretist and a communications specialist."

Tosh sat forward abruptly. "That would be perfect! Is she in the Shield Corp?"

"Unfortunately, no. Ciera is with the Divinity Corp, which as you know has always held an interesting collection of talents all geared toward solving the Divine mystery."

"Bollux!" Castellan sat back in her chair and shut her eyes out of sheer frustration.

She was brought out of her dejection by quiet laughter. "Fear not Commander, all is not lost."

"But if she is neither Defense, nor Shield, your interpretist would not pass the necessary tests!"

General Renou smiled. "You younger generation officers always think the combat corps are the only ones with exemplary skill! I do believe that Interpretist Penn would pass the physical and psyche evals. She has a four rated telepathic channel, as well as a four eidetic memory and threes in both enhanced memory and intuition. Yes, she is quite the intellectual, but also very fit."

"And how do you know so much about Interpretist Ciera Penn? And how was she not steered into Defense during her initial Psi tests?"

Renou touched the side of her nose and winked at Tosh. "She is my sib's daughter. As for her career, Defense was an option for her, as was Academic. Ciera is incredibly well-rounded. But my sib has always been an overly protective father and begged her to steer clear of the military corps. Ciera said that Divinity sounded most interesting of the other two available. I know she loves her job, we have spoken quite a bit. But she is too much like me I think and would welcome a faster-paced career."

Castellan smirked at the general's wistful tone. "But won't your sib be angry if she switches to Shield Corp, after trying so hard to keep her out of the more dangerous professions? How long has she been out of academy?"

Camen Renou's eyes twinkled. "He'll be furious but Steben is my younger sib and has been a pain in my backside for my entire life. I trust you to keep Ciera safe and well managed and I will look forward to Steben's upset. As for my niece, she just turned twenty-five and has been out of Academy for about three rotos now."

"Well, as long as you can convince Interpretist Penn and she passes all the tests, I would gladly welcome her on my team. Will you contact her todae?"

The general smiled broadly. "I can do better than that if you let me use your teleo." Castellan stood and moved the teleo from one side of her desk to the corner nearest General Renou then waited while the general flipped the correct switches and punched in a connection code. After a few secs wait, Renou began to speak. "This is General Renou calling for Interpretist Ciera Penn...yes, I'll hold." A meen went by before Renou began speaking again. "Ceecee? What would you say about an offer to join Shield Corp? Too intellectual? Actually, I've got someone putting together a new kind of team and provided you pass all the usual tests, you have just the skillset she's looking for." A sudden screech could be heard over the handset of the teleo and Renou quickly pulled it away from her ear. She looked at Castellan with a grin and covered the speaker with one hand. "She's excited."

Castellan grinned back. "So I gathered."

Before she could ask another question, General Renou's attention was pulled back to the teleo. "Right away. Yes, as soon as possible. Can you get away? That would be perfect. Meet me down in the lobby in half an oor and I'll turn you over to our testers. And I'm not going to tell them we're related so you better sweat if you expect to pass our evaluations!" When she disconnected the line, she glanced over to where Tosh gave her a curious look. She knew what it was about. "I don't believe in nepotism. Psi Shield Corp has a reputation of excellence and I will not sully that for anyone. She will either pass and you're set or she won't and we'll have to search elsewhere."

Even after being invited to join and requested by the Queen

herself, Tosh still had to go through the grueling Shield Corp tests. She also knew that the general's niece would be with the testers for the rest of the dae so it was unlikely she'd hear anything before the next morning. "Thank you for your help, General. Now with your permission I'd like to write up the unit request for Specialist Lazaro, and the transfer request for Specialist Lear. Then after that I think I'll go speak with Connate Dracore and brief her as to where we stand on her team. I think she will be pleasantly surprised by the group of talents I've put together. Well, I hope."

Well aware of the difficulty that was Connate Dracore, Renou chuckled. "Good luck with that." She abruptly stood and straightened her pin-neat black uniform. "Well, I shall leave you to it then. Good dae, Commander Tosh!"

"Good dae, General!" Tosh saluted her one last time before the older woman exited the office. Then Castellan sat back in her chair and sighed. She wasn't looking forward to speaking with Olivienne, mostly because the Connate had become...testy since going on unofficial holidae. But Tosh couldn't really blame her since she herself was going a bit stir crazy after spending a weke with her nose buried in tedious reports and files. There was a lot to learn and accomplish in her new role and she hoped that she wouldn't let anyone down along the way. Especially the sovereigns.

Chapter Twelve

IT WAS STRANGE spending time at the Shield Corp headquarters after serving her entire career stationed outside the capital on one stint or another. It was stranger yet coming and going in the middle of the dae because the place seemed oddly empty. Most that were assigned duty there spent their daes in office work, something that would have driven Castellan mad. Before she could exit the side door of the massive building, the guardian attending the entrance saluted and called out to her. "Ser! Are you Commander Castellan Tosh?"

She looked at the woman curiously. "Yes, that's me."

Taking a rigid stance, the woman spoke clearly and concisely. "Ser, General Renou asked me to tell you that your vectura voucher came through. She said if you go to the moto yard, you can pick out something to use for the duration of your assignment."

Tosh blinked in surprise. "Oh."

"Ser?"

Shaking free from her shock, she waved a hand at the woman. "It's nothing. I simply wasn't expecting that particular perk of rank. But I suppose it makes sense. On base we'd have a base moto for the officers, but I didn't think about what I would use in Tesseron as a Shield unit leader."

The private looked so earnest. "Ser, if I may suggest?"

Castellan nodded. "Go ahead, Private."

"Ser, my coz'n, Gar Soleng, is on your team and I've heard plenty of stories. Pardon my saying but if you're going to lead Connate Dracore's team, you best pick something fast."

The senior officer smirked back at her. "I'll keep that in mind. Thank you."

The moto yard was in a centralized location where it could be easily accessed by members of both Psi Defense Corp and Psi Shield Corp. Tosh showed her ID to the two privates who were guarding the gate. One checked the slate on his desk, running his finger down the names until he found hers. "Says you're cleared for moto or cycle...oh! Looks like you've got lot six." He looked back up at her, uncertain. "I'm sorry, ser, but anything higher than lot four and I have to call my sergeant in."

The private removed the voteo from his belt and stepped away from the door to verify her clearance. Castellan looked at the other guardian with some concern. "Lot six? Is that good or bad?"

"You're Shield, ser, direct service to Connate Dracore. Lot six means you get your pick of the best."

The Sergeant arrived exactly two meens later and saluted Cmdr. Tosh exactly the way the privates had done when she walked up. "Commander Tosh, good to meet you, ser! I'm Sergeant Demmon. If you'll follow me I'll take you to lot six myself. You need a special key to access that section."

"I see." If there was one thing Castellan had learned in the previous weke, beyond the boredom of looking at stacks of files, it was that her new commission seemed to be full of surprises. It didn't take long for Tosh to find herself walking through rows of all different types of motos. Two doors, four doors, all-wheel power, their design and makeup varied but all were armored and weaponized. She didn't need anything so large and cumbersome within Tesseron so she moved on to the cycles. Her eyes widened at the selection and for a sec she thought maybe she was in love. Castellan turned to Sgt. Demmon, who paced her progress though the rows. "Which one is fastest?"

The man smiled. "Follow me." He weaved them through the rows until they came to a section in the farthest corner. "These five were all built based on the prototype schematics Connate Dracore brought back a few lunes ago."

"You mean the prototype that nearly got her previous captain killed? Are you trying to tell me something, sergeant?"

He looked at her confused. "No, ser!"

She waved him off to indicate she was kidding then stepped closer to one particular cycle that caught her eye. It gleamed with a warm burnished copere color, like the sunset over the Solis Sea. She ran her hands along the gauges and dials, inspecting every single toggle and switch before finally swinging a leg over the saddle. The illeostone tank sat directly in front of the saddle but just behind the steerage bar. Tosh glanced toward the sergeant and with a nod he gave her permission to switch the cycle on. It barely made any sound, with just a quiet rumble and the occasional hiss as built up aether released into the air. "This is the one I want." The cycle was a gorgeous balance of speed and engineering.

"That shouldn't be a problem. If you can just sign this sheet we'll get you set up with a helmet." Within five meens she had filled out the proper document and selected a helmet from the nearby storage unit. The helmet was the same shade of copere as the bike and featured a darkened face shield that could be switched for a clear one at night. The bike had a panier on each side in back, as well as storage beneath the seat. "The seat is made to hold a spare helmet. I recommend you pick one now while the stock is full."

After grabbing a matching helmet from the cabinet, the sergeant showed her how to lock it into the seat bin. "What about gloves or other gear?"

"I'm sorry, ser, but supply doesn't provide that. However, Tesseron has a number of top notch cycle shoppes and I'm sure you can find what you need there." After that Castellan remounted the machine and waited impatiently as he walked her through the extra features on the specialty Shield Corp cycle. "There is a rail gun on the front, mounted to each side of the headlamp. There is also a beacon that will transmit in times of emergency. You can manually turn it on, or it will turn on automatically if the cycle suffers catastrophic gyro damage."

Cmdr. Tosh nodded. "That makes sense since the majority of my time will be spent with Connate Dracore. What else?"

He shrugged. "There's not much more to know. It has light armor and built in stabilizers that help with control at top speed. Oh, and top speed is one hundred and fifty mahls per oor."

"Bollux! You're putting me on, man!"

The sergeant shook his head and tapped the speed gauge. "No, ser. I advise caution whenever crossing the one hundred mahl per oor threshold."

"I should think so! Have no fear, Sergeant, I have full confidence in my ability to ride at high speeds. Even ones this beast can provide."

"Ah, I assumed you'd be a high rating since you're the only commander that's ever taken over a sovereign-assigned Shield unit. Telekinetic?"

"Yes, at a six. I'm also six with intuition and five levitation. I should be fine, sergeant."

A look of shock washed over his face. "How is it you have three high rated channels?"

She sniffed at his awe and tapped her head. "I have five high rated channels. Telepathy and ferrokinesis are in here as well."

"I'm starting to believe the stories about you that have made it north, ser!"

"Pox on those stories. You'd think military would have more to do than gossip!"

"You know how it is, ser."

"I certainly do. All right, Sergeant. Thank for getting me set up here, now I'm afraid I must be on my way. Good dae to you."

The man stepped away from the cycle and gave her a final salute. "Good dae to you too, ser! And good luck." His last few words were lost to her as she rode away.

Castellan made quick time going back through the city toward the Temple of Archeos. She loved the ride of her new cycle and the freedom of the wind tugging at her uniform. As she crossed the great river, Mir Tessere, she could see the temple in the distance. The pyramid shone brightly in the light of the two suns. Tosh thought about what she still needed to do with the rest of her dae.

She needed to speak with Olivienne and the temple was the last place her unit had checked in. With the exception of the three people she had spoken with General Renou about, the rest of the team was in place. She had the original members of the unit paired up with the new ones to better assimilate them into the team. Tosh was no stranger to how things worked within the fighting corps and she trusted those original six to instruct the new people on all the Connate's quirks and foibles.

Castellan had met with all the new specialists individually before bringing them on board because despite how good someone looked on vellum, it was hard to tell what kind of fit a person would be until you met them face-to-face. She was planning an all-hands meeting once the remaining members were official so she could go over their slightly different duties from a normal Shield unit.

Unused to daes of idle time, Olivienne had taken to spending her holidae at the Temple of Archeos. Since the secret of the lost temple was a privilege held by only a few, she had been assisting the two interpretists that had been given security clearance on the project. There were hundreds of untranslated documents in the temple archives and the Connate knew that if she were going to discover the location of Antaeus, they'd have to be decoded. It was also convenient to spend her daes in temple since it was so heavily guarded, it made it easier on her new and still under-staffed Shield unit.

Before she left her office, Cmdr. Tosh had contacted Lt. Savon via the voteo she had clipped to her belt so she could confirm the exact location of the Connate. The temple was a massive place and a person could get lost for daes in the lower levels if they didn't know their way around. He said he would message her if the Connate moved to a different room, or left the temple all together. Unfortunately for Gentry Savon, Tosh was already on her way to the temple when Connate Dracore decided she was done for the dae.

"That's it!" Two of the guardians and one interpretist startled at the outburst though Savon wasn't one of them. He had been expecting her to break for daes.

"Is there something I can do for you, Connate Dracore?" The other interpretist, an older woman named Cadentia, was both calm and thorough in her duty. There was nothing, shy of stripping nude and singing the newest operae, that would startle her.

Anticipating the sovereign's words, Lt. Savon alerted his commander's voteo to let her know he had a message. Meanwhile the Connate stood from the desk she had been working at, stretched, and rubbed the bridge of her nose. "No, I'm just tired of being deep in the bowels of the temple each dae. I'm going stir crazy!" She glanced at the other two interpretists, realizing that it was their job to be there dae in and dae out. "Oh, I mean...it's fine if you like it and you're used to it but I'd much rather be outside."

Both interpretists smiled but it was Cadentia that answered. "It's fine. We know exactly what you mean and both of us love this work. Though I suppose if we didn't, we would not be in this department of the Divinity Corp." Before Olivienne could apologize again, the older interpretist grabbed a stack of translated documents from her desk and walked them over to the Connate. "If you're leaving, you may as well take what we have completed so far. I think it was a good idea to start with the oldest dated documents first. Maybe you can piece together more of the story from these."

Olivienne took the vellum sheets from her before walking over and grabbing both her own translations and those of the other interpretist, Lyndee. Then she bundled them all together and put them in a pack that she had brought with her to the temple. "That is a great idea. Perhaps I'll go find someplace in the suns' shine to begin my notes. Have a good dae, pseras. And good luck!" With that she shouldered her pack and made her way toward the door, only to be stopped by Lt. Savon. She looked up at him partly in curiosity, part in irritation. "Yes?"

"Begging your pardon, Connate Dracore, but Commander Tosh is expecting you to be in the secured interpretist room when she arrives."

"So tell her I'm heading back to my home."

He tried again. "But she is already on her way here, I have no way of contacting her before she arrives."

Olivienne smiled sweetly at the worried man. "Well then, we better hope she arrives before I leave." With those words she walked out of the room. The Connate had been frustrated by Castellan Tosh since the moment of their first meeting. Despite that fact, Olivienne still found the woman attractive and engaging and a sure lure for the sovereign who loved adventure. But since Tosh had become her Shield unit leader, the officer had sadly made herself off limits. While Olivienne received competence and professionalism from the commander in abundance, she found no forgiveness for her actions leading up to the assassination attempt.

It didn't help that flashes of their shared passion together still found their way into her dreams. And there were those occasional moments when the Connate wished she were back in her cabin on the railer, before the ill-fated trip into Penterole. As Olivienne made her way out of the temple nearly twenty meens later, she once again thought back to that time. The passion between them had been explosive and so very memorable.

Before she could trip further down memory lane, her attention was caught by a flash of copere and stele and the breath stuttered in her throat. Olivienne stared intently as Commander Tosh rode into the parking area on her cycle and dismounted from the gleaming machine. Her voice was a whisper when it finally escaped. "Why does she have to make it so hard?"

Lt. Madlin, the new counterpart to Savon, looked at her knowingly. "Did you need something, Connate Dracore?"

Olivienne shook her head and smiled wistfully. "No, just wishful thinking." She looked around then, noticing her surroundings for the first time. "Do we not have a moto for transport yet?"

Lt. Savon shook his head. "No, Connate. We thought you'd be here a whole dae again and it was scheduled for service. I've called for another but it will take a bit for a secured one to be inspected and sent over. My apologies."

"Are you going somewhere, Connate Dracore?" As soon as she rode up, Tosh noticed the on-duty team of Shield guardians milling around outside the Temple of Archeos, along with one sovereign. She glanced over at Lt. Savon who had the grace to blush.

"I tried to contact you, ser, but you were already on your way."

She waved him off. "Its fine, Lieutenant. No replacement moto yet?" She was aware that the Connate's original transportation was due for service and Castellan herself was the one who chose that dae for it to happen. She had no idea that the Connate would reach her breaking point of inside activity so soon. Though Castellan shouldn't have been surprised considering her own breaking point had come and gone.

"No, ser, they said at least another half oor before inspection would be finished."

Olivienne looked at the commander pleadingly. "Can't we just take another back to residence? I really cannot stand being cooped up and pinned down any longer."

As Tosh looked into those purple eyes, she recognized the same spark of restlessness that she knew to shine in her own. Finally she sighed and gave in to the urge that was pushing against the back of her mind. "I think I can do better than that." She reached down and opened the seat of her cycle and pulled out the spare helmet, holding it out to the Connate. "I can provide you with a personal escort back to residence while they follow behind when the secured moto arrives."

Olivienne's face lit up but Lt. Savon's features showed concern. "Are you sure, ser? That seems very...open."

Castellan addressed her senior officer and his concerns. "I take my job seriously, Lieutenant. And you can trust me when I say nothing will touch us on this cycle. I would swallow my own sword if proved wrong."

Lt. Savon winced at his commander's declaration but he had seen the officer in action and trusted her to keep the Connate safe. "Yes, ser, we'll follow as soon as the moto arrives."

Realizing that Olivienne's satchel probably contained secured translations, she opened the seat of her cycle again and nodded toward the compartment. "Connate Dracore, I have space for your pack if you wish to bring it with you."

Olivienne quickly exchanged the pack over her shoulder for the helmet that Castellan held out. "Thank you. Is this one of the new cycles, from prototype?"

Tosh nodded. "It has been built according to the updated schematics you brought back, yes." She stepped out of the way so that the Connate and the rest of her team could look at the cycle. "It has twin rail gun barrels mounted to each side of the lamp, as well as stabilizers to assist with safety when running at top speed of one-fifty."

"Holy sheddech!"

"Son of a sint!"

Castellan wasn't sure which of the guardians muttered the expletives but they were appropriate.

Lt. Madlin raised a dark eyebrow. "Nothing but a railer can top that speed. Impressive!"

Suddenly nervous about sharing a cycle with the woman who had dominated her dreams of late, Cmdr. Tosh remounted the machine. She wanted to get back to the Connate's residence as soon as possible to shorten the amount of time they'd be in close contact. "If there's nothing else, Lieutenants, we should be on our way." She looked at Lt. Savon as Olivienne mounted the cycle behind her and she was glad of the tinted face shield that hid her flushed features from the rest of the team. "Give me a heads up when the team is on their way back. The residence unit can cover until you arrive."

"Yes, ser!" All the guardians in the unit saluted her and Olivienne before Tosh swiftly accelerated out of the lot. The royal estate was not far away, but Tosh wanted to avoid the busy high traffic roads so she opted for the longer route along the speedway. The speedway was a limited access road that circled around Tesseron before branching north in the direction of the dirigible station that was located on the south side of the channel between Instrucia Island and Endara.

Because the Academy, with its officer and standard schools, was located on the large island, the six hundred mahl stretch between the dirigible station and Tesseron was highly traveled. Dirigibles were the only way to safely cross the channel that ran between Endara and the massive island. Boats were too much of a target for the Atlanteens and their creatures of the deep. Speedways actually ran parallel to the railer line all the way around both continents, as well as quite a few locations that didn't have railer service. It made it significantly easier to transport goods and people, though the railers were certainly faster. Not everyone had a prototype cycle.

As soon as they hit the open speedway, Tosh's heart soared with freedom. She increased the speed of her cycle. She felt a faint matching response from Olivienne's mind as well just before the Connate spoke to her via telepathy. *"I wish we didn't have to go back right away. I've been cooped up in that temple room for daes!"*

Tosh was already well aware of the tingling that had started as soon as Olivienne slid behind her on the cycle and she knew she was going to regret the words as soon as she said them. But her heart and mind were too free not to agree with the woman gripping her from behind. *"Care to take a detour?"*

Olivienne's response was immediate. *"Yes, where?"*

Tosh didn't respond. Instead she accelerated onto an exit ramp that led them from the city speedway to the one that would take them north. She watched as the gauge crept up on the speed dial. There were few motos and haulers on the speedway but none were in the far left lane reserved for official use. As they passed one hundred mahls per oor, she contemplated slowing down when a voice echoed through her head.

"Faster..."

Castellan couldn't turn her head to look at the Connate because that would have been a sure way to kill them both. But she responded anyway. *"Are you sure?"*

"Commander, you should know me well enough by now. But in case you haven't been paying attention, I like my cycles the same way I like my sex. Fast the first time and a slow cruise the second." She paused to let her words sink in and then added one last bit. *"As long as you're prepared to bring me home, I have no problems with your speed."*

Olivienne's words within her mind caused things to tighten dangerously while she was in control of such a powerful machine. Since the moment they had met, the violet-eyed woman behind her continued to push and Tosh found herself fast losing the will to resist. And being in such close proximity to the infuriating sovereign was certainly not helping keep her libido in check. Rather than answer the Connate's obvious innuendo, she sent back two simple words. *"Hold on!"* Then with savage twist of the throttle they shot forward at an exponential rate. It was the fastest Tosh had ever gone when in control of a vectura herself. It was exhilarating on a lot of levels, some of which were solely due to the woman clutching her from behind.

Castellan glanced down as the gauge hit its max speed then she leveled it off and maintained a smooth one-fifty. Things were going along well until they came up to a spate of traffic fifty mahls outside the city. One moto decided to move into the official lane, a crime punishable by loss of driving privilege if the driver was not authorized. Olivienne's enhanced awareness kicked in and she telepathically warned Tosh before they'd even come up to that section of speedway. That combined with Castellan's high intuition rating and her telekinesis meant that instead of a fatal crash between moto and cycle, she lifted them safely into the air. It was a feat she had no idea she could accomplish at such a speed.

Rather than try to bring them down to a stop she let off the throttle completely then with extreme focus brought them slowly back to the road. Their momentum kept them speeding along until Castellan could twist the throttle and speed them back up again. She breathed a sigh of relief at the same time Olivienne's voice broke through her racing thoughts. *"That was amazing!"*

Tosh shook her head resignedly as she brought the cycle back down to appropriate speed and moved to exit the moto-way. When they were safely off the road, she braked to a stop and just sat there before she flipped up her face shield and turned to look over her shoulder at the sovereign she had endangered. "It was beyond foolish of me, and I apologize."

The thrill of the maneuver still pounded in both women's veins and Olivienne decided she was tired of playing Castellan's game. She flipped her own visor up and looked at the officer. "Get off the cycle, Commander Tosh!"

Shocked pale blue eyes widened at Olivienne's tone. "Connate Dracore?"

Olivienne gave her a shove from behind. "Off, now!"

Thoroughly confused, Tosh complied with her demands and removed her helmet. Olivienne was right behind her in dismounting from the cycle. Tosh tried again. "Connate Dracore, did I say something wrong?"

Olivienne removed her own helmet and set it on the seat then rounded on the officer. With the first two fingers of her right hand she poked Castellan in the chest with each word, to emphasize her point. "Stop pretending like you don't feel anything! Stop acting like you don't feel the rush the same as me!"

The near death experience and Olivienne's words and proximity only made Tosh's heart race more. As emotion and sexual tension reached their breaking point, Olivienne grabbed Castellan's pristine black shirt and pulled the woman to her. Lips met in an explosive rush and Tosh dropped her helmet to grip Olivienne's head and pull them even closer. Neither was sure who moaned into the kiss but they eventually pulled back at the same time. They stood at the side of the speedway exit ramp with heads pressed together, panting like they had run a mahl, and Tosh gave in to the uncertainty that plagued her. "I don't know what to do here."

Olivienne pulled back and looked into Castellan's icy blue eyes. "Stop pretending like this passion between us doesn't exist."

Regret flashed across the officer's face. "I can't! This is my career, worse yet, this is your life! How do I ignore that, ignore my sworn duty?"

The Connate stepped away from her, regretting instantly the loss of contact between them. "I don't know. But know this, Castellan Tosh, you haunt my dreams."

Tosh bent down to pick up her helmet from the ground. She put it on and walked back to the cycle before meeting Olivienne's heated gaze. "You haunt mine as well. We must get back or they will worry." Before Olivienne could answer, the commander's voteo crackled to life with the alert tone. She took it from her belt and answered. "Tosh here."

Lt. Savon's voice came over the small speaker. "Commander, we've returned to the residence. Are you held up somewhere?"

Tosh sighed and met Olivienne's steady gaze. "No, Lieutenant, just on a joy ride. We shall return shortly." By the time she had clipped the communication device back to her belt, Olivienne had donned her own helmet. "Olivienne...we must return."

The Connate nodded in understanding but threw out a warning to Castellan anyway. "We're not finished here."

Castellan sighed again as the pulse continue to pound through her body in time with her beating heart. The ride back would not be nearly as fun for either of them in their current state. "No. No we're not."

Chapter Thirteen

THE RETURN TRIP to the residence was silent. There were no mental urgings of faster, though after the kiss they shared those exact words rolled through both their heads. While Castellan navigated the cycle within safe limits, she still drove as quickly as possible. She wanted to deliver Olivienne back to her home so she could leave and put some space between them. It was impossible to think with the sovereign molded so tight behind her, with Olivienne's hands circling her waist and grasping at the pressed fabric of her uniform shirt.

Despite the wind and the enclosed helmet on her head, Tosh swore she could still smell Olivienne's scent. It was woodsy and sweet with a vague hint of well-worn leather. The memories would not turn her loose from their time together and she feared the distraction of it all. She feared failing her duty should there be another assassination attempt. But there was a heat between them that Tosh could no longer ignore.

Olivienne was having similar difficulties. As she gripped the officer from behind, memories flashed through her head of their time on the railer, when she had Tosh pressed face first into the soft coverlets. She had the tightly controlled woman's wrists pinned as she kissed her way down the center of Castellan's nude back. The skin below her tongue tasted salty with slicked sweat and the air was perfumed by their mutual arousal as Olivienne moved even lower.

They played for oors, wearing each other out, only to begin anew each time. The sovereign discovered that she loved holding Castellan down, reveled in the control of so simple a thing. And as much as the strong woman squirmed, she never once tried to break free of Olivienne's hold. Her patience was rewarded again and again. Of course Castellan held her immobile as well, only she used a more creative application of her telekinesis to do it.

Olivienne's carnal memories were interrupted when they pulled into the vectura building on the sovereign estate. She sighed before they could even dismount from the cycle. "So much for our talk."

"What?" Castellan looked back at the Connate with confusion.

Olivienne got off the cycle and removed her helmet before pointing out the window where they could see two guardians standing at the front entrance of her residence. "Since Captain Torrin, the head of my mother's Shield unit, is standing at my front door, obviously my mother is inside."

One part of Tosh was relieved because she didn't want to discuss what was growing between her and Olivienne. But the other part was terrified because the Queen's prescience and empathy channels were legendary. The reigning sovereign was sure to know what was going on between her and the Connate and she resolved herself to firm up her mental wall as soon as she entered the door. Then she realized she didn't need to go in at all. "Well as lovely as your family meeting sounds, this is where I let you off. I still have some vellumwork to take care of back at—" She stopped when she felt pressure inside her head and knew immediately who it was. She let the mental voice come through.

"Please come inside with my daughter, Commander Tosh. I wish to speak with you and Olivienne together."

In that moment the profanity she muttered under her breath seemed completely legitimate. "Bollux!"

Olivienne had heard the directive also since the Queen had spoken to both of them at the same time. She snickered at Castellan's sour face and answered. *"We'll be right there, maman."* Once their helmets had been removed and stowed, Olivienne stepped close to Tosh, until the fronts of their bodies were nearly touching.

Castellan's eyes widened in surprise and her furtive whisper came out as a hiss. "What are you doing?" She cast a glance through the window at the guardians that were standing thirty yords away. "We cannot do this!"

The Connate pushed. "We can. I can feel exactly what you want, Castellan. Do not try to pretend it's not the same thing as me."

Tosh sucked in a great breath and felt dizzy with Olivienne's scent and nearness, but Olivienne's mother, the Queen, was inside waiting. "Are you suddenly empathic now? While that may be your mother's channel, it is certainly not yours!"

"No, I'm not an empath." Olivienne reached up to delicately trace Tosh's neck causing the muscle to twitch. "I can see the way your pulse jumps in time with your heartbeat, and it races each instance I come near. I can look into those pale eyes of yours and watch as they grow dark the longer they look into mine. I know arousal, Commander Tosh, I know passion. You feel exactly as I in this and it terrifies the soldier in you to break the rules."

"You know nothing about me!"

Olivienne's hand had made its way up to the back of Castellan's head and when the officer's defiant words spilled from her lips, the Connate pulled her down into a fierce kiss. There was no resistance from Tosh, no hesitance at all as their tongues tasted every ince of each other. When Olivienne finally pulled away with a hammering heart and shortened breaths, she smiled at her Commander. "Don't I?" With that she spun and walked away, toward the residence and her waiting mother.

Castellan waited a meen before following the Connate inside. She spent the time straightening her uniform and getting her own breathing under control. The officer walked up the steps muttering to herself. "She is a vixen and will surely be the death of me."

Spc. Qent and Spc. Dozier came out the front door as she walked up the steps. Qent heard her muttering but not the actual words. "Ser? Is there something you need?"

She paused before opening the door. "Perhaps a new head, Specialist Qent. I fear mine is not screwed on right." His eyes widened and she waved her hand through the air nonchalantly. "I'm only jesting...mostly." The last word was said beneath her breath as she walked inside. Her long strides took her just past the foyer before she was halted by the Queen's voice.

"Ah, Commander Tosh! So good to see you again. Please, come have a seat with us." The Queen was seated on a divan in Olivienne's main room and she gestured to her daughter, who stood off to the side. "'Vienne, won't you be a love and fix us all some scotch."

Castellan raised her hand to stop Olivienne. "Thank you but..." Her words trailed off when the full weight of the Queen's violet gaze met her own. She quickly changed her mind and made her own way to the sideboard where the liquor was kept. "Thank you, but I can pour for all of us. Neat for both of you?" Both sovereigns nodded and Olivienne moved to sit next to her mother.

Once drinks were handed around and Tosh took a seat on a nearby chair, Olivienne broke the silence. "Are you here to check on my progress, maman?" She pulled off the satchel she had re-slung over her shoulders when Castellan put the spare helmet away. The Connate set the leather satchel on the tile floor between her booted feet then unlocked and opened the heavy flap. In less than a meen, she had the translations placed in a pile on the low table, oldest document down to the newest one. Though newest was a relative term since the sheets they were translating were still ones from nearly one hundred rotos past. "We've only been translating, this is the first chance I've had to look at what the vellums actually say. I will not lie...I'm excited to piece together this new facet of the Divine Mystery."

Olivara smiled at her daughter. "I suspect our Commander here is just as interested in the story." Both sovereigns looked at Tosh.

"Indeed I am, my Queen."

The Queen waved a hand through the air. "Please, just Olivara here. What I have to say will take us beyond the bounds of formality."

Olivienne looked down at the stack of vellum and back up at her mother. "You're not here for an update on the mystery, are you maman?"

"No, I am not. I've had a vision..."

Tosh startled out of sheer panic at the Queen's words, certain that she was going to say something about the interactions between her daughter and Castellan. A bit of the scotch slopped onto her hand and the other two women looked at her in surprise. As she sucked the liquor from her thumb, Olivara smirked knowingly. Tosh's face flushed at the Queen's smile. She was saved when Olivienne spoke up. "Does this vision have anything to do with the Divine Mystery and our work here?"

The Queen took a slow drink of her scotch and contemplated her words. "In a way...but it is more to do with Commander Tosh."

Pale blue eyes widened and Castellan took another large gulp of her drink. "Come again?"

Olivienne sighed and set her glass down before turning to look at her mother fully. "I suppose you're here to warn me off from having relations with Castellan. Surely your prescience has told you nothing about me or my future."

"Of course it hasn't!" Olivara scoffed lightly. It was well known that even the Psierians with the most powerful prescient and precognitive abilities could not predict for themselves or those that they were emotionally linked with. That was why the Queen didn't know in advance about her daughter's assassination attempt, a fact that still plagued her. The Queen turned her purple gaze toward Tosh. "No, my vision was about Commander Tosh."

Castellan swallowed thickly but Olivienne was the one who spoke. "And? What about her?"

"She will die."

"Sheddech!"

Olivienne stood abruptly and stared first at Tosh, then back at her mother. "Maman, what do you mean she will die? When? How?"

Olivara held up a hand. "That is the tricky part. I've had two visions, one where Commander Tosh is alone and she dies. The other is where the two of you are together and, while you are each in grave danger, you both live."

After another cleansing swallow of her scotch, Castellan finally found the voice to speak. "What do you mean by 'together'?"

The Connate shot her a strange look. "I'm sure she wasn't talking about that!"

"Oh, I absolutely was talking about that."

"What?" Two voices spoke at the same time then Castellan and Olivienne looked at each other in consternation.

A heavy silence fell over the room and the Queen sat back to watch the interaction between her daughter and the good commander. She smiled to herself. Sometimes two stubborn heads required knocking together. "Is there a problem?"

Olivienne narrowed her eyes in suspicion. "Maman...you have never encouraged my dalliances before. Why now? Why would my interactions with Castellan in any way affect our future?"

"I don't know." The Queen shrugged. "But I saw it and the vision was strong."

The Connate pressed. "And despite tradition, rules, or good sense, our continued dalliance is the safest course of action?"

Olivara nodded. "Yes."

Castellan set her glass down on the slate table and the action caused an inordinately loud *crack,* which startled both mother and daughter. "Do I not have a say in any of this?"

The Queen looked at her seriously and opened her empathic channel. She sensed a roiling mix of emotions just below the surface of Castellan's calm façade. Fear, irritation, and tenderness sat above all the rest. "Of course you do, dear."

Tosh turned to the Queen with a glint in her eye and Olivara's empathic sense abruptly ran into a smooth wall of...nothing. "Neither my thoughts, nor my emotions, are available for casual purveyance. If you please. I would think you of all people should know the law there!"

Olivara nodded her head. "My apologies, Commander Tosh. Please, continue with your argument."

Castellan sighed and looked down, away from two sets of intense violet eyes. "I fear that further...entanglements, be they romantic or sexual, with Olivienne would only compromise my ability to keep her safe. It is against the rules for a good reason, because judgement becomes compromised when the officer is distracted."

"Are you saying I'm a distraction? Should I be worried or flattered?" Olivienne smirked at the commander.

Tosh gave her a wry look in return. "Yes."

The Queen snorted in mirth and quickly hid it behind a sip of her scotch. While Commander Tosh had made a good point, valid given the history of the Shield Corp, she was missing something even more essential. "You forget one important facet of this discussion."

Tosh looked at her warily. "Which is?"

"Which is the fact that you've already saved my daughter while in the midst of your dalliance and distraction as you put it. Your judgement didn't appear to be compromised at all. If anything, I'd say it would be sharper now that you are acting in an official capacity."

Castellan held up a single finger and opened her mouth to disagree, then abruptly shut it again. The Queen made a valid point that Tosh had not considered. Despite the fact that she wanted nothing more than to take Olivienne back to the railer and have her way, Castellan was never distracted when they were wandering about in Penterole. Simply being near the Connate made her more aware of security than she ever had been before. The commander sighed in defeat, but refused to go down without a fight. "Perhaps you are correct in that it is possible to perform one's duty by separating the personal from the professional side of things —" Her words were interrupted by a thought from Olivienne.

"I remember exactly how good those personal things were."

Tosh scowled and put a mental wall up to block the other Dracore in the room as well. She looked from one to the other and couldn't help thinking how curiously alike the two dark-eyed sovereigns were. She cast one more annoyed glance at Olivienne before continuing. "As I was saying...regardless of my abilities to perform my job, I have to be a willing party to such dalliances. I will not be forced into something I'm not comfortable with." She turned back toward Olivienne and watched the Connate's face darken with some unread emotion. "I prefer my relations to happen a little more...organically. I will not have a prophecy dictate my choice in bedmates!"

Castellan's words had only served to raise Olivienne's ire. "Oh? And what pray tell does dictate your choice in a bedmate? It does not appear to be passion or even preference. You espouse duty but when that obstacle is removed you find a million others to take its place." She stood and glared at the calm-seeming officer. "As far as I can see, the only thing that is making your decisions is your stubborn pride!" Before anyone could react to her raised voice and words, Olivienne stalked off to her private rooms upstairs.

"Well *that* could have gone better."

Tosh looked at the Queen in shock and irritation. "Speaking frankly, what did you think would happen? We mix like oil and water and I will not have my life dictated to me when that action would take me outside my honor." She finished her scotch and studied the Queen for a moment longer. "Vision or no vision, I'm quite offended that you would even try to push us together in such a way."

"Watch your tone, Commander. While I admit that I can be a bit manipulative sometimes, I am still your Queen." Seeing that they both had empty glasses, Olivara stood and apported the scotch decanter right into her hand. She diligently refilled both their glasses before sending the bottle back to whence it came. Castellan watched as the Queen sipped from her freshened glass, waiting for the woman to respond. Finally Olivara met Tosh's gaze steadfastly. "I'm going to lay my tiles on the table here. I love my daughter, Commander. That is certainly no secret. But I will be the first to admit that I have not always cared for her *dalliances*. To be honest, she tends to choose more for sport and spite than any actual potential. She lives to torment me with women who are beneath her in either intelligence or in honor. I see acceptable, nay, excellent consorage potential in you, Commander Castellan Tosh. Can you blame me for encouraging a closer attachment?"

Tosh sat back in her chair and swirled the amber liquid in her glass. "I hate to speak crudely, but since we are letting honesty mouth our words, the Connate and I have merely engaged in that sport you so disagree with. It was a simple tupping between two willing adults and nothing more. Your daughter and I are practically strangers and contentious at best. I do not share in your surety of this consorage you speak of. Nor am I looking for any such relationship. Perhaps that is why we initially connected, because neither of us has time nor room in our lives for such deep emotional connections." She paused to take a sip before continuing. "And I'd like to add that this is an incredibly awkward conversation to have with not just my Queen, but the mother of a former lover. I would prefer if you did not bring the subject up again."

Olivara stared at her for a meen longer then smiled and nodded. "Very well. I give my word that I will not bring up your dalliance with my daughter again. And for the record, you have handled this entire visit with admirable aplomb. Cheers!" She raised her glass and downed the rest of the scotch.

Castellan raised her eyebrow at the Queen's capacity for the strong liquor and mirrored her actions. "Cheers."

"Now, I should perhaps head upstairs and mend the rift between me and my daughter."

Castellan watched her climb the main stairs but remained seated herself, deep in thought.

BOTH THE COMMANDER and the Connate kept to themselves until later. It was just going on early supper when Olivienne went in search of Castellan. She paused briefly before knocking on Tosh's door to her private suite. "Commander, are you in?"

Before she could second-guess her request, the door abruptly opened beneath her knuckles. "What can I do for you, Connate Dracore?"

Olivienne sighed and closed her eyes. It was exactly as she expected, the conversation with her mother earlier only served to push Castellan further into formality. "I've come to inform you that I received a last meen dinner invitation from a close friend. The upscale eatery is called Pax Ammond."

Commander Tosh frowned, already thinking on the arrangements that would have to be made for the Connate's safety. "What time is your dinner engagement?"

"Two oors from now. My dinner date will be Benicia Demeer."

A pale eyebrow raised at the Connate's famous date. "The

pipeball player?"

Olivienne watched Castellan's face for a reaction but the officer's features were well guarded, as usual. "The very same, why do you ask?"

As the head of the sovereign's Shield unit, Cmdr. Tosh had been briefed on all Olivienne's favorite places to visit, as well as her history of relationships and dalliances. That meant Tosh was well aware of Benicia Demeer's status as one of the Connate's regular lovers. The resulting burn that information left within Tosh's gut was less than ideal. She struggled to maintain her calm even as jealousy growled within. "I am only asking because I would imagine that Psera Demeer would have some security of her own with her."

"That makes sense." Olivienne was puzzled by the commander's nonchalance about it all and a little hurt that she didn't get a reaction from the woman with too much self-control.

Cmdr. Tosh continued after mulling the situation over in her head for a few secs. "Okay, I will teleo ahead to let the establishment know of our requirements for your safety. I also want six guardians with you all night." Olivienne started to protest but Tosh held up a hand. "This is official protocol, I will not budge. However—" Castellan paused to swallow down her upset. "Should you decide to go someplace more private, two guardians must inspect the place before you go in but afterward they will all remain outside for the entirety of your stay. Is that acceptable?"

Olivienne looked at the neat and emotionless officer and wished that Castellan had put up more of a fight, or any fight at all really. "That is acceptable. Thank you, Commander." She paused for a sec then asked the question that she had been worrying over. "Will you be one of the six?"

Castellan stared at her with an undecipherable look and Olivienne was too much of a lady to pry into the officer's thoughts. Not to mention that the offense of violating someone's mind privacy carried severe punishments in the Psiere Legibus. "Under the circumstances, Connate Dracore, I much prefer to stay at the residence for the evening. I will see you on the morrow."

The remote woman was clearly finished speaking so Olivienne took a step back and nodded. After that she turned to go back to her own suite of rooms.

Dinner was pleasant enough that evening, though most of the conversation was of Benicia speaking of the tournament her team had just won. It wasn't until they were nearly through with the meal that the pipeball player seemed to run out of words. The Connate watched as her friend fell into the old seductive routine that had worked so many times before. "So what have you been busy with lately, calla? I'm assuming your adventures have taken you far afield as you haven't been in the city until recently." Benicia gave Olivienne a heart-stopping smile and reached over to cover her hand. The fact that she had just called Olivienne by her pet name did not go unnoticed. Calla was a night blooming flower that had deep purple petals with a black center. Benicia said the flower reminded her of Olivienne's eyes. "Though you are still as beautiful as ever."

Olivienne allowed the caress for a few secs before pulling her hand away. "As always, you are much too good for my ego, and no drab attraction yourself, Benne. I'm afraid I have been exceedingly busy, and remain so even now that I'm back in Tesseron. I have made a huge discovery concerning the Divine Mystery—" Benicia began to speak but Olivienne held up a finger to stall her. "But, not a discovery I can speak of just yet, I'm afraid. You will have to wait for the official announcements like everyone else." She smiled to take the sting out of her words. She expected the Benicia to continue her attempts to get information from her, or at least begin her seduction game again but Olivienne was surprised when neither of those things happened.

"You've changed, 'Vienne."

The Connate looked back at her in surprise. While Benicia was beautiful and full of copious amounts of energy, she was also reliably self-centered. The sovereign liked that the other woman never fawned over her like some. Olivienne never expected a declaration such as what just fell from her mouth. "How do you mean? I'm the same as always, just busy as I said."

Benicia's face became one of puzzlement. "No, it isn't that. You have never once failed to flirt with me, never once not responded to my cues. Are you involved with someone, Olivienne?"

Olivienne made a face. "I am definitely not involved with anyone else. Perhaps it's because I've been tired of late."

The attractive woman across the table wagged a finger at her. "Bollux! I've seen you come off three straight daes of adventure and still have the stamina for an all-night tupping. No, there is something more..."

"My mother spoke with you, didn't she?"

Benicia's eyes widened. "The Queen?"

Olivienne sighed in exasperation. "No, my other mother! Yes, of course the Queen!"

The pipeball player's appalled look morphed to that of addled confusion. "Of course I haven't spoken to your mother, she loathes me! Why do you ask? Has she been hassling you to settle down again, to give up your dalliances?" The Connate and Benicia had spoken often of the Queen's pressure on her only daughter to become consoral. While Benicia would have loved to be her par, she knew it wouldn't happen. For one, Queen Olivara never seemed to like or approve of her. Beyond that, Benicia knew that she had never held Olivienne's heart and that the Connate had too much adventure in her to settle down. She peered into those purple eyes that had gone dark in thought and waited for Olivienne to answer.

The sovereign sighed and rubbed a finger over the grain of the wood table. "No...well yes. Kind of."

Benicia stilled her hand. "You're being murky."

Olivienne slowly lifted her eyes to meet the other woman's gaze. "My apologies. She is actually encouraging dalliance with someone, and hoping for a consorage to come of it, I'm certain."

"I sense a 'but' coming."

Olivienne nodded. "Yes, *but*, the person is not amenable to such things."

Benicia sat back in her chair and her exclamation of surprise was enough to garner the attention of the other people eating. "What? Who would be foolish enough to turn you down?"

"No, it's not like...she didn't. I mean we have but—" She sighed again. "I'm making a mess of this and I shouldn't be talking about it with you. I am sorry." Olivienne looked back down to the table, unsure of anything in the moment.

"Calla...from the beginning, we knew that there would be no consorage between us. But I'd always hoped we could remain friends when the time came to end our dalliance. I think that time is now. I sense a change in you and I think this person you are referring to has gotten in deeper than you anticipated."

"What good does that do me when I am but a raindrop upon her leaf? She simply doesn't care!" Before Benicia could speak again, Olivienne rescinded her statement. "No, that is not true. She feels the passion between us just the same. But this woman is as stubborn as the dae is long and thinks that it is beneath her honor to give in to that passion. She keeps rigid control over herself, refusing to give in to temptation when we both know how sweet it is. I have tried everything but throw myself at her. I will not beg!"

Benicia tittered with laughter. "Oh calla! I know you, my dear. You could make any woman beg with just a whisper and a caress. I would say that if she is feeling half the passion you speak of, you should be fully capable of breaking through that control." She looked down at the small timepiece strapped to her wrist. "It's just past twenty-one hundred oors now. I think you should find this woman and put those gorgeous lips to use. Show her that control is nothing without knowing your limits."

"But what of you?"

Benicia smirked. "Oh you know me, I'm only alone when I wish to be. Go on, find your lover." She leaned forward to whisper as if in conspiracy. "But don't tell the Queen. Let her think all her machinations and coercing were a failure."

Sensing dinner was over, both women stood and embraced. Olivienne was glad that her past lover understood, and even happier that she gave advice on the topic of a certain commander. "Thank you again. And let us not stop with our dinners as we drift off to new *pursuits*. All right?"

"Oh perish the thought! Good night 'Vienne, and good luck!"

A credit chit had been delivered by Lt. Savon when they arrived so there was nothing the Connate needed to do but return home. As soon as she walked into the residence, she informed the guardians on duty that she was in for the night and not to let her be disturbed the next dae either. Olivienne told them that she felt like lying in. She didn't let herself stop to think when she got home. Instead she immediately made her way to the back of the house where Tosh's suite was located. There she knocked on the door once and when it wasn't answered she impatiently knocked again.

"Who is it—Olivienne?" In her surprise, she failed to use the Connate's title. Instead, Castellan stood slack-jawed as she stared into the eyes of the woman she didn't expect to see for the rest of the night.

Olivienne took in the sight that greeted her from the open doorway. Castellan looked deliciously rumpled. Her black shirt was untucked from her black trousers, and the collar was unfastened to nearly mid chest. Her blonde hair was also in disarray and Olivienne craved to run her fingers through the remembered thick blonde locks. She stilled her impulsive hands and stepped closer to the officer. "Yes, Olivienne. I'm so glad you remembered that I am a flesh and blood woman here."

Too many things assailed Castellan at once. The beauty that stood in her doorway was enough to steal her breath. But the scent of the woman in front of her also left her knees weak and Castellan's pulse began to race when Olivienne slowly licked her lips. Sentences eluded her, only random words were left. "Woman? Flesh?" Another step brought them chest to chest and Tosh gasped even as her cheeks flooded with color.

"Are you going to push me away again?"

"But...but...your dinner engagement..."

"That is not how I wish to spend my evening. I repeat, are you going to push me away again?"

Time seemed to slow and secs scraped by like oors. Olivienne watched as the officer's pale eyes darkened with desire, and her nose flared in excitement. Then, as if their passion carried the strength of the sea, it crashed over the two women. Tosh pulled them together in a desperate embrace, kissing Olivienne's lips with a ferocity she had not shown with anyone else. All the while she backed them into her suite and with a kick of her bare foot she shut the door. The slam reverberated through the wood and plaster walls. Olivienne had her answer.

Chapter Fourteen

THE COMMANDER'S SUITE was fairly simple. It had a decent size sitting room, with two other doors besides the main entrance. One led to the lavatory and the other to the bedroom. But rather than move from their position, Tosh pushed Olivienne forcefully against the newly closed door. With only an ince difference in height, Castellan's hips surged against Olivienne's and their mouths fought for dominance of the kiss. Olivienne tangled her hands in that thick hair to pull Tosh even closer. The officer's mouth eventually moved on, initially causing displeasure. But as Castellan's lips moved to the skin just below Olivienne's ear and teeth came into play, the Connate writhed and groaned beneath her. With such added stimulus, Olivienne left only one hand to grip Tosh's hair tightly and the other traveled inside the open top of the officer's shirt. She was surprised to meet smooth skin then delighted to discover that Tosh must have removed her own bosair earlier in the evening.

"'Vienne...you burn me with your touch." Castellan's words came haltingly, barely a whisper and she shuddered as Olivienne explored as much skin as she could reach before moving her hand up to grab the back of Tosh's neck.

"There is a fire between us. Castellan..." She called softly, willing Tosh to meet her gaze.

Those pale blue eyes were wild and her breath came out in gasps. "Yes?"

"Don't make me wait any longer."

Tosh's smile was feral but their eyes held the same passion. "Never." She grasped Olivienne behind the thighs and lifted the Connate until she could wrap her legs around Tosh's waist. Castellan didn't even use her telekinesis for the short trip to the bedroom. Once there she gently set Olivienne on her bed and as the Connate scooted back, Castellan followed her until she had wedged her hips snugly between the sovereign's thighs. Olivienne wore tight trousers for her evening dinner plans and as such there was not much to protect her from Tosh's touch.

She cried out at the immediate pressure on her most tender parts and raised her hips to increase the delicious contact between them. Sensing that the woman below her was uncharacteristically close, Tosh thrust slowly and gently at the same time she swallowed Olivienne's moan with a kiss. Her hips continued their unceasing rubbing rhythm as the sovereign rose higher and higher.

Olivienne's hands gripped the back of Castellan's loose shirt, clutching desperately as she fast approached the pinnacle of release. She didn't want to fall yet, it was much too soon. She tore her lips away but rather than words, a breathy whine came up from her throat. Finally she was able to speak. "Wait..."

Tosh slowed and looked down into heavy-lidded violet eyes. "Why would I do that?"

The Connate's pupils were dilated and she struggled to think through the sexual haze that Castellan had thrown over her. "But what about yo—" Her question was cut off by another kiss even as Tosh ground into her. "But I want to—bollux!" It happened that fast, Olivienne reached her release in a series of shuddering gasps as Castellan continued to move. When it became too much, Olivienne patted the officer's shoulder to stop. Instead of moving her hips out from between Olivienne's own, Castellan dropped her lips back down to the flushed upper chest to kiss the sweaty flesh. For her part, Olivienne had thrown a forearm over her eyes as she lay panting. "That was borderline embarrassing with its alacrity...the things you do to me."

Tosh looked up at the same time Olivienne moved her arm. "The things I do to you?"

Serious violet eyes met hers. "You make me wanton and needy. And I can't have your boundless stamina showing me up!"

Tosh raised a pale eyebrow. "Oh? And is it my fault that you wind up and tire so easily? I will admit that it can be hard to keep up with me at times—"

Without warning, Olivienne flipped them around until Tosh was on her back and she sat comfortably on the commander's hips. "I should perhaps punish you, make you suffer for your insolence and braggadocious words!"

Tosh licked her dry lips and smiled slyly. "I would be ever so appreciative if you did just that. I would be more delighted if you could start with a kiss though."

Rather than give in to the dashing woman's suggestion, Olivienne began slowly unfastening Castellan's black shirt. Each extra bit of flesh that was exposed caused her pulse to race faster. She had to move back to unclasp the last bit but the effort was worth the reward. Castellan's smooth chest and abdomen showed a soldier's strength. The woman was certainly not limited to stylus and vellum all dae. Olivienne traced the skin and muscle within reach, teasing in the way she studiously avoided the small breasts with their dusty-colored nipples. When she finally brought her hands where Castellan wanted them most, the prone woman moaned with pleasure. "'Vienne, please! You are torturous."

"I believe I owe you a little of such, my dear commander. And you are wearing far too many clothes." Olivienne rolled both Castellan's nipples between her fingers as she spoke, causing the officer to thrust her hips upward as a bolt of arousal shot straight to her core. Then she pulled her hands away and Castellan actually whimpered.

"Me? What of you?"

Olivienne smiled, shut her eyes, and in an instant, her clothing simply disappeared from her body and appeared in a rumpled heap on the floor. She was left sitting nude atop Castellan's pelvis. Then before Tosh could react, she focused again and the officer's uniform disappeared as well. "Is that better?"

Castellan brought her hands up to Olivienne's soft hips as her eyes darkened further with arousal. When their gazes met, Tosh gave the Connate a little mental push, like telepathically knocking on her door. The Connate opened wide to let her in. *"Do you know what would really be better?"*

Olivienne started teasing those delicious breasts again while they were so intimately connected and a multitude of thoughts and images flitted through Tosh's head. The Connate struggled to pick one and Castellan struggled to speak through the pleasure of the sovereign's touch. Finally one image stayed steady and Olivienne smiled down at her lover. *"Ah, that is the one."* Without another word she tamped down her fascination with Castellan's breasts and slowly slid down the officer's body. With a sassy little wiggle, she finished spreading Castellan's legs apart and was left with a most distracting view. She looked up and their eyes met again.

"Please."

Olivienne grinned up at her. "No need to beg, love. I've got all night." Before Castellan could respond, Olivienne lowered her mouth for the most intimate of kisses.

Tosh cried out and had she not gotten her own response under control, she would have rivaled Olivienne in her speed of release. "Oh! I—" She faltered as the actions of Olivienne's tongue drove words right from her mouth. The Connate took pity and slowed her movements just a tetch. She stilled them completely when Castellan gripped her shoulder in desperation. "Please, I will not last long like that."

Olivienne could feel the slight trembling below her and witnessed the dark and wild look within Castellan's eyes. "So I see. Well then..." She paused to tease Tosh's sacred opening with her fingers. "We'll just have to go again, won't we?" Then without another sec of waiting she brought her mouth back down at the same time she entered Castellan, propelling her higher with sure strokes of fingers and tongue. They were still lightly connected through their telepathic channels and Olivienne could hear the other woman's thoughts as she approached the precipice.

"So close...by the Makers I am so close. Feels so good – oh!"

"'Vienne!"

The cry of her name caused her own quim to throb and ache but she continued her ministrations until Castellan feebly tried to push her away. Olivienne stopped and gently removed her hand from that warm and inviting place, then placed a gentle kiss upon Castellan's inner thigh and another on the top of her wet slit. Tosh shuddered and twitched at just that light touch. Another smile graced Olivienne's face as she looked up at her commander. Tosh's eyes were shut tight and a ruddy flush colored her skin from chest up to the roots of her dark blonde hair. "Are you all right, darling?"

Castellan's chest heaved with the strength of her release and she blew out a sigh. "I am well. I just need a meen."

Rather than wait for Tosh's go ahead, Olivienne crawled up the panting woman's body until her own center rested on Castellan's stomach. Her pleasure slicked the skin below and Tosh's eyes flicked open at the feel of her. "Oh! You are so wet! So ready." Her hand moved from the side of the bed to rest on Olivienne's abdomen. The sovereign's eyes widened as it inced downward and a thumb moved into the crease of her labia.

Olivienne threw her head back with overwhelming pleasure as that digit slowly rubbed along the side of her clitoris. The touch was light and teasing and she wanted more. "Yes!"

Just as Castellan hit the limit of her thumb's reach, she reversed course and pulled it back up along the wet folds. That sensitive bundle of nerves hardened further and twitched against the pad of her thumb. Without moving her hand, she sat up and took one of Olivienne's nipples into her mouth, alternately sucking on the hardened flesh and biting lightly. She pulled back slightly and stopped her caress to get Olivienne's attention. "Is this all right?" She moved the thumb again and Olivienne shuddered.

The Connate's laugh ended with a hiss of pleasure as the tightness began to build again. "You will finish me sooner rather than later if you keep that up." She gasped as teeth closed around the other nipple and Tosh continued her gentle stroking.

"Did you not say we have all night? Let us see how many times we can finish each other before exhaustion claims us."

"Your idea has merit —" Olivienne's mental voice abruptly cut off as Castellan increased both the suction of her mouth and the pressure of her thumb. There were no more intelligible words after that. Only sounds of want and need. The air was filled the night through with moans of passion and the occasional pleading whimper. Neither one out-proved the other with her stamina. It was near seven hundred oors the next morning when a rare simultaneous orgasm caused an abrupt collapse to the bed. As they were still connected telepathically, exhaustion washed over them at the same time and their eyes fell shut nearly in unison. Olivienne's last thought was that perhaps stamina could be proven another dae. Castellan's reaction was quiet laughter in her head as they slipped into well-deserved dreams.

ON CASTELLAN'S URGING, Olivienne followed Benicia's advice and kept their dalliance from her mother. The commander didn't think it would be a good idea to make their flaunting of protocol publicly known. Beyond that, she surmised that if someone with nefarious intent suspected her concentration was compromised, they may attempt another attack on Olivienne's life. As for the Connate and the commander, things had gotten decidedly easier between them. Simply acknowledging and acting on their attraction had cooled that contentious fire that filled any room they were in together. It wasn't much of a surprise to discover that they worked quite well together. Nearly a weke after the initial incident, Castellan was glad to admit that they had begun building a solid foundation of friendship. It was much preferable to the constant push and pull of before.

With the vellumwork completed for the team formation and schedules worked out, there was really nothing to do until Olivienne discovered something that would lead them away on the

Connate's next adventurist mission. Because of that, Castellan had taken to helping Olivienne and the other two interpretists with decoding the Antaeus encryptions. That was exactly what the officer was doing late one afternoon.

Olivienne had gone to see the Queen at the main palace, leaving Castellan to work in the peaceful light of the two suns. They weren't scheduled to leave the estate that dae but she was expecting word on the arrival of their last Shield unit member. Lt. Savon had orders to retrieve Spc. Necole Leer from the dirigible station and get her settled into the unit house. The pilot had been flying local trips while waiting for her inter-corp transfer to be approved. Tosh planned to hold a team meeting to introduce everyone to the Connate when Olivienne returned to the residence.

"Ser."

Tosh looked up to see her first lieutenant saluting her from the entryway of the outdoor patio where she had been working. It was a delightful little secluded place, surrounded by a three yord high stone wall. "Yes, Lieutenant? Is everyone settled?"

"Yes, ser. Lieutenant Madlin and I verified the training and duty rosters and posted them on the main board for the unit. We're ready to meet whenever Connate Dracore returns."

"I want double teamwork drills until she's ready to head out, savvy?"

"Yes, ser, we've already informed everyone. And if I may speak candidly, ser?"

Castellan looked at the man curiously. Lt. Gentry Savon had a lot of potential and she was exceptionally glad to have his Shield Corp experience and stability on the team when so many other factors were in flux. "Go ahead, Lieutenant."

He smiled. "I'm really glad you came aboard, ser. I have a good feeling about the team you've put together and about your leadership. Connate Dracore already seems significantly more amenable to your directions than she was to Captain Shendo's command."

She stifled a smile at his words. "Well, let's hope she always remains so compliant to protocol but I would not wager your weapon on it, Savon. The Connate is smart and headstrong and is sure to give us grief at some point."

As Castellan finished speaking, she saw Lt. Savon's gaze flick behind her and his eyes widened even as his face paled. "Um, ser..."

The officer was well aware of the person that had come out of the residence through the door directly behind her lounger. But she enjoyed seeing the panic crawling across the lieutenant's face. She interrupted his attempt at warning. "Yes, we all know that Connate Dracore has a reputation for not following protocol and being generally difficult." A small whine came from the nervous man's throat and his eyes flicked behind her again.

"Is that so?" Olivienne's mellow voice nearly had Lt. Savon in a panic, until he caught the look on Tosh's face. She winked at him then turned in her seat to look back at the approaching Connate she had just been referring too.

"Oh, most certainly! Do you deny the fact that you've driven away all your captains? Well, away or insane. At least that's the Corp gossip I heard." Rather than devolve into a fit of temper as Lt. Savon had expected initially, Olivienne stood behind Cmdr. Tosh's chair and began laughing wholeheartedly. Castellan chuckled along with her, happy that her teasing found its intended response. Savon sighed as well, just glad the Connate had not taken his commander seriously.

The sovereign eventually got control of herself and smile down at Tosh. "Oh, I deny everything, Commander. I have never been anything less that polite and tractable."

Tosh snorted at her words and Lt. Savon hid a smile behind a cough. "Ser?" Castellan looked away from Olivienne and met his gaze. "Now that Connate Dracore has returned to the residence, would you like to schedule the team meeting?"

The commander glanced from Olivienne back to Savon. "Yes, Lieutenant. Let's say a half oor right here on the patio."

"Yes, ser!" Lt. Savon smartly saluted both Castellan and Olivienne before turning on his heel and making his way back off the patio.

Tosh immediately thought of the introductions to come and what she was going to say to the team as a whole. She had met each one individually but this would be the first time some of them had been introduced to Olivienne. Despite their laughter and teasing of the previous few meens, the Connate did have a reputation. She was hoping that all of them could begin on a positive note, make a fresh start. Her deep thoughts were interrupted by fingers combing through the back of her hair.

"You look much too relaxed out here, Castellan. It makes me wish I could drag you off into the residence but a half oor is not nearly enough to satisfy a proper craving. Not to mention that it would only delay telling you the news I've received from my mother." She sighed and took a seat adjacent to Castellan's lounger.

"The Queen? What has she to say?" It had been just over a weke since the Queen tried to push them together, albeit with good intentions. Tosh was curious as to whether the sovereign had experienced any more visions with her prescience channel.

Olivienne grinned ruefully. "Well for starters, she questioned me unceasingly about the two of us. I told her that we had agreed to work out our disagreements and were fast becoming friends. She was quite disappointed to learn that we had not resumed our dalliance." As she said the words, Olivienne directed a wink to her newly reinstated lover. They had only spent one other night tupping but both agreed it was a significantly better way of working out their natural passionate energy. Certainly better than their previously contentious relationship.

Just as the Queen predicted, Castellan had no problems at all maintaining focus while she was in the thick of her duties as commander of the Connate's Shield Corp unit. But in those off times when they were simply socializing with each other or working on translations in the private library, there were moments when the officer found herself intrigued by Olivienne's profile or the highlights in her black hair. She did not speak of those moments to anyone. Rather, she was hoping they would fade with time. She smirked at Olivienne's words about her mother. "Pity. But she really was quite heavy-handed with her meddling. I do understand her concern for you though. She is more than just the Queen in this, she is your mother."

The Connate groaned and rubbed her temple. "I'm quite aware of that but I will not be mollycoddled by anyone!" She turned her violet gaze to Castellan. "Do you hear me, Tosh? Once I am in the field, the job is mine to perform. Yours is to guarantee my safety. I don't mind help but if there is something I need to do or someplace I need to go, that is part of my job. Savvy?"

Castellan leaned over to gently grasp Olivienne's hand. "I'm well aware that you have a job to do and I assure you that you will be allowed to do that job. But please keep in mind that I've spent wekes putting together this team to be able to do more than simply keep you safe. Their secondary purpose is also to assist in an adventurist capacity. But you need to trust me and the team, trust in our abilities and don't go rogue. Promise?"

They stared at each other for another meen before Olivienne

finally nodded. "In other more disturbing news, my mother has received word that there is a conspiracy brewing in Dromea. Because of security concerns, she has ordered the transfer of all untranslated temple documents to her personally. My father has expanded the interpretist team that is in place at the north temple to six in order to sift through the hundred rotos of unknown information."

Tosh nodded. "Has any new information about the third temple shown up in the texts yet?"

"Actually, yes." Olivienne unlocked the satchel she had set next to her feet when she took a seat. She removed a single vellum. "One document was found that distinctly spoke of the Temple of Antaeus, and more specifically about the Antoraestones. Apparently there was an incident generations ago that involved the power-boosting stones, a catastrophe. The Makers deemed the stones too dangerous for Psierians and as a result gathered them all up and locked them away in the newest built temple at the time. Apparently the Temple of Antaeus was the most secure with both its architecture and location and they did not want future citizens to find the stones until their society as a whole was ready to handle such powerful tools."

"One thing that has always bothered me is the lack of written or oral history for Psiere beyond more than a few hundred rotos into our past. Did we once coexist with the Makers? Or are they simply our ancestors and the entire society made a concerted effort to block their origins from future generations? Why all the secrecy?" Tosh rubbed her temple in frustration.

"You may as well ask why the ground is hard or the sky is blue for all the answers you get with the asking of such questions."

Tosh lifted her hand into the air and waved it about. "It's as if we as a people simply...sprang from the aether with our society and structure fully intact. Surely that cannot be the case."

Olivienne gave a small helpless smile. "Darling, it's called the Divine Mystery for a reason."

Tosh chuffed with displeasure. "I suppose it is. And since you have no big answers for me, how about gifting me with a small one. Such as, where is the temple of Antaeus?"

Olivienne laughed and continued with her update. "According to the text I mentioned a few meens ago, the problem isn't necessarily going to be finding the location of the temple. There are also three keys needed to get inside. It was documented that the keys were scattered across the two continents, and the location of the Temple of Antaeus was hidden with the third key."

"Wait, keys you said?"

The Connate leaned forward. "Yes, why? Have you found something?"

Castellan immediately began sorting through the translated papers she had been piling up on the outdoor table that sat in front of her lounger. "Ah ha!" She slipped the vellum out of the stack and placed it where they could both see. "Look here. I discounted it because I thought it was a simple bit of poetry, entertainment and nothing more. But the second stanza references a key." She pushed the vellum toward Olivienne and the Connate scanned the document.

> *In the summer of celestial events*
> *On the fifth and final dae*
> *Cataclysm turned the sky gray*
> *And the land was scored with rents*
> *As awareness slowed by moments*
> *And forethought came into play*
> *Our people recognized a way*
> *First thought of by the docents*
>
> *It was possible to hide the stones*
> *In a place that was most secured*
> *And locked with a triad of keys*
> *On an island of rocks and bones*
> *In the mouth of our mother revered*
> *Lay the first treasure you may seize*

When Olivienne finished reading the vellum through, her mouth was left ajar. "Well that is most fascinating!"

Castellan remained just as puzzled after reading it through the second time as she was the first. "What do you think it means?"

The historical adventurist looked at her commander with surprise. "Why it's quite obvious, my dear Tosh. They hid the stones somewhere, and secured them with three keys. One or all of them is on Mater Island."

"And how do you figure all that? And where is Mater Island?"

Olivienne rolled her eyes and pointed at the second portion

of the poem. "Right here it references the stones and the secured location, as well as the three keys. Those are the first three of the last six lines. Fourth and fifth lines are obviously speaking of Mater Island, locally known as Roc Island. I thought you were stationed on the western most region of Endara. How do you not know about the preserved roc nesting and breeding grounds?"

Castellan grimaced. "I do know about Roc Islands, but I never got around to learning the official name of them. And the poem spells them as rocks!"

The Connate laughed at her and ran a finger across the back of Tosh's hand. "You're not one for the interpretation of the arts, are you my dear?"

Tosh grinned at the subtle flirt. "Oh, I can appreciate beauty when I see it. But I was always more a woman of action than imagination."

"So I've noticed." Olivienne shook herself from the distraction that was Castellan Tosh and got back to the important job at hand. "So we have found our first mission of many. Will your team be ready in time?"

Castellan frowned. "Roc Island is a suicide mission!"

"I concede that it will be difficult but it is my job, and the task of finding Antaeus has been specifically directed by the Queen."

Tosh sighed. "We need three wekes to fully prepare."

Olivienne shook her head. "One weke."

"Bollux! You can't outfit an expedition in a weke, let's call it two and be done. I dislike bickering on such a fine dae."

As they stared at each other, that familiar heat began to rise and Olivienne couldn't help licking her lips in anticipation. The Connate had just begun to lean forward when boots sounded on the patio flagstones. "Connate Dracore, Commander Tosh, the team has assembled for your meeting." Castellan had seen Olivienne's intent for what it was and anticipated the taste of her soft lips. She glanced down at her watch and sighed. Unfortunately for both of them, Lt. Madlin had impeccable timing.

"Welcome everyone, please file in and we'll start. To begin I'm going to tell you that we have our first mission with Senior Historical Adventurist, Connate Dracore. We have two wekes to train as a team while Connate Dracore and I handle the planning and supply portion of the operation. Now, let's get down to the business of introductions. I'm sure the Connate is as excited to meet you all as you are to meet her." Lt. Savon coughed and Olivienne hid a smile behind her hand. Castellan pointed at Lt. Savon since he seemed to have plenty to say. "Go ahead Savon, you can start by telling everyone about yourself." He groaned and the rest of the guardians laughed at their first lieutenant's expense. Olivienne laughed with the rest but her primary thoughts were already racing ahead to the mission. She couldn't wait to begin.

Chapter Fifteen

THE CONVOY OF haulers traveled at a fast clip of one hundred mahls per oor in the official lane of the speedway. After wekes of prep and team building, the Connate and her Shield Corp unit were finally able to set out for Mater Island, off the coast of Endara's western peninsula. Mater was the outermost of two long narrow islands, one shielding the other. Locals affectionately referred to them as mother and daughter, or not so affectionately as the roc islands. The fishing port was located close to the eastern end of the smaller island of Filia.

On Olivienne's urging, Castellan made sure the mission packets for each included information about the islands and their feathered inhabitants. The trip from Tesseron to the fishing town of Natus was one thousand mahls so Tosh had the teams in each hauler rotating the driving duties in shifts of three oors each. With the rest stops, she estimated it would take nearly twelve oors to get to their destination. Once there they would set up a base camp and get a good night's sleep in preparation for travel to the island the next dae.

Olivienne had already hired a fishing boat for the unit that would go to the island. The boat would leave a four person team on Filia as backup and deposit eight on the shores of Mater. The final four were the ones that had the least training to be of use on the island and Tosh chose them to secure the base camp. As much of a danger as it was to take boats across Atlanteen controlled water, dirigible flight was impossible because of the rocs. All fishing vessels were equipped with rail guns, a given when undertaking such a hazardous job. While they rode along, Castellan spent much of her time pouring over the intel they had received about the rocs of Psiere. She was certain that the greatest danger to the Connate would not come from her fellow Psierians, but rather from the monsters of the air.

The massive birds that inhabited the island were incredibly territorial about the air around their nesting grounds. Weighing one hundred and seventy punds, with a wingspan of sixteen yords, and sporting ten ince talons, no one survived a roc attack. They were nearly four yords tall and could pick up a grown man and fly him away. Finding the Key of Archeos would be an incredibly dangerous undertaking.

The only reason rocs were not hunted down and killed long before was unless they were provoked, they left the Psierian population alone. They exclusively hunted the large creatures of the ocean. Because of that, they had formed a symbiotic relationship with the fishing fleets that would go out. They didn't care about the smaller animals brought aboard the boats, but they feasted on the larger creatures that the Atlanteens sent up from the deep to attack the ships. Rocs had enlarged, highly curved talons on each toe that made it easier to catch prey, such as large sturgeous fish, small whals, dolpheens, and sharcs.

Even though the rocs were incredibly long-lived, the oldest recorded being nearly three hundred rotos, the mated pairs only hatched one or two eggs a roto. Because of the sensitivity of roc habitat, the islands themselves were protected land, as dictated by the crown many generations before. The only ones that were allowed on the island were those with special permission from the Queen.

Mater was about six hundred mahls long and about one hundred and twenty-five mahls at its widest point. The island was also covered by massive coniferous trees that stood on average ninety yords high. They were said to be as wide as a small house at the base. Strangely enough, the birds didn't build nests for their young as with smaller brethren, but rather they laid their eggs amongst the boulders on the south shore. The commander was equal parts fascinated and alarmed by all that she had read about the inhabitants of the island they would need to traverse.

Despite making regular stops, the travel dae was grueling. Tosh and a few other soldiers had taken to doing exercises at each break just to get their blood flowing and stay the boredom. The stops weren't long, usually only fifteen or twenty meens, but it was enough to break the monotony of the trip. It wasn't all seriousness though. Once in a while someone would display odd talents or tricks, much to the entertainment of others. It was discovered that Cmdr. Tosh was a decent juggler and that Spc. Holling could mimic more than thirty different animal sounds. Olivienne was seated next to Tosh in the middle hauler. She leaned over and whispered into the commander's ear once they were on their way again. "I had no idea you were so good with your hands."

Castellan looked at her with a mischievous glint in her eyes and kept her voice low as well. "Now that is a poxing lie, Connate Dracore. You know full well how good I am with my hands." Then with a smile she added a bit more with thought alone. *"I remember the incident over the back of the chair quite clearly."*

Even as she heard the words in her mind, Olivienne flashed back to that exact moment. Her face flushed when she remembered the way Castellan had left her shaken and spent. "My apologies, Commander Tosh, you are completely correct." They didn't give in to the fire between them often but when they did it generally turned to a conflagration that would last an entire evening leaving both women worn and satiated.

It was around nineteen hundred oors when they exited the speedway at the point nearest to Natus. Castellan used the voteo to contact the local Security Corp station to let them know that the Connate and her team had arrived. The only lodging available for traveling personnel was the research dorm. Unfortunately for the Shield unit, the dorm was full for the season but the station commander assured Tosh that there was ample room on the property for their camp. The dorm also had full shower facilities that they could use for the duration of their stay.

Sleeping outdoors wasn't a problem since everyone had top of the line gear for the mission. All-weather sleep cubes had easy room for two people per, plus personal gear. Everyone doubled up with the exception of the Shield unit commander and the Connate. Their rank afforded them the privilege of personal cubes. Two larger cubes were set up with the remainder of the unit's gear, such as heavy weapons, tools, components, and long-range coms.

Tosh set her personnel to popping up the sleep cubes and securing them firmly to the ground. There was an option to connect the cubes together at the corners and some elected to do that. To prevent disturbing the group's rest as a whole, she had them rotate through overnight guardian duty in two oor shifts, two person teams. The shift partner would be the person they shared a cube with. While Olivienne and the rest of the group ate a late meal, Castellan went off in search of the station commander. She found him still at his desk, hard at work. She knocked on the open office door to get the man's attention.

He was a few rotos older than Castellan herself. His face was one of surprise when he looked up to see an officer with a black uniform at his doorway. He stood immediately and saluted. "You must be Commander Tosh, with Connate Dracore's unit." Technically, he wasn't required to salute Castellan because they were the same rank. But Psi Shield Corp were a law unto their own and a Shield unit leader on active duty with a sovereign outranked most everyone. He held out his hand to clasp in greeting. "We spoke on the voteo earlier but I didn't get a chance to give you my name, it's Commander Dendin. And I must say that it's a real honor to meet you, ser!"

"I'm not sure what I've done to earn all that honor but thank you."

"Are you putting me on? You, the Hero of Temple Beach? The person who took a shell for Connate Dracore and still managed a kill shot on the assassin as you were bleeding out?" He looked genuinely taken aback that she would question her honorable qualifications. "You're famous in certain circles."

"I'd wager I'm infamous in even more. Anyway, back to the task at hand, Commander. Connate Dracore has chartered a fishing ship to take us to Mater Island tomorrow—"

Before she could go any further he shook his head. "Not tomorrow, there's a big blow coming in from the west."

She looked at him curiously. "Don't the islands protect the waters around here?"

"The big bay shields us from the east, and the islands protect us from the south. But when the storms come in from the west there's nothing to break up the winds. The rocs won't fly in the high wind and without the rocs, the fishing boats won't go out for any reason. The Atlanteens are too much of a risk."

"Sheddech!" Castellan rubbed her temple as she considered the change in their plans. "How big is this storm, will it affect our camp over on the other side of the research dorms? And how long will it last?"

He stroked his stubbly chin. "It won't affect your camp near the research dorm. That's about as sheltered as you can get with the forest on three sides. But the information I got from the weather witch—"

"Excuse me? What?"

He blushed and looked genuinely chagrined. "My apologies, Commander. We have a local Psi with an extremely high clairvoyance channel and it often attunes to the weather. I suppose that's a good thing if you live in a coastal town. But anyway, I don't know where the term came from but people hereabouts just call her the weather witch. She's well loved."

Castellan sighed at the way the man constantly lost track of the conversation. "And the storm?"

"Oh, yes! The weather w...Sarae, she says it will most likely blow for two daes, then clear as can be after that. That's two daes from tonight, so I guess two nights."

"So...the dae after tomorrow will be clear?" She was fast losing patience with the Security Corp officer. He took twice as long to say what he needed because he kept straying off topic. She could already see the wind picking up outside and wanted to get back to the camp.

He looked confused for a second then smiled. "I suppose so."

Glad the conversation was done, Castellan saluted her fellow officer and mentally scoffed at the people they let into Psi Security Corp. While they did well as local law enforcement, Security Corp members were not nearly as disciplined as Defense or Shield. Granted, her youngest sib served with Security, but he was more of an example rather than an exception. "Thank you for the information and I'll see myself out. Good dae, Commander."

Dendin hastily stood and saluted back. "Good dae!"

Back at their camp, Castellan gave a loud thumb and forefinger whistle at the same time she sent a telepathic nudge to her entire team, including Olivienne. Within two meens they had all assembled in front of her. The Connate looked at her curiously but waited to see what she'd have to say.

"I just spoke with the regional Security Corp commander and he said that we're due for a big blow that will last two nights." She pointed to the west where the sky was already turning black with flashes of lightning cutting jagged strips through the gloom. "As you can see it will probably hit within the next oor. We're fairly sheltered here and rain won't come in your cubes but we're going to be pretty isolated in our camp until it clears. I recommend connecting them if you want some social time without getting soaked. Otherwise, everyone should have rations for two daes and a stone heater, one per cube. I apologize about the fact that we're all going to get wet on the trips to the lavatory but at least we'll have a full facility to use in the dorms. If you're on guard detail, make sure you have your weather proof gear ready and dry it thoroughly after each use. Savvy?"

A chorus of voices all responded. "Yes, ser!"

"Did you ask about our charter?" Olivienne looked worried that they may miss their boat.

Castellan smiled in reassurance. "No boats will run during the storm because the rocs won't fly and they provide the majority of the security from the Atlanteens. We should be able to head across to Mater the dae after tomorrow." She scanned the group as a whole just as the first fat drop landed on her cheek. No one spoke so she circled her finger in the air twice to indicate they were dismissed. "Run then, get out of the rain. First detail starts now!" Once they were gone she turned to Olivienne. "I'm sorry your plans got delayed. What will you do now?"

The sovereign gave her a wicked smile and waved toward their sleep cubes. "I took the liberty and connected our sleep cubes. I hope you don't mind."

A lone pale eyebrow raised at the Connate's words. "That's a little obvious isn't it?"

Olivienne laughed. "On the contrary, I told them I needed to confer with you about the coming mission."

Tosh snorted. "And you think they believed that?"

"Does it matter? A third of the team was on the railer when we first began tupping. And I'm sure the team you put together is smart enough to have figured out what's what by now. We are around them most of the time and the fact of the matter, dear Commander, is that I find you much too beguiling." Olivienne smiled and shrugged her shoulders. "Maman always said that while I have her coloring, my eyes showed my mind much like my papan. I'm a terrible liar and worse secret-keeper."

Two more chilly drops splashed onto Castellan's skin and she looked up at the sky. "I suggest we take our discussion on the merits of honesty someplace a little drier." They ran across the grassy site just as the rain came down in earnest and for the sake of entry time, each went into their own cube door. As they had slightly larger than standard sleep cubes, both the sovereign's and Castellan's living space were seven foot by seven foot square with an inside height of eight foot. The cubes could be connected on the corners, which is what Olivienne had directed. Castellan's sleep gear was still rolled tight and none of her other kit had been unpacked since she wasn't the one who had set up her sleep cube.

"I'm soaking wet over here." Despite being less than a yord away, Olivienne's voice came back muffled amongst the drumming sound of rain. "I'm going to string a line and hang my things to dry over the illeostone heater. There's plenty of room for your uniform as well."

Castellan laughed from her temporary living space and began removing her weapons and gear. "That was decidedly unsubtle."

The reply that came back was full of humor. "Well I've always heard that soldiers were a bit thick in the head so I figured I'd help you out a little."

"Funny, I've heard the same about Service Corp...athletes in particular."

The Connate smirked unseen in her cube. "Still jealous about that?"

"I was never jealous." Tosh's voice was unexpectedly loud as she stepped through the connector. The officer was gloriously nude and holding onto her wet uniform. "I believe you offered me a line?"

Olivienne made no secret of her blatant appreciation of Castellan's form. "I'll give you whatever line you need as long as that body is in my bedroll within the next ten secs."

Instead of responding, Castellan strode the few steps to the installed drying line and turned to hang her things. The Connate visually devoured the strong back and tight buttocks that faced her way. "You are killing me over here, Commander. You should not tease a humble psera so."

Castellan couldn't help laughing as she completed her task and turned to face a decidedly heated sovereign. "You give such good advice and when I find a humble psera I'll be sure to follow it."

"You cad!" In less than two secs Olivienne grabbed Tosh's arm and used her leverage to trip the officer onto her bedroll. Then the Connate quickly straddled Castellan's hips and rested her hands on the firm shoulders below. "You surely deserve to be punished for your impertinence!"

The dashing officer's pulse increased at the feel of their nude and slightly damp bodies pressed together. Her pale blue gaze was full of heat as she challenged Olivienne with a familiar raised eyebrow. "And who will dole out such a punishment? For I find myself more than a little wet, and perhaps dirty from our dae of travel. I hardly think the Royal Sovereign Connate Olivienne Dracore would want to sully her fingers with such a punishment."

Her words turned to a gasp as Olivienne reached between them and ran her fingers through Castellan's hot folds. "Oh, I plan on sullying so much more than my fingers." Those were the last intelligible words spoken for many oors between the two women as they practiced their not-so-secret tupping well into evening. Castellan never did get around to laying out her bedroll.

The next dae didn't dawn so much as get measurably lighter

as each sun broke free of the horizon. Tosh had retreated to her own cube earlier to do some basic exercises. Her space was limited but she was able to get a solid oor in of basic strengthening with a little cardio thrown in. Olivienne did a much shorter workout, but only because she was bored and wanted to get her blood pumping. She would have preferred a much more pleasurable way to accomplish that goal but, ever the soldier, Tosh insisted she needed to complete her waking routine. The rain continued unabated into the morning and the grayness outside brought the Connate's mood down as well.

Once her fitness routine was taken care of, Cmdr. Tosh used the voteo to check in with the team. She spoke with both Lt. Savon and Lt. Madlin, as well as the current guardians on duty. Nothing untoward had happened overnight and the team overall was getting a bit stir-crazy. Knowing that they would all appreciate a hot meal, Tosh once again voteod Cmdr. Dendin. "Commander, is there an eatery in this town that can seat and feed sixteen?"

Laughter returned over the small handheld communicator. "Are they going crazy already? It's been less than twelve oors!"

"Yes, well I thought it would be good to take Connate Dracore and the Shield unit out to eat something that tasted better than field rations."

"I hear that particular Dracore is a handful of an assignment. Gone through all her previous captains, right?"

Commander Castellan Tosh had spent her entire career within the Psi Defense Corp before transferring to Shield. She lived and breathed the daily gossip that circulated about officers and civilians both. And it really didn't matter which militia Corp one ended up in, they all had their share of gossip. She didn't usually reprimand anyone for it unless it was detrimental to team or morale because people were people and were bound to speak and speculate. But hearing Cmdr. Dendin speak of Olivienne with anything but the highest respect left her feeling cold. She couldn't explain her need to defend the sovereign, she simply reacted. With as much scorn as she could muster she spoke into the voteo. "Connate Dracore is our sovereign and the heir to the Divine Cathedra. You will speak of our sovereign with respect or not speak of her at all. Is that clear, Commander?"

There was a distinct pause of about six secs before the speaker crackled. "Yes, ser. I apologize for any seeming slight. To answer your question, there is only one eatery that will be open during the storm and that one is only so because the owners live above it. Look for the gray building near the clock tower in the center of town. If I were you I'd teleo ahead to prepare for your arrival but it should meet your needs."

"That will do nicely."

Dendin's voice sounded strangely hesitant when he spoke again. "Will that be all, Commander Tosh?"

She smiled at the special privilege her black uniform afforded her. "No actually. First, I'd like you to teleo the eatery and tell them to expect sixteen for noon meal. Second, I need two of your Security officers stationed at our camp for the entirety of our noon meal. Savvy?"

A few sec pause again and the commander responded. "Yes, ser. I will tell them to be ready for you at twelve hundred oors and arrange for guards for the Connate's camp. Dendin out."

Castellan was satisfied that she got her point across to the Security Corp commander. It wasn't really a dressing down but she took more pleasure than she should have in setting him straight. Rather than use the voteo to contact Lt. Savon, she telepathically informed him about the new plans for the team to take noon meal at the eatery, and that local Security Corp officers would watch the camp. He informed her that he'd relay the message to everyone else. Castellan's thoughts were interrupted by a light mental nudge. She recognized Olivienne's 'feel' in her head. *"Yes?"*

"I don't hear you making friends over there."

Tosh flushed at the notion that Olivienne had heard her words to Cmdr. Dendin. *"The need for professionalism far outweighs the desire of friendship. Dendin was out of line."*

"Since when do you get so defensive of my sorry sovereign carcass?"

Castellan wasn't sure she understood her own action, let alone be able to explain it to someone else. Especially the Connate. She strengthened the wall she had to prevent snooping of her deeper thoughts and responded. *"Despite our dalliance, I do take my job quite seriously. Denigrating our nation's sovereigns is offensive and rude and I will not tolerate it."*

The Connate smiled from where she reclined on her own bedroll, nude as she was the instant Tosh left to go back to her own cube. The tempyrature inside was elevated from the stone heater and she was tired of pouring over documents that yielded no more clues to the specific location of temple treasure. *"Why are you still over there talking to me mind to mind? Why not just come back to keep me company?"*

"Why not?" Castellan smirked at the other woman's reasoning, because there was none other than 'why not.' At that moment there was nothing between them other than casual bedmates. But as much as Castellan enjoyed their dalliance together, she also worried that it would change and go too far if they spent too much time together. Just as she had told the Queen wekes before, she had no time in her life for things such as romance or the consorage it inevitably led to.

If she were promoted away from the Connate's Shield unit in the future, it would be best for everyone if they were not too attached. For Castellan Tosh, her career had always been her compass in life. She wasn't sure what she would do if she no longer had the goal of rising to the top whilst contributing to home and country.

Almost as if Olivienne could hear those private most thoughts, she changed her request. *"Will you?"*

"That depends."

Violet eyes rolled in exasperation. *"Depends on what, Commander?"*

"On whether or not you are as nude as when I left you two oors ago."

Olivienne grinned and responded with mock affront. *"Of course not! What do you take me for, the pampered thespians in the Service Corp?"*

No sooner had she finished speaking when Castellan came through the connector between the cubes. She was looking down when she cleared the opening and turned to re-fasten it again immediately. That was why the Connate's nudity took her completely by surprise. "Sheddech! Why aren't you dressed?" Tosh looked away from Olivienne's laughing face and divine body, hoping to slow her pulse back to its normal pace.

"Oh, don't be such a prude, Commander. You cannot convince me that you didn't appreciate the view. Besides, it's not like you haven't seen me in every state imaginable by now."

Castellan had come into Olivienne's sleep cube in absolute professional mode and it was impossible for her to switch gears so fast. Not completely sure how to act, she kept her eyes fixed on the side of the Connate's cube even as she heard rustling from the nude woman's location. "I appreciate a great many things but we have noon meal plans at the eatery —"

"Noon meal is three oors away. Won't you look at me, just for a sec?"

Olivienne's voice was decidedly closer and Castellan shut her eyes to avoid the temptation. She clenched her jaw when deliciously smooth skin brushed against the knuckles of her left hand where it was clenched at her side. "I should probably return to my cube while you dress —"

A firm hand gently turned Castellan's face to the left and she opened her eyes just as Olivienne brushed her lips with a kiss. The Connate backed away an ince when the kiss was done and met her heated gaze. "You don't really want to do that, do you?" In a blink, Castellan found herself nude as well and watched as her clothes reappeared on a duffel next to the bedroll. Olivienne smirked and that was all it took for the commander to act.

Castellan turned and practically tackled the sovereign to the bedroll, pinning her instantly with her greater muscular bulk. "You are going to pay for that!"

Olivienne tickled her lover's side, causing Castellan to squirm. "Oh yeah? And who is going to elicit this payment from me?"

As it had often been said, turnabout was fair play. And thinking of those words in that moment, Castellan used her telekinesis to completely pin the woman below her. With her channel rating, there was no way the Connate could break free and the look in those dark eyes said that she was well aware of the fact. Alternately, pale blue eyes twinkled with pent up humor. "Who indeed?" Then she adjusted Olivienne's position so that her limbs were spread to all four directions. The throbbing pulse in the Connate's neck increased with the knowledge that she was so exposed and completely at Tosh's mercy. She had never been held so completely before, at least not by someone as powerful as Tosh. It was quite exhilarating knowing that she could not win free.

Instead of struggling, she stared straight into Castellan's eyes and wet her suddenly dry lips. "Perhaps you should deal with your 'handful' of an assignment now, Commander."

Tosh knelt between the prone woman's legs and leaned over until she could whisper in Olivienne's ear. "Oh, I will..." The officer's voice trailed off as she moved her mouth down to lightly bite Olivienne's neck.

The Connate writhed below her. "Don't tease!"

"Who's teasing?"

Castellan moved lower still and Olivienne stifled a whimper. The droning of the rain had quieted somewhat and it wouldn't do for the entire Shield team to hear their goings on. Though she was hard pressed to stay silent when the woman above her took a firm nipple between her teeth. Her voice was a desperate whisper. "Tosh..."

Castellan looked up at the light warning in the Connate's voice. There were a multitude of things swimming in Olivienne's eyes, none of which the officer could decipher. "Does it bother you to be so helpless below me?" Tosh's grin was a little predatory.

Olivienne swallowed at the other woman's hungry look but still answered the question. "It doesn't bother me, per se. But I'm certainly not used to it."

"Does it frighten you?"

Their eyes met and both women felt a moment of truth come over them. "No, I'm not afraid at all."

Tosh cocked her head and peered down at her lover. "You trust me with your passion?"

Olivienne's voice was soft and sincere. "Castellan...I trust you with my life. It cannot get deeper than that."

It was but a mere thought that came back to her. *"I suppose not."* Then before Olivienne could think to decipher either Tosh's mood, or her mental words, she was besieged by a pleasure as the officer began stimulating her in multiple places at once. Tosh kissed her even as she took Olivienne's breasts into her hands. If the Connate were capable of rational thought in that moment, she would have been truly impressed that Castellan could hold her down so thoroughly while engaged in other activities. Not only that, but a startling and titillating pressure had begun to rub along her clitoris. But rational awareness was lost as Olivienne spiraled higher and higher, writhing within the bounds of Tosh's mental grip. It was a glorious way to kill a few oors' time.

Chapter Sixteen

LUNCH WAS MUCH appreciated by the entire unit, especially Olivienne and Castellan. When the meal was finished, Olivienne took the opportunity to speak with the owners of the eatery. Murph and Sarae were a consoral couple, old-timers that had lived in Natus their entire life. She explained that she was looking for something that was only referred to as a treasure, and that she knew it was located on Mater Island. Sarae was striking with her carefully pinned white-hair and an oceanic-blue flowing pantsuit that was exactly the color of her eyes. Her shirt was open at the front, beautifully displaying the matching blue tattoo of consorage around her neck. She looked up from Olivienne's unclassified notes with surprise.

"Oh! Mayhaps you're looking for the Fortuna Ligno!"

Both Olvienne and Tosh's attention focused on the old woman. It was the Connate who spoke up. "Fortuna Ligno? Fortune tree? What exactly is that?"

Murph joined his par where she stood talking to their esteemed guests. "They say it's the tallest tree on Mater. Now I've never been so close as to confirm, but they say that the tip of the tree turns golden when Archeos rises in the morning. Because of its famous size and strange gold tip, the local legend has always referred to it as the fortune tree."

Castellan turned to the experienced historical adventurist. "What do you think?"

The Connate closed her eyes and recalled the texts she had been reading since discovering the Antaeus translation. Finally she opened them again and was caught by the intensity of her lover's gaze. Tosh's eyes reminded her of the pale blue light of Illeos and she had to give herself a mental shake to bring her mind back to the task at hand. "I feel as though we're on the right track." Olivienne turned back to Murph and Sarae. "Do you know where the tree is located?"

The couple shook their heads. Murph looked apologetic as he spoke. "As I said, I haven't been there myself. But you may want to check with a few of those research types at the station. They have all kinds of maps of the island. Perhaps they can help you out. I'm sorry I can't be of more assistance, Connate Dracore."

Olivienne smiled at the older man. "No, you've done plenty already. Your information has aided me considerably and I appreciate it."

"You're much nicer than the publications always say."

Murph's face paled and abject horror crawled across his features. "Sarae! You can't speak that way about a sovereign!"

Sarae looked at him and snorted. "Why not? She seems like the type to appreciate a little truth."

Tosh covered a smile with her hand but Olivienne was unable to stop the laughter from bubbling up at the words spoken by someone easily old enough to be someone's avia. "Actually, I prefer the truth. And to give you a bit in return, I've always taken my job as historical adventurist quite seriously. Unfortunately, not everyone else does. As a matter of fact, it irritates some members of the Imperium that I refuse to quietly settle someplace and wait my turn for the Cathedra."

"Ahh, well that makes more sense!"

Cmdr. Tosh looked at the old woman curiously. "Really?"

Sarae nodded. "Sure. Our government is a system of balance and power. The Queen has the most power so it makes sense that the Imperium would want more. And controlling someone is just another way of stealing their power. If certain members can't control Connate Dracore, then it stands to reason they'd want to control how others see her."

Castellan and Olivienne looked at each other in surprise, then back at Sarae. Olivienne found the words to speak first. "That is surprisingly insightful and does make complete sense. Maybe you should come be my advisor when that time comes that I'm required to make my ascendance as Queen!"

Sarae waved her hand through the air and grinned affably. "Oh, nonsense! I'm much too old for all that. Besides, your dashing companion will give you better advice than most. I think you'll be just fine with Commander Tosh." Her words sent Olivienne deep into thought about her future as Queen. She sincerely hoped it was a long ways off.

Dismayed, Castellan looked closer at the old woman and received a wink for her trouble. She tried to fathom whether or not Sarae was prescient, or if she were just making a random guess. The implication was clear enough, she was saying in no uncertain terms that Castellan would still be around when Olivienne became Queen. Suddenly fearful for the safety of Olivara,

Tosh took advantage of the Connate's distraction. She gave a tele-pathic nudge to Sarae and was lucky enough to discover that the aged psera had the telepathy channel.

"Yes, Commander?"

Tosh sent back the words that had frozen her veins with fear. *"Soon?"*

Sarae gave a small shake of her head. *"No, not for tens of rotos. It will be long after I'm gone and that is all I will say to you."*

"Sarae," Castellan said the name aloud and suddenly it clicked. "You're the weather witch that Commander Dendin was talking about!"

Olivienne snapped out of her reverie. "What's that?"

Sarae shook her head ever so slightly at Tosh so the com-mander kept quiet about what had been said. "She's the one that predicts many of the storms for the area."

The Connate grinned anew at the old woman. "Well that is certainly handy in a coastal town!" She looked at both eatery owners with appreciation. "I can't stress enough how grateful I am for your help todae."

Murph finally spoke up. "The pleasure is all ours, Connate Dracore. It was an honor to serve you and Commander Tosh, as well as your fine guardians. Please don't hesitate to stop in again before you leave."

Olivienne glanced at Tosh then smiled at him. "Perhaps we will." It was still raining when the large group left the eatery. Tosh set up a rotation for the guardians to cycle through the dorm shower facilities. She and Olivienne took a team of six to the research station office to inquire about possible maps of Mater. Much to their pleasurable surprise, they not only acquired a map, but it had the location of the Fortuna Ligno clearly marked on it. It wasn't precise because researchers had to rely on their channels to get most information. But at least it was a start.

When they returned to the camp, Olivienne opted to go with the second to last shift of guardians to the dorm for her own shower and Tosh retreated back to her cube. The old woman's words gave her much to ponder. Did they mean that her career was destined to stall, thus guaranteeing that she'd wind up as the Connate's Shield Commander for the rest of her daes? Then Cas-tellan thought on what else Sarae had said, that when Olivienne is Queen, she would be taking advice from Tosh. Advising the Queen was not the typical role of a Shield Corp captain. The role of advisor was usually reserved for the King...her own thoughts ground to a halt on that scenario. "Sheddech." The profanity slipped from between Tosh's lips as the true meaning of Sarae's words dawned on her.

She stopped thinking after that, instead reviewing the plan that she and Olivienne had put together for their trip to the island. Castellan had no time for idle wanderings and half-worked premonitions of an old weather-teller. She had a job to do.

That evening after their meal, Olivienne, Castellan, Lt. Savon, and Lt. Madlin went over the plan one last time. The main island team's goal was to make their way undetected through the forest until they came to the Fortuna Ligno. After that, six people would scour the tree from bottom to top, looking for anything that didn't seem to belong and the other two would stand guard and watch for rocs.

Castellan was certain that she had chosen the right mix of individuals to go to Mater. She tried to select only specialists that had hard channels, assuming they would be the most help if things went sour with the rocs. Spc. Devin and Spc Qent were from the original unit and while Qent had no hard channel, he had a sub-degree as a historical adventurist and was the only one with advanced water training. Spc. Yazzie was the medican going to Mater and she had a telekinesis rating of four, as did Lt. Madlin who was also chosen. Spc. Legget was an engineer and had a ferrokinesis rating of four, and Spc. Dante Lazaro was the communications specialist and he had an apportation rating of three. With a three rating he could easily grab sixty pund objects at a time with minimal effort. One potential use for Lazaro's ability was to apport stones above any rocs, should they happen to attack the team.

It was near twenty-two hundred oors when the two lieutenants finally went back to their own cubes. That left Olivienne and Tosh in the silence of the commander's cube. It didn't escape the Connate's notice that Castellan had carefully laid out her bedroll in preparation for the night ahead. She half expected the officer to invite her to stay, hoped even, but Tosh never made mention of wanting a bedmate for the evening. Finally she stood and stretched, ignoring the cautious gaze of her Shield unit commander. "Well, I think I'm going to bed down. We have to be at the boat at second sunrise tomorrow, and morning comes early."

Castellan's response was just as careful as her eyes. "Yes, I suppose you're right."

Olivienne smiled ruefully. "I don't know what is more exciting, finally beginning this portion of the adventure, or the thought of seeing the suns again after daes of rain. Though I'm sure your main thought is on the adventure ahead and the safety of the sovereign under your protection."

"Honestly?" The Connate nodded. "I could do without the rain as well. And the adventure itself is exciting too. I've read so many documents with you that I feel as though I'm half adventurist myself!"

"Well, you're certainly more qualified for the role than any other officer I've met."

Tosh smiled and some of the awkwardness between them dissipated. "Well, I'm not just any officer. According to Commander Dendin, I'm *famous* in certain circles!"

Olivienne laughed at Tosh's sarcasm-laced declaration. "I'd be willing to bet you're infamous in many others!"

Her stoic shell cracked and Castellan burst into laughter. "That is exactly what I told him!" She shrugged as her humor settled. Silence descended on the cube again as the rain pattered against the fabric around them.

Seeing she wasn't going to receive an invite to stay, Olivienne turned toward the connector that led back to her own cube. "Goodnight, Commander, I'll see you in the morn."

Their eyes met just before Olivienne went through the doorway and Castellan nodded back to her. "Good night, Olivienne." Tosh stared at the opening for nearly five meens after it shut behind the Connate. She could see clearly what Olivienne had wanted, it was written in those expressive violet eyes. And it took all her self-control not to issue the invitation. Castellan needed a clear mind for the mission ahead and she would not have that advantage if she woke wrapped in the Connate's warm embrace. Too much was happening between them that she didn't understand. The confusing roil of emotions kept her unsteady and off-kilter and she wasn't a fan of the lack of control she felt. Tosh was afraid that continued intimacy while she felt as such would mean a head left anything but clear when they set sail for Mater. And Psiere could ill-afford a lapse in diligence where one of the sovereigns was concerned.

THE SEA BREEZE and smell of salt in the air was exhilarating in the early morn. Olivienne stood at the bow of the large fishing vessel as it plunged through the two-foot waves that were the only remnants of the storms. Olivienne was frustrated because Tosh had reverted back to that professional officer with the coming dae. She had felt the other woman pull away the night before and it stung, but her rational mind knew that they had to focus on the mission ahead. She didn't have to like it though.

"We're approaching the drop off point for Lieutenant Savon's team now."

She startled when Castellan interrupted her ocean gazing. Olivienne moved over and made room at the railing for Tosh. "He didn't seem too happy last night when you told him he was directing the backup team on Filia."

Castellan smirked. "Is that your empathy talking now, Connate Dracore?" She teased with a referenced channel the Connate didn't have but Olivienne remained serious.

"No. I've known Savon a few rotos now and I don't need empathy to see how he's feeling, just my eyes." She turned to look fully at Castellan. The officer wore the black uniform so well, so strong. "Are you sure of your choices in this?"

"As sure as I can be. I refuse to second-guess myself now. I spent too many oors putting together your Shield unit, and even more selecting the teams for this particular mission. I know that Specialists Soleng, Dozier, Penn, and Calderon were disappointed at having to remain at base camp but the others had skills more qualified for this particular mission. The camp needs to be secured so they were chosen. But that will not always be the case and I made that very clear to them. Each mission we plan will require a unique set of skills and I did my best to make sure all skills were accounted for in this unit. Small teams are mutable and who knows what we will need in the future. Besides, this will encourage the younger ones to continue their advanced training and certifications. It never hurts to keep growing your skills, right?"

Olivienne wasn't surprised that Castellan had put so much thought into her guardians, and the team placements for their current mission in particular. She looked up at the officer then and noticed a small lock of hair had come lose from her otherwise pristine appearance. They finally neared a small strip of beach on the eastern end of Filia and the boat began to slow. Before they could be distracted by the exit of Lt. Savon and Specialists Lear, Meza, and Holling, Olivienne reached up to smooth that distracting bit of hair. "And what skills have you been growing, Commander?"

Castellan recognized Olivienne's grin for what it was and appreciated the small break in seriousness for the moment. She gave the Connate a wicked grin in return and let playfulness color her voice. "Why my dear Olivienne, you don't know? Between the two of us, I think we've elevated dalliance to an art form worthy of Service Corp appointment!"

"It's no wonder you're infamous in those circles." The Connate gave the officer a slight shove. "Now go see your team off so we can get on with the rest of the trip!" Tosh saluted her smartly then walked toward the stern of the ship and Olivienne was left in thought. Had she not been watching the officer's face when she mentioned their dalliance, she may have been stung by the words. The Connate had finally admitted to herself the night before that her feelings for the staid and stubborn officer went beyond mere dalliance. But as she had just told Tosh, one didn't need an empathy channel to see someone's feelings. Sometimes their eyes told more than any words from their mouth, and those pale blue eyes held more than Tosh's proclamation of dalliance. Only time would tell if Castellan's lips would hold more as well.

The ship they were on was quite large and they used a smaller boat to ferry the team to the island. The owner of the vessel informed them that Lt. Savon and the others should be safe and secluded from the rocs that soared the ocean breeze above. There were no eggs or hatchlings on Filia, just an abundance of giant trees and black sand. It had taken the ship two oors to get to the first island and the steersman said it would be another oor before they arrived at Mater. Olivienne requested to be deposited as close as possible to the eastern end of Mater. That would give the team good tree cover for the entire trip to the interior of the island where the Fortuna Ligno was supposed to be located.

The remaining eight occasionally looked up and see the rocs circling high above. "They don't look that big, nothing like our briefing vellums stated." It was Lt. Madlin who spoke her mind, but the other specialists nodded along with her words.

The steersman laughed heartily. She was big-boned with fair hair and a face reddened by salt, wind, and suns. She glanced at the group of black uniformed Shield Corp guardians on the deck of the ship. "You only think that because they're so high up." She pointed at Spc. Lazaro who was the tallest of the group at six foot six inces. "Those rocs up there are probably near twice his height, and they're strong enough to pick up the biggest of you and fly away."

Castellan gave her a sober look. "Any advice you can give us about the island?"

The steersman nodded. "Don't go near the boulders on the south shore, that's where they lay their eggs. And they're drawn to movement so avoid attracting their attention at all costs."

Olivienne spoke up next. "How do we do that?"

The weathered sailor grinned and showed strong white teeth. "Don't run."

A little over an oor later, the small team of eight was deposited on a strip of black sand not even big enough to call a beach. The tree line came nearly to the water so it was no great effort to scramble up the slight hill and into the cover of the thick canopy. While the air still smelled of salt and sea, it took on a different quality within the forest proper. Their boots made a muffled sound as they walked across the needle-covered loam and nearly half the light of the suns was blocked by the canopy above. "It's no wonder they said we'd be safe from the rocs while in the forest!" There was a feel to the area that prompted Olivienne to keep her voice low. They weren't really sure how good the hearing was of the mammoth birds, but no one wanted to chance it.

Tosh consulted the map that they were given at the research station. "According to our map, we've got approximately a sixty mahl hike to the general location of the treasure. Or at least what we guess is the treasure. You've been keeping in top condition and I'm going to warn you that this is still going to tax you. We've got twenty mahl hikes ahead of us for the next three daes in order to reach the interior where the Fortuna Ligno is located." Someone in the group groaned and she cut a glance toward the sound. "Problem, Specialist Qent? Is that too far for your lily feet?"

The guardian's eyes widened and his cheeks flushed at her words. "No, ser! The distance isn't a problem, I've done adventurist missions in the past. But I've never done them kitted out with Shield Corp gear."

Castellan frowned. "I know it's going to be rough and we haven't had nearly enough time to train for this but I have confidence in this team. All your packs are between fifty and seventy punds, easy enough for any of you to handle. I've lowered our loads as much as possible while still having the minimum to do our job. What is our job here?" No one answered as she glanced around at the six guardians. Olivienne watched and waited for Tosh's next words. "Our job is not to protect the Connate—"

"Ser?" The interruption came from Spc. Yazzie, one of the unit's medicans.

The commander shook her head and kept going. "Our job is not to assist with Connate Dracore's historical adventurist agenda." She paused as all six faces looked back at her in confusion. "No, this team is part of a new type of Shield Corp unit. We will be performing both tasks, and must prepare for both. I know it is difficult and more challenging than standard duty but I have faith that every one of you has the skills to succeed. You have the finest gear available, the lightest boots the Corp provides, and I've lightened your loads to thirty-five percent of your body weight. And the only reason it is that much is because we need gear for the adventurist side of the mission, on top of the things we need to keep the Connate safe. Do you have any more questions or concerns? Because if you don't think you can make it at this point, I'm going to send you out to the beach to wait for the boat to come back around."

A chorus came back in response. "No, ser!"

She nodded. "Good. The dae is already ahead of us so we need to make haste if we want to reach our distance goal by evening." With those words she turned on her heel and began trekking toward the interior. She had checked her compass when they arrived and knew the direction they needed to go.

After walking for nearly an oor, Olivienne caught up with Tosh and looked at her with concern. "I had no idea they were carrying so much. My own gear is significantly lighter."

Tosh looked at her companion, the rest of the guardians had spread out in the four cardinal directions to provide the most scouting and cover. "You're not wearing armor, nor are you carrying weapons other than your pistol. We have basic kit we are required to carry that you never would need as an adventurist. Some of the team members are only able to carry their primary task kit, so the rest of their gear is spread out to the others."

"Task kit?"

"Yes. Take Specialist Lazaro over there..." She pointed off to their right where the man in question was hiking along. "As our communications specialist, he's the one who has to carry the long range voteo. The amount of illeostones needed to power that thing means he can't carry much more than the communicator. He's got his rifle, pistol, and a canteen, but that's it. His cubemate is carrying the cube, as well as the rest of his gear. And over there..." Castellan trailed off again as she pointed out Spc. Yazzie.

"Our medican has to be better prepared than those normally in the field because one of our charges is you. Your health takes higher priority than any other wounded corpsman. I had to be sure my medicans had the best training, and also the best equipment. So her primary task kit is also extensive."

Olivienne's awe of both Castellan's leadership skills and her team's grew the more she learned of what went into her protection. The Connate had spent many rotos complaining that her Shield Corp guardians had no understanding of the work and expertise that was required of her as a historical adventurist. But for the first time Olivienne realized that she had no clue about what went into being her guardian. She found herself looking forward to learning more about her commander and the team as a whole.

There was a slight incline on the first dae but it eventually leveled out as they made their way toward the center of the island. Every member of the group was glad when they hit relatively flat ground because even the slight incline was enough to add weight to their steps as they hiked through the initial twenty mahls. Castellan made sure they stopped every two oors for a break of water, food, or rest. She herself carried the condenser that provided water for the team once their canteens ran out. At the end of the second dae, they made camp by a small stream. It was the first water that they'd seen and Tosh opted to follow it the next dae since it was running in exactly the direction they needed to go.

It was easy enough to become agoraphobic as they walked through the massive tree trunks. Each one was wider than a hauler at the base. On the morning of the third dae, Olivienne made a remark that sent a chill through Tosh's bones. "They say these trees live for thousands of rotos. A person could feel small indeed within the press of such immense age."

"I'm not gonna lie, this place gives me the creeps." Spc. Qent was the youngest on the Mater team at only twenty-one rotos. He jumped as they heard another shriek echo through the forest.

Every so often they'd see vague shadows flickering from where the rocs circled overhead. Castellan had a feeling the birds knew they were on the ground below, but she figured they wouldn't attack as long as the team was in the forest proper. There wasn't nearly enough space for such a massive wingspan to be maneuverable. As luck would have it, those were the words that haunted her late on the third dae of hiking. They had to leave the stream around midafternoon in order to follow the compass point. It was only a few oors after that when they came to the edge of a clearing. As the group looked out from the safety of the tree line, Castellan's attention was caught and held by the multitude of circling shapes in the air. "Bollux! A pox on those beasts I tell you!" She was so focused on what was in the air above them that she failed to notice the most important part of the clearing.

"Tosh."

Castellan looked to where Olivienne stood at her left side, then she followed the Connate's pointing finger to the largest tree she'd ever seen. It easily rose another twenty yords above the other greatwood trees that ringed the clearing. "That's it!"

Lt. Madlin stood to Tosh's right side. "Clearly that must be the Fortuna Ligno but how will we get across the clearing?" She squinted toward the massive tree. "The distance looks like it would take us a little over a meen to sprint without gear. So maybe five hundred yords? We could try circling around to see if it's closer to the tree line on the other side but I'd wager not."

With another glance at the sky, Cmdr. Tosh made an easy decision. "It's near enough to the end of the dae and we're all exhausted from the march in so let's pull back farther into the forest and set up camp for the night. Then Connate Dracore, Lt. Madlin and I will confer on what options are available to us in the morning. Savvy?"

All seven people nodded in agreement, six of them responding with a hearty, "yes, ser."

While camp was set, Castellan called both Madlin and Olivienne to walk with her along the edge of the clearing. "I have an idea but it's dangerous."

Olivienne raised a dark brow at her words. "Is there any realistic plan that would take us through that field and not be dangerous?"

Tosh looked at her. "You mean besides killing all the rocs ahead of time? No, probably not."

"What about camouflage, Commander?"

Tosh pointed at her lieutenant and smiled. "Exactly. The field is full of tall grass that is in all manner of disarray. From the information in the mission packet, we know that the birds hunt primarily sea life, so they will be attuned to spotting prey that is in the water. Their middle talons are longer to facilitate 'fishing' for their dinner. I have a hunch that they won't see nearly so well when peering down at the grass instead of the waves. We can cut swatches to tie to our backs and do a field crawl across to the tree. Once under the canopy of the Fortuna Ligno, we should be safe again from their prying eyes and sharp beaks."

"I'd say that sounds like a reasonable plan." Olivienne nodded unconsciously in approval.

Lt. Madlin looked at her with concern. "Connate Dracore, will you be able to do the field crawl?"

Castellan hid a smile behind her closed hand as she watched Olivienne's face turn red. "I'll have you know, Lieutenant, that I was crawling through mahls of cave tunnels, many of which were coated in rancid batt dung, before you had even entered officer training!" She snorted in affront. "Of course I can do the field crawl!"

The lieutenant flushed with embarrassment and Tosh thought it wise to save the poor woman. "It was a valid concern but rest assured, Connate Dracore is tougher than most." She grinned at Olivienne and got a scowl in return.

The first sun had yet to break the horizon when Castellan rose for the dae. She stood at the edge of the clearing with a hot mug of pekoe, watching the sky lighten. Something in her awareness told her that another person was approaching from the darkness behind so she wasn't startled when Olivienne stepped into the space beside her. The Connate had her own hot mug that she sipped from. "What do you think we'll find? I don't look forward to searching that entire tree."

Tosh shrugged. "I'm not really sure, this is your bailiwick now. I'm nothing more than a poor officer charged with saving your skin should you get foolish. Your head guardian."

Olivienne turned to her in the twilight of early morn. "You speak untruth as smooth as you shoot a pistol."

"Oh? And which of my words were untrue? Are you denying that you have a penchant for leaping before you look, implying that you don't perform foolish things on occasion?"

"No, I am disagreeing with the words that said you were nothing more to me than a guardian. You are more, you know. You —" Her words were interrupted by Spc. Yazzie as she walked up from the camp.

"By the Makers! Have you ever seen such a thing?"

Castellan and Olivienne followed her pointing finger to stare in awe at the top of the Fortuna Ligno. The rising sun of Archeos had bathed it in golden light. "Murph was right!"

Olivienne's voice came softly on the heels of Tosh's words.

"It's beautiful."

They had no more time to admire the treasure tree because Lt. Madlin broke their collective reverie with her voice and her approach. "Commander, I instructed Specialist Devin and Specialist Leggett to cut tall grass to use as camouflage before suns' rise. We're ready to equip and head across.

Castellan grinned at the news but when she turned toward Olivienne, she caught a fleeting look of disappointment. The Connate's moment of admission was lost with the onrush of dae and she wasn't sure she'd have the constitution to bring it up again. Tosh hadn't invited her to share a bedroll since base camp and she worried. Olivienne felt as though a distance had grown between them and she had no clue as to why the commander had pulled away.

Rather than dwell on that loss, she shook free from her maudlin thoughts to focus on the task at hand. When she looked up again, Castellan was looking at her strangely with those pale blue eyes. Tosh just wanted to get the mission complete so she could get the Connate back on safe ground. She had a job to do and could not afford to be distracted. Their reasons were different, but both knew that focus on the mission was more important than anything else.

Chapter Seventeen

IT TOOK NEARLY an oor for the team to slowly make their way through the field to the massive tree. Once all eight people had assembled beneath the canopy, Tosh split the group in half to walk around the perimeter of the residence-size trunk. When the two groups met on the other side, they stared up in awe at the immense opening. It was easily five yords tall and two across and the base. It looked as if a giant had split the wood open with its hands.

"I suppose that's where we need to go." Olivienne couldn't take her eyes off the black fissure in the trunk. It was already gloomy beneath the massive canopy but the blackness was especially dark inside the hole. Dim light only extended a few paces inside and highlighted the walls of a wooden tunnel of sorts.

Castellan glanced from the opening back to the Connate. "I should go in first—"

Her words were interrupted by a sharp look and quick response from Olivienne. "And do what, exactly? I am the adventurist here, Commander. Or did you forget?"

Tosh's face darkened. "I have not forgotten, Connate Dracore. But I and my team are responsible for your safety and none of us know what is inside."

"Exactly."

The commander looked at her sovereign in surprise, not expecting that answer. "Come again?"

Olivienne sighed and pointed toward the opening and the rest of the unit spread out around the trunk to both, give the pair space, and to watch for any incoming threats. "I said, that is exactly my point. While you may be a highly capable and experienced officer, I am the one with experience in this arena. As you stated before, this is my bailiwick. I've found traps and other sensitive setups during my adventuring. You would neither know what to look for, nor would you know how to disarm such things if you haven't seen them before."

Castellan's face took on a familiar obstinate look but her voice was quiet when she spoke. "If something happens to you..."

The Connate's breath froze and she wondered what words

would come from her difficult lover's lips. When Tosh's words trailed off, Olivienne was prompted to speak. "If something happens to me, what?"

"If something happens to you the entire nation of Psiere will be in a panic and your mother will surely have my head."

The sovereign sighed as Castellan once again took the safe road. "Tosh, trust me to do my job here. We all have our strengths, and I'm very good at what I do. I *need* to be able to do my job."

After a few secs pause, the commander finally nodded her assent. "You're right and I apologize. However, Specialist Qent and I will accompany you inside."

Seeing a fair deal when it was right in front of her, Olivienne nodded as well. She knew that Tosh was worried about her beyond the job at hand, regardless of what the officer did and did not say. "Fine."

Tosh gave a mental push to the entire team then spoke telepathically to them all. *"Connate Dracore and I will be entering the tree and we'll take Specialist Qent with us since he's the only other one here with adventurist training besides the Connate. Lieutenant Madlin will take command outside until we return."*

Qent came around the tree to the large entrance while the other six spread out to cover evenly around the trunk. "I've only gone on a few adventures when I was getting my sub-degree. What are we looking for first?" Spc. Qent seemed nervous but Castellan had faith in him.

Olivienne rifled through her pack and pulled out an illeostone powered light and the other two followed suit. "I'll go in first and you two will follow close behind. I've had caves and other structures that had intricate traps upon entry. Some just have puzzles to solve before doors would open."

Tosh nodded. "I read that the great pyramids had hundreds of such puzzles and traps when we first got them open generations ago. Why did the Makers make artifact and document retrieval so hazardous?"

"I read a translated document once that spoke of tests of skill, courage, and tenacity. From what I gathered, the Makers believed that knowledge should be earned and not given freely to people who have neither the capacity, nor the will to see it implemented in a safe and beneficial way. Truthfully, I'm not expecting much because of the remote location and the fact that the chamber is inside a living tree. I don't think the Makers would want to harm the tree in any way so they'd be limited with what they could do in the space available. I'll watch for wires, either above or down at trip level. We should also keep an eye on the ground. I think we're fairly safe if it has a dirt floor but you can never tell. When we enter we should watch for patterns on the floor of the opening. Ready?"

Both the Shield Corp members nodded and Olivienne turned to enter the tree. The pace was kept slow as Olivienne constantly checked the walls and ground in front of them. They walked through a tall vertical tunnel for about nine yords before they came to a chamber. As soon as they broke free of the entryway, all three stopped in awe at what they saw. Their eyes adjusted to the gloom and they were able to see the entire perimeter of the inner tree with the glow of their lamps. "Sheddech!" The word may have come from Qent's mouth but all three were thinking it.

Three lamps illuminated a roughly round space in the center of the tree. It extended more than twenty yords across and with a height that was difficult to determine. Olivienne would have loved to light it up even more with her channel but pyrokinesis was too much of a risk inside the greatwood. Perhaps the most fascinating thing about the hollowed room was the steps carved into the inner wall that circled upward, spiraling around inside the trunk. "Looks like we're going up. Look sharp though, the stairs are narrow."

"Yes, ser." Olivienne smirked at Castellan's response then started a slow ascent up the carved wooden stairs.

Castellan shined her light on the wall and took special interest in the carvings. "Look..." Olivienne was ahead of her and Spc. Qent followed a step behind. "Is there special importance to an eight pointed star?"

The Connate shrugged in the dim light. "Not that I know of. They seem to be carved right next to each step. Let's keep going."

As they were only four steps up, the Connate continued slowly. When she stepped onto the seventh step, Tosh got a feeling that came straight from her intuition channel. "Wait!" Everyone froze and the commander shined her light farther up. "There's no carving next to the eighth step."

Olivienne knelt down on the one she was on so she could peer closer at the one above. She shined her own light on the roughly thirty ince wide step and called for Tosh's as well. "Shine right here, please." Castellan adjusted her beam and Olivienne pointed at a faint line that outlined the eighth step. "See there?"

Both Tosh and Qent leaned closer.

"What is it?"

Qent whistled softly. "Looks like a step trap. But what does it do?"

The sovereign shined the light farther up. "I've seen a few different types. Some drop away once your weight is pressing down, others will trigger other contraptions or weapons." She looked around the shadowed interior of the hollowed out great-wood tree. "I can't see anything obvious but a weapon could come from anywhere. They're usually projectiles and it would be impossible to determine exactly what in this light."

"Should I go ahead of you?"

Olivienne narrowed her eyes at the commander. "Just follow my lead and don't put any weight on that step for any reason." Sure enough, every time there was a step that didn't have a corresponding carving, Olivienne made sure to guide them over it. After climbing more than a hundred stairs, they finally found themselves on a platform large enough to fit five people. When they shined their lanterns on the wall of the tree, the Connate grinned to see a metal box set into the wood.

"Is that grown into the wall?" Tosh reached up to touch the wood that seemed as if it had grown around the box, trapping in in place. The only thing they could really see clearly was the intricate lock on the front. "Will you just cut it away?"

Qent shook his head. "You can't just cut stuff like that because you don't know how delicate either the box is, or whatever is inside the box. You could damage the treasure you seek."

"He's right. I've dealt with similar things before because so many of the artifacts left by the Makers have been lost for generations. It's easy enough to strip away small bits of the surrounding wood using apportation."

Specialist Qent shined his light farther above them but only saw darkness. He had no idea how high the hollow of the massive tree rose into the trunk. "What do you need us to do while you work?"

Olivienne pulled her gaze away from the box and shined her own light around. "Just keep an eye out for any movement, listen for any sounds that don't seem as though they belong. I don't want to accidentally set off anything while I free this."

It took about twenty meens to remove enough wood for the box to pull free of the wall. It was painstaking work to carve it out bit by bit but eventually she was able to take it in hand. "Should we open it here?"

Castellan looked at the metal box in Olivienne's hands. It was about eight inces wide, two tall, and five inces deep. "I have a three rating ferrokinesis, I could probably remove the lock, or even put a crude hole in the side. Though Leggett has a higher rating and could probably do either with more accuracy." She started to reach her hand out then stopped again.

"What is it?"

Tosh answered Olivienne's question without taking her eyes off the box. "We should wait. I'm certain that we should have Lieutenant Madlin put her hands on it before we go any further." When the Connate gave her a curious look, she elaborated. "She's rated four in psychometry, she'll be able to give us some history before we do anything rash."

"You're right, that's a resource I didn't consider at all." Olivienne turned to Castellan with a big smile on her face. "There may be some merit to your special team after all!"

Tosh grinned back. "I have my moments."

As soon as Olivienne moved from the platform onto the top step Qent paused. "Can you hear that? It's coming from above us."

Without another word from him, Tosh used her telekinesis to sweep all three of them off the supportive steps and platform into the blackness in the center of the tree. But rather than free fall to the ground, she controlled their decent to the center of the chamber with her levitation. When their feet hit the ground, all three people shined their lanterns above and Spc. Qent's eyes widened. Crashing sounded above and they ran toward the place where light was streaming in through the tunnel. As soon as they reached the outside of the tree, they collapsed to the ground and a muffled *whoomp* followed their relief as well as a goodly amount of dust. Castellan looked at Qent in the dim light of the suns as it filtered through the canopy above. "What was that?"

He gave her a wide-eyed look, clearly still shaken. "I don't know, but it was massive and it fell from the ceiling. Our weight on the platform itself must have been a trigger, which released as soon as Connate Dracore stepped off and the weight on it was decreased. "

Olivienne groaned as she stood and inspected the entrance to the middle of the tree. "Bollux, I should have known to look for that! I'm such an idiot!"

Tosh stood as well and put her hand on Olivienne's shoulder. "It's all right, we all survived."

"It was that close." Tosh followed the Connate's finger to see what she was pointing at only to find smooth wood at the end of the short tunnel they'd come through. Whatever had fallen from the ceiling inside the hollowed out tree had filled the entire space at the bottom. They would have been crushed flat.

"Close only counts when you're pitching dung. Is everyone okay?" Lt. Madlin had come around the base of the tree to see what the commotion was about.

Cmdr. Tosh gave her a tight smile. "We're fine." Truthfully they would have been because Castellan was certain she could have held the falling object long enough for them to escape but it was good she didn't have to. No sense draining her energy when they were only halfway through the adventure. "We need you to see if you can get a psychometric read on the box we brought out."

Olivienne held it out for the lieutenant to grab with both hands. Lt. Madlin closed her eyes and stiffened for an instant before relaxing once again. "I sense danger. Something small and pointed, perhaps spring-loaded—"

"Can you tell anything about who left the box there?" The Connate leaned forward, nearly as curious about who put the treasure in the tree as she was about the actual treasure.

Lt. Madlin focused harder and lines formed between her eyes as dark auburn eyebrows drew together. "Gray ones...eyes black and long fingered hands...three and one not five..." She trailed off.

Tosh tilted her head whilst trying to make sense of her lieutenant's words. "Three what? And what do you mean gray ones?"

"I don't know." It was the strangest psychometric reading that Lt. Auda Madlin had ever experienced and she handed the box back her sovereign. "I'm not sure what the rest means but I got a definite sense that the box is dangerous to open."

The Connate turned to Tosh. "Her reference to needles indicates it's probably got a spring trap. I've seen it before where there is a small hole with a poisoned needle inside. The needle is spring loaded so if you try to pick the lock, or just open the box you'll get stabbed with it. Based on what I've encountered in the past, I think your idea of opening a hole in the side has merit."

"Leggett!" Tosh gave a mental shout that anyone in the vicinity with telepathy was sure to hear.

Spc. Branda Leggett jogged around the trunk of the tree to their location. "Yes, ser!"

Olivienne carefully set the box on the ground and stepped back then Castellan pointed at it. "We need an opening made in the side facing the tree. Delicately. Do you think you can handle that?"

Leggett smiled. "Yes, Commander." Tosh directed the rest of them away from the box and Spc. Leggett went to work. She focused her ferrokinetic channel on the back side of the box and slowly a hole began to appear. She kept going until it was nearly two inces across. "How is that?"

Tosh walked closer to the box on the ground and gave a little tap with her foot. A *shickt* sound came from the small rectangle and a collection of sharp pins shot out of the hole and stuck into the bark of the tree. "Sheddech!" Tosh jumped back in reaction. She glanced at Madlin with more than a little shock. "You certainly weren't kidding around about the danger."

No one seemed particularly willing to move so she stepped forward and gave the box a little tap again. When nothing happened, she used her telekinesis to lift it and tip the opening toward the ground. The sound of something sliding inside had them all nervous until a decorative pendant fell out and landed in the dirt below. Tosh carefully discarded the box off to the side then bent down to pick up the artifact that had fallen out. She didn't inspect it herself, because it wasn't her place. Instead she held it out to Olivienne. "I believe this is yours."

The few guardians that were on their side of the tree crowded around as the Connate took the treasure in hand and examined it. It was an intricate representation of the highly familiar temple symbol. The interwoven circle and triangle were made of two different metals. The triangle appeared to be copere and the circle made of stele. It was a little over an ince across and prominently featured a blue gemstone set in the center. "It's beautiful...but how is this a key?"

Tosh shrugged, having no answers for Olivienne. "I can't and won't pretend to understand the ways and workings of the Makers but if it is supposed to be a key, we'll treat it as such."

Olivienne pulled a length of cord out of her pocket and threaded it through the pendant before tying it tight around her own neck. She glanced at Tosh and shrugged. "For safekeeping."

Everyone was happy to leave the tree and get back to their camp in the forest proper. Tosh was the last one to crawl out of the exposed field and gave a sigh of relief when the danger was successfully past them. A low beep sounded from the supply cube and Spc. Lazaro jogged over to answer the voteo alert. The commander called out to the rest of the team. "I want to break camp now and start back. It's still fairly early in the dae and we can make good progress back to the beach if we leave now" Afterward, she followed their communications specialist to the cube with the long-range voteo, curious as to why one of their other two teams would contact them.

Specialist Dante Lazaro was younger at only twenty-two rotos, but he seemed to know his way around the equipment quite well. He cued the mic. "Mater base receiving, request ident. Over."

There was a brief hiss then a familiar voice came over the small speaker. "Filia base, Lieutenant Savon. I have a message for Commander Tosh, over."

Tosh took the mic and cued it. "Tosh here, go ahead Savon."

"Commander, the channel between the islands is clogged with Atlanteen guests, I think somehow they've figured out we've got people on the island. I don't sense they'll leave anytime soon and the ships won't come into the channel even with rocs as cover. I also had a vision that your team would be picked up on the eastern beach instead."

Olivienne had walked up in time to hear Lt. Savon's transmission. "Isn't that near the roc's nesting grounds?"

Tosh nodded and cued the mic again. "Lieutenant, your prescience says it's safe despite being near the location of the roc hatchlings?"

"Yes, ser."

Commander Tosh blew out a long breath and shut her eyes to consider her lieutenant's prescient warning. "I've got a bad feeling about this and I want to get back to the mainland as soon as possible. What do you think?"

The Connate frowned. "I think it's a trap. The Atlanteens are looking to pinch us between their creatures of the deep and the rocs. They know if we get near the nesting grounds, we'll be in danger of attack from above but what choice do we have? If the channel is impassible then we have to rendezvous with our boat elsewhere."

"I don't have as much experience with Lieutenant Savon, has his prescience ever been off?"

Olivienne shook her head. "Never."

Tosh didn't say anything to acknowledge the statement. Instead she pulled out the map she carried in the pocket sewn onto the outer thigh of her trousers. "Look at this." She pointed at the area they'd have to traverse to get to the new rendezvous point. "The eastern beach is half as far from our location as the north one we landed on. And it's downhill so it will be a considerably faster march on the way out." She cued the mic again. "Roger the east beach, Savon. Convey to the captain that we will rendezvous directly east of the marked Fortuna Ligno tree on the map. That is around the bend from the south beach and I'm hoping that will be enough to keep us out of rocs' sights. Copy?"

"Yes, ser. ETA?"

Castellan glanced at the map again before responding. "Thirty-eight oors which is nine hundred the dae after next."

"Yes, Commander. I'll let them know. Savon out."

"Tosh out." She handed the mic back to Lt. Lazaro and he quickly powered down the machine back to its receiving mode and began packing it up for the trip to the eastern beach.

They traveled the rest of that dae before making camp, then had another dae's travel after that. They set up camp within sight of the beach where the ship would collect the team. Tosh addressed Olivienne and the six guardians while they ate their evening meal. "I want to break camp at first light tomorrow and be on the edge of that beach by eight hundred."

Their original plan called for the ship captain to pick up the team on Filia before coming to collect the team on Mater and the commander never specified different the previous dae. Even though the pickup for the Connate's team was farther away than expected, the ship wouldn't have a problem performing both retrievals on time. "I don't want to expose our location until we receive communication from Lieutenant Savon." A chorus of affirmation met her words.

Tosh eventually grabbed her own meal and sat next to Olivienne to eat. The Connate had the pendant removed from her neck and held the piece in the palm of her right hand, cord dangling down between her legs. "It is beautiful, the closest thing to art I've ever seen from the Makers."

Castellan set her empty tray aside when she was finished eating and held out her hand. "May I?" Olivienne gave it to her and Tosh turned it between her fingertips, looking at all sides. It was circular and flattened, but not nearly as thin as a coin. The detail and artwork that went into the interwoven metal shapes was breathtaking. And the gem sparkled in the dim firelight. "I don't see how it could be a traditional key unless the shape matches up to a cutout somewhere."

Olivienne shook her head slowly and took the pendant as Tosh handed it back. She tied it back around her neck with a double knot for safekeeping and tucked it down the front of her shirt. The commander watched in fascination as the artifact nestled into the cleavage that she could see peaking from between open buttons. When Tosh raised her eyes, she was caught in the dark gaze of her sovereign. Some of the pressure of the adventure was off them with the retrieval of the artifact and Castellan felt the first stirrings of her passion return as she looked upon Olivienne's face. The shadows flickered across the planes and valleys, making the sovereign's image jump around. She was startled by Olivienne's quiet voice. "Do you need to look at the pendant again, or perhaps you would be more interested in discussing strategy in my cube later?"

Castellan flushed at Olivienne's implication but smiled rakishly in the firelight. "Perhaps a long...strategy session is in order. We're fairly safe here after all, and near enough to the end of our journey."

Both women reveled in the thought of another night of dalliance but neither would say why. Oors later, when all was done, they were much too exhausted to part company afterward and Tosh fell asleep pressed tight behind Olivienne. She worried for a bit before sleep could fully claim her. Each new intimate act seemed to draw them closer together and she didn't know what to make of the connection. One thing she knew for certain though, it was going to affect their future in one way or another.

AT EIGHT HUNDRED the next morning, the team was fed and fully assembled with their gear nearby and their weapons at the ready. They had taken positions just inside the edge of trees where the forest grew right up to the rocky beach. There were rocs circling in the air high above but it was off to the south and a fairly good distance from their current position. The team was in place for nearly thirty meens when desperate screeching off in the distance could be heard, steadily rising in intensity. At the same time, Lt. Madlin called out to Tosh in a panic. "Commander!" She staggered and grabbed her head, nearly falling to her knees in the loam near the forest edge.

Tosh rushed to the stricken lieutenant. "What's wrong?"

"Distress...my animal empathy is resonating so much fear. I

think something is happening down beach."

"That must be why they're kicking up a racket." Olivienne got out her spyglass and tried to see more. "I see an unusual amount of roc activity in the sky—bollux!"

Castellan pulled out her own spyglass from the pouch at her waist. "Tentacle! We've got a leviathan off the south beach. Specialist Lazaro, best inform Lieutenant Savon and the ship." The guardian in charge of communications quickly fired up the machine he carried on his back and sent an urgent message to Lt. Savon.

"Ser! The leviathan is heading for the rocks where the young birds are located."

"They're all afraid. The fear is nearly overwhelming, Commander." Lt. Madlin still had her eyes closed and Tosh debated what to do. She contemplated letting the scene between the leviathan and the rocs play out simply because they were not equipped to interfere. Their small team didn't have the firepower to take on something that could drag entire ships beneath the waves with little effort.

Olivienne broke through her thoughts. "You can't leave it to take their young! Rocs only lay a few eggs a roto!"

Castellan turned to her with a pained look. "Connate Dracore, we do not have the resources to meet the challenge of protecting the young rocs, not to mention the adults would attack us as well. Ultimately, we are responsible for your safety and I will not jeopardize our objective."

Olivienne looked at Tosh with something close to fury. "What is protocol two of the Sovereign Code, Commander?"

The officer looked back at her like she'd gone mad. "Protocol two dictates that no subject of Psiere may lay a hand on a sovereign without their express permission, nor are they allowed to use their channel on a sovereign without the same permission. I don't see what this has to do with—"

Her words cut off as Olivienne abruptly dropped her pack and took off like a shot through the forest, headed in the direction of the south beach. Based on where the cries were emanating, they were at least five meens away at a run. Panic filled her as she realized what Olivienne was doing. "Sheddech!" She quickly called out all to the team. "Lazaro, stay with the gear and the long-range, tell Savon that the Connate has gone to engage the leviathan and that we are heading to the south beach. The rest of you leave the gear but bring any weapons you have. Follow the

Connate!" She wasn't carrying her own pack but she grabbed her bolt rifle from where it was leaning against a nearby tree and took off after the foolhardy sovereign. Per the code she had just recited, she knew she couldn't stop Olivienne without risking exile to the prison island of Iuvenis. All she could do was follow and protect her to the best of her ability.

When she broke from the trees onto the south beach, utter chaos met her gaze. Olivienne was ahead of her, scrambling over large boulders to get to where a tentacle was creeping toward one flightless roc juvenile. The adult birds were taking turns diving at the beast and raking it with their claws but it was having little effect. Castellan used her telekinesis to pitch one tentacle back into the water, away from the Connate and a cycle-size bird while Olivienne was using her pyrokinesis to burn another that came near. The commander pitched a boulder toward the great eye of the leviathan where it had broken the surface of the water. The other guardians arrived and began firing their rifles into the creature as well. Unfortunately, such small weaponry had no effect and two more tentacles broke the waves onto the rocky shore.

The battle itself seemed suicidal unless the ship came around and brought its big guns to bear. The eye of the beast was frightening enough at twelve inces across and they could see it from where they stood on land, nearly thirty yords from where the leviathan sat in the water. The average tentacle size was around one hundred and forty foot and the monster that had washed ashore rotos before weighed nearly five thousand punds. They were massive and deadly. Not only were those long tentacles covered in suckers with jagged teeth ringing the inside, but they also had claws along the edges of each appendage that could rotate or even retract. Two screams tore through the air, one avian and the other more familiar.

"Tosh!"

The commander looked around and watched in horror as the leviathan had taken the Connate and one of the baby rocs into its grasp. As if that had been the creature's intention all along, the tentacles began a slow withdrawal back out over the water. Thinking fast, Castellan grabbed the creature with her telekinesis to prevent it from sinking below the surface and called to the others. "Don't fire projectile weapons! Devin, Yazzie, Madlin, grab it with your channel. Don't let it go below the surface!"

Even though the claws near the end of the tentacle had already pierced her clothing and skin around her torso, Olivienne worked feverishly to free the young roc that was caught by the nearby tentacle. Her pyrokinesis flared as she worked at burning through the tough rubbery skin of the monster that had ensnared them. She sent a mental push outward, casting her thoughts toward shore. *"Tosh!"*

She was answered immediately. *"We're trying to hold the beast, can you free yourself?"*

"I'm freeing the baby first!"

"No, please!"

Tosh's words did no good. *"I'm almost through, get ready to grab the bird — now!"*

The commander didn't consider her actions, she abruptly let go of her mental grip on the leviathan to grab the falling baby roc. With her lapse of concentration the burden of the entire five thousand pund beast fell to three guardians whose collective power didn't even come close to the commander's. It wasn't their fault that the leviathan began to slip away. Between the three of them, they had less than a tun of capacity lift per oor, whereas Castellan could and had lifted three thousand pund armicrustes. Just as she set the young bird onto the rocky shore, Lt. Madlin called out frantically. "Commander, we can't hold it!"

Tosh turned back to the horror in the water just as it sank below the surface, taking Olivienne with it. "No!" The scream tore from her just as her power cast out over the water until it could grab onto something that was much too large. Tapping into every bit of resource she had, Castellan mentally pulled the leviathan toward them as the exhausted guardians could only stare in awe. The commander screamed again as the large body of the beast was pulled into the shallows, along with a motionless Connate. Then before the leviathan could drag itself back out again, she grabbed the largest boulder she could and sent it crashing into that staring, baleful eye.

With its immediate death, Lt. Madlin grabbed the sovereign with her telekinesis and sped her toward the shore where Spc. Yazzie started pumping her chest and breathed into her mouth. After a meen of working on the Connate, Olivienne abruptly convulsed and they turned her to the side as she coughed out a wash of water into the pebbles on the beach. She gave a hoarse cry and grabbed her left side at the same time. Madlin called out with a triumphant smile. "Commander, she's okay!" She turned and was dismayed to see Tosh lying on the ground ten yords away.

Spc. Qent and Spc. Leggett were also busy working on their

commander just as Yazzie had been working on the Connate. Qent was giving chest compressions and glanced up at the lieutenant. "She dropped as soon as she had the beast nearly ashore. She's not breathing, Lieutenant!"

Lt. Madlin tried to push into the commander's mind and found her still aware. *"Commander, you have to breathe! The Connate is safe, breathe – breathe!"*

Without warning, Tosh gave a great gasp as her back bowed off the ground, then she groaned and grabbed her head as she rolled to the side and vomited. Before anyone could say anything, the heroic woman fell unconscious again. Lt. Madlin was concerned still, looking at the woman who had blood trickling from her nostrils and ears, but at least the officer was alive. Another cry split the air and the hairs on the back of Madlin's neck stood on end. She felt a great wash of air buffet her back and turned slowly to take in a sight that both terrified and exhilarated her. Devin raised his bolt rifle and the lieutenant held her hand up to stay him. "Don't fire, I'm not sensing any aggression from it, just curiosity."

"But, ser!"

Lt. Madlin made eye contact with Devin then swung her gaze to take in the rest of them as the roc stepped closer to the Connate. "Hold, guardians! Any aggression on your part could get our sovereign killed right now. Do not engage! Savvy?"

They all nodded but none answered. The team was frozen in fear and Madlin could feel the anxiety practically radiating all around her. It spiked when the roc leaned down from its nearly four yord height and nudged the Connate with its beak. Olivienne was in pain but awake and stared at the creature with wide violet eyes. The roc cocked its head to one side, then the other, taking in the sight of the prone sovereign with each eye. Everyone held their breath as Olivienne lifted a single hand up to touch the razor sharp beak. "I won't harm you. We saved your baby."

Madlin felt new emotion then. "Connate Dracore, the roc...it is grateful, relieved. I think it's just saying thank you."

Olivienne smiled as the enormous bird stepped back again. "You're welcome." With those last words, the giant avian gave another squawk and took to the air. It swooped over to the chick and snatched it with its claws before flying off. The rest that had been circling followed it farther down the southern coast. Olivienne heard steps running toward her but was too sore to move. "Where's Tosh?"

Madlin came into view with concern darkening her face. "Commander Tosh is down. Can you be moved? Is anything broken?"

Olivienne tried to take a deep breath and winced. "I think some ribs are broken, and I feel like I got chewed on. There was something sharp on the tentacles that cut though my clothes. I—" She gasped and grabbed her left side as she tried to sit up. "Definitely broken. If you help me up, I believe I can walk on my own. What's wrong with the commander?"

Devin and Yazzie helped the Connate stand and steadied her when she swayed slightly. Madlin glanced to where Tosh lay farther down the beach and her brow furrowed. "The commander is, well, I'm not really sure what is wrong. She's in great pain but I have no way of saying if anything else ails her. I suspect she overextended her channel pulling the leviathan in—"

"She what?" Olivienne looked from Lt. Madlin to her fallen lover then turned and caught sight of the beached leviathan that lay like a mountain behind her.

Devin was on her right side and spoke quietly into her hear. "When you got pulled under, she just—I've never seen anything like it. She screamed and her face looked like madness had come and left her scoured in its wake."

Olivienne turned to look at the man who had served on her Shield Corp unit for nearly a long as Lt. Savon. He appeared to be in shock. "What is it, Devin?"

Their slow pace took them ever closer to the prone woman on the ground and Spc. Devin's gaze seemed fixed on the downed officer. "I heard the story about Temple Beach, we all did. But I never really thought someone could have that much power. It's a little frightening."

"Let's just be glad she uses it for good and not for other more nefarious purposes then, shall we?"

His answer was a whisper. "Yes, ser."

Olivienne called out softly to Tosh's mind. *"Castellan?"*

A whimper came from the other woman and Olivienne immediately withdrew. "She's in shock, we need that ship now!"

Luckily for everyone, Spc. Lazaro had gotten in touch with the ship while they battled the sea beast and it was already within sight of the belabored group of guardians.

Spc. Leggett took measurements and recorded images of the leviathan while they waited, if only for the official report later. Within ten meens, a small boat had come to retrieve their partial

team. It was a painful ride for the Connate. Every small bump
and wave shot agony through her broken ribs, even as she tried to
hold her side steady with her hand. Once they were safely aboard
the large vessel, the ship took off up shore to collect Spc. Lazaro
and the rest of their gear. Lt. Savon was the first to reach them as
they made it aboard. Castellan was placed on a stabilizing plank
even as Yazzie and Holling conferred on the best course of action
for treatment of the Connate. "What happened?"

It was Olivienne herself that answered. "The leviathan came
up to the edge of the south beach where one roc chick was
located. I tried to keep it from taking the baby, but it grabbed me
as well. I was able to burn one tentacle to free the young bird but
I made the mistake of yelling for the commander to grab the freed
chick. The other telekinetics couldn't hold the beast by themselves without the commander's help and it pulled me under. I
don't know what happened after that."

Savon turned to take in his fellow lieutenant's pale face.
"And after?"

Madlin shook her head slowly as she watched Spc. Holling
check Cmdr. Tosh's pupils with a light then administer a pain
reliever. "She just...she — she pulled the poxing thing up all by
herself! She's burned out I think, but I don't know because I
didn't see her drop as I was the one bringing in the Connate at the
time."

Her own pain reliever was making her sleepy but Olivienne
found the energy to assuage the lieutenant's fears somewhat. "It's
not your fault, Madlin. Tosh did what she was trained to do. She
did what she always does. There is no other action you could
have taken to prevent this."

Lt. Savon clasped Madlin's shoulder and smiled at her.
"She's right, you grabbed the sovereign, which is the correct
thing to do. If Commander Tosh were awake right now she'd tell
you the same."

Lt. Madlin rubbed her own head, not used to using her telekinesis to such an extent. As senior lieutenant of their team, she
knew Savon would take charge of the group until the commander
was able to resume command. "Yes, ser. If you don't mind, I'm
going to grab a pain reliever for my own head."

"Absolutely. Grab some downtime, we've got oors before we
get back to the mainland. Nice job, Lieutenant, the situation could
have been a lot worse." Savon looked down to the padded bench
where the sovereign had slipped into sleep and heard Madlin

mutter quietly as she walked away.

"It could have been a lot better too."

Chapter Eighteen

CASTELLAN NEVER EVEN woke when they made it back to the dock and loaded her into the waiting hauler to be taken to the nearest med center. Olivienne had come around again though and dreaded the call she would have to make to the Queen as she was loaded into the hauler with Tosh. As they rode through the streets of Natus, the Connate grasped the medallion that still hung beneath her shirt and gazed down at the haggard features of the woman who had once again nearly died to save her life. They were going to have to talk, and soon.

The small fishing village wasn't substantive enough to warrant a full hospital but their med center served most purposes for the residents. Olivienne was taken to a private room and Lt. Savon made a schedule to keep at least six guardians on duty at all times until the Connate was released. He had the displeasure of contacting Gen. Renou to inform her of the events that led to the Connate's injury, as well as the current state of Cmdr. Tosh. He was told to inform Connate Dracore to expect a teleo call from her mother. As for Olivienne, she was treated for puncture wounds from the leviathan's claws, as well as the abrasions from the rings of denticles within each sucker. Other than that and three broken ribs, she was fit as a flightless bird.

The sovereign was deep in thought when Lt. Savon entered her room. "Connate Dracore."

She looked up immediately. "What is it Savon, do you have any word on Commander Tosh's condition?"

"The news is not good, ser —"

Panic washed across the Connate's face. "Bollux! What has happened to her? I need to see her right now!"

"No, Connate Dracore, Commander Tosh is in a deep sleep and receiving intravenous fluids for pain and dehydration. The news I was referring to comes from the capital. Regretfully, I had to inform General Renou of the events over the past weke and the injuries that were sustained in the battle against the leviathan. She informed me that you could expect a call from the Queen." His gaze flickered toward the teleo that sat on the table next to the Connate's bed then back to her pale face.

"My mother?" He nodded and she groaned before covering her eyes with her right hand. "I really have no energy to speak with her right now."

He shuffled uncomfortably, unsure how to help his sovereign. "Um, I could maybe answer and tell her that you're asleep?"

She peeked from between her fingers to take in the loyal lieutenant who had served her for rotos. "As much as the offer is appreciated, lieutenant, I need to speak with her about a number of things so best that I just answer and get it over with."

He bowed, looking relieved. "Yes, Connate Dracore. If that is all, I should probably see to the rest of the unit and arrange to have our supplies taken back to the base camp." Savon turned to go but Olivienne called out to him.

"Lieutenant."

"Yes, ser?"

Olivienne smiled at him, and though it was tired and filled with discomfort it was also genuine. "Thank you for your warning yesterdae, and thank you for all you've done over the rotos that I've known you. You're a good officer and I'm glad you're on my team."

Pride filled his eyes then and he saluted her. "Yes, ser. I'm happy to serve." He turned and made his way out.

The quiet of Olivienne's room didn't last long as the air was split by the ringing of the teleo. Even though the Queen seemed quite calm, Olivienne could hear the panic in her mother's voice. "I'm fine, maman, I promise." She paused as she listened to her mother speak. "Scrapes mostly, and three broken ribs. I'm afraid that Commander Tosh bore the brunt of it as she has not awakened yet. The doctore on staff thinks that she burned out all her channels." Another pause. "No, I didn't see it but I heard after...yes, an entire leviathan." Olivienne sighed as her mother continued to speak and pushed away a few stray hairs that had come out of her braid and hung down in her face. "Truthfully? I don't know. I wasn't aware she was capable of that much power."

The next spate of questions took the Connate by surprise. "I—I don't know what you mean." The next words caused Olivienne's heart to race. As much as she and Tosh had tried to keep it a secret, her mother already knew of their dalliance. Worse yet, she suspected the depth of Olivienne's feelings. "Maman, I cannot say—fine, *will* not say then. I have to speak with Castellan first and she's not..." Olivienne's voice trailed off and her mother remained silent. Tears sprang to Olivienne's eyes as she thought about how close her lover had come to dying. "Oh, maman...she has to wake!" Before their conversation could continue further, a knock sounded at the door. "I have to go." Olivara asked another question and the Connate answered. "Yes, Savon says we'll leave tomorrow whether she wakes or not. She'll get better care in the capital anyway. Yes, maman, and thank you. I love you too."

The call disconnected. "Enter!"

An older gentlemen wearing a warm fishing sweater walked through the door carrying a small tablet and stylus. He saluted her and smiled warmly. "Good afternoon, Connate Dracore, it is an honor to officially meet you. I'm Doctore Strem."

"As the man who patched me up, believe me when I say the honor is all mine. So when can I leave?"

He glanced at his tablet then back to her. "Truthfully, you can leave at any time. I'll give you some analgesics for the pain but I'm afraid there's nothing I can actually do for the ribs. Time will be the best healer for—" He paused and chuckled good-naturedly. "I forgot who you were for a sec. I supposed the Queen will have a telesana healer tend to you as soon as you enter Tesseron, so my words of advice may be for moot."

Olivienne smiled in acknowledgement. "How is Commander Tosh?"

Dre. Strem frowned. "She is physically hale, but still sleeps. I think that her channel was so badly burned by the actions against the creature that any amount of stimulus is painful. I'm keeping her sedated for now. I recommend doing a telepathic check every oor and if she gets to the point where she doesn't react with pain then she will be safe to stop administering the sedative. I'd like to keep you both overnight for observation and I'll sign vellum for your release in the morning."

"Can I see her?"

He touched the side of his nose, indicating a secret shared. "She was muttering your name in her sleep so I feel as though it is my duty to have her bed transferred to your room for the night."

The doctore left after that and a little while later Lt. Savon came back. He informed her that the team would be packed and loaded for the trip back to Tesseron the next morning. He was leaving six of the best rested guardians at the med center for her protection and would return in the morning. When Castellan was wheeled in a few oors later, Olivienne had to hold back tears. Her brave officer was pale as she lay on the bed. Tosh's hair was in disarray and she had disconcerting dark smudges beneath each eye. The Connate missed the blue of her lover's eyes as they looked upon her with mirth and she missed Castellan's smile. She spent oors by the unconscious woman's bedside, just holding her hand, until exhaustion pulled Olivienne back to her own bed for much needed rest.

"'Vienne."

The Connate woke the next morning with Tosh's voice in her head. She moved carefully to get out of the med center bed and made her way to once again sit next to the commander. She took Castellan's hand and gently stroked the pale skin. *"I'm here. I'm right here."*

"Head hurts."

"I know, love. The doctore says you burned your channels. Do you remember?"

Castellan shifted in the bed and moaned as her hand clasped tightly to Olivienne's. *"Don't leave me!"*

Olivienne gently ran her fingers through her lover's hair, straightening the oddly mussed pale strands. *"I'm not going anywhere."*

THE RETURN TRIP to Tesseron was miserable for all. There was no light-hearted banter within the unit at each stop. No one liked the fact that their sovereign had been injured and the entire team was distraught about Castellan's more grievous seeming ailment. They had come to love and admire their commander in just a short time and all felt partially responsible.

Despite the depressive atmosphere in the haulers as they headed east along the speedway, they made better time returning than heading out. It was eighteen hundred oors when they hit the city outskirts. Per the Queen's instructions, Lt. Savon directed the haulers to head straight to the main hospital facility within Tesseron where there waited a team of doctores, including one with a telesana channel. He worked on Olivienne first and within twenty meens all her injuries were healed. Then he spent another two oors of healing on Tosh, but was not able to bring her up to full strength in one go. He said he'd have to rest and complete her healing the next dae. It was enough to have her awake and ready to return home, albeit more grumpy than normal with a persistently throbbing head.

Later that evening found Tosh lying in her own bed, cursing her impulsive foolishness and nursing that aching head. A knock sounded at her door and her crankiness caused her to be more terse than normal. "I told you I'm fine and I don't need more coddling!" She thought it was Olivienne coming to apologize again and she didn't need that. One thing Castellan had realized as she came out of sedation was that she would risk everything again and again to save the Connate. Olivienne had thoroughly and definitively found her way inside the commander's defenses and she wasn't sure what to do about it. But Castellan also hated being so weak and pained, and as a result she was a terrible patient.

The voice through the door was muffled but Cmdr. Tosh blanched when she recognized it. "I have no intentions of coddling anyone, especially not an experienced, if cantankerous, officer of the Shield Corp. May I enter?"

Castellan attempted to straighten her appearance as well as she was able without aid of a mirror or comb. "My apologies, Queen Olivara, you are more than welcome."

Olivara walked through the door wearing tight riding breaches and a flowing white shirt. Her hair was pinned up in her usual coif. She seemed comfortable and relaxed but it was her intense violet eyes that gave Castellan pause. They were so like Olivienne's, yet the Queen's eyes were not full of guilt like her daughter. "I would ask how you are but I already know."

Cmdr. Tosh saluted from her bed but did not attempt to stand. "My apologies for not greeting you properly, my Queen—"

The supreme leader of Psiere waved off her apology and pulled up a chair next to Tosh's bed. "It is of no matter, Commander. I'm quite aware of your doctore's orders. So, how are you?"

Castellan felt the slightest pressure from the Queen's telepathic probe and winced in pain. "Please don't. I'm afraid I can't stop you todae and it is exceedingly painful."

"It is I who owes you an apology but rest assured I would not have breached your privacy. I only meant to perform my own assessment of your condition."

A little humor came back to the commander's face, even if the color had yet to return. "Oh ho, so are you a doctore now, my Queen? Perhaps that is where Olivienne inherited her penchant for claiming abilities she does not possess."

Olivara smiled and let the dig slide, after all, Castellan was destined to become part of the family. "I see your spirits are high enough even if your capacity is low. Have no fear though, Commander, the doctore will be here first thing tomorrow to finish up your healing."

Castellan nodded. "That is what your daughter said earlier." There was an awkward pause before Tosh prompted the Queen about the reason for her visit. "Have you come to see Olivienne?"

"Actually, I've come to see you. It seems I chose well when I begged you to take control of my daughter's Shield Corp unit all those lunes ago. Not only have you put together a top-notch team, but you've once again sacrificed yourself to save my daughter. That is an action for which I can never truly repay you." She reached over to gently grasp Tosh's hand. "Thank you for bringing her back to us."

Uncomfortable with the Queen's words, Tosh shrugged. "I only did what I was trained to do, my Queen. I would give everything I have for my home and country."

"I'd like to think it was more for Olivienne than for Psiere that prompted you to accomplish such impossible feats."

Tosh looked at her uneasily. "I beg your pardon?"

"It's quite simple, Commander. I know of your dalliance. After all, I was the one who promoted it to you. And I am more convinced than ever that the bond you have forged is what saved you both on that beach. Tell me, Castellan Tosh, do you have feelings for my daughter?"

The officer stiffened at such a personal and difficult to answer question. "Ser!"

Olivara narrowed her eyes shrewdly, knowing that she was putting the officer on the spot. "I asked you a question, Commander Tosh, and I expect an answer."

Castellan swallowed thickly. "Of—of course I have feelings for her! Your daughter and I have become lovers and we've grown close as friends. As a matter of fact, she is one of the best friends I have ever had."

"That is not what I meant and you well know it. Do you love Olivienne?"

Tosh's anger grew at the Queen's sheer audacity. "I cannot answer that."

Olivara wasn't just a sovereign, trained all her life to rule and understand the nature of the people around her, but she was also a politician and knew how to get the answers she sought, sometimes pushing on a stubborn door just right in order for it to open. "I think you can."

Piqued by the continued request for her innermost thoughts,

Castellan forgot who she was speaking to and slammed a fist into the bed at her side. "I *will* not then! My feelings for Olivienne are for her to hear before all others!"

"Thank you." Castellan abruptly paled as she realized she had erred two-fold, first with her tone toward the Queen and second with the words that slipped from her mouth while anger blinded her. Rather than call her out for the disrespect, the Queen nodded, smiled at her, and stood. "The doctore will return early tomorrow morning to finish your healing. At nine hundred there will be a meeting in my private chambers for everyone on the task force that is currently in Tesseron. More documents have been translated and my husband will present the location for the Key of Illeos. I estimate you will have two wekes to prepare for the next adventure once the meeting is finished."

Dread washed through the commander at Olivara's words. "My Queen, are you certain that is wise? This last adventurist mission ended with poor results."

"On the contrary, Commander, it has taught us a lot. I will go over the reasons and other problems you will face tomorrow at the meeting. Until then." She nodded her head in clear dismissal and Tosh was left to salute the retreating figure. She had much to think about and time slipped through her fingers like sand. A conversation with Olivienne was imminent but she didn't see the Connate again until the following morning when the doctore arrived.

It took less than thirty meens for him to finish the healing and Castellan was ever so grateful for his attention. She stood tall and held her hands out to her sides as she explored the boundaries of each one of her channels. He did a deep healing, not like what Gemeda had performed on the railer during her trip to Tesseron. In order to repair all her channels, he had drained his own capacity significantly, which was why he had to do it in two different sessions.

With his exit, Tosh found herself in high spirits and she felt calm enough to probe the emotions that the Queen's words had stirred up the night before. When Olivienne knocked on her door and entered her private suite meens later, she saw the Connate through completely different eyes.

Olivienne was distracted, both by her feelings for the commander and her fears about the upcoming meeting. "Tosh, I—" She looked up abruptly when she felt a gentle pressure along her telepathic channel. "What is it?"

Castellan could only stare at her as emotion hammered at the walls she had erected to keep such things away. "You're beautiful."

"Are you mad?" Despite her exclamation, Castellan's words caused the Connate to suck in a surprised breath.

Tosh shook her head and smiled. "No, I've not gone off the rails. I've got all my wits and faculties about me. Everything seems to be the same as it was before the incident on Mater, with the exception of one thing."

The doctore had warned that with severe channel burn, sometimes the person never fully recovered their previous strength. The channels would be permanently damaged. She stepped close in concern and took Tosh's hand in both her own. "What is it?"

"I've realized something important in the past dae and a half of recuperation."

"And?"

Taking a chance, Castellan brought Olivienne's hands to her lips and kissed the back of each. "Despite my best efforts against such an impossibility, I've gone and fallen in love with you."

Violet eyes widened and Olivienne pulled a hand away to cover her mouth. "Oh!"

Tosh's pale brow furrowed. "Oh? Is that all you can say when I make a declaration of heart to you?" Her eyes grew bright when Olivienne still hadn't spoken and she attempted to pull her hand away. "I see. Your 'oh' was your way of saying my depth is not returned. My apologies, Connate Dracore. I did not mean to be so forwar—"

Her hurt words were cut off by Olivienne's passionate kiss. When the Connate pulled away again she had tears in her own eyes. "That was merely an 'oh, she feels the same as I,' you frustratingly handsome woman!" With Olivienne's words of reassurance, Castellan dropped those walls she had been clinging to so tightly. They both sucked in a breath when the emotion rose between them. Despite neither being an empath, they had somehow formed a connection. Dalliance was no longer their game, things had gotten decidedly more serious. Unfortunately they couldn't spend any more time in consideration of their feelings for each other because they had to rush to make the meeting across the royal estate. The Queen and King would be gathered with the other members of the task force, waiting on them to arrive.

They stole one last kiss before heading out the door and Olivienne cast her thoughts out to her lover. *"My mother is sure to be pleased."*

Castellan laughed aloud, startling both the Connate and the guardians on duty as they exited the residence. At Olivienne's questioning look, she replied. *"The Queen already knows. Who do you think told me?"*

KESHIEN DRACORE MOVED his gaze back and forth between his daughter and the good commander. His wife had told him they had deep feelings for each other but he initially scoffed at the idea. Olivienne had never been known for pursuing anything meaningful in a relationship. Even as her father, he had to admit that his daughter always held a part of herself separate from any of her dalliances in the past. Then there was the Queen to consider. It was a lot of pressure to have one's mother as Divine Cathedress, and Olivara never made a secret of how much she disliked her daughter's past acquaintances. His thoughts were interrupted when Olivienne met his gaze with eyes so like her mother's. It was eerie the way she seemed to read his mind but in truth he had been looking back and forth between them so his thoughts were fairly obvious.

"I love her, papan."

He smiled as General Renou finished reporting on the state of unrest on the southern continent and the Queen began to speak again. The same unrest that Keshien had become convinced had its stirrings much higher up. He shunted his thoughts back to the conversation with his daughter. *"Does she love you the same in return? I have heard many good things about her."*

"She does and all the things are true. Castellan is the most honorable person I've ever met, her spirit shines more pure than any other." Their private conversation was interrupted when the Queen finished out the meeting.

Olivara rapped her knuckles twice on the table as she gazed around the room. "Finding the first key is proof that generations of rumors are true. We are on the cusp of great change, I can feel it! However, we need more answers on some of these new questions before Olivienne can pursue the next lead in our search for the Temple of Antaeus. That is why I would like Commander Tosh to head up to the Academy on Instrucia. She will remain in Scola for a weke while she goes through re-testing. The rest of the unit, under my daughter and Lieutenant Savon's command, will resupply for the trip south to Navis. Commander Tosh will instruct her unit todae and leave on the northbound railer first thing in the morning.

"What?" Olivienne's voice cut through the small room like a pistol shot. The thought of her lover leaving for a weke after only just confessing her feelings filled the Connate with dismay.

The Queen glanced from her husband to her daughter with a scowl on her face. "If you'd been paying attention you'd know the details. I think you can ask Commander Tosh when you leave because this meeting is now finished." She sent a mental request to Keshien, requesting that he escort Cmdr. Tosh outside while she took a meen to speak with Olivienne alone.

People filed out of the Queen's chamber and the King gave a slight nod to his wife then turned and winked at his daughter. "Commander Tosh, a word if you please."

Castellan paused to look at Olivienne, then turned her attention back to the King. "Yes, ser." They walked out together leaving the two sovereigns behind.

"I asked your father to speak with Commander Tosh because I need to discuss something with you."

With a final glance at her departing lover's back, Olivienne moved to sit in the chair near her mother's desk. "Is it really necessary for you to send her north? And if so, why can't I go with her? Savon is fully capable of handling the prep for Navis."

Olivara leaned forward and rested her elbows on the desk, her fingers folded below her chin. "You know, when I first discovered your dalliance with the good commander, I was fully prepared to dislike her. You've never chosen wisely in the past, 'Vienne. You don't tend to pick your *acquaintances* for their heart or their head."

A sigh came from the Connate's lips. "Maman, I dallied with plenty who had good hearts or heads, and all had fine stamina."

"And Commander Tosh?"

A smile washed over Olivienne's face, transforming it to a shape her mother had never seen before. "Castellan is—" The breath seized in her throat as she thought about all that Commander Castellan Tosh had become to her. "She is everything!" Fearful violet eyes turned toward the Queen, well aware of her mother's usual disapproval. "Please say you understand because I've never been serious about someone the way I am her."

Olivara melted at her daughter's frightened and unsure look. "Oh my love, I said I was prepared to dislike her, not that it would be at all possible. If I had to choose one person in all of Psiere that embodied the qualities I would wish for you in a royal consorage, it would be Castellan Tosh. But I do have one last warning, another vision about your commander."

Those violet eyes went dark with real fear. "What is it?"

"I have seen how Commander Tosh is, and how she values duty and honor above all else. In my dream last night, these words resonated through me over and over 'til I woke. In the dream I was here in my office, partaking this exact wisdom to you. But make no mistake about it, the dream was about your Castellan Tosh." Olivienne leaned forward a bit in anticipation and waited for her mother to speak. "Duty will best be served if you never let it come between you and the one you love. Honor will always be upheld if you don't grasp it too tight."

"That's it?" Olivara nodded. "But what does it mean?"

The Queen shrugged. "Like most prophesies, you won't know until you know."

Olivienne rubbed her temple in frustration. "And why does she need to travel north for testing again?"

"After hearing the story of Castellan's actions with the leviathan on Mater beach, General Renou asked the doctore to probe her channels to see if he could discern any changes. There was nothing he could report other than your commander had full capability after her second healing. But the general raised a point that I had not considered before, Commander Tosh seems to be getting more powerful. The instructors will run tests and study her channels at the Academy and compare them to her original test results. Then they will report back to me and the general when they're through. Instrae Greene herself will be overseeing the tests. Rest assured, daughter, she will be in good hands and will return to you before you even know she's gone."

Olivienne sighed at her mother's words and collapsed back into the chair. "I'm afraid that's impossible, maman. She merely has to look away and I miss her. Any distance would be too great."

Chapter Nineteen

CASTELLAN AND OLIVIENNE were busy for the next two oors after the meeting with the task force. They had to speak with Lt. Savon and Lt. Madlin, then the entire Shield Corp unit as a whole. Tosh wanted to get the team squared away on assignment rotations and training exercises for the weke that she would be in Scola on Instrucia Island. Even though their morning was filled with serious business and preparation, neither woman could help stealing little looks and touches when they thought no one was watching. As a result, there was a building tension between them, a rising emotion that had been turned lose with the admission of their mutual feelings for each other. They made it back to the residence a little past thirteen hundred, after lunching with the team lieutenants.

As soon as the front door of the Connate's residence shut behind them, they stopped and just stared at one another. Olivienne was the first to break the silence. "Tell me again."

Castellan knew exactly what she was asking and took a step closer. "I've gone and fallen in love with you."

The Connate smiled. "Again."

Another step closer, until they were nearly touching. "My Royal Sovereign Connate Olivienne Dracore, I've fallen in love with you."

This time Olivienne's voice was a whisper. "Again."

Castellan pressed close and took Olivienne into her arms. "I love you." Then to prevent more requests, she sealed her love with a kiss.

Their kisses didn't end in the foyer of Olivienne's residence. They continued down the hallways and around corners until they came to Tosh's suite of rooms. Before they could go through the door, Olivienne pulled them to a stop. "Do you have any more meetings or commitments todae?"

The officer gave her a perplexed look. "No, not until the railer leaves in the morn. Why?"

Olivienne gave her a wicked smile. "Because you're mine for the next eighteen oors."

That smile turned into something infinitely more tender with

Castellan's response. "I certainly hope you'll want me longer than that."

The Connate reached up to caress Tosh's cheek. "Well, Commander, we'll just have to see when your time is up now, won't we?"

"Vixen! You minx, you, you...infuriating tease!" Laughing, Castellan picked up the other woman and swiftly carried her into the suite, not stopping at all until they arrived at her private bedroom. There she gently placed Olivienne in the center of the bed and began removing her own officer's kit and accessories while the Connate apported her own boots off her feet.

"You know I could just—" Olivienne waved her fingers through the air in the vague direction of the officer's clothing to indicate the use of her apportation but Tosh just shook her head.

"Not todae, I want to take my time with you."

Olivienne was curious about Tosh's motive but she didn't disagree with her words. "Yeah? Why is that?"

Tosh smiled and finished undressing then crawled up on the bed to kneel over Olivienne, where she lay propped on her elbows. With deliberately slow movements, she unclasped the Connate's soft white shirt. Tosh spoke while her strong fingers were kept busy with their task. "Because I've gone and fallen in love with you and I plan on spending the next eighteen oors showing you exactly how much you mean to me." When Olivienne's shirt was spread wide open, Castellan leaned over and deposited a series of kisses along the cleavage that showed at the top of the sovereign's bosair before reaching around beneath her shirt and removing the strip of material. Even as Olivienne's respiration increased with her arousal, Castellan moved farther down the bed so she could reach the fasteners of Olivienne's trousers. Once they were open, she deposited a kiss at the last bit of skin where it disappeared beneath the fabric of the Connate's unders. Tosh hooked a thumb beneath each side then gazed beseechingly up at her lover.

With a flushed face and parted lips, Olivienne could only stare down the length of her own body at the woman that had taken her life by storm. Nothing in Olivienne's past could have prepared her for the depth of emotion she felt whilst gazing into those pale blue eyes. "Would you like my help, Commander?"

Rather than answer, Castellan used her tongue to trace along the skin exposed by the open trousers, ever so often nibbling or kissing little bits on her path from left to right. Finally Olivienne could stand it no more and she lifted her hips to aid Castellan's quest in undressing her. Tosh slid everything off all at once and laughed. She placed her right hand flat against Olivienne's abdomen. "Are we getting impatient, Connate Dracore?"

Olivienne grabbed that hand with her own and pushed it slowly toward the area she wanted it most. "No, my love. I throb for you and my will is that you will show me this love you promised sooner rather than later." Both women moaned when Tosh's fingers met the moist lips of Olivienne's labia. Her clitoris was already hard and distended and Tosh brought her other hand to play. She held the Connate's gaze as she gently caressed both sides of the sensitive bundle of nerves with the pad of each thumb. Olivienne whimpered and her eyes rolled back with pleasure but Castellan's weight had settled over her lower legs, preventing the prone woman from writhing like she wanted to. "Please, Castellan!"

The officer responded to that plea by removing her hands and sliding even lower on the bed. Olivienne parted her legs to let Castellan settle in and shivered when the other woman blew across her throbbing flesh. "Slowly, 'Vienne. Patience is a virtue."

The Connate shivered when those teasing lips came in to kiss a bit more of her moist flesh. "I'm not feeling very virtuous right now."

Pale twinkling eyes took in the trembling body below her. Olivienne's skin was flushed and carried a sheen of sweat. Her breasts were bared with hardened nipples where the shirt had pulled apart to expose them. And her eyes were shut tight as she quivered with every kiss. "I could talk you through it if you like—"

Violet eyes popped open. "No more talking!" And following her sovereign's orders, Tosh didn't do any more talking, at least right away.

They made love to each other, with lips whispering words that each had never promised to another. And their eyes made promises that had never once whispered from their lips in all their past dalliances. Olivienne thought of it as a new adventure of sorts, one she had never come across before. And Tosh willingly and pleasurably gave the Connate something rare and precious, her future. Oors of loving left them spent and half-starved so they raided the kitchen pantry and raced back to the bedroom. Then once their commonplace hunger had been assuaged, Olivienne and Castellan made love again.

Sometime near evening meal they finally lay together, basking in the aftermath of their immense passion, reveling in the connection of heart they had found. The room was awash with the smell of sex and light from the suns slanted lazily through the curtain over Tosh's west facing window. Silence reigned but Castellan's imminent departure had Olivienne's mind turning at a rapid pace. The Connate startled her lover when her soft voice cut through the dim room.

"What do you think of this theory that your channel ratings are changing?"

Castellan glanced over to where Olivienne lay pressed against her side. It was nearly eighteen hundred oors and they were sweat-covered and completely done-in at last. In the cool air of her room, Castellan considered the question. "I'm not really sure what to think. We all go through the same tests when our powers emerge and once our ratings are established, it's been assumed that is the level we'll be for the rest of our lives."

Olivienne traced a scar on the shoulder closest to her head. "What was your telekinetic exam like?"

The commander blew out a sigh. "Probably much the same as any of your hard channels. In the beginning they tested me for strength, starting with the heaviest weights first then working my way down until I found one I could lift. I was fifteen and so amazed that I could move something the size of a moto!"

"Yeah, I'll admit that my pyrokinesis scared me at first. It is both destructive and beautiful in a way."

They laughed at the wonders of youth then Tosh continued the explanation of her testing. "Once they established my strength level, then they tested for distance in order to factor the true rating." She smiled at Olivienne, whose dark hair fanned across the pillow next to her head. "My maman was so surprised when I not only tested for two level six channels, but that I had three more high to middling channels to boot. My soft channels were a little different. They gave me a series of puzzles and tests to gauge if I had the intuition channel and — oh! The first time I heard someone talk in my head it was strange. I was one of the younger ones to experience telepathy, maybe because my mother is so strong."

"And your academy test for it? I assume it was no big deal for you. I remember my first time, I was not an early bloomer like you. First I felt a pressure, then a little tickle. After that a voice that was unlike my own internal voice started asking me questions." She picked up the hand that had been tracing her scar and delicately wove their fingers together.

"What about your other channels? How do they test for enhanced awareness?"

Olivienne was blissfully happy and enjoyed just spending time talking with Castellan. There were so many things she wanted to know and she truly regretted that they'd be apart for a weke. "Believe it or not, it was an obstacle course. They made me run through, all the while slinging objects at me. There are some traps, but mostly it is designed to see how aware of your environment you are and test your reflexes. I don't think the soft channels are as easy to pin down with a rating but the Academy has been using the same system for at least fifty rotos now, so it's the best we have."

Tosh shivered as her skin finally dried from their all-dae activity and she used her telekinesis to pull the coverlets up to their shoulders. Olivienne smiled and hugged her closer. Thinking back on the original question, Castellan shrugged. "As for increasing one's strength...I know that all our channels pull from the same core capacity within us. That is the first thing we're taught after we get our channel ratings. And the size of our capacity determines how fast we recharge. Perhaps it's not my channel that is increasing, but my capacity. Or maybe it's neither of those things but rather that I am recharging faster. I really have no idea and I suppose that is what the tests will tell me when I go up to Scola."

"I heard that they sometimes have a hard time calculating channel ratings when the Psierian has multiple channels because even if your channel limit was say three thousand punds for your kinetics, you could lift that limit over an over until your capacity ran out. I heard you were lifting and pitching the armicrustes when you were dubbed the Hero of Temple Beach. How many?"

Castellan grimaced at that. "Must you use that horrific moniker?" Olivienne grinned unrepentant and Tosh thought back to the crustacean massacre that turned into a boon for the local food supply. "Hmm, only twice. They were right at the limit of my telekinesis. After that I started pitching rocks until I was forced to swing my sword."

Olivienne turned those violet eyes up to meet Castellan's gaze. "You strained yourself then too, right?"

"Barely. Nothing like on Mater. Though I'll admit that when I lifted myself, along with the woman and child, out of harm's way,

I nearly passed out in the few secs after I set us down. But I soldiered on."

The Connate caressed Tosh's jaw and placed a kiss on the spot nearest to her. "My strong brave commander. There is no way you'd let your subordinates see you weak."

Tosh colored slightly because she knew Olivienne's words were true. "I have to say though, I've never been taken so close to my established limits until the last roto. It seems like every time I turn around I'm flinging large beasties here or there." She laughed. "Perhaps I'm just building my mental muscles much the way your athletes build their physical ones."

"My athletes? What exactly does that mean?"

Castellan grinned at her. "You know what that means. After all, you're the one who preferred to dally with the slow-witted oxen in your past history of tuppin—" She was unable to finish her statement because Olivienne crawled on top of her and pinned her to the bed.

"Let's make something clear right now, Commander Castellan Tosh. There is only one dim-witted oxen welcome in my bed now and that is you!"

Her eyes grew wide when Castellan abruptly flipped Olivienne onto her back and nestled her hips firmly against the apex of the Connate's thighs. With a roll of her own hips, Castellan rubbed herself against the woman she had grown to love above all others. Just meens before, she thought them worn out for the evening but Olivienne's eyes rolled back at the delicious pleasure that radiated from their joined hips. The Connate's dark lips parted and Tosh leaned down to gently nip at the jawline just to the right of her chin. She continued kissing farther to the side as her hips moved slowly but firmly. When her own lips reached Olivienne's ear, she whispered to her. "I am no oxen, Connate Dracore. I am a tigre searching for a feast." Olivienne whimpered and pulled Castellan's hips into a faster pace. "I know for a fact that you taste divine."

Those words set off a shudder through the body on the bottom and the quiet whimper turned into a moan. "Please!"

"'Vienne." The Connate's eyes fluttered open and her purple gaze met Tosh's pale blue eyes. "I'm hungry." With those words Olivienne moved her hands up to the Castellan's shoulders and began pushing the commander farther down her body.

"I expect a thorough job, Commander."

Tosh laughed lightly as her lips skimmed the flesh of each

breast. "Yes, ser!" It would be another couple oors into evening before they had an actual meal.

WANTING TO GET to know the team of men and women that Castellan had put together, Olivienne used the next weke to speak with each and every one of them. She worked closely with Lt. Savon and his new counterpart, Lt. Madlin. She found both capable, with interesting insights about not only her protection, but her historical adventurist career as well. It was almost as if Castellan's words alone to the team had elicited a shift in mentality that Olivienne hoped would make her own adventuring significantly easier. She spoke with each member at length about their training and goals, thus sealing their loyalty as they realized she was legitimately interested in them as individuals.

To further bond with her team, she even began drilling with them. If they surprised her with their width and breadth of knowledge, she certainly surprised them with her physical ability that was nearly on par with the men and women in those infamous black uniforms. What the Connate lacked in strength, she more than made up for in her prowess with a pistol. She bragged that she could outshoot anyone in the unit and even gloated a bit as she bested each one in turn. News of the friendly competition got back to the Queen and she showed up with her own custom pistol, putting an end to Olivienne's bragging. No one was a better shot than Queen Olivara.

Even keeping busy as she was, the weke crawled slowly by. The two lovers got to speak via teleo in the evenings but the channel testing usually left Castellan too exhausted to talk for long. The commander was also ready for the weke to be over. The thing that Gen. Renou didn't tell her was that after her preliminary tests to establish a new baseline on the first dae, she was run beyond her limit each dae after. The Academy employed multiple doctores with telesana so at the end of each dae she would be healed of her inevitable channel strain. But exhaustion would suck her down into a solid ten oors of sleep each night. It saddened her that most evenings she could barely manage to talk to Olivienne for ten meens. She fell asleep missing Olivienne every single night she was in the Academy city of Scola.

Both Gen. Renou and Gen. Leniste had made the trip up for her sixth dae of tests. They didn't run nearly as long and by thirteen hundred oors, Castellan, Gen. Renou, and Gen. Leniste all sat in the office of the Academy's elected head. Ins. Keeley Greene was the youngest leader the Psierian institution had ever seen. At just over forty rotos, she seemed impossibly young in such a position of high responsibility. It didn't help that the dark-haired woman was short and androgynous, lending to her youthful air. She held a stack of vellum in her hand and once the rest were seated, she made her way over to their chairs and handed each a page from the pile.

Tosh looked at the results and a single pale eyebrow rose with surprise. "Instrae Greene, surely there must be a mistake."

The instrae shook her head and took a seat behind the desk. "I assure you, Commander Tosh, there is no mistake. Your new baseline is significantly higher than the original test when you first entered Academy. Not only that, but after pushing you to your limits a number of daes in a row, you've succeeded in increasing your baseline again. As such, your telekinesis has actually gone beyond our current scale of measurement. Based on the scaled weights per rating, you, Commander Tosh, are now a level 7."

Gen. Renou looked up in shock. "How is that possible?"

"There must be a mistake!" Leniste seemed just as dumbfounded.

Keeley Greene shook her head. "There is no mistake. For the last few daes, we had one of our instructors observing Commander Tosh's sessions. Instrae Kenton is one of the few people with the aetherkinesis channel and he reported findings most strange. Apparently every time Tosh completely drained her reserve, the aether began flowing slightly faster into her. It was as if her absorption rate increased. On top of that, when Commander Tosh was fully charged again, she held more aether in her cells than before." She shook her head in consternation. "The reason this has never been discovered before is because we train all Psierians to conserve their channels, to moderate how much they use of their reserves. And if the training weren't enough, there is the real consequence of channel strain to dissuade those that push the boundaries."

All three sets of eyes turned toward Castellan. "It's not like I set out to strain my channel. I was merely doing my job."

Gen. Renou smiled at the woman who had become a highly capable commander in such a short amount of time. "It is your diligence and dedication that has resulted in your recordable increase in strength. That's certainly nothing to scoff at and it will mean an entirely new direction of channel research going forward."

"Think of the potential applications with those Psierians going into the Defense and Shield Corps if we could increase their ratings early!"

Tosh shook her head. "I don't think it would be a good idea to make this knowledge public — ".

"What?" Gen. Leniste's face darkened at her words. "The program would benefit immensely if our soldiers had higher channel ratings." He looked to Renou for support but she was busy staring at Castellan with a new kind of respect.

She smiled and addressed both Leniste and Keeley Greene. "I see what she is trying to say. If we made it public knowledge that pushing your limits could lead to increased channel ratings, our medican centers would be flooded with people who had drained themselves nearly dry. We would have accidental deaths on our hands because as we all know the higher the channel ratings, the more career opportunities will open. People would overextend themselves, and on what? Damage and injury for bystanders would certainly increase as a result. It could be dangerous to the public in general, as well as to the individuals trying to increase their power. Permanent channel damage is a recordable detriment."

Castellan added another point that Gen. Renou had not covered. "It's not only that, General, but we really don't know the long term effects this increase will have. Will I eventually burn out? Will my cells break down faster? Psierians are fairly long-lived with our life expectancy near one hundred and forty rotos, but will the changes in my cells and aether replenishment affect my longevity? We don't have answers to any of these questions." She turned her head in an arch to meet each person's eyes. "Honestly, if it were me I would not trade ten rotos of my life for a little bit more power. It's just not worth it."

General Renou sighed. "I hate to say it but she's right. This is something that is completely unknown and perhaps unpredictable. While I don't think it is anything to be concerned about insofar as Commander Tosh's current assignment, I have to counsel against making it public knowledge. And if research is to be continued, it should be in a highly classified manner."

Instrae Greene nodded. "I have already spoken with the Queen at length explaining the results. Strangely enough, she said nearly the same thing as General Renou. She pointed out that the current regime has enemies and we do not wish to give them the knowledge to become more powerful. Unrest and protests have been cropping up in the southern continent and she is concerned for the safety of citizens down there."

"I've not even been gone half a roto yet but I don't remember anything but the rare protest when I was stationed in Ostium. I wonder why the increase now?"

Gen. Leniste leaned forward wearing a keen look. While he was well known for being stubborn and resistant to change, he was also a brilliant tactician and often surprised his counterparts with how well he kept track of the many people under his command. He had been following Commander Tosh's career since she was a mere lieutenant, long before the strong and well-respected officer was poached by Shield Corp. "I think the answer is you, Tosh. You were a strong leader, a solid presence in the southwestern region of Dromea. I think perhaps someone is taking advantage of your absence and the placement of someone less capable in command. I will send out inquiries, circumspect of course. I've never liked that Pon Havington."

"Ser, if I may?" Tosh was only slightly surprised to learn that Leniste didn't like the Praefectus of Dromea. The general gave a nod and she continued. "It was a well-known secret of the mutual dislike between me and Havington. At the time I left I had my suspicions, especially when further concern was brought up to me by one of my lieutenants. I trust her implicitly and gave instructions to keep an eye on things down there once I was gone. So if you need a contact on the inside, I would recommend First Lieutenant Cando. She's probably due for promotion soon too."

Gen. Leniste grunted at her news. "Lieutenant Commander Bello is in your old position, correct?"

"Yes, ser." While she agreed with him, it was obvious in the tone of her voice that she didn't particularly care for Bello any more than she cared for Havington.

"I'll most likely have to initiate a full-scale investigation of the Ostium base but it helps to know who I can trust. Thank you for the intel, Commander."

"Back to the business at hand, which is the channels of Castellan Tosh." Three sets of eyes turned toward the Academy head. "The Queen suggested I put together a classified team of researchers who will report only to me. I think it would also be beneficial to send out lunely reports to Queen Olivara, as well as the both of you. What say you?"

Leniste gave a familiar grunt. "I'm amenable to that plan."

Gen. Renou also nodded. "As am I. However, I would like to add one thing to that plan. I think it is necessary that Commander Tosh come up every half roto for re-testing."

Castellan abruptly sat straight as a rod at that news. "I must protest, General!" She paused when Renou turned a hard-eyed gaze to the lower ranked officer.

"I know you haven't been working for me long, Commander, but I don't usually like having my orders questioned."

Tosh grimaced. "Ser, I'm not questioning your orders, I would merely like to suggest once a roto, rather than twice a roto. With my duties to the Connate, it would be difficult to arrange a weke out of every twenty-five to come up for testing at the Academy. She is sure to be ramping up on her adventurist missions with the emphasis that the Queen has placed on finding the Temple of Antaeus."

Tosh waited nervously for the general to deliberate her suggestion and finally Renou sighed. "You're probably right. Fine, once a roto and I want the full battery of tests. As long as the research team isn't actively trying to increase your power like they were this time around, it shouldn't take more than a few daes." She scanned the three other people in the room. "Are we finished here? I'd like to get back to Tesseron sooner rather than later. Pendar celebrates his dae of birth tomorrow and I still have things to arrange."

Ins. Greene stood and waved her hand through the air. "Of course, by all means. I think we've covered all the bases going forward and I'll make sure a copy of the test results goes into Commander Tosh's record."

Before leaving the office, Tosh saluted Gen. Leniste who stayed behind to speak with the instrae then followed Gen. Renou out the door. Her thoughts whirled with all that she had just learned about herself and channels in general. So much was Castellan in her head that she failed to hear Renou call to her the first time. " — I asked if you were already packed, Commander Tosh."

Startled, Tosh met the smaller woman's piercing eyes. "Yes, ser. I've actually left my duffel at the downstairs desk."

Gen. Renou smiled at her. "It's been quite a weke for you, hasn't it? I bet you can't wait to get on the dirigible that will take you across the cut to the railer station."

"Yes, ser."

It took them nearly ten means to navigate the maze of hallways and corridors before they arrived at the welcome desk near the ornate entrance of the primary building. Tosh retrieved her duffel from the desk officer and they made their way outside into the duel suns' shine. While the season had been getting noticeably warmer in Tesseron, it was still quite chilly in Scola. It was the norm given the fact that they were nearly a thousand mahls north of the capital of Endara.

Castellan pulled her jacket snug and flagged an Academy moto for transport to the airfield. The ride was short and they were in luck in that a dirigible was scheduled to exit within ten meens of their arrival. Gen. Renou smirked at Tosh as they settled into the passenger seats of the well-appointed official section. "Looks like Leniste will have to take the next one out two oors from now. Which means he'll be stuck at the railer station barracks overnight until the next railer departs. As it is, we'll just be catching the last one out at twenty-one hundred." Wisely, Tosh didn't reply to Renou's glee at the other general's discomfort.

It was roughly three hundred mahls by flight from the dirigible station in Scola to the small railer station across the cut of sea that divided the island of Instrucia from the mainland. Dirigible was the slowest of all transports, with a top speed of around forty mahls per oor. The problem didn't lie with propulsion, but rather with the rigidity of the air bladder that held it aloft. The aether driven props could drive them faster but the flexible balloon itself collapsed underneath the press of air to the front section. They tried a rigid bladder but the gas they used inside to keep it aloft was not light enough to lift that along with supplies and a gondola full of people. Unless dirigibles switched to either a lighter toxic gas, or one that was lighter but highly flammable, the air transports would be limited in speed.

After the rigorous testing over the previous weke, Tosh took the opportunity to doze for the first few oors of the flight. She woke when a porter came around and asked her preference on evening meal. She took her dinner with Gen. Renou then they shared a snifter of brandy. After speaking on a variety of subjects, Renou broached a subject that had Tosh feeling flustered and highly uncomfortable. "So the Queen has filled me in on your *situation* with Connate Dracore."

Castellan downed her drink in one large gulp then turned her pale eyes to meet the general's. "I know that I've broken protocol..." She looked down and trailed off, prepared for the worst news from her superior.

"I think it's grand."

Tosh's head jerked up. "Pardon?"

Renou laughed and leaned over to clap Castellan on the shoulder. "Easy there, Commander. The Queen also told me that she all but demanded you and her daughter continue the dalliance you began on the train."

"Oh." Tosh's face was blank with shock.

Gen. Renou smiled, then called for another refill on their drinks. She sighed and took another sip of hers after the steward walked away again. "You may not know this, Tosh, but the Queen and I have been friends all of our lives. I'm actually Olivienne's heart mother, or was rather. I suppose she's old enough now to not need such a thing. But my point is, that girl has been wild from the moment she emerged squalling into the world. But since you came into the picture, she's changed. No one thought the Connate would settle down but I've seen a difference in her the last few times we've met and I believe that difference is you." When Castellan continued to look worried, Camen Renou reassured her. "That is a good thing, Commander."

Tosh swallowed thickly. "Erm...thank you, General." She took a healthy swig of her brandy to calm her nerves and nearly spit it across the aisle with Renou's next words.

"So what are your intentions for the future, Tosh? My heart daughter is currently in need of a par. I think you'd make fine children with the Maker's splicing technol—"

"General!"

Renou laughed at her discomfort. "What?"

"That is an incredibly personal question to come from my commanding officer. Olivienne—I mean, Connate Dracore knows of my feelings and intentions. Can we not just let it be for now? I do not wish to make a path public news until we can be sure where we are going."

The general swirled her drink again and smiled benignly. "Very well, I'll leave off for now. But I want a good seat at the Consorage Ceremony, savvy?"

Tosh choked as the brandy burned its way down the wrong pipe. She looked at her watch only to see they still had another oor on the dirigible, then another four oors on the railer before they were scheduled to arrive back in Tesseron. When she glanced back up at the general, she received a wink for her discomfort. It was going to be a long night.

Chapter Twenty

IT WAS MUCH too late, or perhaps too early, by the time Castellan arrived back at the residence. She had not given Olivienne a time of arrival because she didn't know if they'd make the connectors in time for the railer departure. She thought she'd put her things away then go upstairs and surprise her lover. Instead it was Tosh herself who was surprised to find Olivienne sleeping soundly in her bed. There was something touching about the fact that the Connate had chosen to sleep in her room while she was in Scola. She took a quick trip through the facility to remove the travel grime from her body then quietly crawled into her bed and moved to hold Olivienne from behind. However, she froze and a ball of dread formed in her stomach as her lover pulled her closer and whispered four unwelcome words.

"Gwennette...back so soon?" Angry and hurt, she started to pull away but Olivienne began laughing and refused to let her go. "Get back here, Commander! I was only teasing you."

Tosh blew out a shaky sigh. "Good to know."

When Olivienne turned to gaze at Tosh, light from a lamp on the property outside filtered through the windows and illuminated her face. "Surely the fact that I'm sleeping in your bed instead of my own should tell you how much I've missed you." She leaned forward and gave Castellan a much needed welcome home kiss. "Your coverlets smell like you."

"Oh? And what do I smell like?"

Instead of answering, Olivienne pulled her into a tight embrace and changed the subject. "What did you find out from all the testing?"

Exhaustion suddenly caught up with Castellan again and she nearly split her jaw with a yawn. "I'll tell you tomorrow, but for now I must sleep. All right?"

Olivienne smiled and snuggled into the commander's arms. "More than all right."

THE PAIR SLEPT late the next morning and even after they woke, they continued to dally in bed, catching up on a weke's absence. After bathing, they had a leisurely morning meal on the back patio. Tosh told Olivienne all about the testing and the surprising results, and Olivienne filled her in about the upcoming adventurist mission to Navis. When they ran out of words, Tosh's gaze was caught by the depth of Olivienne's violet eyes. She leaned toward the Connate for a kiss but was interrupted by the beat of heavy-soled boots on the stone steps leading up to the patio.

"Connate Dracore, everything is s—Commander Tosh!" Lt. Savon looked up from his slate as he noticed Castellan sitting with the sovereign. "I didn't know you were returning todae!"

She shrugged. "Ah, well, I wasn't sure how long I'd be up there and I came in late so..."

Gentry Savon smiled good-naturedly and didn't remark on the color that had risen on Tosh's face. "I'm glad you're here, Commander. Per Connate Dracore's instruction, everything has been prepared for the trip to Dromea. We have chartered the railer for our entire team to head south, including cargo segments that will carry the haulers. The railer will take us to Vesper, the little village we stopped in when Commander Tosh saved those children from the flood. From there we'll follow the jungle road to the fishing village of Wahnish where we can charter a dirigible over to the island of Navis."

Olivienne raised her dark brows at his words. "Do fishing villages down south normally have a dirigible available?"

"No, ser. It will leave from the station in Cordeesh and meet us there."

"What about pyroclastic displays from Mount Ignis?" Castellan lived on the southern continent long enough to know all about the active volcano that was located on the northern end of large jungle island off the west coast of Dromea. There was a reason it was uninhabited.

Savon responded to her question with ease. "I was informed that winds typically carry the debris in a northerly direction, the same direction that the lava flows when there is an eruption. As long as the wind doesn't change, the dirigible will be safe enough. The fishing boats will not travel so far as the island because of the Atlanteens. They only have railer gun coverage along the coast of the mainland."

"Hmm..." Tosh's eyes were unfocussed as she thought about the information presented.

Olivienne looked at her. "Is that a good hmm, or bad hmm?"

"Mostly good. I wasn't looking forward to tramping across that blasted island to the southern cliffs. The jungle road will be bad enough. I've heard enough tales to know that we'll all feel like our spines have been bent out of shape by the time the journey is done."

Savon shook his head with a grin. "It's not as bad as it once was, ser. My coz'n is actually with the Engineering Corp down there and he said they finally smoothed and coated the jungle road a few roto's back. He said we could achieve fifty mahls per if we had good drivers, but told me to watch out for the howlers at each stop. They'd steel the tires off our haulers and boots off our feet if we weren't paying attention."

Olivienne burst out laughing. "You cannot be serious!"

"No, ser. But they are tricky little primates just the same."

"He's right. They'd come to the country markets outside Ostium and beg for fruit or other food and if you didn't give them just a bit, they'd steal something from your person and take off. I lost a timepiece when I was first stationed down there."

"A timepiece?" The Connate looked at her in disbelief that the small animal could get a timepiece off the commander.

"As he said, they are tricky." She looked back at Savon. "I'm assuming the entire team is going on this one? I don't remember seeing anyone scheduled for leave."

"Yes, ser. I think the unit has really begun to come together and Connate Dracore impressed them so much while you were gone that they're quite excited to share her next adventure."

A slow smile graced Castellan's face as she turned to look at her lover. "Oh really? And what were you doing that was so impressive?"

Olivienne smirked. "Just outshooting everyone with my pistol."

Her smile turned to a little frown when Savon added his piece. "Everyone except for the Queen."

Olivienne waved her hand through the air dismissively. "Yes, well, you can't win them all, Savon!"

Castellan laughed heartily until she was gifted with Olivienne's scowl. "When do we leave, Lieutenant?"

Lt. Savon stood straighter with his slate held down at his side. "Eight hundred, the morning after next, ser."

Tosh tried to think of any other information she needed to know or impart to her lead lieutenant. "We're going to count on Specialist Dozier on this one, Lieutenant. Make sure she has everything she needs for both rappelling down the cliffs and for the cave exploration. Use these two daes to hold clinics with her and the rest of the unit. Not everyone has cave experience and we'll end up splitting up into search teams when we get down there because the cliff is riddled with caves. You're dismissed, Lieutenant."

"Yes, ser!" Savon saluted both of them, turned on his booted heal, and quickly walked away.

THE DAES FLEW by for everyone and before they knew it, the departure time to Dromea arrived. The Connate's team had three railer segments all to themselves, on top of the added open segments that held the haulers. They arrived in Pentole just past seventeen-thirty oors and departed the Pentole station on time, thirty meens later. But during that thirty meen interim, Olivienne and Castellan sat quietly in the sitting area of the Connate's private segment. Suddenly Olivienne shivered. Sensing something off, Tosh glanced up from her book to catch a look of naked fear on her lover's face. "What's wrong, 'Vienne?" The Connate stiffened, not expecting Castellan to notice that her mood had changed. "It's nothing, go back to your book. I'm fine."

Rather than do as directed, Tosh marked and closed the book then moved over to the couch where Olivienne sat. "Is it Penterole? This is the first time you've been through since the assassination attempt. I can understand if that would upset you."

Olivienne looked down at her clasped hands. She wasn't used to feeling weak or unsettled, and she was less familiar with actually showing such weakness to another. "I'll admit that it is somewhat unsettling. But that is not what made me feel as though someone had dipped me in an icy lake." She looked up to meet Tosh's pale blue eyes and her own reflected sadness. "I barely knew you then but something inside me nearly broke while I watched you bleeding out on the stones of the marketplace." A tear broke free from her dark lashes and she tried to laugh as she told Castellan what upset her most. "And there you were, dying painfully yet calm as you please shooting assassins down from bell towers. I was then, and continue to be, amazed by you on a daily basis. And..."

"And?"

"I couldn't bear it if something were to happen to you, if you were to be taken away from me."

Castellan smiled and gently cupped Olivienne's cheek. "Well then, I shall endeavor to make sure nothing untoward ever happens to my fair flesh and functioning mind. And just in case you wonder, I feel the same about you. Clearly if the beach battle on Mater told you anything, it is that I'm quite taken with you." Then as if she were announcing the dae's weather, she said four more words. "You hold my heart."

The second leg of their trip was much longer and Olivienne and Castellan opted to share the Connate's private cabin overnight. They had another thirty meen layover the next morning in Gomen, just before ten hundred local time.

It was a short four oor jaunt down to Vesper after that and both Olivienne and Cmdr. Tosh were surprised to receive a hero's welcome when they stepped off the railer in the small river town. Because of the impromptu celebration and lunch, they didn't start down the jungle road until nearly sixteen hundred oors and Castellan knew it would be a long trip for everyone. While they had plans to stop every few oors on their way to the coast, it wasn't recommended they make camp because the local flora and fauna was notoriously inhospitable to Psierians. Carnivorous nocturnal animals and poisonous plants and insects were no way to start a successful adventurist mission.

"I hope we don't have to search too many caves to find the one with the key." Olivienne was studying her pile of vellum and locally drawn maps that she had brought on the trip. It was twenty-one hundred and they still had four oors more before their scheduled arrival at Wahnish.

Tosh glanced down at the translated page that was on the top of the stack. "There were no other clues given, other than it was in one of the Caves of Navis?"

"I forgot, you haven't actually read the translated text. Just as with the other reference to the key, it doesn't specifically call out where the location is. We knew it was the correct text because the beginning of the poem is identical, but the end changes to speak of a different place." She held out the page for Tosh to read.

In the summer of celestial events
On the fifth and final dae
Cataclysm turned the sky gray
And the land was scored with rents
As awareness slowed by moments
And forethought came into play

Our people recognized a way
First thought of by the docents

A pendant for each temple door
Collect the three to enter
All of them a different gem
The second on a fiery shore
Holes a'stern left of center
The Key of keys will open

Tosh read it silently while the hauler bounced along and she raised an eyebrow at its conclusion. "Well at least the Makers made it obvious that this text is related to the other. I think our clue can be found in the last two lines."

"How so?"

The commander tapped Olivienne's folded map that was given to them by the surveyors. "How many caves are listed in the cliff face? Does it say how many are large enough for a Psierian?"

Olivienne handed the mission folder to Tosh so she had a little more space to unfold the map. It was large for the space available so she kept the top half of the island folded over and they studied the bottom. Surveyors had drawn an exploded section showing just the cliff face and they counted eighteen different cave markings. The surveyors had used a sonal ocilloscope or sonalscope as it was often called, to read the initial depth of each cave. Tones produced by the machine, most likely mounted on a dirigible, would be sent out to strike the cliff face. They would then reflect back to the scope and give a calibrated distance. The sonalscope would gauge cave depth based on the difference between the external rock face and the sounds returned from within the caves themselves.

Unfortunately it didn't work if the cave took a turn in one direction or another. But initial depth and height readings would perhaps narrow down the field of choices, as well as taking into consideration the fact that the cave was left of center. Tosh casually grabbed the stylus that Olivienne had tucked behind her ear and drew a light line down the center of the cliff region. Then she put a check mark next to any cliffs that were large enough to explore. That brought the list of searchable caves down to six. "Thank the Makers!" Olivienne leaned over and kissed Tosh straight on the mouth for her deductive work and Lt. Madlin snorted from the front seat of the hauler.

There were only four in their hauler, with Spc. Calderon driving that particular leg of the trip. The other twelve were split up between the two haulers behind them. Even so, it was still more witnesses than Castellan was comfortable with. Tosh flushed and looked up abruptly to meet the lieutenant's eyes. "Erm..."

Taking pity on her commander, Madlin pretended like she had seen nothing and Olivienne spoke again. "So we've narrowed it down to six, have we? We have gear for four caves at a time so hopefully we nail down the correct one in the first go 'round. But what about the last line?"

Castellan shook her head. "I don't know. It could have to do with the pendant you already have. It's the only key I know of. Perhaps it will make more sense when we get there."

The Sovereign nodded, also flustered at her show of affection in front her guardians. "Hopefully."

The haulers were hot in the stifling jungle humidity. Even with the windows open they didn't do much to cool the passengers. The Connate was ready to arrive at the coast where at least they'd have the breeze coming off the ocean to refresh them. Howlers, the small primates with loud voices, could be heard over the drone of the engines of the mini-convoy. When they'd stop for breaks to stretch their legs or in some cases eliminate a short ways into the trees, the sounds of the fauna would increase exponentially.

By the time they had gotten though the last scheduled stop before Wahnish, Spc. Lear had lost her tinted spectacles and Spc. Lazaro had lost his voteo. After repeated screeching and howls came over all their portable communication units, Tosh ordered the entire team to adjust their voteos to a different frequency. While she chewed the man out publicly in front of the team, she and Olivienne laughed in the privacy of their hauler. Every time they'd calm down, Tosh would grab her voteo from her belt and make the classic howler face and that would set them off again. The Connate was pleased to see such a lighthearted side of her lover. Tosh made stones look jovial at times and Olivienne was honored to be graced with the commander's humor. And after catching Lt. Madlin glance at them from the front, Olivienne had a feeling that the rest of the unit would also be in on the joke and would in turn tease Lazaro mercilessly.

It was just after one hundred oors when they arrived in Wahnish. The Connate's group drove straight to the local Security

Corp station and made camp in the green space behind it. Tosh
spoke with the officer on duty and asked him to teleo the nearest
Shield office and let them know that the Connate had arrived
safely in Wahnish. They had plenty of time to catch up on their
rest since they weren't scheduled to leave on the dirigible until
twenty-two hundred the next evening. That gave Castellan time
to organize the teams and double check equipment, as well as get
the dirigible loaded that had shown up the afternoon after their
arrival.

The captain of the air ship said she preferred to travel to the
volcanic island at night because they could better see if any hot
bits were in the airspace they'd be travelling. It made no difference to the unit since the dirigible was both comfortable and
secure and they'd all be guaranteed a good night's sleep for when
they arrived at the cliffs at seven-thirty.

It was a strange experience to stand in the open air section at
the stern of the dirigible's gondola. Tosh had stayed inside to
speak with her team when they lifted into the night breeze. With
no more preparation needed on her end, Olivienne went to watch
the few twinkling lights from the fishing town slowly disappear
behind them. The night was pitch black, with only a blanket of
stars in the sky to guide their way. The Connate marveled at how
the tapestry changed whenever she traveled to the southern continent.

At loose ends, she thought on her developed closeness with
Castellan. Though she would never admit it to the Queen, she had
secretly dreamed of finding someone who suited her as well as
her papan seemed to suit her maman. But she was also aware that
she had a duty to fulfil as Royal Heir to the Divine Cathedra.
Even if she had no par, she would be expected to go through fer-
tilization at the temple by the age of fifty rotos to produce a Connate of her own.

She wasn't ready to settle down any time soon, nor did she
want to become a mother just yet, and she had given up on finding someone who accepted both her career and her royal status.
Over the rotos, she had also given up on finding a person who
could match her intellect and her passionate drive. Olivienne
wasn't looking for just a lover, she wanted someone that would
challenge her and rival her own curiosity when it came to the
Makers and the history of their world. She craved a partner in
adventure.

As she continued to gaze into the inky blackness, with matching dark hair loose and swirling around her head, Olivienne felt a little hope that maybe she had found all she'd given up on in one Castellan Tosh. Then as if thoughts alone had pulled her from the sea air, Tosh's arms snaked around the Connate and together they watched the fading shoreline.

ONE OF THE steersman aboard the dirigible was forced to shoot an anchor harpoon into the rock atop the windy and barren Cliffs of Navis the next morn. After reeling the airship down to the ground at the top of the cliff, the Connate and her Shield Corp unit disembarked and unloaded their adventurist gear. On their initial approach, Olivienne asked the captain to bring them in from the south side of the island, facing the cliffs, so they could shoot dye pellets at the top of the cliff to mark out the location of the cave entrances they needed to check. That way the individual teams would have a marker to set up their rappelling lines. Specialized pistols were used to shoot anchor bolts into the rock and lines were clipped to the anchors. Then the entire unit did one last buddy check of their gear and split into teams to start their decent.

Spc. Soleng and Spc. Lazaro were disappointed to be assigned topside but Tosh wanted a few guardians left outside the caves in case something untoward were to happen to the rest of the team. She figured that a quick-thinking engineer and one of their communications specialists were the best ones to leave with the dirigible. Olivienne, Castellan, and Spc. Holling would be going into the first cave, the one just to the left of cliff center. Holling was an experienced medican who had worked with the unit for three rotos and had proven to have a level head on his shoulders. He also had a small amount of cave training. Castellan didn't tell the Connate that the main reason she was bringing the man was because he was a medican. Tosh couldn't bear if something happened to Olivienne again.

The next cave team would be led by Spc. Qent since he was another guardian with a sub-degree in historical adventurism. His team consisted of the salvo and rescue trained Spc. Devin, Spc. Yazzie who was the team's other medican, and Spc. Leggett. Three of the four cave two team members possessed hard channels and Tosh had confidence they'd come through all right in case of an emergency.

Cave three team was led by the adventurist with specific cave training. Spc. Dozier had done a fine job getting the unit up to speed with basic spelunking training and would be taking Lt. Savon, and Spc. Penn into the darkness.

The fourth and final cave team was led by Lt. Madlin. She would take another four person team consisting of Spc. Lear, and Spc. Calderon. Her final member was Spc. Meza who was another guardian trained in salvo and rescue.

They had all seen the first key, a medallion, and they'd all been warned to watch for traps. The one group that didn't have a historical adventurist with them was actually instructed to simply hold position and voteo Connate Dracore if they came across anything that seemed out of place. Olivienne was the first of her team to clip onto the line and rappel the ten yords down to their cave. Castellan followed, then Spc. Holling swung in last. Despite being high above the ocean waves, the cave was cold and damp and smelled of salt tang and old fish. All three turned on their headlamps as soon as they were inside the cave proper. Once they were in, Olivienne pulled the remaining line inside and all three clipped back to it. It was better they stayed together and had some sort of safety line in case there were holes or other traps farther in.

After about fifteen meens of walking along a twisting and turning passageway, the cave abruptly came to an end. "Well clearly this isn't the one." Olivienne sighed and rubbed her head while Tosh pulled the voteo from her belt

She cued the alert button then spoke. "Tosh, checking status of cave two. Over."

Spc. Qent's voice came across the small speaker. "Qent here. Cave two status incomplete. Still walking, Commander."

"Roger status, Qent. Keep walking and report any change."

"Affirmative, Commander. Qent out."

Olivienne looked at Tosh and Holling in the dim light of their lamps. "Well, no news is good news I guess. At least their cave is still viable—" Her words were cut off by a frantic transmission over the voteo.

"Maydae, maydae, maydae! Cave three. Med red, med red, med red! Cave three!"

The three Psierians looked at each other and Tosh responded. "Team one on our way!" Then they started running toward the cave entrance. As soon as they got to the opening, Tosh peered out toward where the cave three team's line hung down from the top of the cliff. The cave was twenty yords farther west of their own, and ten yords lower. "Sheddech! We don't have time to climb up then back down to their cave again!" Before Olivienne could start brainstorming for other ideas, Castellan unclipped from their own line.

"Unclip, I'll take us over and we can clip to their line when we get inside cave three."

The Connate looked at her with concern. "Are you sure? We're pretty high off the water, I know that makes it harder to levitate..."

Tosh shook her head and smiled grimly, knowing that every single sec counted when it came to a medican alert. "Don't worry, I'll still have plenty in reserve should there be more trouble in the cave."

They all quickly unclipped from the line and with supreme focus, Tosh swept them from the cave and lowered them over and down to the cave three entrance. As soon as they were inside, they all clipped to the cave three line, with Tosh at the front. They took off at a fast pace along the smooth corridor that pitched down at a fairly steep angle. Moisture leaked from the ceiling and walls making the going pretty treacherous. More than once Holling, who was off balance from the med pack, slipped and fell backward. He learned to clamp his gloved hands tightly onto the rope brake to prevent further sliding, and Olivienne did the same every time she heard him fall. It would help no one if they all arrived at the bottom in a tangle.

Eventually they could make out the headlamps of Spc. Dozier and Spc. Penn. They were on their bellies peering over the edge of a drop off. The blackness beyond and below swallowed the light shining from their helmets and when Tosh spoke, the words echoed disconcertingly. "Dozier, what's the status?"

Both Dozier and Penn carefully stood, holding tight to the line in front of Tosh but it was Dozier who answered. "Lieutenant Savon was at the back and he kept sliding down the hill behind us. When I saw the drop off, I installed anchors to the walls on either side of the passageway and ran another line, assuming we'd have to belay down. Penn and I clipped to the line as Lieutenant Savon came down the path. When he tried to stop, his braking mechanism snapped and the clip that held him on the line malfunctioned. Ser, he just went right over the edge and we can't see him from up here." Sorrow washed over her face. "I failed my team, ser. I failed my lieutenant."

Tosh patted the specialist's shoulder and turned to Olivienne. "Can you light it up so we can see a little better?" All three newcomers clipped to the shorter anchor line that Spc. Dozier had strung across the passageway and Olivienne focused on making a fireball out in the darkness. Tosh shaded her eyes as she peered down into the gloom. As soon as the flame of the Connate's pyrokinetic channel lit the chamber, Castellan could make out the body of Savon lying near an underground river some ten yords below them. "There he is and I can hear his unconscious thoughts in my head! I can just lift him up from here, no need to go down."

"Ser..."

Four sets of eyes turned toward the medican. "He needs to be stabilized before he can be moved. I will need to go down there and assess the situation, ser."

Castellan nodded and pulled another line from her pack and tied it to the new anchor line since the original from the cave mouth didn't go more than a foot beyond the drop-off. "I'm going to lift us down but I want to clip onto the line just in case." They clipped onto the new line and Tosh quickly lowered them into the cavern and set them down on the rock floor near Savon. Right away they could see his helmet was cracked and his arm lay at an odd angle. "He probably tried to grab onto the wall to break his fall—"

"Look there, ser! You can see where his helmet struck the rock." Holling pointed toward a bright mark left from when the colored helmet impacted the wall on his way down. Holling knelt swiftly and began an examination of Savon. The most he could discover was that the lieutenant's upper left humorous bone was broken. He stabilized Savon's neck with a brace and splinted the arm as best he could with supplies from the med pack then stepped back. "If you could keep him as level and stabile as possible when you lift that would be optimal."

Castellan called out to the three people standing above. "Clear a space, I'm going to lift Savon up to you!" The commander stepped back as far as she could in the chamber until the small underground river blocked her way. She would rather telekinetically lift the unconscious man than levitate all of them at once. It was about energy consumption and she knew she should keep some in reserve. But to lift him, Castellan needed to get a good line of site up to the ledge. "Connate Dracore, can you light it up again?"

No sooner had she finished speaking when the cavern was lit from high above. Just as she was getting ready to lift the unconscious lieutenant, her voteo crackled with the alert tone and Lt. Madlin's voice came over the speaker. "Cave four reporting a large chamber straight back from the entrance, Commander. There is a panel with twenty-five buttons on the far wall, other indicators are placed around it, and a series of numbers. Team status is green and need instruction. Over."

Castellan grabbed the voteo from her belt and keyed the com. "Tosh here. Roger status, cave four. Return to the cave entrance and hold position, we are in the process of evacuating Lieutenant Savon to the dirigible."

"Roger for return. Madlin out."

Commander Tosh knew that Lt. Madlin would inform the dirigible crew to ready their own medican. If Lt. Savon looked in more serious condition when they got him topside, she was prepared to send the dirigible back with him alone and keep the team on the cliff until they returned. They had shelter in the caves and enough rations to last for a few daes. Water would be the only difficulty but Castellan figured she could just take the saline filter and levitate herself down to the ocean surface to fill their canteens. She looked down at Gren Holling, the man who had been the Connate's medican for a few rotos. "Ready?"

"Yes, ser!"

Making a last meen change in decision, she unclipped her harness then pointed at his. "Unclip. I was going to lift him first and bring us up second but I think I'll just take us all at once. I have the power, it just takes a lot of focus." He nodded and did as she asked then she carefully but swiftly lifted them the ten yords to the ledge where Olivienne stared down at the trio worriedly. Tosh reassured her. "He's not critical, just unconscious and as far as Holling can tell has a broken arm. The return trip is a little far and the ceiling is too low for me to just float us all out so we're going to have to climb back up the incline the hard way. I will use my telekinesis to float Savon though, horizontally in front of me. When we get back into the main cave proper I'll levitate the two of us to the top so the ship's crew can care for him. While I'm up there, maybe you can check in with the remaining team and get a status report."

The Connate nodded and all five healthy members of the group clipped onto the original rope coming down from the cave mouth and made the slow trek back up the slippery slope. Olivienne called out to the rest. "Easy does it now, we don't want anyone else taking Savon's slippery adventure slide." She joked because even if they all knew the lieutenant wasn't in serious condition, they were still worried.

It took nearly thirty meens to make it back to the cave opening. Olivienne watched Castellan lift herself, Savon, and Holling out into the empty space some fifteen yords above the crashing water below. She pulled her head back in when she lost sight of the three as they went up to the top of the cliff. After that, Olivienne unclipped the voteo from her belt and gestured toward the climbing line. "I'm going to contact the cave four team and see if they've found anything else. In the meantime you two can start climbing."

Spc. Penn frowned. "Begging your pardon, Connate Dracore, but we're supposed to keep you secure and we can't do that while hanging from a line over the ocean. You should bring up the middle, ser."

"Someone experienced should bring up the end, Specialist."

Dozier held up a hand and Olivienne stopped. "If I may, I'm from over by Dara Mountains, that's why I'm specially certified in caves and mountain training. Been doing it practically all my life, ser. I can bring up the rear."

Olivienne sighed at the seriousness with which Castellan's team took their job. There was a time when no one would argue with her, just let her go about her duty. But she had to admit that both guardians had a point and they had certainly been useful during their adventures so she let it go. "Fine. Specialist Penn, start us off and I'll begin my ascent when you're halfway up." She turned back to Dozier. "You can contact the cave four team and let them know we'll meet them at their cave mouth after Savon is sorted out."

Spc. Dozier gave Olivienne a salute and a grin before pulling her voteo from her belt. "Yes, ser!"

It wasn't long before all teams, minus cave four, were back up to the top of the cliff. Lt. Savon had been taken aboard the dirigible and the ships medican, along with Spc. Holling were treating him for a broken arm, a concussion, and possible fractured fingers. Both Castellan and Olivienne spoke with him before heading out to meet with the rest of the team. They left Savon awake and hurting but in good hands.

Once again at the top of the cliff, Castellan spoke with the remaining members of the unit. "You may have heard Lieutenant Madlin say that they've found something in cave four. Connate Dracore and I will go down there to investigate." She pointed out names as she called them. "I want Qent, Dozier, and Yazzie to come with us, the rest of you stay topside and guard the cliff. And thanks for the good work so far, just a little longer and we'll get to head home. You're dismissed to assume your stations!"

Olivienne held back a smile when the entire unit saluted Tosh all at once. They had a lot of respect for the woman who had claimed the sovereign's heart. Instead of commenting on it, Olivienne turned to Castellan with a look of eager anticipation. "Are you ready?"

Now that the fear of Savon's injury had tempered, the excitement of discovery had begun to rise again. Tosh gave a nod and a grin to the sovereign. "Of course! After you, Connate Dracore."

Chapter Twenty-one

LT. MADLIN'S TEAM was waiting for them, helping to pull each one in as they lowered themselves to the cave entrance. "It's really straightway down the passage, Commander. The chamber is fairly small but it's dry with no hidden surprises that we could ascertain."

"Thank you, Lieutenant Madlin." Unfortunately for the lieutenant, the next thing Tosh did was order her and the rest of her team topside. "You've done good work here, all of you. But with Lieutenant Savon down, I want to make sure we don't have all the team leadership stuck underground. Also, these caves aren't very big so I'm taking the ones with the most adventurist training below and one medican, no more. Savvy?"

Understanding washed over the lieutenant's face and she nodded to Tosh before turning to the rest of her group. "Yes, ser. Come on you lot, let's head up." As the original four person team began clipping in and ascending the line up the cliff, Olivienne turned on her headlamp and led the other four deep into the recesses of the cliff.

Twenty meens later they came into a small chamber, just as Madlin described. The light of their headlamps showed a large panel of buttons, twenty-five by twenty-five square. Each button had a number written on it and above the panel was a horizontal tube mounted to the wall, no more than a finger's width in diameter. It looked like a clear glass ampule that has been segmented into three sections. Along the right side of the button panel were tiny square slates showing numbers, each number appeared to correspond to the row of buttons to the left. And along the bottom of the panel was the same thing, with the tiny number slates corresponding to the column above. "How peculiar." In all her rotos as a historical adventurist, Olivienne had never seen the like.

Castellan looked at her and grimaced. "I'm not even sure where to begin but strangely enough I don't get the sense of danger with this one that I had back on Mater."

Olivienne tapped her chin as she studied the panel. "Me either. Look here, notice how the rows and columns of numbers each add up to sixty?"

Spc. Dozier shook his head. "The last column and last row add to sixty-one. That's strange."

"But what are the slate numbers off to the side? Spc. Qent pointed at the ones to the right of each row and called them off. "Fifty-three, forty-five, thirty-eight, fifty-one, and sixty-one. There is no pattern that I can detect!"

Castellan cocked her head and studied the buttons in the combined light of their headlamps. "Could there be maths involved? What if we subtract the slate number from the total?"

Olivienne pulled out a stylus and small slate from her belt pouch and wrote down the row totals in a line. Four were the number sixty and the fifth was the number sixty-one. Directly below that line she wrote out the second group of numbers and started subtracting. She wrote the remainders in a third line at the bottom. "Seven, fifteen, twenty-two, nine, and zero...that still makes no sense!"

No one in the little group had a clue as to the meaning, none could find a pattern. But before frustration could mount further, the voteo at Castellan's hip sounded an alert tone so she responded. "Tosh here. Over."

"Madlin sending, Commander. Specialist Meza has had a clairvoyant episode. She's asking me to send Specialist Penn down to your location. Over."

Olivienne looked at Tosh with confusion. "Why would we need Penn?"

The Shield Corp commander thought for a meen then abruptly snapped her fingers. "Penn has interpretist training! What was the last line of the poem?"

The sovereign's face suddenly lit up and she reached down to pull the translated poem from her waist pouch. She followed the lines with her finger until she came to the last one. "The Key of keys will open." Then she looked back up at the panel of buttons. "That's it, we need to use the key...not the pendant but the translation key!"

Tosh smiled. "That makes sense, do you know it?"

The experienced historical adventurist snorted at the humor of such a question. "I've been translating texts, albeit slowly, for rotos. Of course I have the numbers memorized by now. The first key was for the Temple of Archeos so I'm guessing this one will be Illeos or Antaeus."

"You want me to cancel Specialist Penn?"

Olivienne was already writing the name of Illeos out on the

slate in her hand and trying to remember the corresponding letters as well as numbers from the much read cypher. "Yes, prob-
abl — er, wait. I really only have the key numbers for the
established temples memorized, and I don't have the full alphabet with me. See if she knows the full alphabet so we can translate
Antaeus to numeric value." Tosh took a meen to communicate her
request to Madlin, who in turn put the request to Penn. Indeed
she did have the entire twenty-six character cypher memorized
and they translated both remaining temples into number form.

The team gazed up at the panel of buttons and compared the
numbers available to the two sets of temple digits. Dozier pointed
at the first row of buttons. The numbers across read eighteen,
five, twenty-four, seven, and six. "Look, one of the numbers in
the first row is also found within the Illeos set, and it is the
remainder of our maths. Seven."

Qent pointed at the second line. "This one is the same pattern. The remainder of the maths was fifteen and fifteen is also
found within the Illeos set. But the third one..." He shook his
head.

Olivienne started writing on the slate. "If the pattern holds,
then the button should be twenty-two, which was the remainder,
however that is not a number in the temple key. So could there be
more than one button in that row?"

"Tricky." Tosh pointed at the buttons, careful not to depress
any. "It could be one and twenty-one. Or it could be one, ten, and
eleven together. And it looks like the fourth row also accounts for
multiple buttons but the only combination available is the eight
and one to make nine. How do we figure it out for certain?"

Olivienne carefully traced each column down. "Look at column one, the remainder is one so that must be the only button
pushed in that column. Now let's look at column two, the only
remainder is fifteen, which we established was the button to push
in row two. That means the ten button in row three can't be one of
the ones depressed, because it's also in column two with the fifteen button. So it has to be one and twenty-one!"

Castellan looked at her with amazed affection. "Brilliant! So
let's check it out, yeah?"

Ready to complete their second temple mission, Olivienne
began pressing the six deduced buttons in order from left to right.
Each time she pushed one in, the panel gave off a *psst-chshhh*
sound, as if aether were escaping somewhere behind it. When she
was finished with the last one, the horizontal indicator mounted

above the buttons flashed and red liquid filled the first of three segments of the glass ampule. Nothing more happened. The Connate growled her displeasure. "Bollux! I was sure we had it."

"What if you press them in order of the key, I, L, L, E, O, S?"

The Connate looked at Castellan worriedly. "But what order to push the one buttons? There are two of them."

Tosh shrugged. "Maybe it doesn't matter, or try both if the first one doesn't work. By the looks of the indicator, you have two more tries. What does your gut tell you?"

She got a finger wagging as a response, then Olivienne smiled and answered her. "You're the one with the highly rated intuition. What does your channel say, oh great Commander?" Though they were all anxious to discover the secrets of the Maker's mysterious panel of buttons, Qent, Dozier, and Yazzie all laughed with the Connate and their Cmdr. Tosh.

Castellan rolled her eyes and pointed at the panel. "Try them in order."

Even Yazzie, who had been off to the side with nothing to do since she was only in the cave for her capacity as a medican, leaned forward as Olivienne pressed the buttons in order. With each number pressed, the sovereign recited its corresponding letter, her whispering voice nearly drowned out by the hissing of the mechanism inside. "I, L, L, E, O, S." When the last number had been pushed in, the indicator flashed again and the red liquid drained out of the glass ampule above the panel. Then a series of mechanical clicks sounded. "That's it?" Olivienne gripped the sides with her fingertips trying to swing it open but it wouldn't budge. "Maybe it's stuck?"

Tosh waved all of them away from the panel. "Let me try something." Focusing her mind, she used her telekinesis to pull the panel toward her and ince by ince it began to slide out from the wall.

Yazzie gasped, recognizing the motion and container for what it was. "It looks like the place bodies are kept in hospital, a mortum drawer! I had to do a rotation at the one in Cordeesh as part of my medican training before I transferred from Medi Corp to Shield Corp. But something is different about this one." She stopped talking as the stele drawer finished sliding out from the wall. The difference became obvious as the drawer stopped much too short to house an average Psi.

"Is that a child?" Spc. Dozier's voice was quiet as the partially disintegrated skeleton came into view.

Yazzie stepped near and Olivienne backed up to let her look. "No, definitely not." She pointed toward the arm and leg bones that were still intact. "For one, these upper and lower arm bones are the same length as are the ones in the legs. Psierians are proportionally quite different. Also look at the head? It is unusually large for the body size and the intact right hand only has four strangely-long digits. We have five. Either this is the skeleton of someone with a significant physical deformity, or—"

"It's not Psierian." Olivienne finished Spc. Yazzie's sentence then cast a quick glance at Tosh. This was not at all what they intended to find.

Qent pointed a slightly shaking finger into the drawer, near a pile of ash in the general location of the chest cavity. "What's that?"

The other four noticed the metallic shine as he pointed it out but rather than just reach right in for it, Olivienne grabbed the stylus from her pouch and carefully lifted the pendant out. It looked identical to the first one found on Mater Island, except it had a green stone instead of a blue one. "Interesting." She pulled a rag out of her waist pouch and cleaned off the pendant, then strung it on the cord with the first one. They made a dull clanking sound when they swung together.

Castellan abruptly stepped back from the drawer and ran a hand through her neatly ordered hair, effectively sending the fine strands into disarray. "Sheddech!"

Spc. Qent looked at her with concern. "Commander?"

Castellan leveled a look at the entire group in the cave. "This discovery is top secret, no one is to speak of the additional find, not even to the rest of the team. Absolutely no one beyond this chamber, Savvy?" The three specialists all looked slightly frightened at the tone in her voice but they gave their assent quickly enough.

"What's wrong, Tosh?" Olivienne moved away as well and placed a hand on Castellan's tense forearm. "I know this isn't what we expected to find but you have to admit that the nature of this is fascinating..." Her voice trailed off when she saw that Tosh's gaze had gone distant as she assumed a thinking stance.

The commander didn't respond for a few secs then she sighed and pulled the voteo from her belt. "We weren't expecting this at all but we can't leave it here. I'm going to see if the dirigible has some sort of airtight container they can send down, one that will hold whatever is in that drawer."

Olivienne watched as Yazzie, Dozier, and Qent stood near the drawer talking to each other, gesturing toward the bones every so often. She switched to telepathy. *"Castellan, this is a huge discovery. No one has ever found anything like this, or any reference at all as to whom the Makers were. We are the first, isn't it exciting?"*

Two small lines creased the skin between Tosh's eyebrows. *"When you look at it that way, I suppose it is. But I find it more disconcerting than anything. The Makers are clearly nothing like us, which raises more questions than we had before. Who are they? More importantly, who are we?"*

The sovereign realized exactly what the commander was trying to say and suddenly, as the future leader of her people, she found herself with the same concerns. It didn't take Cmdr. Tosh long to message the dirigible and arrange for a large sealable container to be sent down. She sent Qent off at a sprint to fetch it from the cave mouth. Inside they found that the dirigible crew had provided clean cloths per Yazzie's request and she pulled some medican gloves from her kit. She was the one who volunteered to get the skeletal remains stowed away in the sealed bin. They were halfway back to the cave entrance when Tosh's voteo crackled to life. "Madlin to Tosh, we're under fire! Over."

Castellan, who was the one carrying the surprisingly lightweight bin, turned to the group and shouted. "Double-time!" They took off running and when they reached the cave mouth, they could clearly see another dirigible coming in over the ocean. The black air bladder of the ship grew closer by the sec as it came in across the shimmering blue water below. "Jump, I'll lift us!" It was both a testament to the faith the entire team had in Tosh as well as proof of her immense power. As soon as they were outside the cave, she snatched them up in a massive show of concentration and strength and pushed her levitation channel to its limits in order to quickly lift them to the top of the cliff. She staggered as she landed, nearly dropping the bin. Levitation was hard enough at one's limit, but to lift five people in the air on top of being so high up was incredibly taxing.

Seeing her dilemma, Olivienne grabbed the bin and pushed it into Qent's hands. "Here, get this stowed aboard the ship!" She touched Castellan's shoulder but the officer had already recovered from her stumble.

"Get the rest of those rail guns set up and keep firing!" Cmdr. Tosh turned back to Olivienne as the enemy dirigible continued to approach. "What's your range for your pyrokinesis?" She didn't even flinch when a shell ricocheted off the rock not more than two foot away from where they stood. Nor did she acknowledge when their own moored dirigible began returning fire. However, Olivienne remained frozen as she watched the ominous ship approach so Tosh snapped her fingers in front of her face. "'Vienne, range?"

The sovereign jerked her head around to meet the fearless pale blue gaze. Drawing on Tosh's solidity amidst the chaos, Olivienne answered with narrowed eyes. "I can certainly hit that blasted ship!"

Lt. Madlin called out from where the rest of the unit was lined up on the cliff face, firing on the approaching dirigible. "Commander! Our shells aren't penetrating the bladder, it must be one of the new ones made from kevlan."

"Aim for the gondola then, Lieutenant! All of you, aim for the gondola." Unfortunately that was easier said than done. The gondola was a small target in comparison and Tosh assumed that would be armored as well. She turned back to Olivienne and grimaced. "It's all on you. Fire it up, Connate Dracore."

Olivienne shut her eyes to focus her channel then opened them again to see what she wanted to burn. Suddenly the entire side of the black kevlan bladder lit up with flickering flames, visible even in the light of the twin suns. Just as quickly, the flames flickered and died. She turned to Tosh with a frown. "There is nothing there to burn. The kevlan is inflammable!"

"Focus on the lines again, be more precise and concentrate your channel on those small areas. We need to separate that gondola from the bladder or things will go poorly for us in a few more meens!" A yell split the air as one of the ship's crew members cried out and fell back clutching his thigh. Immediately after that, Spc. Soleng took a hit to his upper arm.

Cmdr. Tosh stood in front of the Connate to shield her body and pulled the spyglass from her waist pouch. She observed the approaching airship, hoping beyond hope that Olivienne would be successful. With a cry of relief, she watched as one line glowed and snapped, then three more lines followed suit. "That's it, keep going!" The abrupt tilt of the gondola precipitated a cease-fire on the pirate's side, but the Shield Corp unit never stopped. Two more lines snapped and the gondola tilted so precariously that she watched the shape of three bodies falling toward the water. "Good, ya bastards!"

Even as she said it, Castellan saw another body fall and with the greatest focus she could muster, she grabbed the person with her telekinesis. At that distance, the strain was nearly unbearable but she quickly lifted the body over the line of fire and set him down on the cliff about five yords in the opposite direction as the ocean. Just as Tosh released him, a triumphant cry went through the combined forces of both Shield Corp guardians and the ship's crew. As she turned around, she caught a glimpse of the foreign dirigible as the gondola broke free and crashed into the waves below. She also grabbed Olivienne as the Connate sagged and nearly fell to the ground. The exhausting pyrokinetic display had clearly taken a lot out of her. Once she had Olivienne settled, Tosh spun around to deal with their pirate only to find him drawing his pistol and aiming at the woman at her side.

"Oh no you don't!" With the remaining bit of her nearly exhausted reserve, Tosh mentally stripped the man of his gun and charged him. He scrambled backward but Castellan caught him secs later. Then with both fists holding the front of his shirt, she lifted him off his feet and slammed him backward into the ground. He lost consciousness as soon as his head made contact with the rocky cliff surface. Energized by the encounter, she began calling out to the unit. "Madlin, status report, Holling, check on Connate Dracore." She paused and caught two guardians at loose ends. "Leggett and Calderon, get this shell sucker tied up and stowed on board! Move people, I want off this Maker-forsaken cliff yesterdae, we don't know if they have more than one ship!"

"Are you all right?" Olivienne stood at Tosh's left side as she called out orders.

The commander grimaced. "I'm fine, just drained. You?"

Olivienne tucked a loose dark tendril of hair around her ear and raised her arm with a wince. "I caught a graze from one of the shells, more of a burn really. I think I strained my channel with the distance on that dirigible. I've got a headache that would drop a roc."

Tosh smiled at her tenderly. "Show off." She was about to say more when she was interrupted by the captain of the dirigible.

"Commander, I've got everyone aboard and all the wounded have been placed in the med room. Nothing critical, ser." Captain Seema Velten saluted Tosh when she walked up, albeit begrudgingly. She was a tall woman with the whitest blonde hair that Castellan had ever seen. She wore an armored jacket and black trousers with tall black boots. And not only did she carry a pistol on one hip, but also a sword on the other. Captain Velten was perhaps one of the most sternly serious people Tosh had ever met and from the tone of her voice she did not enjoy the fact that, despite titles, Cmdr. Tosh outranked her simply because she was a Shield Corp commander on active duty with a sovereign. However, if one could ignore the slight attitude, Velten was an excellent ship's captain.

"Thank you Captain Velten, we will board immediately then." She glanced around one last time and noticed someone had pulled in all the ropes from the cliff anchors, and another of the ship's crew stood by to release the anchor line for the dirigible. She shook her head and led the way back to the airship. Once they were aboard, she turned back to Capt. Velten. "Do you have someplace secure that we can keep our prisoner until we reach the Defense Corp office in Wahnish? It won't do to leave him trussed up, the circulation would be cut off and therefore dishonorable to keep him in such a state. Also, did the ship hail you at all before the attack?"

Before the captain could respond, the dirigible gave a jerk as it was released from the mooring point and they all felt when it began to rise. "They did hail us, Commander. I was told that if we gave up the Connate, we would be free to leave unmolested. I could see that it was one of the new kevlan ships out of the shipyard in Soflin, but I would be derelict in my sovereign duty as a Psierian if I let any harm come to Connate Dracore! We had no choice but to fight, *and how*." She turned an appreciative eye toward Olivienne. "Well done by the way, I don't think I've ever seen a display of power quite like that before."

Olivienne inclined her head. "Thank you, Captain, but I only did what I had to do. Everyone knows that the royals have high rated channels. It would be a crime not to use it when people's lives were at stake."

Capt. Velten bowed to her. "Just as it would be a crime not to have evening meal with me tonight."

The good captain could not see Tosh's face, which had darkened like a thundercloud behind her. However Olivienne was a witness to the reaction and her violet eyes crinkled with humor. "Actually Captain, Commander Tosh and I would love to take dinner with you this evening. I was impressed with both the size of your ship and the capability of your crew and I'd like to talk to you about another mission coming up later this roto."

"Oh." A quick glance over her shoulder showed a fully composed Tosh and the captain was thrown off at Olivienne's subtle rebuff. "I would be happy to host you both at my table this evening. We can speak more of your proposed trip then. Now if you'll excuse me, I have to attend the bridge."

As soon as she was out of earshot, Olivienne began laughing. "Your face! No gems or precious metals could buy such an equally gobsmacked and angry look as that!"

Castellan ignored the jibe. "Are you sure we can trust her? I'm assuming you're inquiring to see if she'd be a good fit to take us to wherever the third temple is located. It must be far off if the adventurists haven't found it yet. But Velten..." She grimaced with distaste.

Olivienne put a reassuring hand on Tosh's forearm. "Such a face, but have no fears with the captain. She had a chance to turn us over to a superior ship and did not. I'll accept that loyalty and reward it with a contract if I can. And as for anything else, you have nothing to fear there either, my love. You and I belong together and that is a fact, no dashing captain or *shell-sucker* can take that away." She snickered then as she repeated Castellan's phrase from the top of the cliff and Tosh blushed.

"I was angry."

"Clearly. I must say though, your display of that physical anger was more than stimulating. Perhaps you can show me some offensive moves later in my cabin?"

Tosh smirked. "I guarantee that nothing I do later will be offensive. As a matter of fact, I quite think you'll like it."

Olivienne playfully ran her tongue along her bottom lip then bit the lip for good measure. "I'm sure I will."

The move caused Castellan to groan quietly and wrench her eyes away. "You torture me, 'Vienne. Come, we must check on the unit. Some were injured and while none were serious, I still want to be sure of their health for it will be another long trip back to Tesseron."

Olivienne sighed but didn't dispute Tosh's words. Instead they left the vestibule of the ship together and made their way to the med room.

IT WAS NEAR twenty-two hundred oors when the airship arrived back at Wahnish. At dinner Captain Velten had warmed considerably to both the Connate and the commander. Perhaps it was Castellan's demeanor, but Seema Velten no longer displayed any blatant interest in dallying with Olivienne. She also thanked the Connate for the opportunity to join them on their future adventurist mission and suggested that when Olivienne had a set date she should send a missive. Velten also cautioned she'd need at least two weke's notice to restock and make it north to Dromea. When the meal was complete, Tosh thanked her for the service she had performed and even authorized a bonus as payment for the captain and crew taking fire.

Once all the gear and injured had been unloaded, the dirigible left toward the southeast, back in the direction of its home port of Cordeesh. Both Lt. Savon and Spc. Soleng were taken to the local medican center while the rest went back to make camp behind the Security Corp office again. The doctore that was on duty said both men should be fine to make the long trip down the jungle road the next dae but she'd send some anesthetics and infection blockers with them until they could get to another treatment center.

The bin of bones had already been stowed and locked away in Olivienne and Tosh's hauler. They had a prisoner who was cooling his heels in the Security Corp lockup, a prisoner that hopefully would give them clues as to who had been sending the assassins after the Connate. While the pirate hadn't spoken yet, Castellan had no doubt that General Renou's team would be able to get something out of the man.

The one other bright spot was that after contacting Renou, the general decided to send an investigation team down to Dromea so that Tosh wouldn't have to bring the man north with them. Cmdr. Tosh was glad of a mission fairly well done, even if it was a bit chaotic and they discovered a lot more than they bargained for. With so much uncertain and the sands of knowledge shifting below their feet, it was nice to count on the bright spots when they appeared.

Chapter Twenty-two

BOTH LT. SAVON and Spc. Soleng had their arms in slings for the journey back to Vesper. They had originally planned to leave around five hundred but the doctore wasn't scheduled to arrive back at the med center until six hundred and he was the one who needed to sign releases on the two guardians. Olivienne also had her minor arm wound seen to before they left. Castellan contacted the Security Corp office in Wahnish the night before, while they were flying back from Navis on the dirigible, so the district commander could make sure the railer departing from Ostium the following morning would be prepared for the Connate's team. They would need a secure VIP segment as well as flat segments enough for their three haulers when they made a special stop in Vesper.

While the trip down the jungle road was eleven and half oors heading out to the coast, the later departure from Wahnish made timing a concern. The railer was scheduled to stop in the tiny river town a few meens before seventeen hundred so on Tosh's direction, they pushed their speed up to sixty mahls per oor and made it there in ten oors.

There was no fanfare upon their arrival, just efficient action. It took almost twenty meens to load the haulers and get the rest of the team and their gear on board. Olivienne didn't want the sealed bin with its strange skeletal contents in their cabin so Tosh ascertained that the next safest place would be to lock it in the armored hauler where most couldn't reach it on a moving railer. But just to be sure, she set up a guardian rotation for each stop on their way north.

With so much on their minds, neither woman felt like dallying on the trip back to Tesseron. Cmdr. Tosh had an abundance of reports to write pertaining to their mission, reports that included write-ups for the prisoner, the skeletal remains, and the injuries sustained by all the team members. The medican report even included the minor injury that was taken by the Connate herself. It was just past nineteen hundred oors local time the next evening when the railer arrived at the Tesseron station. Castellan had sent an encrypted voteo missive ahead to General Renou and the leader of the Psi Shield Corp was waiting on Tosh when she arrived. A significant look passed between Castellan and Olivienne. *"I wish I could go back with you, but between the prisoner and the skeleton we found, Renou is insisting on an official debriefing. I'll head back to the residence as soon as I'm able."*

"I'm probably just going to bathe and go right to bed, I'm exhausted and my arm is tender. Wake me when you come in?" Castellan nodded and the Connate climbed into one of the unloaded haulers to go back to the residence with the rest of the unit. The bin of bones had been placed in the storage compartment of the general's private moto so Tosh loaded herself as well.

Castellan was as tired as Olivienne professed to be, even though she had plenty of time during the trip north to recover all her channel strength lost during the incident on Navis. She was lucky that she didn't strain her channels at all. The commander was surprised when the moto did not turn down the familiar roadways that would take them to the Shield Corp main office. "Ser? Are we not going back to headquarters?"

Renou frowned. "I'm afraid not, Commander. The Queen has been briefed on the events on Navis and requested this meeting as soon as you got in."

"Why wasn't Connate Dracore requested as well? After all, it was her historical adventurist mission."

"Connate Dracore is not a Shield Corp officer and would not have the training to recognize potential threats and implications of all that occurred during your trip. Also, the Queen informed me that the Connate will have her own debriefing with the King upon her return to her residence. It seems the location of the final key to the lost temple has been identified and he will be presenting her with the research materials. He has also taken the liberty of arranging supplies and a dirigible for the trip since the Queen wants your team to leave as soon as your Shield Corp unit is at full strength." The moto bounced as they turned off the roadway and Tosh's head reared back as she looked upon the serious face of her commanding officer. Questions whirled through her head. But before she could ask any more of General Renou, they pulled up to a side door at the main palace complex. Renou glanced back at her as they exited the moto. "Bring the bin, Commander."

Tosh retrieved the bin and followed the general up the steps. Black clad Shield Corp agents saluted both as they approached and one man opened the door for them. The group waiting in the Queen's private office was a small one. Besides Olivara Dracore, there was General Leniste, Captain Torrin, and Instrae Greene. Castellan was surprised that Keeley Greene had made the long trip down from Schola. She set the bin along the far wall and saluted the lot before taking a seat at the oval table in the Queen's meeting room. The Queen was the first to speak. "Commander Tosh, did you bring your reports with you?"

"Yes, ser." She reached into her satchel and pulled out the stack of vellum, then passed it down the table. Queen Olivara scanned the pages with one dark eyebrow raised. Then she turned her gaze to General Renou. "When will the prisoner arrive?"

The small woman seated to Tosh's left cleared her throat. "I confirmed the arrival time just before picking up Commander Tosh. They should be here in the next twenty-four oors. The specialist team has orders to take the man straightaway to the secure underground facility below Shield Corp headquarters."

General Leniste grunted. "You going to put the serum to him?"

Renou shrugged. "I've got a pair of interrogators assigned to that case. I suspect they'll use traditional techniques first and if that yields no results then they'll switch to chemical."

"If in the end you get nothing from the scoundrel, I'd set the telepaths on him. We've got a level six in Defense Corp I can loan you." Leniste was known for his occasional ruthlessness when it came to getting a job done.

"No!" The Queen's cold response cut through the tension of the room. "I would no more authorize the rape of one's mind than I would their body. We will find a way to get the information we need legally."

Secretly Castellan was relieved. After all, if they broke from the Psiere Legibus, how easy would it be to keep breaking their sacred laws? Sensing a lull in the conversation, Tosh brought up the thing that most concerned her. "What about the skeletal remains? What is to be done with that?"

Instrae Greene chimed in. "That is where I come in, Commander. I will take the bones with me back to the research center at the Academy. I have a team of experts set up to analyze the remains as soon as I get back. We got your report and that of your medican stating that they were suspected not to be of Psierian origin but we want to run tests to be sure."

Queen Olivara quickly spoke up. "I want those bones secure at all times. I'll send soldiers up with you if I have to. And Tosh, I trust you put a gag order on your team about the bones?"

Castellan nodded. "Yes, ser. The only ones who know what's in the bin are those few that were in the cave with us at the time."

General Leniste held a hand aloft. "Actually, Queen Olivara, I think sending soldiers is an excellent idea. Besides discovering the location of the third temple, the remains may be the most valuable find in all of Psiere."

The Queen nodded. "Make it so, Leniste."

He nodded. "Yes, my Queen."

With that portion buttoned down, the Queen moved on to other news. "We've also received further intelligence from the southern continent. On Commander Tosh's suggestion, we tapped First Lieutenant Cando as our person inside. She has discovered that Tosh's replacement in Ostium is receiving cred chits from someone that goes by the name of Ser Gannon. As some of you may not be aware, Ser Enik Gannon has been on the list of most wanted criminals for a variety of Corps. He is a profiteer and pirate and has provided rail guns and other weapons to the rebel factions that protest the current system of rule. They've also been spreading tales that the Makers and the Divine Mystery are nothing more than a giant hoax perpetrated by the government to keep technological advancements from the people. He is powerful and dangerous, and no matter how much we plot and plan, the man always slips through our fingers."

The Queen paused to take a drink and General Renou took over speaking. "Along with the intel that Lieutenant Commander Seevert Bello is in a traitorous partnership with Gannon, we also have heard a whisper that Gannon himself reports to someone higher up. The Queen and I have our suspicions but we will not sully your minds against the character of what could be an innocent man. Because of the heightened danger to the royal family and other government officials, General Leniste, Captain Torrin, and I will draw up a plan to increase security in the capital that will encompass both Defense Corp and Shield Corp agents. The safety of the people is a priority."

Tosh drew in a surprised breath when the general spoke of the man suspected of employing Ser Gannon. One name popped into her head as the person that would have the power and money to control such a massive operation. She felt a little mental tickle and looked up into the violet eyes of the Queen. *"Yes?"*

Olivara answered. *"You know, don't you?"*

"I suspect, same as you."

The Queen narrowed her eyes as Renou continued to deliver

the information they had about rebel movements on the northern and southern continents. *"Tell me."*

"Ser Pon Havington, the Praefectus of Dromea. We never got along during my stint in the south. That man set my intuition channel jangling every time we met in person. Havington is self-serving and power hungry and I never once trusted him. He also has the means to fund such an operation. Am I correct in my assumption?"

Olivara gave a discreet nod. *"You are correct. Now that I think on it, he seemed most adamant that you be recalled to the north after your accomplishments in Ostium. I thought he simply wanted you to be rewarded for your immense success but his tone always rang false to me. Perhaps you were too successful in ensuring the safety of the region and he wanted to get rid of you in a way that would not raise any concerns. If it is Ser Havington, we have a problem."*

Tosh blew out a sigh. *"No proof."* Before the Queen could respond, Castellan caught her name uttered aloud during Renou's briefing and refocused her attention on the general.

"...don't think it is necessary to increase Commander Tosh's current Shield unit numbers but the entire team is to remain on high alert until the head of this serpent of unrest can be cut from its body." She held up a hand to tick off items on her fingers. "Our priorities right now are the safety of the sovereigns and the royal family, discovering who is the financier and brains of the rebellion, finding the location of the Temple of Antaeus, and researching the origin of the remains found on Navis."

Renou looked right at Castellan as she gave her next directive. "Tosh, your duty is three-fold. Obviously you need to use every one of your unit and channel resources to guarantee the Connate's safety. You need to help her successfully complete the search for the last temple pendant key. And you need to start putting together a long-term mission team as well as a list of equipment and other resources you will need for a possible expedition to the lost temple. Since we've never stumbled across the third pyramid in all our previous exploration, the general conclusion is that it is beyond our usual range, which means you will have full support and the best the Psi Shield Corp can offer in terms of supplies."

Castellan grinned. "Does that include one of the new armored dirigibles coming out of Soflin? Because I can tell you that was tough to beat down on Navis."

Olivara was the one who answered. "Count on it! I want my daughter protected, Commander. And I want the temple mission to be a success when it happens. As you and I discussed in the past, there are other factors involved with the temple mission that need a smart and decisive mind. I don't want those Antoraestones to fall into the wrong hands. If it came to that, I'd rather they were locked away until they could be examined fully or destroyed." She looked around. "Is everyone in agreement on that?"

Gen. Renou and Ins. Greene quickly agreed but Gen. Leniste looked like he wanted to argue the point. "But, my Queen, there are so many positive uses for such power —" He stopped for a sec then frowned and shook his head. "Blast it, you're right. Without knowing the limits, it would be disastrous for such a thing to fall into the hands of our rebels or their mysterious leader. Yes, the magnification stones should be locked away or destroyed if there is a chance that they can be used against us. Such a waste —"

"I agree, General, it will certainly be a waste of resource if we are forced to destroy them but I'm hoping it will not come to that. The Makers themselves locked the stones away for a reason. Clearly they are dangerous." She leveled a piercing look at Castellan. "I will put my trust in Commander Tosh that she will handle the discovery with absolute secrecy and a fair amount of finesse."

Castellan nodded solemnly. "It will be as you wish, my Queen."

"Good! And on that note, I think we all have our tasks assigned and we can conclude this meeting." Everyone stood but Olivara called to Castellan before they could file out of the room. "Commander Tosh, a word in private, if you will."

Tosh nodded and waited until the door shut behind Captain Torrin before returning to her seat. She took the initiative, suspecting what the Queen had to say. "I well understand your concerns where it comes to the Antoraestones. Have no fear that I will make the safest decision when the time comes."

Olivara smiled. "I trust you, Commander, or I would have never placed such an onus on your shoulders. However, I have another concern about the situation and it has to do with my daughter."

"Olivienne — I mean to say, Connate Dracore? What is your concern?"

The Queen smiled. "You forget that I'm well aware of your relationship with my daughter, Commander. Just as I'm well aware of how persuasive she can be when she sets her mind to

something. I fear she will try to talk you out of destroying or locking away the stones should the moment arise. Where does your
loyalty lie, Commander Castellan Tosh?"

"My loyalty lies with Psiere, and with its Queen by extension.
I will follow your directive when the times comes, I know my
duty." Tosh paused. "Is that all you need from me, my Queen?"

"I have one more thing. My daughter, what is your intention
with her?"

A surprised look washed across Castellan's face. "What do
you mean? I intend to serve to the extent of my duty to keep her
safe, of course!"

It was a different kind of smile that the Queen wore, one not
like any other she had previously graced upon Castellan. It was
the smile of a mother. "No, Commander. I'm referring to your
romance. Do you see yourself in a future consorage? Romance
with an heir to the Divine Cathedra is no mild matter."

Tosh sat in stunned silence for nearly a meen before she
could answer. "Well I—truthfully being someone's par is not
something I've given a lot of thought with my career such as it is.
And I suppose I never considered the implications of a royal
romance."

"And now?"

The officer cocked her head to the side, pale eyebrows raised.
"I don't know, I suppose that depends on Olivienne and her
wishes on the matter."

Olivara tapped a nail on the table in front of her. "There is
one small matter besides my daughter's wishes, Commander."

"Please, call me Castellan when we speak of matters outside
my career as an officer. I feel as though it would be
unprofessional elsewise. And what is this other issue?"

The Queen's voice was serious as she responded. "To put it
succinctly, me. Unlike any other par on Psiere, an heir to the
Divine Cathedra is required to have her consorage sanctioned by
the Queen. So you see, my questions are not without validity or
merit."

Castellan abruptly sat back in her chair. "But what if the
suitor does not ask, what if it is the heir?"

Laughter poured melodiously through full, dark lips. "Well
she would have to request permission from me as well."

The fair-haired commander made a face. "It sits poorly with
me, having someone dictate my feelings and future."

More laughter followed her words. "Oh my dear Castellan,

you are an officer. Has your entire life not been about someone else dictating your future? This is your opportunity to make the future what you will, to take love and destiny into your own hands."

"You seem a little too eager for our oathing, why else would you be telling me all this now?"

The Queen shrugged. "Perhaps I am. But that has no bearing on the truthfulness of my words. I'm only asking you to consider the idea and to remember the rules should you decide yay instead of nay. That is all."

Tosh nodded, feeling a host of unease at the Queen's words. "I'll take all you said into consideration."

"Thank you." The Queen stood again and gestured toward the door. Their meeting was clearly over and for that Tosh was immensely glad.

"PAPAN, I'VE BEEN considering Castellan as a possible par. What do you think?" Their official meeting was over and father and daughter had spent the past oor catching up on personal affairs. Olivienne was sitting on her well-worn lounger with her arms wrapped around her bent legs and her chin propped up on her knees. It was a casual and relaxed pose that she could assume around few others. There were many expectations of propriety when one was the heir to the Divine Cathedra.

Keshien Dracore thought hard on his daughter's words. While they weren't completely unexpected since she had already admitted her feelings for the commander, he never seriously thought he'd see the dae that his daughter was ready to settle in with just one person. He was both elated and sad to see Olivienne finally growing into her own powerful woman. The two had always enjoyed a close relationship and he feared the moment that someone would come along and take his little girl away. That dae was rapidly approaching. Seeing that she was expecting an answer, he shook himself free from his thoughts. "I think that if she makes you happy, if she compliments you and grows with you, then you could ask for no better. You have my blessing to offer your oathing if that is the case. However, it is not mine that you need."

The younger woman blew out a sigh. "I know, but I hate having to ask permission. Her meddling irritates me to no end!"

"I know, my darling, but she is the Queen. Just as you will be somedae, and it will be your permission needed for your children's consorage. And besides, despite how buttoned down your mother is, I suspect she adores Commander Tosh as much as you!"

Olivienne laughed. "I hardly think it is possible for anyone to adore her more than I." She gave another sigh, only it had a more dreamy quality than the frustrated ones she usually let loose.

The King smiled indulgently at his eldest child and gave her knee a brief squeeze. "It looks good on you."

"What is that, papan?"

He smiled again with a twinkle in his eye and answered her before rising to his feet. "Love, of course. And when you are ready, I will gladly welcome Castellan Tosh into the family as another daughter."

Olivienne stood as well and embraced her father with tears in her eyes. "Thank you."

The King took his leave but before stepping outside into the night, he turned and wagged a finger at her. "And talk to your mother!"

Olivienne laughed and shooed him out. Castellan arrived back at the residence a short while later looking uncharacteristically rumpled and tired, but her face lit with a smile as soon as she met Olivienne's violet eyes. The Connate met her halfway across the room and they reunited from their brief separation with a slow and sweet kiss. As they walked up the stairs to Olivienne's room, the sovereign glanced back at her lover. "How was your meeting?"

Castellan sighed with exhaustion at the responsibility that had been placed on her shoulders. She didn't answer until they began to undress for bed. "Our prisoner should arrive within the next twenty-four oors and he's set to be interrogated by one of Renou's special teams. Unrest in the south along with rumors of a cred man at the top of the list for assassination suspects has both Renou and Leniste increasing security on the royal family." She held a hand out at Olivienne's look of dismay. "Fear not, our unit will not change. The nature of our missions dictates the necessity of a smaller team and also makes it more difficult for would be assassins. They seem to think you're safe enough with me."

"Because I am."

The look of absolute certainty gave Castellan pause before once again continuing on. "Instrae Greene was down for this debriefing."

Olivienne raised dark eyebrow as she slid beneath the cover-lets. "Oh?"

"Yes, it seems she will be taking the remains we found back to the Academy for research and the entire discovery is to be kept under tight wraps. General Renou assured me that someone of discretion already spoke with my team to impart the news." She got between the coverlets herself and groaned as her nude body slid against the cool and clean material.

"It was actually my father that debriefed the team. He spoke separately with those of us that were in the cave and discovered the bones. He was here waiting for us when we got back with the haulers. Lieutenant Madlin said they will return them to the moto yard in the morning."

Tosh shut off the light that was near the bed and turned toward Olivienne. The Connate's room was dimmer than her own, as the lamplight from outside didn't seep through the blinds as much on the second floor. "And how was your meeting with the King?"

Olivienne scooted closer until she could wrap her arm around Tosh's upper body. "We have a new mission in two daes. He's assured me that we already have all the supplies we'll need."

"Where is the mission this time?"

The Connate closed her eyes remembering the last stanza of the third key poem. "Amongst a sea of scaled beasts, north the tallest mountains tall, an island of breeding danger lies. Beware the place wyrms feast, centered on the lake of blood and gall, for below is where innocence dies."

Tosh snorted. "I have nowhere near the brain power to deal with such riddles this evening. What does it mean?"

Olivienne laughed quietly. "There is an island in the middle of Dir Nubila, Serpens Island..."

Castellan sucked in a breath at the danger that had suddenly multiplied in her mind. "Dir Nubila, the same inland sea that is full of drakes that are easily twice the size of rocs and who spit boiling acid when they attack?"

"The very same." Castellan barely made out her nod in the dark. "Anyway, the drakes breed on Serpens Island. And in the middle of Serpens Island lies another lake, Dir Sanguis. They say it is named so because it is red like blood from the high acid content and strange algae blooms. Whatever we seek is in the middle of Dir Sanguis."

The officer coughed. "Convoluted and mysterious." She tried to remember the map of Psiere that had been drilled into her head since her time at the Academy. "I'm assuming we'll take a railer up to Baene, then dirigible out to the island? That's going to be a long trip, though not nearly as dangerous since we'll be coming in above the island, out of reach of the drakes."

"My father said the same thing."

Tosh continued her line of thought, guessing times and distances as she went. "So about seventeen oors from Tesseron to Baene, including the brief stop at the Academy station. From Baene it will be another...sixteen oors out into the sea. I'm just guessing based on where I remember Serpens Island to be from our Academy maps."

Olivienne caressed her cheek. "Very good guess, love. It is nearly exactly that."

The commander shrugged depreciatively while lying on her right side. "I've always been good with figures."

The sovereign grinned lasciviously, mostly unseen in the near dark of the room. "You're good with much more than that."

Castellan laughed quietly as she picked up Olivienne's less than sleepy thoughts. "Aren't you tired?"

Olivienne made a sound low in her throat. "Not any more. You?"

The answer whispered from between Castellan's lips as she leaned toward her lover. "Not at all." Olivienne's final thought before Tosh proved how good she was at other things, was that she really needed to speak with her mother. The dashing officer had decisively won her heart and it was Olivienne's sincerest hope above all others that Castellan would want to oath and eventually consor with the future Queen of Psiere.

Chapter Twenty-three

THE AIR WAS cooler near the Dara Mountains. After a grueling seventeen and a half oors on a railer, they arrived in Baene with all their gear. The team had the luxury of overnighting in the northern city and they didn't leave again until fifteen hundred the next afternoon. The King had chartered a local dirigible to take them south to the inland sea, inaccurately referred to as Dir Nubila. But at eight hundred mahls long and almost half that wide, the body of water was so big it had its own micro-climate. The sea itself was just north of the Dara Mountains and a lot of cold air bathed the eastern end, the region between Baene and Nubila. Not only did the dirigible have to travel seven hundred and fifty mahls southwest from the northern city to their adventurist location, but they had to fight a cold head wind the entire way.

Leaving Baene in the afternoon meant the team would sleep on the dirigible for half the trip, similar to what they had done when traveling to Navis. The captain informed Olivienne and Tosh that they'd make one stop at an illeostone supply station halfway there, but it wouldn't take more than twenty meens to exchange their spent stones for charged ones. Most dirigibles had a max range of fourteen hundred mahls when the illeostone tank was full so they wouldn't have to make any additional stops on the way back to Baene. No one was sure what they would find when they flew over Dir Sanguis. They were not expecting much initial danger from the drakes while so high in the air. The real danger would come when the team landed. They weren't even sure what to look for, if there was a cave or other structure that housed the third key.

Olivienne shivered in the breeze of the observation deck located at the stern of the airship. She left Tosh a half oor before so the commander could hold a quick briefing with her team. Olivienne was planning on heading to her cabin soon but wanted a chance for some quiet contemplation first. There were so many thoughts and emotions going through her and she feared a loss of concentration when it came time to complete their mission. One new worry to Olivienne was the concern she now held for her team's safety. It was never something she had considered before. But after working closely with the men and women of her Shield Corp unit for nearly half a roto, she had come to admire and like every one of them. Castellan had certainly done an exemplary job putting the group together.

The Connate smiled as her mind veered along another track. Then there was Tosh. The upright officer had in turns vexed and excited her more than any other person Olivienne had met. It seemed as though each dae taught them something new about each other. And Olivienne wanted many more of those daes, nay, all of those daes. It was then, standing at the rail of the dirigible at near twenty-two hundred oors, she knew she had to ask. Olivienne Dracore could not wait a meen longer. She spun on her heel to go search for her lover and ran directly into a solid body. "Oh!"

"I would have warned you that I was here but you seemed so lost in thought. I didn't want to disturb you."

Castellan's eyes shone pale in the dim lamp that hung from a ceiling post of the deck. The only other light around them was that of the endless and swirling stars above. The night was clear and black and a sense of waiting hung in the air. The Connate briefly wondered what it must have been like to have a moon in the sky, before the destruction of Antaeus. "I was just coming to find you." Olivienne reached up to caress Tosh's cheek and the pale-haired officer shut her eyes at the feel of it. "Besides, you could never disturb me."

Castellan smiled as she opened her eyes again. "You know, as much as discussing my feelings is far outside my ken, I cannot help admitting that I fall deeper in love with you each dae."

The sovereign sucked in a surprised breath and a smile broke over her face. "I was just thinking something similar when you walked out here. I was wondering where the search for the lost temple will take us, and I was speculating where we ourselves will go."

Castellan cocked her head, trying to decipher Olivienne's words. "Where we will go? How do you mean? If you're speaking of us, I should warn you now that I don't see an end."

It hardly seemed possible for Olivienne's smile to grow wider but it did. "That is wonderful news and to that, I have something important to say to you." She paused and Castellan squeezed her hand in encouragement.

"Well go on then, what is it?"

Before she could second-guess her actions, Olivienne went down on one knee. "Commander Castellan Tosh, I have no token to give you save my heart. And within that heart I hold all the things one should feel for a future par...passion, love, honor, respect, truth, and kindness. It is because I hold these things within me that I offer you my Oath of Consorage."

For Castellan Tosh, time seemed to inexplicably slow to a stop. She no longer noticed the chill air, the flickering stars above, nor did she notice the way the wind mussed her hair, leaving her less than reputable. All she could think about was the woman who knelt in front of her. Not just any woman, but a sovereign and heir to the Divine Cathedra of Psiere. Olivienne's dark eyes stared up at her, waiting for an answer to a statement Tosh never dreamt she would hear or speak. She cleared her throat and her lover's gaze never wavered. "You...are you oathing to me?"

Rather than take affront at Castellan's lack of reaction, Olivienne smirked. After many lunes together, she knew how the officer's mind circled a thought fully, trying to understand every aspect. "My, you are certainly slow on the uptake this evening, Commander. But to answer your question, yes. Though it is not official until it's...well, official. Being who I am, there will have to be a public announcement of course."

Castellan pulled Olivienne to her feet so she could see her eye to eye in the dim light. "But, are you sure?" She paused and blew out a breath at Olivienne's annoyed look. "Of course you're sure. I know you would not have asked otherwise. But the Queen, my career—"

"The Queen has already approved, mayhap a little too readily I might add. I dearly hate giving my scheming mother exactly what she wants but in this instance it perfectly aligned with my own wants and needs. And what about your career, did you expect to get promoted away from me?"

Tosh's face darkened. "Frankly, yes. You know this relationship has been hard for me with the conscience of my duty tugging me this way and that. In the past I've always feared a lack of challenge if I stayed in the same position too long. And I certainly don't want any accusations of nepotism! Fie on that!"

Olivienne could see that Tosh's mind was still working at the statement and knew it was only a matter of time. But she couldn't help laughing at the dashing woman's words. And Castellan Tosh was dashing and so much more as she stood in the dark of the night with her pale hair blowing in the wind and the light of those pale blue eyes gazing on her with all seriousness. "Did you just say fie? Oh my dear commander, nobody says fie any more. How antiquated of you!"

"Are you mocking me?"

The Connate leaned into Castellan and ran a finger along her strong jawline. "Of course not. But look at it logically, do you really think leading a Shield Corp unit for a historical adventurist is going to bore you? In the time you have known me, have you ever lost interest in your job?"

Castellan finally cracked a smile. "I've certainly rued it some daes but never once have I gotten bored. And you can promise that no favors will be awarded me by the Queen?"

More quiet laughter from the sovereign. "Oh my dear Tosh, somedae I will be Queen so I can certainly not guarantee the Queen will abstain from giving you favors. And if you consor with me, somedae you will be King."

"That is a daunting thought."

Olivienne's face softened as she recognized the core of Castellan's worry. It was fear. "I know it is but do you love me?"

Castellan pulled her even closer. "Of course I do! It is as if you are—" She paused to slip her hand between their chests and placed her own directly over her heart. "I feel you right here every single dae. And I worry for you whenever you are not near."

"And do you want me in your life, do you want to be with me for the rest of your daes? I can think of no better person in all of Psiere to be my protector, to be my King, nor to be my love. It is you and no one else I wish to have by my side."

"I—" Castellan swallowed thickly and looked down to gather her emotions. Not having full control was difficult for the regimented woman. "I wasn't sure how deeply you felt. I only know what is inside myself and truthfully we don't speak of this love between us much. It is a secret after all."

Olivienne pulled Tosh's chin up and deposited a sweet kiss on her lips. "Well, I don't know about you but I'm ready to put this secret to rest. Aren't you?"

Castellan's voice was quiet. "I am."

"And do you accept my oath?"

Instead of immediately answering, Castellan dropped to a knee in front of Olivienne. "My Royal Sovereign, Connate Olivienne Dracore...I, Castellan Tosh, pledge my heart and my future to you. Those things you hold within your heart—passion, love, honor, respect, truth, and kindness—I too hold. I accept your Oath of Consorage and pledge my own in return. Let neither our vows of oathing, nor our future vows of consorage ever be broken." She stood again and sealed her words with all the passion she could muster. As their lips met, all thoughts of mission, worries of future, and even the night sky, simply dropped away. It was no longer a matter of admitting their love for each other, it had become a promise between them.

They started to pull away from each other but Olivienne's grip in the back of Tosh's hair was firm and she pulled them back together. Neither heard the door open onto the observation deck. But the sound of Lt. Savon's voice brought them out of their kiss as fast as a bucket of water. "Commander Tosh, we have confirmed the gear...oh sheddech!" Lt. Madlin was pacing him and pulled up short when she saw the embracing couple. Only instead of going red-faced like the senior lieutenant, she wore a self-satisfied smirk. Savon stumbled over his manners briefly before saluting and looking away. "My apologies, Connate Dracore and Commander..." Madlin snickered at the flustered man and gave her own salute.

While Olivienne was trying her hardest not to laugh, Tosh had turned all business once again. "At ease, Lieutenants!" She watched closely the reaction of her two officers as she spoke her next words. "Though we've tried to keep our relations a secret, it seems obvious that at least a few deductive individuals have figured out that Connate Dracore and I have been engaging in dalliance for quite some time now." Olivienne snorted at Castellan's use of the word dalliance but let her continue. "What you may not know is that this has been sanctioned by not only General Renou, but also the Queen herself. So there is no risk to you or your career over my behavior."

Lt. Madlin spoke up. "Pardon my truth, ser, but it wouldn't matter to me if it weren't condoned. I would still follow you because you're a great leader and this is the best team I've ever been a part of. Not only that, but I both admire and respect Connate Dracore and I think you make a good match."

"And you, Savon?"

Gentry Savon cleared his throat and looked up to meet their eyes. "I've worked with you for a handful of rotos now, Connate, and I don't believe I've ever seen you happier. And I know I've never had the confidence in our Shield Corp unit that I currently have under the direction of Commander Tosh. At this point in my career, I'd be hard pressed to accept a promotion were it offered, simply because this is the best post I've ever had."

Tosh smiled at the man who had flourished in his role over the past half roto. "Good to know."

Olivienne reached over and took Castellan's hand then. "What your commander hasn't told you yet is that we've just oathed to each other. It will not be official until the announcements can be made upon our return to Tesseron, but you are the first to know."

"Congratulations, I look forward to the ceremony!" Lt. Auda Madlin leaned forward. "You will have seats for us, right?"

"I'm afraid not, Lieutenant." Auda's face fell until Castellan spoke again. "You will all be there, of course, but the entire unit will be working that dae. After all, we can't leave our sovereign unprotected now can we?"

"I suppose not, ser."

Savon grinned and could barely contain his happiness. "Congratulations to both of you. May your consorage be long and fruitful."

Tosh turned to Olivienne and stilled when her gaze was caught. In the silence that followed Savon's words, the four of them seemed frozen. Then with as much tact as she could muster, Lt. Madlin gave Lt. Savon's telesana-healed arm a poke and spoke up. "Well, we'll just be going now, and well done again." Then before the Connate or commander could respond, she all but dragged her fellow lieutenant back through the door of the observation deck.

Olivienne laughed and blew out a sigh. "It took them long enough."

Tosh laughed with her. "It certainly did. We can follow if you like."

"Or we can stay right here. Though it is a bit chilly."

"I hear the Connate was given the nicest cabin aboard ship. Perhaps we should check it out?"

Olivienne smirked at Castellan's wile. "And who are you to think you'll be invited in?"

Tosh bent and lifted Olivienne into her arms before twirling the sovereign around. "Why, I'm the Connate's future par! She has gifted me with a precious promise, an oath of her future. I merely want to show my appreciation and give my heart in return."

"Oh, put me down! I refuse to be so coarsely handled on my way to the room!"

Tosh raised a single pale brow in the darkness. "Oh really?" Her skepticism was obvious but she acceded to Olivienne's wishes.

Once the Connate was standing, she took a step toward the door and turned back to crook a finger at her lover. "Mmm hmm, however once we are inside my room..." Tosh gave her a dashing grin and both took off with speed to the sovereign's cabin in record time.

LIGHT OF THE first sun was just filtering over the horizon when the dirigible had Serpens Island in its sights the next morning. While it was easily seen from the height of the airship, the approaching island was still shrouded in twilight. They had been traveling over open water the night before and it was a shock to see the forested landscape of the island as the light grew brighter. Perhaps it was because the land was so green that the inland lake glimmering on the island seemed so out of place. There was no vegetation in the vicinity of its shore. As Illeos also rose above the horizon, the light nearly doubled and the red lake that drew ever nearer shone with the ominous visage of blood. Tosh stood on the staging deck on the port side of the airship. She was startled when Spc. Holling stepped to the rail next to her.

"Dir Sanguis. A lake within an island within a lake. Dangerous and as of yet unexplored."

Commander Tosh shot a sideways glance at the original medican for the Connate's unit. "Like two mirrors turned toward each other, a reflection within a reflection within a reflection. Nature is certainly strange."

Holling seemed more talkative than normal and they still had nearly twenty meens before arriving at their destination so Castellan let him go on. "Did you know that the red of Dir Sanguis is caused by a mix of toxic algae bloom and high acid content of the water?"

Tosh smiled at the man's bout of loquaciousness. "I had actually read that somewhere."

Holling held up his finger. "Ah, but did you know that the lake algae is an essential part of the drake's diet? That is why their young are hatched on its shores. The drake's abdomens have two chemical filled chambers that combine during emesis. The resulting spray is an acid that has been heated to more than two hundred pyrs! Not bad for a dumb water dragon, eh?"

"That sounds rather unpleasant and dangerous. How do you know so much about drakes?"

Gren Holling closed his eyes briefly, as if to see the memories that prompted his words. "I grew up on the southern seashore, in a small town that lies between the Dara Mountains and Dir Nubila. I've always been fascinated by the large sea serpents and when I got my secondary medican training in animal biology, I chose drakes as the subject for my dissertation."

The pale eyebrow of his Commander rose. "Oh? And what was the title of your paper, Specialist?"

Holling blushed. "The Symbiotic Relationship between Psierians and the Drakes of Serpens Island."

Castellan looked at her guardian with new eyes. "And what was your conclusion?"

"I believe the drakes to be psychic. Not on the same level as the Atlanteens, but certainly with more intelligence and understanding than say the average fish. Animal empaths have gotten flashes of emotion when near the great beasts. I would guess very much like what the team experienced when they encountered the Rocs on Mater. The drakes seem to understand that the Psierians that go out into the lake are no threat so they leave our fishing boats alone. In return we stay away from their island and its surrounding waters. Most anyways. And just like the rocs, they don't seem to tolerate trespassers in their territory."

Castellan knew that the medican had animal empathy as one of his channels and assumed that he had felt such emotion. The people of Psiere could do much worse than to admire the greater and lesser animals of the land. She clapped him on the shoulder with a smile. "Well I'm certainly glad you're along on this journey with us. Now tell me, worst case scenario, what are the effects if someone goes into Sanguis?"

Holling rubbed his chin. "Hmm, the lake itself is not hot. However the acid content will cause moderate to severe burns to the skin. It will most likely cause blindness if it gets in the eyes and extreme pain no matter where it touches."

"Well as you were informed in my briefing, we don't actually know where the object we are looking for is located. We are hoping to see a sign when we approach from the air. But the encrypted text specifically mentions Sanguis. So we all have waterproof suits to protect our skin and special full face masks in case we have to go beneath the surface."

The medican nodded. "I've seen the suits and read their

specs. They will be sufficient. There have been many samples taken of the lake over the rotos. The scientists all come in via dirigible, just as we are, and lower sample tubes down to the water below. That is the only way to test the fauna and waters of the island."

Olivienne walked up closely followed by Lieutenants Madlin and Savon. Castellan held up her hand to forestall any comments from them because she still had one more question for her talkative medican. "And what of exposure to the drakes' spray? What is the worst case damage if someone is hit?"

Holling blanched and shook his head. "They'll die. I'm sorry, Commander, but even the suits will not protect us from a drake's spray. Between the tempyrature and the volatile acid, it will melt both the suit and skin right from our bodies."

Both lieutenants looked pale at the medican's declaration and Olivienne spoke quietly in the lull. "We just came to tell you that we're in position but perhaps we should rethink our plan, Tosh. We don't even know what we're looking for down there."

Rather than answer her worried statement, Castellan pulled her spyglass from the satchel that was slung across her chest and peered down at the red lake below. It was much larger than she anticipated. "It's huge! Why, it must be at least fifteen mahls across!"

Lt. Madlin nodded. "Yes, ser. Most people don't realize that the lake within an island is the same size as Dir Altum that lies just east of Nubila."

Holling spoke next. "It's not widely known because Serpens Island is uninhabitable and unexplored."

Castellan contemplated their lack of information and rubbed her eyebrow thoughtfully. "Are there any islands within Dir Sanguis?"

Again, it was Holling who answered. "Yes, ser. There is an island near the center of the lake. It's probably two dirigibles in length and naught but bare dirt. If you notice, the high acidity guarantees that nothing can grow right around the lake itself, so the island has no vegetation."

Tosh looked at Madlin. "Please go tell the captain to head for the center of Sanguis, and hover us over the bare island. That has to be the place!"

Olivienne looked at her in surprise. "Are you sure?" Tosh tapped her head and smiled. "Ah, your intuition channel has decided to kick in, eh? Good to know."

Suddenly Lt. Savon stiffened and his eyelids began to flutter. Both Olivienne and Castellan grabbed him to prevent the man from falling to the deck as his knees buckled. Their touch only served to make his prescient vision stronger. "Blood...blood everywhere! The Makers of above and below, the gray ones will flood the menagerie...beware the rope...the seed is in the soil."

Just as fast as the vision came on, it left Savon once again. He stiffened and opened his eyes fully as the other three stared at him. After a few calming breaths, the lieutenant spoke in a shaky voice. "That was...intense. Did it make any sense to you?"

Olivienne looked back at him in thought. "Blood would be an obvious analogy for the lake. I don't understand the part about the gray ones and the flooding of the menagerie. Nor the bit about the seed and the rope."

Tosh snapped her fingers. "Back on Mater, Lieutenant Madlin mentioned gray ones in her psychometry reading! And the rope..." She grabbed her voteo to contact Lt. Madlin. "Tosh here for Lieutenant Madlin. Find out what the anchor line for the dirigible is composed of. Tosh out." She turned to Savon and Olivienne. "Perhaps the vision references something happening to the anchor line. If it's made of standard rope instead of cable, it would be at risk should the drakes engage us. After all, the anchor line is also what we will rappel down on."

Spc. Holling's had been watching the exchange and his face abruptly lit up. "Ser! When a seed sprouts into a flower, it opens. Perhaps they mean the opening of the place we seek is below the soil."

"Yes!" Olivienne jogged her fist in the air in agreement with the medican. "Well done, Specialist Holling!"

The commander's voteo crackled and Madlin's voice came over the line. "Madlin here. Captain confirms the anchor line is standard woven rope. We should be wary on the descent, ser. Over."

"Confirmed. Gather the rest of the unit to this deck, descent in ten meens. Tosh Out."

As Castellan, Olivienne, Holling, and Savon all began stepping into their harnesses, the rest of the unit trickled onto the deck. A few of the ship's crew also joined them. They would be handling the anchor gun that would fire into the ground below. There were also spotters posted on all sides of the airship's decking to watch for activity in the water. The commander was going over details with Lt. Savon when Holling approached her again. "Ser!"

She turned and leveled a look at the man for interrupting. "Yes, Specialist?"

He quickly pointed at one of the crew members manning the rail guns. "They're using standard issue, ser. The drakes are a protected species, we cannot use lethal force against them, per the old Queen's directive that was signed into place after the Gammen incident. Article twenty of the Psiere Legibus states that lethal force may not be used upon a greater beast within their protected territory. The same law would have applied to the rocs as well, not that we needed to use such force then."

"Sheddech!" Tosh abruptly took off at a jog, taking the outer stairs of the dirigible to the bridge where the captain was located. Capt. Tomas looked up from his map of the region when Tosh entered the abundantly windowed space. "Captain, your crew may not use standard rail guns on the drakes below, even if my team is in danger. You must switch to non-lethal concussive shot instead."

The man's face blossomed deep red at being given orders by someone twenty rotos younger and of lower rank. "Listen, *Commander*, my crew will use whatever means necessary to guarantee the safety of this airship. And if I tell them to use rail guns, then by the Makers, that is what they'll use!"

Castellan's anger blossomed in the face of such insubordination but she did not let it outwardly show. Instead she calmly stood ramrod straight and looked the man dead in the eye. "My name is Commander Castellan Tosh of the Psiere Shield Corp. I am on active duty in charge of Her Royal Sovereign, Connate Dracore's personal Shield unit, and on direct duty for the Queen herself. You, ser, are out-ranked!"

Capt. Tomas's face went from red to pale and rage-filled in an instant. "No one out ranks me on my own ship, least of all some—"

He never got to finish his sentence because in the blink of an eye, Tosh had pulled her pistol and aimed it straightaway at his head. She paused to telekinetically immobilize the livid man and addressed the rest of the crew on the bridge. "Your captain has been relieved of duty per article two, section three of the Psiere Legibus for insubordination and mutiny. The rules of our governing system state that an active Shield Corp unit leader holds seniority over all other officers where a royal's life may be in danger. Do any of you disagree with my assessment?"

Six shocked faces looked back at her and after a few secs

delay, voices responded. "No, ser!"

"Good, now who is next in command?"

A middle-aged woman with tidy short dark hair and a trim fit to her uniform stepped forward smartly and saluted Cmdr. Tosh. "Lieutenant Bescal Greem, ser!"

Tosh nodded. "Good. Will you submit to a trust reading, Lieutenant Greem?"

The officer paled but nodded her head. "Yes, ser."

Telepathically a person could not lie so Castellan asked the lieutenant a series of questions to determine her loyalty. *"Who holds your pledge of service?"*

"The Queen, ser." Lt. Greem's mental voice was strong and resolute.

"Do you agree with my assessment of Captain Tomas in regards to rank and the articles of the Legibus?"

Again, Greem's answer was solid in Tosh's head. *"Yes, ser!"*

"Will you have trouble with the rest of the crew when we head down to the island?"

Lt. Greem glanced around the bridge and gave a minute nod of her head. *"Some crew have been with Captain Tomas a long time, I think we will have problems with them."*

Castellan grimaced at the voice in her head and grabbed the voteo from her belt. "Tosh to Savon, over."

Savon's voice came clear over the speaker. "Savon here, over."

"Change of plans, Lieutenant. We need a team of—" She looked back at Lt. Greem and the woman's voice came back into her head.

"I think four of your black-shirts would be enough to steady the loyalists."

"Fine." Aloud, Tosh spoke into the speaker again. "I need either you or Lt. Madlin to stay aboard the ship, and select three more of the unit to stay with you. Suspect mutinous element with the removal of Captain Tomas. Copy?"

Savon's response came back immediately. "Yes, ser! Give me five to make the selection and hand out orders. Savon out."

By the end of the five requested meens, Savon himself had elected to stay, in case he had any more visions. Spc. Holling was also selected for his animal empathy to better gauge the drakes in the area. He also chose Gen. Renou's niece, Spc. Penn, and the unit's hulking man of an engineer, Spc. Gar Soleng. Castellan had full confidence in the topside team and left Lieutenants Savon and Greem on the bridge to deal with the shackled captain. When she returned to the staging deck on the port side of the ship, she found Olivienne, Madlin, and Leggett huddled around a portable sonica cradled in Leggett's hands. "What's this?"

Madlin and Leggett both saluted and Olivienne turned to her with a smile. "Everything sorted out up there?"

"As well as could be I suppose, but he will face charges when we get back to Baene." Movement farther down the deck caught her eye and Castellan watched as the ship's crew unloaded the rail guns and replaced the shots with concussive marks instead. "All that's left is to get down below and start digging, though I'm concerned about how long it will take to find a possible point of entry."

"Commander, I believe we have an answer to that problem. Lieutenant Madlin thought that perhaps we could make some adjustments to the wavelengths used by the sonica so that it would read differently between organic material and much more solid material. And if that does not work, we can try the Pyrometer that we have stowed in the gear. Maybe the entrance would hold a different heat signature."

Castellan grinned broadly at her enterprising guardians. "Excellent ideas, both of you!" Since the anchor bolt had not been fired, the ship moved farther down the small barren island until it sat roughly over the center. "Start there!" Tosh pointed right below them.

As luck would have it, the sonica read an anomaly just to the right of where the airship hovered. Without waiting, Tosh focused on the dirt thirty yords below and began scooping the earth away from the spot with her telekinesis. Olivienne quickly caught on and used her apportation much the same way. Soon enough they'd dug nearly a yord deep and stared upon the exposed hatch in awe. There was a wheel connected to the metallic looking door similar to what could be found on both dirigibles and sailing vessels and Castellan quickly addressed the crew member operating the anchor gun. "Belay anchor, we're ready to head down. Fire to the left of the hatch below."

The man saluted Tosh and did as directed. Rather than a dull sound of the anchor bolt hitting dirt, or the sharp crack of the bolt imbedding in stone, there was a muffled boom below and the lake water rippled around the island. Olivienne looked at Castellan with some concern. "Well that was decidedly odd."

Castellan frowned in concentration. "It certainly was, and

perhaps it is a sunken ship, but it was also our signal to make haste. It will not be long before the drakes come investigate the intruders into their territory and we will be especially vulnerable on the ground so we must hurry." She turned to the remaining ten members of the Shield unit. "Begin descent!"

One by one the guardians clipped onto the anchor line and slid to the ground below. As originally directed, Spc. Branda Leggett was the first down the line. As an engineer she would have the best knowledge and skill to open any doors, though the visible hatch seemed straight forward enough. She had it open with no sign of alarm by the time Olivienne and Castellan made their descent. Olivienne marched to the door and made to enter when Tosh lightly touched her arm. "Please, Connate, allow me. It will not harm your adventurist reputation to let me go first for safety's sake. This discovery is yours and yours alone."

Olivienne looked down into the opening of the hatch. Stele rungs descended into the darkness. She nodded and waved Tosh forward. "Be my guest, Commander."

Chapter Twenty-four

ALL TWELVE MEN and women on the ground turned on their headlamps and started the climb down the hatch. Lt. Madlin was the last one in and she called down to Castellan in the artificially lit darkness. "Commander, should I shut the hatch? There is a wheel on the inside for locking, it may prevent possible danger if the drakes should come up on the island."

Castellan quickly weighed the danger of the drakes entering against the danger of not making a quick enough exit. She decided that if worse came to worse, she could blow the hatch with her telekinesis. "Go ahead and close it up, Lieutenant. Best be safe than sorry."

Despite wearing waterproof full-body suits equipped with gear pouches, the soles of their suits had surprisingly good traction on the rungs and were only a little bulky going down. The full face masks for the suits hung off the back of the kit belts for easy retrieval. Even though the commander had set a fairly fast pace down the ladder, it still took nearly ten meens before they reached another access hatched in the floor of the vertical tube. Once it was open the team dropped into the space below. Then much to everyone's surprise, the entire tunnel abruptly lit up from panels placed at regular intervals near the ceiling.

"What in the Maker's metal is this?" Tosh stared in awe.

"I believe you just answered your own question." Olivienne's reply was forestalled when a rumbling sound echoed up and down the length of the lit space and they all felt the shaking in the soles of their boots. "I don't like the feel of that."

A strange automated voice sounded from speakers hidden along the tunnel. "Warning. Hull integrity at ninety percent." Despite the worry that clouded her head, Castellan couldn't help the thrill of realization that they were indeed in a sailing vessel of sorts.

"Commander!" She looked over to where Spc. Eliseo Calderon, one of their pilots, pointed toward the wall. There was a list of strange writing with numbers and arrows scribed next to it.

Castellan glanced toward the sovereign and Olivienne shook her head. "I've never seen the like."

Tosh looked around the group. "We have a lot of minds here, does anyone have a suggestion? An adventurist mission is more one of discovery and not strong on intel. I chose this team to be flexible and intuitive. And from the feel of that shaking, we're under a time crunch here! Think people, think!"

Spc. Meza raised her hand. "Ser, I'm getting a sense that we should head that way." She pointed down the tunnel to the left and Tosh, knowing about the young woman's level four clairvoyance, accepted it as fact.

The tunnel was more of a hallway than anything else, with walls made of the same material as the long entry hatch. Olivienne too had come to the conclusion that it was a ship of some kind. The fact that it sat below a lake led to the obvious thought that it had sank beneath the surface somehow intact. She also wondered if the high acid content was in any way related to the compromised vessel, or if it was from their belayed anchor bolt. Either way, it was too late to second-guess decisions already made. Guided by Meza's clairvoyance, the entire Shield unit marched past large windows that were spaced out approximately every twenty yords.

Each window featured more strange writing next to it. They suspected a room on the other side but the light from the hall was not enough to penetrate the darkness beyond the glass. After walking by the third such room, Tosh instructed Olivienne to hold her headlamp directly to the window and she cupped her hands to peer inside. "Bones." She whispered the word aloud and saw Yazzie shiver nearby. "There are large skeletons lying on the floor, though of what I do not know. Larger than a Psierian, a beast of some sort perhaps." They stopped at a few others and only found more skeletal remains of various sizes in each.

Lt. Madlin threw out a guess. "Was this a prison, ser?"

Tosh shook her head. "I don't know. Perhaps it is the menagerie that Lieutenant Savon's vision spoke of." The structure around them groaned again and Castellan decided not to investigate the mystery any further.

"Warning. Hull integrity at seventy-five percent." Cmdr. Tosh's intuition channel screamed danger with each new tremor and subsequent warning and she instructed the unit to pick up the pace.

Twenty means and two flights of strangely shortened stairs after they arrived at the base of the hatch, they found themselves in a chamber. Per the most recent announcement by the mysterious voice, the hull integrity was down to sixty percent and every member of the team was filled with a sense of great urgency. As soon as the last guardian passed through the entryway, a door that had been recessed in the wall slid shut. The Connate made no secret of her displeasure at not predicting such an obvious trap. "Bollux!"

Cmdr. Tosh quickly went into action, calling out orders to her unit even as Olivienne moved forward to examine the only other door in the room. "Lazaro, update the crew topside on our location and current situation. Madlin, Leggett, Lear, and Devin, get to work on that door. Madlin, use your psychometry and maybe you'll get lucky and get an image of the operating mechanism. I don't like being trapped in here against our will. Yazzie, stay close to the Connate. Qent, Dozier, Meza, and Calderon, I want you to walk the perimeter to look for traps or other dangers. Heed Meza's clairvoyance if something comes to her." When she was finished doling out orders, she joined Olivienne at the far door.

The room wasn't large by any measure, maybe ten yords square. But Castellan didn't like being trapped inside just the same, especially with the rumbling and ominous voice calling out their mortality in percentages. As they studied the panel next to the door, they saw four buttons placed along the bottom of a dark screen. It looked almost like glass but black, so black that at first Tosh thought it was made from the natural mineral, obsidae. She reached out to touch it and all four buttons lit up. "What—" Olivienne's words were cut off when Spc. Qent called out from behind. Everyone in the chamber spun to stare toward the ceiling in the center of the room. A fine mist emanated from three pipes that had lowered from the ceiling and Castellan's mind scrambled for a solution to the rising panic among her team. "Masks!"

The unit was well versed and practiced in the use of the full face mask, with the exception of Olivienne. But even so, the mist filled the room so fast that every one of them received at least three breaths of it before masks could be pulled on. Despite their obvious exposure, no one had any adverse effects. Olivienne turned to her with wariness in her violet eyes and her voice sounded distorted through the large clear mask. "That is strange, I feel fine but a cloying flavor has coated the back of my tongue. I have never experienced it's like before."

"I have." Tosh immediately removed her mask and clipped it back to her kit belt. At the Connate's look of dismay, Castellan grimaced and shrugged. "It is harmless, never fear." Then she raised her voice louder and addressed the entire unit. "The gas is harmless, it is polycyclon. Though you may be more familiar with its other name, truth spray. It leaves a bad taste like sweet rotted fruit and nuts on the back of your tongue, but it will not harm you. Keep your masks handy and resume your current tasks while we investigate the other door."

When she was finished speaking, the Connate looked at her with much concern. "Why would the Makers administer truth spray to the entire room? What could possibly lie ahead of us?"

A strange mechanical voice came from the speaker in the panel, startling everyone. "Terra Halcyon two-four-seven-nine cargo storage is locked to all unauthorized access. Security protocol Gamma-tau-five to commence." A serious of high-pitched tones sounded through the chamber then the voice resumed. "Requesting illuminated guest to please step to the panel and state your intent."

Castellan gestured Olivienne forward. "Go on, Connate Dracore, it's your mission."

Olivienne shook her head and pointed at the floor below them all. It was comprised of a grid-like pattern and the squares below and around Spc. Yazzie's feet were lit. "Looks like it's Yazzie that needs to answer."

The medican looked down and was startled to see that the floor was indeed glowing below her boots. "Me?" They nodded. "But ser, I don't even know what to say!"

Tosh gave the woman a wry smile. "Lucky for you, Yazzie, you'll only be able to say the truth. The effects of polycyclon last for hours but I don't want to be down here that long so hop to it, Guardian!"

The medican's eyes widened at the commander's decisive tone and quickly strode the last few steps to the panel. "Specialist Almeta Yazzie and my intention is to open this door." The panel flashed red and a tone sounded that was so low and loud that it vibrated the bones in Tosh's ears.

"Answer is unacceptable, please state your intent."

"Yazzie, it's looking for the base reason. While your statement was technically true, it wasn't absolute truth. You're here because you're on the team, you're on the team because..." She looked pointedly at the woman, then moved her gaze to Olivienne. And the answer dawned on both at the same time.

The twenty-six roto old Shield Corp guardian tried again. "Specialist Almeta Yazzie and my intention is to heal and protect my sovereign, Connate Dracore."

That time the panel flashed green and the voice spoke again. "Answer is acceptable. Illuminated guest, please step forward."

It was Tosh's boots that were outlined in the pale light so she moved to the panel as Yazzie moved away from it. "Commander Castellan Tosh of the Psiere Shield Corp, here to lead this team — " She paused for only a sec before quickly amending her statement. "Here to protect Olivienne Dracore." Again the panel flashed green and Castellan suspected that the Connate would be the next one called, since it seemed to be going in order of who was closest to the panel.

"Answer is acceptable. Illuminated guest, please step forward."

Indeed it was Olivienne and she was prepared to answer after witnessing both Yazzie's and Tosh's answers. "Olivienne Dracore, here to retrieve the Key of Antaeus." The panel didn't flash that time but rather turned yellow and stayed yellow.

"Please hold, accessing Antaeus files." A mild tone beeped and repeated every ten secs after. Olivienne looked back at Tosh and the commander could only shrug. Finally, after nearly two meens of beeping, the voice came up again. "Antaeus file access complete. Illuminated guest, please state reason for your Antaeus Key request."

"I wish to learn more about the Makers."

The low tone sounded again, even louder than the first time and more than one of the people in the chamber gritted their teeth in pain. "Answer is unacceptable, you have one falsehood remaining. Please state your intent."

Olivienne took a deep breath and tried again. "My name is Olivienne Dracore, Royal Heir to the Divine Cathedra, Sovereign Connate of Psiere. I wish to improve the lives of my people using the knowledge locked away in the Temple of Antaeus, left behind by the Makers."

Everyone blew out a sign of relief when the panel flashed green and both doors slid open. "Psionic resonance frequency of Archeos and Illeos temple keys detected. Answer is acceptable. Access granted."

"That's it? And how did it know I had the pendants on me?" Olivienne peered inside a room that was so small it was nearly a closet. Lying on a shelf among a multitude of other cases and containers was a box roughly the size of a sheaf of documents. The Psierian temple symbol that matched the pendants around her neck was embedded in the lid. The Connate raised a dark eyebrow with a skeptical look on her face.

Castellan was quick to call her out. "Just be glad you were wearing them and don't question the voice. Instead, let's retrieve the key and get out of here. Something is off about this place." Her words proved to be prescient, despite her lack of channel because as soon as she stopped speaking, great shaking erupted again nearly knocking the team off their feet. An alarm claxon sounded and the voice came across speakers that were hidden somewhere overhead.

"Hull breach in sector seven. Please exit Terra Halcyon two-four-seven-nine in a calm and orderly fashion. Full submersion in T-minus thirty minutes."

Despite the unfamiliar word, it was close enough to their own word of thirty meens for the unit to extrapolate the meaning of the warning. "Sheddech!" Olivienne darted into the small room and snatched the box from the shelf and stuffed it into her satchel. She gazed mournfully at the other boxes but quickly dashed back out without grabbing any.

Lt. Madlin called out from the far door. "Commander?"

Tosh let out her own curse and pointed back the way they had come from. "Run!" The team sprinted down the corridors and up the flights of stairs they had descended not long before. The automated voice sounded every ten meens, pushing them ever faster.

"Warning...full submersion in T-minus twenty minutes."

They were passing the first of the glass cells when Spc. Lear stumbled and went to the ground. Tosh waved everyone on. "Keep going!" Olivienne began to slow and Tosh gave her a telekinetic shove. "Go now, I'll be right behind you!" Then she turned Lear over and took in the pilot's sweating face and blue lips.

"I'm sorry, Commander. I think that I'm allergic to the truth spray. I have a mild tree nut allergy that I didn't mention before joining the team..." Her eyes fluttered shut and her voice trailed off as she struggled to breathe. Tosh quickly removed Lear's mask from the kit belt and clipped in in place, then turned the oxy content up to high to aid with the specialist's breathing. The tank would only last for twenty meens but that was long enough to get them out. She shouldered the woman and took off at a run. Seeing that the main unit had fully gone from her sight, she decided to speed their travel with her levitation and the glassed rooms passed by at a blur.

"Connate, you have to go now!" Castellan caught up with the group as they were beginning their ascent up the hatch tunnel. The Connate had already ordered the rest of the team up the access tunnel and Lt. Madlin was pleading with Olivienne to enter the hatch herself but the sovereign just stared worriedly back the way they came. The look of relief on her face was obvious as Tosh came into view carrying a limp Necole Lear over her shoulders.

Another round of shaking nearly took the officer off her feet but she managed to stay upright and yell at the Connate at the same time. "Up the hatch, we don't have much time!"

"Warning...full submersion in T-minus ten minutes."

The place shook again and Olivienne scrambled into the vertical corridor, climbing the rungs as fast as she was able. Madlin followed her and Tosh drew up the rear. She floated Spc. Lear above her in the passage as they raced up the rungs. The space was too narrow so she couldn't just push them all out like she had in the giant tree on Mater. She could do more harm than good if one of the team struck their head on the side or a rung. More shaking occurred and she locked her arms around her current rung to prevent coming loose. She heard swearing above and suspected one of the guardians did not take such a precaution. Olivienne's worried voice called to her from above. "Tosh, we're not going to make it!"

Castellan grunted as they began to move again ahead of her. "Climb!" At least the commander had the foresight to close and latch the lower hatch before starting her ascent. She wasn't sure how much time it would buy them but she hoped it would be enough. As soon as she saw daelight above, she paused long enough to grab the voteo from her belt. "Tosh here. Situation dire, ready for team ascent!" She didn't bother waiting for a reply, merely clipped the voteo back to her belt and resumed the climb.

Spc. Devin's voice called out from above. "Ser, the island is sinking!"

She used her telepathy to instruct them, saving her breath for the climb. *"Put your masks on and clip to the line for ascent as soon as you reach the surface!"* She was relieved when Spc. Lear's body cleared the hatch and she pulled herself into the light of the two suns. However that relief was short-lived as she saw the red water swirling within two yords. She slipped her own mask on and activated the breather and stared up at the people strung out along the anchor line of the dirigible. Illeostone-powered drivers clipped to their harnesses pulled them up the line at a slow but steady pace. She clipped Lear's driver to the line first and turned it on. Tosh knew someone at the top would grab her and pull her into the airship. When enough space had passed she clipped in her own driver.

A horrific groan filled the air, then a series of muffled booms and the hatch abruptly sunk below the surface of the lake. The dirigible above jerked in the sky and Tosh had the intuition to grab her knife and cut the anchor bolt free from the bottom of the line. She called a warning to the entire team. *"Hang tight!"* The rope swung wildly in the air below her but they were safe enough as they continued to rise above the water. Then as if to prove their dae could indeed get worse, two serpentine heads rose above the red lake and looked up at the line of climbers. Remembering Lt. Savon's premonition, Tosh whispered to herself. "Beware the rope — sheddech!" She called out with her mind to every member of her team. *"Lock your drivers now!"*

She didn't know what the range was for the drake's spray but she had to be fast to catch them all if the beast burned through the rope. She could only hope it wouldn't hit any of their team members. Sure enough, three secs later, one of the drakes gave out a great roar and steaming liquid shot into the sky, perfectly severing the rope between Meza and Calderon. With supreme effort, she caught all six of them that had been cut free from the anchor line and prevented the disastrous fall into the water below. The guardians still attached to the dirigible began climbing again and the second drake reared back as if to spray its own boiling acid into the air. Not wanting to stick around to see the results, Tosh lifted them all straight up toward the rapidly rising dirigible. The distance was significantly greater than she had gone when they flew from the cliffs of Navis and she stumbled with exhaustion when she landed on the staging deck once again.

"Castellan!" Olivienne fairly flew into her arms whilst both Holling and Yazzie began working on Spc. Lear.

Castellan called out to them to speed up the diagnosis. "She said she thinks she's allergic to the polycyclon. She'll probably need a stimulant and something to counteract the respiratory distress."

Holling nodded. "Yes, ser!"

Once that was done, she turned to address her lover and

future par. Olivienne had grabbed Tosh in a tight embrace and buried her face in the crook of the commander's neck out of sheer relief. Castellan tried to get her attention. "Olivienne." When there was no response, she tried again. "'Vienne." The sovereign pulled her head back and looked at her with emotion filled eyes and Tosh's words were a whisper. "We did it."

The words were repeated, as if Olivienne didn't quite believe they were true. "We did it." Together they looked around the deck and watched as Spc. Lear sat upright on her own. Her lips were still tinged blue but she smiled at them and gave the sign for all clear. Other guardians were busy stripping from the uncomfortable waterproof suits and gathering their other gear on the deck.

Lt. Savon came clattering down the stairs from above and clapped Lt. Madlin on the shoulder before turning to the Connate and his commander. "Did you find it?"

Olivienne pulled the box she had retrieved from her satchel and after checking thoroughly for traps, unclasped and opened it. Inside was a stack of vellum, and on top of that lay the third pendant with its gleaming red stone. She pulled the pendant out and glanced at the detailed map of an island and pointed at the coordinates written in scripte in the bottom right corner. Not wanting to chance the wind blowing the vellum pages away, Olivienne quickly shut and stowed the box back in her satchel then held the pendant up to catch the light of the two suns. She looked up at Castellan and smiled. "We did it. We have the coordinates for the Temple of Antaeus and all three keys!"

A massive cheer went up among the members of the Connate's Shield Corp unit when they saw the purpose of their mission lying safely in the sovereign's hand. Members of the airship's crew gave a hearty cheer as well and Tosh shook her head at their antics. "Savon, report."

The man saluted but he couldn't seem to lose the grin. "Ser, the captain and five crew members have been locked in a cabin for the return trip. The mutineers were quickly rooted out with Lieutenant Greem's assistance. We should have clear sailing and a tailwind back to Baene from here."

Castellan looked down at the lake below. They had gained enough altitude that she could no longer make out the shapes of the drakes in the water. Gone too was the long dirt stretch of the unknown island with its curious ship's hatch. Having sunk into the bloody water, the patch of land had become only a memory. It seemed as though every new answer to the mystery they found only provided more questions. What kind of sailing ship would sink in a caustic lake and remain intact for so long? How long had it been hiding below the surface of the water, and how big must it be to hold such an immense length of corridors? And the menagerie...Tosh didn't yet know what to make of the rows of glass fronted cells or the long-dead beasts they once held. Perhaps she would never know the answers but at least she had the right person by her side should she ever decide to go searching.

Olivienne looked at her curiously, noting the faraway gaze in those too-pale eyes. "What are you thinking?"

Castellan focused her sight on the woman she had grown to love beyond all else. Neither doubts nor fears could stand in the way of their future. "I was thinking that you are just about perfect."

The Connate raised a dark eyebrow and smirked at her lover. "Just about?"

Tosh shrugged but couldn't hold back the smile. "Well sure, no one is completely perfect."

Olivienne's voice was soft and nearly unheard as the dirigible moved forward at a fast enough clip that the wind whipped by them. "You are."

The commander shook her head in denial. "'Vi—"

A finger covered her lips, prompting silence. "You are perfect for me."

Castellan had no choice but to kiss her in response. She didn't need a clairvoyance channel to know that you shouldn't argue against a sovereign of Psiere.

Glossary

Aeons [Measurement] – Ages, eons, a long time

Aether [Natural] – Enhanced radiotope gas that is produced by archeostones and illeostones. Archeostone aether reacts with illeostone mineral and charges the illeostones. Illeostone aether is emitted and used to power gadgets and machines. The Archeostone aether changes babies at a genetic level while in utero. The more exposure the more power.

Aetherkinesis [Channel] – The ability to sense and physically manipulate aether, with the mind.

Amita [People] – Family. Aunt, female sib of parent.

Animal Empathy [Channel] – The ability to communicate and read emotions mind to mind with animals. (Soft Channel)

Antaeus [Planetary] – Exploded moon, source of the Archeostones and half source of the fused Antoraestones.

Antoraestone [Planetary] – Pieces of powerful fused rock created when the asteroid Torae collided with the moon, Antaeus. The power imbued within provides 10x magnification of illeostones or Psierians.

Apportation [Channel] – The ability to instantly physically move objects within your sight from one point to another, with the mind. (Hard Channel)

Apree [Measurement] – Second lune (month) of the roto (year).

Archeos [Planetary] – Larger yellowish-orange sun, first to rise in the morning. Part of a binary stars set.

Archeostones [Planetary] – Fist size and glow yellowish orange, very rare. These charge illeostones with two days of exposure.

Armicruste [Natural] – Giant aggressive armored crabs sent by the Atlanteens. 3000 lbs.

Arslick [Society] – Expletive, curse. Derogatory term for someone of ill character.

Atlanteens [People] – Race of humanoid fish people who live in the seas and hate the Psierians. Cannot survive on land any more than Psierians could survive under water. They have telepathy and empathy, but no other known channels.

Automaton [Mechanical] – Robot powered by a single illeostone. Controlled by a specialized soldier programmer.

Avia [People] – Family. Grandmother, mother of parent.

Avus [People] – Family. Grandfather, father of parent.

Barde [People] – Writer, poet, storyteller, and more.

Bollux [Society] – Expletive, curse.

Bosair [Society] – Bra.

Calla [Natural] – Beautiful.

Cathedress [People] – Title for the Queen, the ruling sovereign, the current seat of the Divine Cathedra. (throne)

Chemistrae [Natural] – Chemistry.

Clairvoyance [Channel] – The ability to gain information about an object, person, location, or physical event. (Soft Channel)

Coacas [Natural] – Coconuts.

Connate [People] – Immediate heir.

Consor [Society] – Marry.

Consorage [Society] – Marriage.

Consoral [Society] – Married.

Copere [Natural] – Copper.

Corm [Finance] – Money, currency delineation = 1 corundem.

Corma [Finance] – Money, currency delineation = $1/10^{th}$ of a corm or ten cred.

Cormi [Finance] – Money, currency delineation = $1/10^{th}$ of a corma, segmented to break into halves or quarters.

Corundem [Natural] – Super hard precious stones found in blue, red, and white. Used for mining, communication, jewelry, science, and as a base for the Psierian financial system due to its value in all parts of society.

Coz'n [People] – Family, child of an aunt (amita) or uncle (patruus).

Cred [Finance] – Money, slang general term.

Credit [Finance] – Money, general term.

Cycle [Transportation] – Two-wheeled vehicle 120 mph standard max (prototype 150)

Dae [Measurement] – Day

Deka [Measurement] – Tenth and last lune (month) of the roto (year).

Dir [Planetary] – Lake

Dirigible [Transportation] – Air zeppelin filled with heliopus gas, powered by aether driven props. Max speed 40 mph. Max distance at full capacity of illeostones is 1400 miles.

Divine Cathedra [Society] – Royal throne. Set with two Archeostones. The throne has existed for the entirety of written Psierian history. The Divine Cathedra can only be held by female sovereigns of the family and is inherited by the first born woman of each generation. It can be held in regency by a male, if no other female heirs exist, until the next female in the royal line is born.

Doctore [People] – Doctor. Psi with advanced training in all healing techniques.

Dolpheens [Natural] – Dolphins

Dowsing [Channel] – The ability to sense the location of water.

(Soft Channel)

Dromea [Planetary] – Southern continent. Population: 11 million. Sq. Miles: 1.5

Eidetic Memory [Channel] – The ability to perfectly recall the details and image anything that it seen. (Soft Channel)

Empathy [Channel] – The ability to communicate and read emotions mind to mind. (Soft Channel)

Endara [Planetary] – Northern continent. Population: 19 million. Sq Miles: 2.5

Enhanced Awareness [Channel] – A superior ability to sense and react to every physical thing around you in faster than normal time. (Soft Channel)

Enhanced Memory [Channel] – A superior ability to store and recall all information you are exposed to. (Soft Channel)

Ferrokinesis [Channel] – The ability to physically manipulate iron, with the mind. (Hard Channel)

Foot [Measurement] – 12"

Gozen [Natural] – Goose

Grav [Natural] – Gravity

Guardian [People] – This is a soldier serving in the Psi Shield Corp, placed in protective duty of a sovereign

Hand [Measurement] – 6"

Hauler [Transportation] – Six-wheeled vehicle for supplies = Max speed 100 mph

Humore [Society] – Humor

Illeos [Planetary] – Smaller blueish-white sun, second to rise in the morning. Part of a binary stars set.

Illeostones [Planetary] – Mineral that releases aether in the presence of water. Size can vary from larger down to microscopic elements that can be found within the bodies of all living things on Psiere. The stones glow blueish white when emitting aether and are fairly common. Full Illeostones release aether which powers machinery and other devices.

Imperium [People] – The elected body that rules Psiere in conjunction with the Queen. The Queen has the majority of the power. The King is an automatic member of the Imperium and is responsible for presenting the Queen's agenda as well as breaking voting ties when enacting new laws and governing Psiere in general.

Ince [Measurement] – 1"

Instrae [People] – Professor, researcher, teacher.

Interpretists [People] – Citizens whose sole career is translating ciphers, ancient artifact schematics, and other texts of the Divine Mystery.

Intinerist [People] – Scheduler, administrative assistant.

Intuition [Channel] – A superior ability to understand something immediately, without the need for conscious reasoning. (Soft Channel)

Judex [People] – Judge.

Juni [Measurement] – Fourth lune (month) of the roto (year).

Leviathan [Natural] – Giant squid, a beast of the Deep, controlled by the Atlanteens. Has an average weight of 5000 lbs, tentacle length of 140 foot, and a 12" eye. The tentacles are covered in suckers with jagged teeth ringing the inside, and feature claws along the edges of each appendage that can rotate or even retract.

Levitation [Channel] – The ability to physically lift yourself, with your mind. (Hard Channel)

Lune [Measurement] – Month (Marte, Apree, Maia, Juni, Quinta, Sexte, Septa, Octobra, Novea, Deka).

Mahl [Measurement] – Mile, 5280 foot.

Maia [Measurement] – Third lune (month) of the roto (year).

Makers [People] – Race of unknown people responsible for creating the pyramids and all the artifacts and documents.

Maman [People] – Family. Mother, informal like mama.

Mamanar [People] – Family, Mother-in-law.

Marte [Measurement] – First lune (month) of the roto (year).

Medican [People] – Medical professional.

Meen [Measurement] – Minute, 60 meens in an oor.

Mir [Planetary] – River.

Moto [Transportation] – Four-wheeled vehicle for passengers, average max speed of 100 mph.

Novea [Measurement] – Ninth lune (month) of the roto (year).

Oathing [Society] – Betrothing.

Oath of Consorage [Society] – Betrothal.

Obsidae [Natural] – Obsidian.

Octobra [Measurement] – Eighth lune (month) of the roto (year).

Oor [Measurement] – Hour.

Operae [Society] – Opera.

Ova [Natural] – A mature female reproductive cell.

Papan [People] – Family. Father, informal like dad.

Papanar [People] – Family. Father-in-law.

Par [People] – Family. Spouse.

Paren [People] – Family. Parent.

Parsib [People] – Family. Sibling through consorage. Brother-in-law or sister-in-law.

Patruus [People] – Family. Uncle, male sib of parent.

Pelma [Natural] – Palm tree.

Polycyclon [Society] – Truth serum in gas form, nut derivative.

Portea [Planetary] – Port, distilled wine.

Praefectus [People] – Continental governor.

Prescience [Channel] – The ability to know something before it takes place, foreknowledge. (Soft Channel)

Preservist [People] – Salvo Corp personnel. Search and rescue, fire, life guard, and more.

Psera [People] – Madam, honorific.

Psero [People] – Mister, honorific.

Psi [People] – Citizens of Psiere, Psierian.

Psi Academic Corp [Citizen Corp] – Instructors, and teachers at the academy, and other primary schools around the continents.

Psi Codice Corp [Citizen Corp] – Psi that deal with Psierian law in some capacity. Telepath/ psychometry teams, executioners, security specialists for the islands, judex, and judiciary reviewers, etc.

Psi Defense Corp [Citizen Corp] – Soldiers and officers that are tasked with defending home and country. Military corp.

Psi Divinity Corp [Citizen Corp] – All professions related to solving the divine mystery. Adventurists, interpretists, engineers and other professions assigned to adventurist teams. Funded partially by the government and partially by the schematics, inventions, and artifacts found on their expeditions.

Psi Engineering Corp [Citizen Corp] – Psi whose responsibility lies within public service works, roads, bridges, inventions, schematic adaptions, research, etc.

Psi Medi Corp [Citizen Corp] – All medicans. Doctores, caretaker, therapist, etc.

Psi Politia Corp [Citizen Corp] – Imperium officials, governors, representatives (all elected). Kings have the option to transfer to Politia Corp upon ascendency to King, or they can decline and remain in their original Corp. Elected Politia help define problems in regions and potential solutions. Organize all the other corps.

Psi Resource Corp [Citizen Corp] – Psi that work with all parts of the resource industry such as mining, for stones, gems, minerals, as well as wood and other building materials. Also responsible for illeostone recharging and recirculation throughout Psiere.

Psi Salvo Corp [Citizen Corp] – Preservists. Fire and rescue, cross-over medicans and caretakers for rescue missions.

Psi Security Corp [Citizen Corp] – Law enforcement in the towns and cities across Psiere. First enforcers of Psierian law.

Psi Service Corp [Citizen Corp] – All other customer driven industries, such as art, entertainment, eateries, shoppes, and more.

Psi Shield Corp [Citizen Corp] – All personnel related to sovereign security. The military Corp personnel with the highest and most varied training of all others. Best of the best.

Psi Stock Corp [Citizen Corp] – Responsible for all Psi involved with food harvesting. Farmers, Fishers, hunters and more.

Psiere [Planetary] – Planet and country name.

Psychometry [Channel] – The ability to discover facts about an event or person by touching inanimate objects associated with them. (Soft Channel)

Pund [Measurement] – Weight measurement, pound.

Pyrokinesis [Channel] – The ability to physically create and control fire, with the mind. (Hard Channel)

Pyrs [Measurement] – Degrees, Fahrenheit

Queen [People] – Divine Cathedress, Her Royal Highness, Supreme Sovereign. She is the head of Psiere with an overall say in government decisions and direction, but she leaves the day to day running of the nation to the Psi Politia Corp.

Quinta [Measurement] – Fifth lune (month) of the roto (year).

Railer [Transportation] – A Train fueled by aether, with supplemental carts attached to hold illeostones and water. Passenger and goods conveyance on two rails sent on the ground. Max speed 100 mph.

Roto [Measurement] – 1 Year (10 lunes).

Sec [Measurement] – Time measurement, second. 60 per oor.

Seg [Transportation] – A shortened form of segment, slang.

Segment [Transportation] – A single car of a railer.

Seme [Natural] – Male reproductive fluid.

Septa [Measurement] – Seventh lune (month) of the roto (year).

Ser [People] – Military honorific, Sir.

Sexte [Measurement] – Sixth lune (month) of the roto (year).

Sharc [Natural] – Shark.

Sheddech [Society] – Curse.

Shell [Mechanical] – Metal bullet fired from a pistol, rifle, or rail gun.

Sint [Society] – Curse. Derogatory term for someone of ill character.

Sonal Ocilloscope [Mechanical] – Sonar using sound for depth measurement. Sonal ocillator with scope.

Sonica [Mechanical] – Radar, frequently used in dirigibles to scan around them and below.

Sovereign [People] – Any member of the royal family with a direct line to the Divine Cathedra, including both the Queen and the Connate.

Stele [Natural] – Steel.

Sturgeous [Natural] – Sturgeon, giant fish and common food source.

Sub-Connate [People] – Supplemental or secondary heir, not in line for the Divine Cathedra.

Sub-Instrae [People] – Assistant, lower level. Also an instructor.

Telekinesis [Channel] – The ability to move and manipulate physically objects, with your mind. (Hard Channel)

Teleo [Mechanical] – Wired communication device, like a telephone.

Telepathy [Channel] – The ability to communicate and read thoughts and words mind to mind. (Soft Channel)

Teleport [Channel] – The ability to physically move yourself from one point to another point that is within sight, instantly. (Hard Channel)

Telesana [Channel] – The ability to physically heal the body, with the mind (subtle vibrations that speed bone repair, blood flow, disease eradication). (Hard Channel)

Telesthesia [Channel] – The ability to see a distant and unseen target using extrasensory perception. Far sight. (Soft Channel)

Temple Charging Rooms [Society] – All expended Illeostones from around Psiere are returned to the nearest temple and sealed into a room with the Archeostone to charge. Five days in room with max capacity, about 3000 stones. (Small room 500 stones is 2 days) Charged stones get shipped out to the entire continent as discharged ones are brought back in. Each temple has 4 stones.

Temple of Antaeus [Society] – Lost pyramid of unknown origin on the island of Magna.

Temple of Archeos [Society] – Great pyramid of unknown origin near Tesseron, the capital city of Endara

Temple of Illeos [Society] – Great pyramid of unknown origin near Ostium, the capital city of Dromea

The Divine Mystery [Society] – Origin of life on Psiere. Who were the Makers, where did the Makers go, and why is there no history for Psierians beyond a few hundred rotos?

Tinkerist [People] – Hobby inventor.

Tracker [Transportation] – Treaded and armored military vehicle that can go nearly anywhere.

Tun [Measurement] – Weight measurement, ton (2000 punds).

Vectis [Society] – Tax on wages to pay for medican services and academy training.

Vectura [Transportation] – Transportation or vehicle.

Vineo [Natural] – Wine.

Vinier [People] – A vintner, or person that makes portea and other vineos.

Voteo [Mechanical] – Wireless communication device, like a walkie-talkie but longer range.

Weke [Measurement] – Week (6 day).

Whal [Natural] – Whale.

Yord [Measurement] – Distance measurement, yard (3 foot).

About the Author

Born and raised in Michigan, Kelly is a latecomer to the writing scene. She works in the automotive industry coding in Visual basic and Excel. Her avid reading and writing provide a nice balance to the daily order of data, allowing her to juggle passion and responsibility. Her writing style is as varied as her reading taste and it shows as she tackles each new genre with glee. But beneath it all, no matter the subject or setting, Kelly carries a core belief that good should triumph. She's not afraid of pain or adversity, but loves a happy ending. She's been pouring words into novels since 2015 and probably won't run out of things to say any time soon.

Other K. Aten titles to look for:

The Fletcher

Kyri is a fletcher, following in the footsteps of her father, and his father before him. However, fate is a fickle mistress, and six years after the death of her mother, she's faced with the fact that her father is dying as well. Forced to leave her sheltered little homestead in the woods, Kyri discovers that there is more to life than just hunting and making master quality arrows. During her journey to find a new home and happiness, she struggles with the path that seems to take her away from the quiet life of a fletcher. She learns that sometimes the hardest part of growing up is reconciling who we were, with who we will become.

ISBN: 978-1-61929-356-4
eISBN: 978-1-61929-357-1

The Archer

Kyri was raised a fletcher but after finding a new home and family with the Telequire Amazons, she discovers a desire to take on more responsibility within the tribe. She has skills they desperately need and she is called to action to protect those around her. But Kyri's path is ever-changing even as she finds herself altered by love, loyalty, and grief. Far away from home, the new Amazon is forced to decide what to sacrifice and who to become in order to get back to all that she has left behind. And she wonders what is worse, losing everyone she's ever loved or having those people lose her?

ISBN: 978-1-61929-370-0
eISBN: 978-1-61929-371-7

The Sagittarius

Kyri has known her share of loss in the two decades that she has been alive. She never expected to find herself a slave in roman lands, nor did she think she had the heart to become a gladiatrix. But with her soul shattered she must fight to see her way back home again. Will she win her freedom and return to all that she has known, or will she become another kind of slave to the killer that has taken over her mind? The only thing that is certain through it all is her love and devotion to Queen Orianna.

ISBN: 978-1-61929-386-1
eISBN: 978-1-61929-387-8

Rules of the Road

Jamie is an engineer who keeps humor close to her heart and people at arm's length. Kelsey is a dental assistant who deals with everything from the hilarious to the disgusting on a daily basis. What happens when a driving app brings them together as friends? The nerd car and the rainbow car both know a thing or two about hazard avoidance. When a flat tire brings them together in person, Jamie immediately realizes that Kelsey isn't just another woman on her radar. Both of them have struggled to break free from stereotypes while they navigate the road of life. As their friendship deepens they realize that sometimes you have to break the rules to get where you need to go.

ISBN: 978-1-61929-366-3
eISBN: 978-1-61929-367-0

Waking the Dreamer

By the end of the 21st century, the world had become a harsh place. After decades of natural and man-made catastrophes, nations fell, populations shifted, and seventy percent of the continents became uninhabitable without protective suits. Technological advancement strode forward faster than ever and it was the only thing that kept human society steady through it all. No one could have predicted the discovery of the Dream Walkers. They were people born with the ability to leave their bodies at will, unseen by the waking world. Having the potential to become ultimate spies meant the remaining government regimes wanted to study and control them. The North American government, under the leadership of General Rennet, demanded that all Dream Walkers join the military program. For any that refused to comply, they were hunted down and either brainwashed or killed.

The very first Dream Walker discovered was a five year old girl named Julia. And when the soldiers came for her at the age of twenty, she was already hidden away. A decade later found Julia living a new life under the government's radar. As a secure tech courier in the capital city of Chicago, she does her job and the rest of her time avoids other people as much as she is able. The moment she agrees to help another fugitive Walker is when everything changes. Now the government wants them both and they'll stop at nothing to get what they want.

ISBN: 978-1-61929-382-3
eISBN: 978-1-61929-383-0

Running From Forever

Sarah Colby has always run from commitment. But after more than a year on the road following her musical dreams, even she yearns for a little stability. Her sister Annie is only too happy to welcome her back home. When she meets Annie's boss, Nobel Keller, she's immediately drawn to the woman's youthful good looks and dangerous charisma. The first night together leaves Sarah aching for more, but the second shows her the true price of passion.

ISBN: 978-1-61929-398-4
eISBN: 978-1-61929-399-1

SOME OTHER REGAL CREST PUBLICATIONS

Brenda Adcock	Soiled Dove	978-1-935053-35-4
Brenda Adcock	The Sea Hawk	978-1-935053-10-1
Brenda Adcock	The Other Mrs. Champion	978-1-935053-46-0
Brenda Adcock	Picking Up the Pieces	978-1-61929-120-1
Brenda Adcock	The Game of Denial	978-1-61929-130-0
Brenda Adcock	In the Midnight Hour	978-1-61929-188-1
Brenda Adcock	Untouchable	978-1-61929-210-9
Brenda Adcock	The Heart of the Mountain	978-1-61929-330-4
Brenda Adcock	Gift of the Redeemer	978-1-61929-360-1
Brenda Adcock	Unresolved Conflicts	978-1-61929-374-8
Brenda Adcock	One Step At A Time	978-1-61929-408-0
K. Aten	The Fletcher	978-1-61929-356-4
K. Aten	Rules of the Road	978-1-61919-366-3
K. Aten	The Archer	978-1-61929-370-0
K. Aten	Waking the Dreamer	978-1-61929-382-3
K. Aten	The Sagittarius	978-1-61929-386-1
K. Aten	Running From Forever: Book One in the Blood Resonance Series	978-1-61929-398-4
K. Aten	The Sovereign of Psiere: Book One In the Mystery of the Makers series	978-1-61929-412-7
Georgia Beers	Thy Neighbor's Wife	1-932300-15-5
Georgia Beers	Turning the Page	978-1-932300-71-0
Lynnette Beers	Just Beyond the Shining River	978-1-61929-352-6
Tonie Chacon	Struck! A Titanic Love Story	978-1-61929-226-0
Sky Croft	Amazonia	978-1-61929-067-9
Sky Croft	Amazonia: An Impossible Choice	978-1-61929-179-9
Sky Croft	Mountain Rescue: The Ascent	978-1-61929-099-0
Sky Croft	Mountain Rescue: On the Edge	978-1-61929-205-5
Mildred Gail Digby	Phoenix	978-1-61929-394-6
Cronin and Foster	Blue Collar Lesbian Erotica	978-1-935053-01-9
Cronin and Foster	Women in Uniform	978-1-935053-31-6
Cronin and Foster	Women in Sports	978-1-61929-278-9
Anna Furtado	The Heart's Desire	978-1-935053-81-1
Anna Furtado	The Heart's Strength	978-1-935053-82-8
Anna Furtado	The Heart's Longing	978-1-935053-83-5
Anna Furtado	Tremble and Burn	978-1-61929-354-0
Melissa Good	Eye of the Storm	1-932300-13-9
Melissa Good	Hurricane Watch	978-1-935053-00-2
Melissa Good	Moving Target	978-1-61929-150-8
Melissa Good	Red Sky At Morning	978-1-932300-80-2
Melissa Good	Storm Surge: Book One	978-1-935053-28-6
Melissa Good	Storm Surge: Book Two	978-1-935053-39-2
Melissa Good	Stormy Waters	978-1-61929-082-2
Melissa Good	Thicker Than Water	1-932300-24-4
Melissa Good	Terrors of the High Seas	1-932300-45-7
Melissa Good	Tropical Storm	978-1-932300-60-4

Melissa Good	Tropical Convergence	978-1-935053-18-7
Melissa Good	Winds of Change Book One	978-1-61929-194-2
Melissa Good	Winds of Change Book Two	978-1-61929-232-1
Melissa Good	Southern Stars	978-1-61929-348-9
Jeanine Hoffman	Lights & Sirens	978-1-61929-115-7
Jeanine Hoffman	Strength in Numbers	978-1-61929-109-6
Jeanine Hoffman	Back Swing	978-1-61929-137-9
K. E. Lane	And, Playing the Role of Herself	978-1-932300-72-7
Jennifer McCormick	Tears of the Sun	978-1-61929-396-0
Kate McLachlan	Christmas Crush	978-1-61929-195-9
Kate McLachlan	Hearts, Dead and Alive	978-1-61929-017-4
Kate McLachlan	Murder and the Hurdy Gurdy Girl	978-1-61929-125-6
Kate McLachlan	Rescue At Inspiration Point	978-1-61929-005-1
Kate McLachlan	Return Of An Impetuous Pilot	978-1-61929-152-2
Kate McLachlan	Rip Van Dyke	978-1-935053-29-3
Kate McLachlan	Ten Little Lesbians	978-1-61929-236-9
Kate McLachlan	Alias Mrs. Jones	978-1-61929-282-6
Lynne Norris	One Promise	978-1-932300-92-5
Lynne Norris	Sanctuary	978-1-61929-248-2
Lynne Norris	The Light of Day	978-1-61929-338-0
Nita Round	A Touch of Truth Book One: Raven, Fire and Ice	978-1-61929-372-4
Nita Round	A Touch of Truth Book Two: Raven, Sand and Sun	978-1-61929-404-2
Nita Round	Fresh Start	978-1-61929-340-3
Nita Round	Knight's Sacrifice	978-1-61929-314-4
Nita Round	The Ghost of Emily Tapper	978-1-61929-328-1
Kelly Sinclair	Getting Back	978-1-61929-242-0
Kelly Sinclair	Accidental Rebels	978-1-61929-260-4
Schramm and Dunne	Love Is In the Air	978-1-61929-362-8
Rae Theodore	Leaving Normal: Adventures in Gender	978-1-61929-320-5
Rae Theodore	My Mother Says Drums Are for Boys: True Stories for Gender Rebels	978-1-61929-378-6
Barbara Valletto	Pulse Points	978-1-61929-254-3
Barbara Valletto	Everlong	978-1-61929-266-6
Barbara Valletto	Limbo	978-1-61929-358-8
Barbara Valletto	Diver Blues	978-1-61929-384-7
Lisa Young	Out and Proud	978-1-61929-392-2

Be sure to check out our other imprints,
Blue Beacon Books, Mystic Books, Quest Books,
Troubadour Books, Yellow Rose Books,
and Young Adult Books.